MW00653447

# THE DO-NOTHING

To Temple:

Thanks so much for coming to the Book Club and all your kind comments. So glad you enjoyed the book.

PERKISON

Best,

Bran

Copyright © 2014 Perkison
All rights reserved.
ISBN-13: 9780615980232
ISBN-10: 0615980236
Library of Congress Control Number: 2014904241
LCCN Imprint Name: Rabbitboy Books, Dallas, TX

# Contents

# THE ROAD TAKEN

I think I just killed my father.

In the rear view mirror, Texarkana. It rapidly diminishes, disappears behind a tree-crowned hill. Roadway scrolls behind me; rolling pine forest is before me. Buzzards spiral upward on thermals, watching. I clench the wheel with both hands, and my nails claw white half-moons in the crusting old rubber. The car is screaming in protest. Tears are streaming down my face, torrents of them. Let them come.

I didn't mean to, I didn't. It was just a push.

He hadn't been happy with me allright; he'd come up to throw me out. That much I'd guessed, but the rage in him, all those things he said; he'd been apoplectic. He'd pushed me and pushed me and pushed me until I couldn't stay quiet anymore. I couldn't take it anymore. Finally, I pushed him back. Physically. Brutally. He was standing at my door with that loose handrail not three feet behind him, and he never saw it coming, never expected resistance from me. I should 'a stayed quiet, just one last time, but I didn't; oh, God, no I didn't.

Now he's dead. My father is dead.

I shouldn't have run. What else was I supposed to do? I'm an idiot. He was right. In a whole world full of idiots, I'm the worst. What was I thinking? I wasn't. I wasn't thinking at all. I just ran. There's no way out of this. No way except for the brown clanging of barred doors upon barred doors upon barred doors, an orange jumpsuit, or worse. I didn't mean to, I really didn't. But I did push him. I meant to do that.

John Sharpe, murderer. Me, a patricide, a fugitive. Me.

Goddamn you, why'd you have to fall? Why? You're bigger than me, stronger than me. Were. A father like you should never fall. But you did. "I'm sorry. Christ, I am so sorry." It's not enough, I know it's not enough, but I am sorry, mostly for being me.

Choking, I pull off onto the narrow shoulder and stop. I just sit there in the baking sun with my head on the uncaring steering wheel. A convoy of logging trucks roars by, tilting crazily as they swerve to avoid me. Turbulence shivers through my car. Bark and debris fly off as they pass, some of it pelting me sharply. One of the morons lays on his horn. An irritated "get the hell outta' the road," fades away with the whining thump of bald tires. I raise my head and yell back at him and beat the wheel with wet fists, but it's totally lost in the dank boiling air, impotent. Other cars blow past. No one stops. And what if someone does?

Don't mind me, I just killed my father.

God, is it possible to feel more wretched? But the tears have stopped now at least. I have to think now. Try and think.

"He did throw me out first."

Alone in the house, he could've fallen. He *did* fall.

"Anyone could have." No one has to know. No one.

But when they find him, what then? Someone will tell them that I was still living there. That'll take all of five minutes to figure out. And no one just accidentally crashes through a second floor handrail. They will come. They could be there now.

Mom. Would he have told her?

Would he have called his ex-wife to tell her that he'd had enough, that he is finally throwing me out? No, not a chance. I pull out my cell phone and look up her number. I stare at it a long time. Telling her I left yesterday is a pretty weak alibi; even I know this.

What if she answers?

"She never answers her cell phone. Go on."

The phone rings an interminably long time. A machine answers.

"Please leave a message at the tone."

I try to say something, can't, try again, my voice rises only to a whisper: "Mom, Dad threw me out yesterday. I turned down another one of his jobs, and he came home and threw me out and... and I'm not sure where I'm heading. Mom, I..." I can't do this. She'll know this isn't the truth. I hold the phone down in my lap, fingering the end-call button.

Turn around right now.

I pick up the phone again and put it to my ear. "Mom, I've got to give up the cell phone now. I've got a little money, but." But nothing, I've got absolutely nothing, barely ten dollars in my pocket. My tennis rackets are all that's in the car. "It'll be a while before I get in touch." That's true at least, every word of it, and there's nothing else I can say to her now, maybe ever. "Goodbye." I disconnect and throw the phone into the trees. It hits one hard and clatters apart in pieces. Seeing the phone shattered is oddly satisfying.

I start the car back up and pull onto the road, accelerating up to the speed limit, not more. The tears on my face run back behind my ears with the wind and dissolve into mist; it's cooling, calming me somehow. Hot air gusts through my hair, and I feel the rhythm of the forty-year-old car running beneath me and through me, growling.

The car I talked him into. A car I love—a bright yellow Porsche 914. A car Dad really bought for himself, but wouldn't ever admit it. No, instead, he had to ridicule me for it. What a piece of crap, John, he'd said when he saw it sitting on the lot. It's not even a real Porsche, got a VW Beetle engine in it for Chrissake. Of all the cars in the world, you want me to shell out for this? But still, he examined it, kind of approvingly, I think, and I know he was surprised that I spoke up for something on my own. Well, he finally said, meaning he was going to get it, I suppose I'll be paying for it every time it breaks down, too, which will be all the time. Still, he never brought himself around to driving it; big Fund Manager like him has to drive a Benz, not some antique little yellow toy.

A pretty conspicuous toy.

I am out somewhere on Highway 59 South, and—if this is any consolation to you Dad, wherever you may be—I already know that I will re-live this scene the rest of my life. The way that banister just folded under you. And you toppled, plunging down headfirst through the empty space like the archangel himself, all the way to the bottom stair with not a sound coming out of your mouth. The sickening, hollow thud of your head on the wood reverberates over and over. I ran down and shook you and shook you, but you didn't wake up. And your lifeless eyes wide open the whole time. It was unnerving. I panicked, and who wouldn't? As I tore out of there, I expected to see storm clouds gathering above the gables, winds howling, flocks of crows screaming. But there was nothing. Just a bright, blue day with white cottony clouds, serene. Like nothing happened at all.

But it did.

And just where do I go now?

There's nowhere to go, and I'm homeless. I bang the steering wheel hard with the palm of my hand. Bang it again harder and harder until my palm tingles numbly and the shocks shiver up to my shoulder. Until I feel it.

"Damn it, damn it." I lay my head back and I scream it. "Damn it!"

Then I notice the cop. He's driving right up beside me in his black and white Cop-Camaro, cruising there in the passing lane. Just staring at me and tapping his steering wheel, a casual disapproving tap of a black gloved finger, a contemptuous frown on his preternaturally smooth face.

Jesus, I look like a drunk. Or a psycho killer.

I sit up higher in the old vinyl seat, let off the accelerator a little, and look straight ahead at the road. He lingers there for a while, watching me, hating me it seems. I know it's coming now. Didn't even make it two hours.

I wait for him to turn on the sirens, but he doesn't. He doesn't need to. He just points to the side of the road, sharply with two fingers like he's shooting a gun and mouths the dreaded words: "pull over."

This doesn't mean he knows anything. In East Texas, they pull seventeen-year-old kids like me over just to be asinine. Just to mess with you. This doesn't mean anything.

Don't run; don't do it.

Still. Something in me. Not quite a panic, but a something that says run. Hesitating, I eye the straightaway ahead of us. No way can I run flat out against that thing he's driving. Maybe I could lose him on some of these serpentine little backroads, but there's no turnoff here. Nothing. No way. Don't try it. A quick glance back at him; anger's spreading across his face. He knows what I'm thinking. He hits his sirens for a second and he shoots his fingers again and he's saying something I can't make out, but it sure isn't friendly. Nodding, I get a glimpse of another plan. I pull over and stop, but leave the car running.

The cop cuts his car over right in front of me, locks up the brakes, and jumps out of his door, almost before he's even stopped. He's storming over with his hand on his revolver, and I think he's going to draw it, but he doesn't.

God, now I've done it. This won't work. Now he's really mad. He'll haul me out of my seat and beat the crap out of me right here beside the road. He'll handcuff me so tight it'll bleed and he'll haul me in half-dead, saying I resisted.

Nothing I don't deserve.

"Why didn't you pull over?" Angry words from the cop, suddenly standing right over me. He's big and he's fit, and he is challenging me. Say something smartass, his attitude says. Just try it and see what happens.

I don't. I shrink down into my seat instead. But I don't turn off the car. He doesn't seem to notice. He thrusts his glistening face right down through my open top. "You weren't thinking of running, were you?" asks the trooper. He smells of leathery cologne and fruit chewing gum. "Surely not in this piece of crap?" He cuts off the last word in his dangerously aggressive voice with a pop of his gum.

"No, it's— I mean. No, sir. I... I'm sorry," I stammer, leaning away from that terribly smooth face and trying to twist around to meet his watery eyes. "There was nowhere to turn off... I'm sorry. I wasn't running."

His eyes hold mine and his gum pops at me until I bow my head in submission. "Driver's license and insurance," he snaps. Fumbling around to find them, I can't stop shaking. The insurance is in my Dad's name. Even an idiot could make the connection. Finally, I hand them over. But he doesn't even look at the insurance. He keeps looking back and forth between me and my license, scrutinizing every detail. He must know what I've done. He knows he's ID'd the wanted man. I try not to think about a lifetime in prison or execution by electric chair or the sleeping death fed through a cold IV. This is Texas; anything is possible. I want to blurt out that I didn't mean to, that it was all an accident.

"This doesn't look like you," he says.

"What?"

"Get out of the car. Hands behind your head." I've got no choice. I do as I'm told. "You're taller than five-eight," the cop is saying as he walks all around me, almost sniffing me up and down and popping his gum furiously. "Your hair's black, not brown."

"I grew. I changed, it's true." And it is true. I've grown five inches at least since Dad exploited the hardship loophole to get me licensed at fourteen. "I'm not lying. That picture is from three years ago."

The cop stops right in front of my face, examining me from an inch away. "John Sharpe, John Sharpe," he says, more to himself than to me. Now an order: "Back in the car. Stay there." I sit down and shut the door as he walks to his cruiser to call me in to the station, looking back over his shoulder at me the whole time. Maybe he hasn't figured it out yet, but they'll know back in his office. They'll tell him allright. He'll be coming back with a pointed gun.

When he's not glancing up at me in his rearview mirror, I quickly depress the clutch and snap the stick into first gear.

His door opens. A shiny black boot emerges, followed by the man.

Just a little head start, that's all I need.

He's walking back now, still looking at my license. The pistol's not drawn. That's good, but it doesn't mean anything. I can hardly breathe, I'm so tight. Relax, relax, get ready.

"Sharpe," he calls, when he reaches the left front fender, "isn't your father Chip –"

"No!" I scream.

I pop the clutch and gun the engine in the same instant. The car lurches forward, wheels spraying gravel. Somehow I miss him as he instinctively jumps away, and I cut the wheels hard left. Gas pedal's floored. Tail's sliding towards the cop cruiser.

Correct, correct.

I cut the wheels hard again, expecting the crunch of metal on metal, but it doesn't come, missed his bumper by less than an inch. Rocketing away, a brief glimpse in the rearview mirror, and I see the gun come out as the cop sprints for his car.

Oh hell, I'm in for it now.

It's just a glimpse because I'm already over the small rise and speeding down the other side into a hard descent. I carry the momentum up the hill in front of me, and it is so steep, I can't see beyond it. I'm flying off a cliff, flying into nothingness. I shoot up and over the apex just as a pistol shot goes off and the car goes airborne, floats out over the drop for a sickening moment then settles down onto the road again with a whump and a trailing metal screech. With the impact, fire sparks blow out and into the cockpit to swirl around me like a thousand Fourth of July sparklers and it is so beautiful and I am so alive that I swear it is happiness I am feeling.

Can't be, shouldn't be, but it is: pure, unadulterated happiness.

Another glance in my rearview mirror. Nothing there yet. This might just work.

The sound of his siren starts wailing after me. I hear him top the big hill, coming hard.

Get off the highway. Now.

One of the hundreds of side roads out here comes into view. I downshift hard into second and careen into the turn just as a huge diesel 4x4 pickup is roaring up to the stop sign. The guy swerves off to the side to avoid me, and I go speeding by with a new sinking feeling.

What rotten timing: the only person within five miles of this place saw the turn I took.

I floor it again and run the 914 up into fourth and let instinct take over.

Another turn-off comes up, and I take it, and another and another until I know not what direction I am heading or why I am taking any of these roads. All I know is that I am away and there is neither sound of pursuit nor any human sound at all. Just the thrumming insect sound of river bottoms and the hot closeness of dense forest pressing in and no time at all to think about the course in life I have just chosen.

Been running around for an hour or more now, and I seem to be back on a familiar road. That's no good. Intermittently, I've heard distant sirens echoing in the trees, caught glimpses of cars behind me, too, but nothing for a while now. I know they're still after me.

I assess the situation and it is not so good either. A quarter of a tank of gas left, and hell if I know where to go. A map would be good, but I do not have one. Not that it'd help; I'd bet none of these little roads here are even on a map.

Where to go? Let's see: they'll be expecting me to try one of the east crossings into Louisiana or Arkansas. Those'll be staked out for sure. North is out, too, and there aren't so many bridges across the Red, anyway, even if I could sneak around Texarkana and get up into Oklahoma. Can't go west either; eight hundred miles of open country on the run down to Mexico is too stupid even for me to consider. So that leaves south. South might work. But hell, I don't even know what direction I am heading at this very moment.

I look up to the late afternoon sun to get my bearings; it's still burning down through the open Targa top, but now it's sinking down in my rearview mirror. Must be heading east then.

No good.

My exposed legs are fused to the vinyl seats in one sticky mass, and I let off the accelerator to pull my leg free of the upholstery, nearly peeling the skin off as I do. I eye my surroundings closely. The forest hasn't changed too much. Still in the huge bottomlands formed by our big, nasty rivers: the Sulpher, the Saline, the Red. So I gotta be close to the Louisiana border. Way too close. I've been down here only once or twice before, and the last time was that family camping trip on the Arkansas side—what, five years ago now? Yes, it was. God, but I never wanted to come back here.

Well, not much choice now, because here I am.

Suddenly, off to my right, a black gash tunneling through greenery. I lock up the brakes and skid to a halt, eyeing the remains of the blacktop. The road is so overgrown and broken it's more of a greenway. Weeds waist high. Barely wide enough for a single car to pass, it looks like one of the very old roads, built right on top of the original settler's trails. Like the one by Granpa's house. I wipe the sweat off my brow and flick it away. And that road ran all the way down to the Galveston ferry, never crossing over a highway once.

"Probably, it just dead ends in a crick or somebody's fishing hole or something." Or maybe not. Maybe this little road here leads to one of the true places?

The kinds of places ol' Ishmael said are not found on any map? Someplace, where I can just start over.

Around the bend before me, the deep sound of a big engine, coming fast.

No time to think now. Gotta go.

Quickly, I ram the stick into first and run the car in fast until I am swallowed up completely by the mass of vegetation, and the view behind me is nothing more than brown grass wrapped in deep shade. Drooping branches reach out and scratch at the paint, the windshield, almost with a purpose. I hear the muscular engine rumble off, and he does not turn in.

The road is surprisingly solid beneath the mat of grass. A few bends later, the trees open up a bit. The grass on the road looks cut, like somebody's bushhogged it. Still heading south. With no sign of the police, though, a different kind of nervousness is setting in, like the times I've been in foreign countries. There are signs of people now. Junk heaps, refuse of all description, a landscape of perverse contrast: beautiful tall forests and crappy, broken-down shacks. Sprung couches and moldy armchairs sit on dilapidated porches, still showing the impression of their owners, but no one's in them, as if these people all up and fled away at my approach. Stranger coming, stranger coming, get off the porch! And if I thought this road was narrow, everywhere out here are smaller ones still: gravel roads, red-dirt roads, and roads that are nothing more than two dried-mud furrows through the grass of a clearing.

Who made them, and where do they go? And who the hell lives way back here, anyway?

Felons, perhaps.

Felons. Like me.

⋏

# BOX OF EMBERS

In the progression of years some memories stand out, simple and desolate, like glowing embers from a fire to be plucked out and packed in earth and damp leaves and saved in your little wood box and kept there nearly forever, never burning out.

Until you feed them into flames again.

It was my Granpa who told me how to keep a fire, and he knew, too, because he'd done it back in World War II. He'd survived cold nights and black nights like that as he tried to escape through the dark forests of Europe in the middle of the winter. And, he'd said, we seen things out there in the pitchblack that we couldn't rightly explain, and it didn't matter whether they were real or not, because they was there all the same. And at the end of it, the monsters that came snarling out of the night with their teeth and their claws, they were real enough.

Used to think the only thing that really makes us different from an animal is our ability to make fire, he told me then, as he crouched there, shakily feeding our own campfire with wood shavings cut from his worn pocketknife, but not anymore. They caught us all, but shot only half of us, he said, I never knew why.

My mother had pulled me on my feet then, and I could feel her angry look at my father who was just sitting there staring into the fire himself, as if he hadn't even heard Granpa's story. She asked what that had to do with anything, and got no response, and then she said something about how telling me these stories was only going to make it worse, and what were they thinking? Couldn't they see I was having trouble enough with my fears as it was? I was about in tears already, and she looked for some support from Dad again, but got none. As usual. Dad and Granpa never even looked up; they just sat there with their faces flickering in and out of the red firelight, like old pagan idols made from stone. So she'd marched me off to my sleeping bag and stayed with me a little while I cried inconsolably. Weary and exasperated, she'd finally just left me there, lying by myself in the dark and terrified of a Thing I'd seen out there, skulking after me in the night.

Is that where I lost him? That camping trip? Seems to be the weekend where he just gave up on me for good, where everything changed for both him and me. That was the last time I saw it. The last time Dad really got angry with me, too. After that: five years of nothing and us barely talking to one another, unless it was for some job he ordered me to do.

Before today, that is.

Now I stoke up the little smokeless fire and lay on a tin of Vienna sausages rummaged up from the litter of this abandoned gas station. Orange and purple flames suddenly flare up, consuming the paper wrapper whole and licking at the meat a moment. Then they're gone.

What a stroke of luck, finding this place. A good place to stop, think things through, and wait out the cops until after midnight. I'd hoped to find an old road map here, too, but couldn't. While my dinner heats, I risk slipping out to the road to double check the car.

Well, it really is hard to see it there in the ruined garage bay, especially in this dusky light. There's no door left to shut, but I've covered the car up with a moldy tarp and piled on some of the millions of newspapers littering this place. Not likely a cop would get out and move things around. Looking around again, somehow, I get the feeling that I'm not the first person to take refuge here, and I'd swear those cans of food were cached.

Back inside the station, I look to my meal. The gelatin boils over the sides of the metal tin and the cylinders of meat bubble and pop. "Your dinner is served, sir," I say with my best English butler accent, bowing down to grab the can off the fire with a greasy rag. I pull at the warm sausages with bare fingers. Pieces tear out in soft, slick gobs. Nothing to wash them down with, but I'm too ravenous to care.

After a dinner that takes all of five minutes, I squat down on my haunches by the fire, not daring to sit on anything. So strange here in this light. The station is a boarded up piece-of-crap kind of place that could never have been decent, even on its opening day. And now the dilapidated plywood and rusted metal structure glows eerily inside, bathed in the crisp white light of a rising moon that is brighter than my small fire. The quiet of rot and neglect reaches out and wraps itself around me. My skin crawls. The sensation of someone else hiding in here is strong. I can't get the Thing out of my mind.

That was the last trip we ever took together as a family. Dad struck camp early the next morning, and Granpa went home in his blue and white work pickup while we made the long trip back in our car, hardly looking at each other, speaking in only the barest of grunts. I kept my nose to the window, trying not to think about the early exit or the lines of disappointment etched unmistakably in Dad's crag of a face. Industrial-scale chicken houses were springing up everywhere then, perched on the sides of hills, angled in rows in clearings in the woods, all glowing with efficiency in the darkness of the lowland morning. So sterile and alien and quiet on the outside, I couldn't have smelled them if I'd had the window down. And I wondered at all those short lives spent in there entirely in the light, standing in their own shit with not enough room to even perch, and yet every one of those birds' lives had a value, every one of them had some worth. To someone. Finally, the chicken farms gave way to tree farms and paper mills. You could sure smell them. The rotten, chemical smell of those massive works permeated even the air-conditioned, micron-filtered cocoon of Mom's shiny SUV, staying with us almost all the way to the outskirts of town where our big, new house squatted in a burb-like development. We'd been there a year, and still I could distinguish it from the other houses only by its larger size. After that trip, I always thought, that's us, just on the Texas side of the smell.

That night, I hid in the laundry closet off Mom and Dad's bedroom. Enveloped in the metallic and firesmoke smell of Dad's sweat-stained camping clothes, I heard everything. The words, the words, they wouldn't stop coming. Sticks and stones, sticks and stones, a father's rant I'd never heard. The words worked their way into that dark cube and into my covered ears and into my brain until they became my own thoughts, echoes that never quite die.

He was sounding off at Mom in his frustration, his voice dripping with blame. He decided the outings were all a "net loss." He'd been trying to force me to "conquer my fears," and "be independent," but I wasn't getting it. John's hopeless, he'd told her. Then she'd said, why do you have to do everything for him? Just put him in Boy Scouts or something, if you're trying to teach him independence. Why, he'd yelled back, why? Open your eyes, Diana. Haven't you seen him? Because he can't handle it. What's wrong with him? He's like some kind of idiot now. All he wants to do is go play tennis or bury his nose in some crappy book he doesn't even understand. Used to be nothing but stupid shit coming out his mouth, blab, blab, blab. Now he never says anything, just stands there like a dolt, waiting for you to order him around, like there's not a single circuit firing in that brain of his. Chip, that's cruel, she'd finally interjected, you know how sensitive he is. He's a sweet boy. He does well in school. You never give him a chance. But she wasn't disagreeing with him, not really, and he just kept going off. And what kind of twelve-year-old is still scared of goddamn monsters? He asked the question, but he didn't expect any answers, and he got none, certainly not from her. Even then, I could hear her turning on her autopilot, like an almost audible click and whirr, cruising speed reached, thankyouverymuch, enjoy your trip. Then he said, why am I even talking to you, and he turned out the lights. I heard him go straight for her then, grappling her to the bed. And she didn't say anything, but she must have scratched the hell out of him, because he roared like a beast, and then I heard her thud hollowly on the wooden floor, and her whimpers of pain were muffled by his big, muscular frame, and she took the thumping quietly, right there on the ground. Quietly, quietly, quiet. I know how to be quiet too.

I awoke the next morning to him looming over me. And the look on his face, it was horrible: enraged and disappointed at the same time, like he was wishing for another son, any son besides me. Like he hated me. What are you doing in there, he said, menace in every word. I couldn't make myself look at him. Couldn't stand the sight of his face like that. Answer me, he'd yelled at me, answer me. But I didn't. My lips moved, but nothing came out. God, but he got angry then. He jerked me out of that cubbyhole by the arm with force enough to dislocate my shoulder, and that's when the belt came out. There was no stopping him. Little pervert, he was yelling at me as Mom scuttled out of the room.

When the doctor asked what happened to my arm a few days later, I didn't tell the truth. Playing tennis, I told him. Mishit a serve so bad my arm popped out. And I managed to get by without anyone seeing the bruises.

As I found out later, all that was just after they'd been told that I was the only one; there wouldn't be any more kids. Not from him, anyway. I hope he felt like shit. Like absolute shit.

Mom walked less than four months later. Gave up custody, too.

Granpa died that same year.

So here I am now, five years later, hiding in a pile of garbage, a criminal, and not knowing what I am going to do next, or how I am going to get out of this. Not knowing at all, and all I can think of is Granpa's little box of embers, and how they'll never die.

Through a gap of the window boards, a bright white light, growing brighter.

The sound of the big engine idling up.

Quickly I dash out the fire with my foot and spring to a knothole in the boards. A county police cruiser is coming up slowly, the officer strafing the station with a spot-light. He stops the car in the middle of the road and fixes the light on the garage for a long moment. Then he turns it back towards me with a suddenness that's hard to duck. His windows must be rolled down because I can hear him calling another unit on his radio.

"Papa-102, to Charlie-101," he says. "Come in."

"Charlie-101, here," replies an aggressive voice that I can recognize even over the crackle of the radio. "P-102, do you require backup?"

"Negative C-101, but stay close. Checking out the old Donald filling station now."

Oh God, don't let him get out and come in here.

"Repeat, P-102. Did you say the Donald filling station?"

"That's affirmative, C-101."

"Request that you wait for backup, P-102," replies Charlie-101. "Do not proceed."

"That's a negative, C-101. Proceeding with search. Request that you stand by only."

"Affirmative, P-102. Don't think he could've gotten out that way, but I am standing by."

"Ten-four," says the policeman who is not twenty feet away from me. "Stand by."

I'm looking around for a stick, a crowbar, anything like a weapon, but there is nothing. Now he turns the car into the parking lot and his headlights light it up inside the station like it is broad daylight, and I cower behind the wall, wondering what I will do when he comes in here. I'm as good as caught. Good as dead more like it. But I will not go back.

I will not go back.

Another peek out the knothole reveals P-102 opening his car door and stepping out with his gun drawn and mag light shining. Another big one, this guy. Thick as a side of beef, he's probably got the better of me by fifty pounds at least. Frantically, I look around the station.

Shit, I haven't figured a back way out of this place. Dad's voice coming at me now: what were you thinking? How the hell could you be so stupid? Think, he thumps me on the ear hard enough to raise a welt. Think, he screams it at me.

I screw my eye back to the hole. P-102, paused in the act of shutting his door, seems to be reconsidering his decision to come in here alone. In fact, he looks scared as hell. Does he know something I don't? Just as he works himself up to do it, his car radio comes back to life.

"Papa-102," says a different voice, a deep bass. "This is COM. Come in, Papa-102." My policeman reaches back in his car for the microphone.

"Papa-102, in. Go ahead COM."

"Proceed to checkpoint," says COM. "Repeat. Proceed immediately to checkpoint."

"Ten-four, COM. Proceeding to checkpoint. Papa-102, out."

And with that, Papa-102 jumps back in his car and is gone.

Something is freaking those guys out.

And it isn't me.

This won't do at all. On trembling legs, I stamp out the remains of the fire, gather up a few cans of meat and run to my car. Throwing off the tarp and papers, I get in the Porsche and run her out hard, flying off into the night.

A long while later and, damnit, feels like I've gotten east again, but I couldn't have crossed into Louisiana. No, still must be in Texas. Somewhere. And I have got to get going south again. But I don't really know south from north or west from east out here in this gloom. Surely there's some place around here where I can ask someone, just a place to get gas, any place. But there's nothing. No, something. Everything I see is crawling, decayed, haunted.

Don't be stupid. Calm down.

Really though, these few houses here, they've long gone to pot. Dilapidated shacks stand behind rotten fences; weed-choked dirt lanes end in nothing more than ruined walls of broken windows. Old brick chimneys stand alone in arrested freefall, like ancient monuments beyond memory. All is blanketed beneath a jungle thicket of trees and vines. Shadows stand between every tree, yet nothing moves.

And now the mist quickly settles down in the dark spaces between the tree boles. Thin strands of cloud obscure the moon; it's just a pale flat disk floating high above the ragged fringe of the forest. A claustrophobic darkness descends. The forest comes alive, and I'm surrounded by the loud, animal noises of unseen things, thrashing in the night.

Suddenly the pavement ceases altogether. What had only been some oil mixed with sand drops off to just a washboard gravel, punctuated by thousands of potholes. Both hands death-gripped to the steering wheel, I try to relax. But I can't. I'm going fast again, too fast. I'm just looking for any sort of normal habitation at all to appear around the next bend in the road.

But, it doesn't. Of course, it doesn't. No, instead, there's a Y-fork in the road here. I slam on the brakes. The car immediately slides sideways, and I correct it into an abrupt stop. In the dim beams of the headlights, I can just make out sticks marking each branch of the fork. On the left, an A, hand-painted in red; a faded B is splashed on the right-hand stick in blue.

Neither of them looks to be heading south. Nothing feels right about this. I slump down in my seat and close my eyes tightly, feeling overwhelmed and confused, like nothing I am going to do here will be right, like nothing I am going to do from here on will ever be right.

Stop wasting time, yells my father, just choose one. Or do I have to do it for you?

"No, Goddamnit," I whisper to him, opening my eyes again. "No. You don't."

I put the car back in gear and thrust it forward, heading down the A fork.

The road is tolerable for a few miles, but I'm speeding up recklessly now, even as the track deteriorates, runs down into and merges with a dry stream bed. I tell myself it's not safe. I seem to be heading nowhere fast. And yet, it is oddly liberating. I feel it now, feel the road, feel the little Porsche fishtailing out around the loose gravel bends, beyond any car's gripping limits. I'm the dirt-track speed racer now. I'm the one who's going to take the cup home. Going to spray the wild crowd with cheap Brut champagne. I'm the one, and it is thrilling to be power-sliding through the corners, and the adrenaline of the moment has me thinking I know what I'm doing. Of course, I don't.

I plow on at high speed even when the track bursts through the woods, leaves the stream bed and becomes just two spurs through a clearing dense with enormous weeds. I charge over them, reveling in the satisfyingly rhythmic sound of plants being slapped to the ground. The car leaps and skitters convulsively; dirt flies from the tires; rocks smash into the undercarriage; debris sprays up around me. A sharp bend appears, coming fast. I power into it.

And then it happens. Of course it happens.

What an idiot I am.

A metallic cracking sound. Something in the transmission. Something breaks, locks; it locks hard. The car comes out from under me with a furious spinning of gravel, weeds, and dirt. A slowmo: a tunnel, a lifetime, both spinning. All around me. A centrifuge of mist, of dark forest, all swirling. All around me. Unthinking simultaneous stomping of the clutch and the brake—both feet slamming with inhuman strength—exactly the wrong the thing to do. I know it the instant I do it. The absolute wrong thing to do.

Something tall in the clearing in the blink of a revolution, a ragged corruption of darkness, moving.

It comes for me.

▲

# ALIVE

At the bottom of the steps, Chip Sharpe blinks his eyes, once, twice. He stares up at his own photograph swimming into view on the stairwell wall. He doesn't know where he is or how he got here, and it seems strange to him that he's looking up at a younger self between his own good, brown shoes, stranger still that his own two feet are laced within them and that he seems to be falling away from himself. Backwards.

He is laid out with his back flat on the landing and his legs angled down the last few stairs awkwardly. Broken pine balusters from the platform above him lie around him like kindling. Pain is rising everywhere in him, but especially in his head and in the wrist that snapped cleanly while arresting his fall just enough to save his life, but not enough to prevent the terrible concussion he has suffered.

The scene comes back to him slowly, in reverse. He grabs one of the snapped spindles with his left hand and throws it at his own picture, but misses and hits a picture of his grandfather instead, cracking the picture glass of the old man who raised him.

"Cheap crap."

Groaning, he flails his feet helplessly a moment, stops.

Now the memory of the push returns just as electrifying pain courses through his limbs, his wrist. That surprisingly strong shove, striking him with a speed and power that caught him totally off of his guard.

"John!" he yells, "John!" but there is no response. "Where's he hiding."

The pressure swelling behind his temples is becoming more intense, but it's not alarming him quite yet—he's used to pounding headaches—rather it's giving his thoughts an unusually introspective, detached quality, and he does not like this sensation at all. For some reason, he feels like this was all his fault. But his anger and embarrassment help force the thought away.

With his good hand, Chip awkwardly pulls himself the rest of the way down onto the landing and slowly attempts to stand. Quickly, the pain in his head intensifies, but he perseveres, grasping his temples tightly between his long, thick fingers, and pressing, as if to force out the matter in between. Then he staggers slowly over to his living room mini-bar.

"I ought to kill him," he mutters pouring himself a very tall Scotch and quaffing it together with four ibuprofen in one seamless, practiced motion. "When I find him." He places his finger tip on the reader of the small safe under the bar, and the lid pops open. The semi-auto .45 is unloaded, but the clips are full, and he locks one in. He attempts to pull back the slide, but he cannot manage it.

"John!" he screams, dropping the gun and holding his throbbing wrist.

Again there is no response, and the shouting is hurting his head horribly so he stops and shoves the gun back into the safe and slams down the lid. Then he pauses, opens the safe back up, drops the clip out of his gun and shuts the lid softly this time. He drains his drink and pours another.

The feeling of tiredness is working through him, and he cannot seem to hold onto his anger any longer. He is having trouble even remembering what has happened to him. All he is left with are notions of his own inadequacy in the face of his son's actions and a distinct lack of coordination in the whole episode. Both of these ideas give rise to very new feelings that he is trying on, almost like a new suit that's too tight around the chest and too short in the legs. Taking off his tie and dropping it to the floor, he looks longingly at his wingback chair, the soft couch. More than anything, he wants to sleep now.

"No. Can't. Not now," he says, thinking of John again and determined to find him.

Glass in hand, he mounts the first four stairs, kicks aside the debris, nearly falling again as he does so, and looks up through the broken banister to John's room. The door is closed. He halfway expects John will be up there, laying on the bed, looking up through the skylight.

Wearily, he finishes climbing the first run of stairs, pausing on the landing to rest and take down his own picture. This he tosses onto the carpet below, and then he tackles the second flight slowly, not knowing whether he wants John to be in there, or not. Again, this feeling he can't quite put a word to. Disappointment?

Chip opens the door. John isn't there. Curiously, some of his clothes are laid out along with a duffel bag, as if he had been packing to leave but stopped. Chip notices for the first time that his kid had been taking down the posters in his room, which is unusual now that he considers it. John hadn't changed his room since they moved into the new house, more than five years ago. Chip shakes his head; fixing up his own room is one of the few things John ever insisted on doing himself.

"Until today." Chip rubs his head gingerly now, for in giving voice to the words, the memory of the argument has come back to him abruptly. "I threw him out today. That's why." Chip whispers the words into the empty space, remembering the yelling, no, screaming at his son. Because John hadn't gone to the job Chip had set up for him. Again. John never even called to let anybody know; he just never showed up. Chip hadn't meant to get so angry, but he'd left work worried that something might be wrong, and then found John, just laid out on his bed, doing nothing at all. Well, he snapped, and he snapped in a major way. Only this time, it had all been different.

This time, John had stood up to him. This time, he'd fought back.

Chip rolls the cold sweat of the glass across his aching forehead.

"Some thanks I get for giving him every Goddamn opportunity in the world," he says.

But why is he always screaming at John? Why the rage? Chip asks himself the questions, but he doesn't have an answer. It's an anger that no one else—not his clients, not his ex-wife, not even his worst enemies—gives rise to. Hell, even as a young man, he'd never yelled at anyone like that. No one ever sees him lose it like that. No one but John. And when Chip does lose it in his encounters with his son, it's as if every frustration he has ever had or ever will have all come spewing out of him, uncontrollably, violently even. And he hates losing control, hates it above all things. But John, Christ Almighty, John; it's as if nothing Chip says ever seems to register on the kid. John just stands there silently and stupidly and takes it all with his mouth slightly open and his head bowed, not looking you in the eyes, until it makes Chip angrier and angrier, and then it's too late.

And Diane, she was no help. She'd just say, he's your son, Chip, don't you bring me into this. When she was here that is. Always working, gallivanting around the country doing her "business consulting" bullshit.

Chip stares into his drink, which doesn't taste so good to him all of a sudden.

John, who never asks for anything. Who never thinks of anything on his own either. Can't seem to think for himself at all. God, but that kid has to be told every single thing to do.

Over and over again.

But all these thoughts and self-examination start making Chip angry all over again, shocking his head into paroxysms of pain. He throws his glass violently against John's wall and watches as it shatters into wet fragments, leaving nothing but an amber starburst of Scotch that runs down the wall in tiny rivulets, forever staining the sheetrock beneath.

And this, his only son. Now and forever more.

Calming himself once more, he looks around the room again. He sees anew the bag, the posters, the clothes, and the realization finally comes to him: "He was already leaving. I came up here to throw him out, but he was already leaving." On his own. "Jesus H. Christ, John," he says, going back downstairs, "why don't you ever say anything?"

Chip heads straight for the garage. Even before all the lights come up on the clinician clean, he can tell: the Porsche 914, the collector's car he's paid for ten times over in repairs, is gone. The garage door is open. Night has come. Chips looks at his watch.

"Christ, I've been out for hours."

He examines the burnt tire marks on the triple-coated floor, and then he sees the house keys. These he picks up thoughtfully, and that's when it clicks. He sees the whole scene. First he stares, then he rubs his head, his wrist, and then: he vomits. He just barely keeps himself on his feet as the thin whisky and acid smelling bile sprays out across his pristine floor and dribbles down his crisp dress shirt, his slacks, his wingtips, despite his best efforts to keep them all clean. He watches in disbelief, hands on his knees, until his gorge curdles up in an oily pool by the drain and he finally stops his retching. Emptied out now, he's beyond his anger in a way he can't quite understand and doesn't want to, but he knows one thing for sure: his only son ran and left him for dead.

Head reeling, wiping his face with a sleeve, he staggers back into the doorway. Then he turns to look into the half-empty garage. Another thought voices itself: "He'll be back. Just see that he won't. He won't even last a day." He closes the garage door. "Thank God he didn't take the Benz." Then he turns out the light.

Back in the house, he picks up his phone and finds the number for his buddy, the County Sheriff, who, like all of his buddies, owes him something.

But no one answers, and he catches himself just breathing into the receiver, and he hangs up without leaving a message. So tired. He sits down in his chair to rest a moment. Sleep, it's all he wants to do, though something tells him not to, and when his eyes begin shutting on their own, he forces them back open by squeezing his broken wrist. He thinks of calling John's cell phone, and he thinks of calling 911, but he cannot bring himself to do either of these things.

The phone rings and Chip rouses himself to answer. It is Sheriff Dodgen.

"Bill," he answers.

"Chip, you just call? I'll bet you're looking for your son?"

"Yeah, Bill. How'd you know?"

"We found him. Scared as hell from the sound of it."

"Where is he? What'd you do with him?"

"Nothing, Chip, because he got away," answers the Sheriff with a question in his tone. When Chip doesn't offer up anything, the Sheriff continues: "One of my officers pulled him over for driving erratically. Your boy stopped at first, but then he just took off and damn near hit the officer and the cruiser, too. You know, running from the police is no joke. Now, I wonder, what'd get him worked up enough to go and pull a damn crazy stunt like that?"

Chip says nothing. He holds the phone down in his lap a moment and closes his eyes.

"Chip? Chip?" He can still hear the voice coming up from the tinny speaker. He puts the phone back to his ear. "Chip," says the Sheriff suspiciously, "you okay?"

"Yes, I'm allright."

"You don't sound so okay. But, now, don't you worry, we'll find him. We been looking for him all afternoon. Don't know how he managed to get away driving that little toy he's in, but he's been leading them boys on a merry chase, I can tell you."

"Listen, Bill," Chip whispers into the phone, "what happens when you catch him?"

"Well, we'll bring him in and process him for resisting arrest, that's for sure. Night in the drunk tank, maybe. But so far, that's all, unless you can tell me why he's running around like a lunatic in the first place? Did he do anything I need to know about?"

Chip thinks a moment. He thinks of the yelling and the anger and of the very many things he's never told John. He thinks of his own divorce and his estranged grandfather, who he used to call "Father," dead these last four years. He thinks of John's clothes up there on the bed, ready to be packed, the bag half-filled. Finally, he thinks of the push and the anger flashing across his son's face for just that one moment. A reaction that Chip would have never thought possible. The face of a monster he'd never seen before.

"Chip? You there?"

"Yes, I'm here. Bill?"

"Yeah?"

"Let him run."

"But, Chip, he's —"

"Goddamnit, I said let him go. Just let him go."

Chip hangs up the phone and turns it off and tosses it onto the couch.

He closes his eyes a long while and then snaps them wide open with a start. He gets up, and drives himself to the hospital, wondering where John is and what he is doing. Deciding that whatever predicament his son finds himself in is John's problem and John's alone; it's a punishment that fits the crime. Deciding to stay dead to his son.

Dead.

Until John comes crawling back for the leavings. And begs for forgiveness.

⋏

# A Spinning

I awake in a car in the woods in the middle of the night. I know this much, but nothing is really clear, nothing. Ringing, ringing, nothing in my head but this noise, this high, vibrant sound. There was a bang, an explosion. Now there is nothing but this noise, this singing? No, something else. A salty, coppery taste in my mouth, I lick the corners. The prickling feel of my own stubble on my tongue, I can feel each individual hair; they're sticky with this liquid taste. Licking it, licking it, I almost have it, this strangeness. I'm drinking it, choking. My head lolls back. A pale, full moon reels above me, in and out of a scum of clouds. And the clouds are here around me too, in this clearing, in these woods, in the middle of the night. I blink stupidly. Focus. Night noises magnified through the singing, wood noises screaming, a cacophony of life noises, nothing human, all exploding in my head. I was dreaming of Granpa, of Dad, by the fire, camping together all those years ago. Dad, goddamn him. And why? The smell of burning. Not wood, not a campfire: burning rubber, burning electrical, gas, oil. I cough violently, that salty taste again. Sweat? Blood. My blood. I start violently, but I'm pinned. Pain shoots through me. I can't feel my legs. My car. This is my car, my old Porsche. Lost. The curve, the gravel like ice. I was too fast, too fast, panicked. Panicking again, I try to struggle free. Can't, can't break free. Something else is here. The night noises that were everywhere: gone, nothing left but this discordant song, a single shrieking note. The moon's gone. No, no it's not, it's there, a form behind an immensity, behind a presence, wrought in a pale ragged crown. Something looms over me, blotting the feeble light. Wildly,

24

I struggle, but it's no use. A cracking and splintering of the dash, the steering column is simply pushed aside. I'm picked up, wrenched up, my legs are free. The strength of this thing, the strength of this thing is immense. Incredible. I'm hurled through space, gravity free. The world spins, or I spin, or both. I'm crumpled up in tall, dense, sweet-smelling weeds, looking up at the moon again. The blood still streams in my mouth. Curling up, I draw the plants around me, make my nest. But I can't hide, and I can hear it back by the car, and the unwashed smell of it is all around me.

Tears streaming now, the salt on salt of mingled blood and tears. I'm crying, and Dad's voice cuts through the wailing of my head. You're a Sharpe for Chrissake, he's saying, almost gleefully. Then his voice laughs and laughs and laughs. Rage and terror shudder within me, fighting, clawing together in a mortal struggle. Granpa's face then, in blood-red profile, shimmering in the heat of a fire. His lips don't move, his disembodied voice says, the monsters that came in the night, they were real enough. I thrash futilely, groping out blindly with both hands for anything. My right hand finds it: a racket, one of my very own, thrown from the car. I grasp it tightly, lovingly. Leaping up, I stumble forward, not looking back, and not the way I came, because it is there. Choking back blood, limping, I run.

A long roar erupts. Indescribable, unbelievable, a two-tone resonance of profound power and depth and a shriek all at once, I feel it all the way into the marrow of my bones. I drop down in the weeds again in a shivering heap.

Again the call sounds, almost a voice now: horrible and unique, otherworldly, with the sense of physical mass. Somehow, too: a lament. It is all of this, all in a moment.

It is not a hundred yards away.

And it is coming after me.

I get up again, and I run unsteadily for an opening into the forest on quivering legs. With this action, strength flows into my limbs, and I burst into the forest. I'm in a never-ending tunnel, a dark downward pipe, never bending, never branching: straight down. I sprint in a once-in-a-lifetime output and the trees part and the brambles shunt aside and the roots pave my way for mile upon frantic mile. I run until my whole body is aflame and my legs are leaden, thudding in agony, until my breath comes in enormous wheezing gasps. Stars burst before my eyes.

I can run no longer. I drop to my knees, tearing at the air in ragged gulps for what seems like hours, until I begin to wonder at the madness of this night. I assess myself. Surprisingly, I seem okay. Gashes down my leg, they're bleeding still, but not profusely. Bruises everywhere. My jeans are shredded. A cut across my face feels long but not deep. My lip's busted bad, the steering wheel perhaps. There's nothing worse. I catch my breath, and I listen. There is still a hint of something in the depths of the darkness, but it's far away now, and there are the normal sounds of the night again. I exhale and breathe deeply a moment. Just breathe, just breathe. Finally, I pick my battered body up and jog again, wincing in pain and in terror at the sound of my own crashing footsteps.

I watch and listen and jog until I come upon a light shining out ahead, just off of the forest path. Seeing this single small light piercing the forest gloom is a relief so welcome I could shout with gladness. I jog to the source, joyfully swinging the racket I still clutch in my hand, as if hitting imaginary balls. My step becomes lighter now, and I literally spring down the path in the direction of the blessed electric glow. In no time at all I'm on the front porch of an old wood frame house. The whine of a diesel generator, a man-made music, fills my ears.

I'm out. I'm safe.

Even as I raise my hand to knock on it, the door is opened wide by a woman, like an apparition, in a flowing white nightgown. She squints a little in the bright porch light, pale, smiling, not the least bit afraid of a stranger. God, she's, well, she's beautiful. Auburn hair, soft and full, pulled loosely back and falling below her proud shoulders. Delicate features belie some strength. What I must look like: filthy, crazed, wet with sweat and blood.

Like a serial killer.

Then I remember I have my racket in my hand. I tuck it behind my back quickly.

Maybe not a serial killer.

God, how could I've missed it? In her hand, held casually: a shotgun, an old double-barrel with antique triggers. I step back a pace or two, and she sees me looking at it but doesn't put it down.

Behind her, hanging back hesitantly, but still smiling, are two more women, also pretty, also gowned in ethereal white. They whisper to each other excitedly.

I take them to be the door-woman's sisters but can't be sure. Older than me, but still young, or not so young. I don't know.

"We heard you crashing through the trees a mile away," the woman says, leaning the shotgun up against the doorframe and stepping forward. "What on earth is a fine young man like yourself doing running around in the woods carrying a tennis racket, and..." Then she gets a better look at me, and she catches her breath in a little gasp as the smile drops from her face. She brings a hand to her mouth. The twitter of the women behind her goes silent. She doesn't wear any rings on her fingers. None of them does.

I should say something to explain myself, but I don't know what. I'm struck dumb now. To suddenly find these women right before me, glowing white and radiant, after I've been running witless from a vision, from a sound, from some Thing that I've been told is never truly there: incredible. Dad would be saying that I imagined the whole thing, that I was thrown out of the car, that I heard some animal (a damn big animal), and my panicked fears and disorientation magnified all of it into something else entirely.

There are no monsters, John, he says. Not now, not ever.

If he was alive that is.

But it lifted me out of the car.

The woman moves close now, looking up into my eyes with serious concern, scrutinizing me. She's small, petite. I try to make a comment, but it comes out a stutter.

Get yourself together.

"I wrecked my car back over there," I finally manage to say. "This Thing came and... or, well, I heard something. Something mighty weird. Whatever it was, I think I lost it."

My words raise an excited whisper from the two women in the house, but the door-woman hushes them into silence with a backward wave of her hand. The concern forming into her face grows as she studies me until I have to look away. The paint on the house is peeling; the wood of the door frame is exposed and bare.

At last she says: "You mean that old Thing? We ain't scared of him. But you now, well...." she takes my hand in her own, "seems to me, you're the one we need to worry about."

I look up at her again, thinking she's making fun of me, and I do see something like mirth twinkling there in those gray liquid eyes. But something else is there too, and now it's my turn to stare. She doesn't shy from my look, welcomes it even. She seems to understand my thoughts—all of them—and she seems to accept it and forgive me, and the color rises up in me and the sensations sharpen until I can feel every cut and every bruise and every drop of sweat and blood. Everything. Quickly, I look down at my feet.

"But, you've been hurt, and you look about half scared out of your mind, and I know you're lost," she says softly, tugging me in close and putting a finger gently to the gash on my face. "Come in, and we'll get you cleaned up and fix you supper. We just ate, but we got plenty of stuff left."

She stands aside and beckons me in with a graceful gesture, guiding me by the hand all the time, like a dancer leading a partner. I come over-willingly, practically leaping into the house, but she holds on to my hand and gives it a comforting squeeze. Hers is calloused, but it's warm and small as a child's, and I try to figure out what she's saying with it.

Inside, a single tidy room with wide plank floors. No carpets of any kind. Beneath a corner window is a small kitchen, a finely cut table sitting in front of it. On the right is a sparse living area with nothing but a couch and two love seats to shape the space around a whitewashed old brick fireplace. There's a fire burning there despite the warmth of the night and a little antique sewing table standing by. No TV anywhere. A hallway opens off the back wall and I can see three more doors with old glass knobs closing off some other rooms. It's all spotlessly clean, comfortably so.

"Nice," I say, and I mean it. Granpa would like this place, I know. Suddenly the women are all around me, and the door-woman comes in closer still, squares off facing me, her small, pert bosom nearly touching my chest. She puts her free hand on my shoulder; it's a touch of feathers, electrifying, oblivious to my filth.

"Girls, could you two see that he gets a bath and something dry to put on?" She leans back and pinches my t-shirt, scrunching up her nose. "Lord, he's soaked through and through."

"Sure," they say in perfect unison, "come on now, follow us."

I start to go, but now the woman's hand is on the racket I'm still trying to hide behind my back, and she tugs on it, pulling me back, almost into an embrace. She laughs softly, saying, "You won't need this in the bathroom." I quickly let my racket go and stuff the free hand in my pocket as she dances aside, showing us the hallway with a hand. How the woman does move, so sweetly, lightly on tiptoes.

Walking behind the two 'girls', I can hardly think straight at all. In the dim, soft light of the house, I decide they might be in their early twenties. They're graceful, too, taller than the other woman, and so close in appearance to each other, they could be twins, but I don't think they are. Beautiful red hair falls down to narrow waists and seems to float of its own volition, like it's underwater. I wonder about boyfriends, and what they do out here, where they go, and I try to think of something cool to ask, something witty, but, as usual, I can think of nothing. I just follow quietly, guiltily conscious that I cannot stop watching how their gowns catch and fall round their lovely bodies as they walk.

The girls pass some clothes to me in the bathroom and shut the door behind themselves with a quiet giggle. There's no lock. The knob doesn't even turn; apparently nothing save gravity keeps the door closed. I examine the clothes under the single light bulb. They're used but clean. Obviously some guy's stuff: new plaid boxer shorts, a threadbare pair of gray Texas High gym shorts, a soft old black concert t-shirt with the band's trademark lightning bolt cracked into pieces, like dried yellow mud.

Maybe they just like to wear men's clothing to sleep in. Maybe. More than likely one of them's got a metal-head boyfriend. He'll be out raising hell right now in some crappy dive in Louisiana, and sometime in the early morning he's going to come lurching back, drunk off his ass. Probably armed with a semi-automatic. And here I'll be. Just sitting around with his women in his very own boxer shorts and his favorite shirt. I put the things down on the toilet seat, eyeing them while I undress delicately. My clothes cleave to my body like snake skins. Painfully, slowly, I peel them all off to stand there naked before the big bathroom mirror, examining myself. The big gashes on my leg have re-opened all on their own, and thick blood beads up within them. I trace the wounds with a finger, imagining how she'll dress them for me. They'll leave scars, like claw-marks. If I live that long. God, how everything hurts.

Groaning rusty pipes cough up sulfurous well water in hardly more than a trickle. I step in the scrubbed claw-foot tub and stand under the showerhead. There's no shower curtain. I try to shake off the visions of the three of them. Can't stop seeing them in here with me. Damnit, just stop it. I'm parentless, homeless, feel like I've been run over by a truck. Probably every cop in Bowie County is out looking for me. And still this.

A cake of soap looks homemade, and probably is. The water's so soft you hardly need soap anyway. Sweat and blood and dirt wash off slowly and spiral lazily through the punctured metal drain cover. Looks like it's been shot. I look down there for the slug, wondering whether this thing empties straight out to the river or not.

There's a soft knock on the door, and it cracks open. I slip and nearly crash trying to cover myself with my hands while the dropped soap clatters down into the bottom of the tub.

A soft laugh, then through the gap: "You allright in there?"

"No," I blurt out, too fast, "I mean, yeah, yeah, I'm allright, I'm okay." Spinning away from the door, my elbow catches a shampoo bottle, and it goes flying. I try to catch it, miss, and punch the wire-metal shelf instead. The whole thing—shelf, razors, bottles, and all—leaps off the wall. I try to catch that too, wagging everywhere, missing everything. A terrific clangor you can hear in the whole house, the whole forest. Before I know it, I'm down. The tub rings like a gong, water rains down on my back; the shampoo bottle's crushed underneath me.

I groan.

Out of the corner of my eye, I see the door open a bit more. She doesn't know what to do, and I can't seem to move. The shower trickles on in the silence. She steps through the door.

"I'm okay," I manage to mumble quickly.

She hesitates. "You sure?"

"Well."

A laugh escapes her, and she pulls back out of the room.

"I'll be out in a minute. Really."

The door closes all the way, and she's gone. I sit and draw my knees up, letting the water pour down on my head and across my open eyes, until the room is swimming liquid light.

No telling how long I sit like that. Could be five minutes, could be an hour. Then the unmistakable smell of fried cornmeal finds its way in, and suddenly my mouth is watering. I am finally able to screw myself up to turn the shower off. I dry off slowly and put the fresh clothes on, concert shirt and all. Lyrics from the band in my head: she rocked me all night long; I'm back in black. Yeah, I'm back in black.

God, what a mess I am.

In the dining room, they are all sitting at the table, still in their thin nightgowns. They're all looking up at me, smiling, in kindness. Or is it sympathy? I quickly sit, drawing my chair deep underneath the table, draping my napkin tightly about my lap.

"Here honey," the woman says from across the table as she rises and bends over a big brown crock to serve me. I can see right down her nightgown, all the way down to her bellybutton. She is as white and smooth and firm as newly polished marble. No bra under there, no nothing. She doesn't seem to notice.

She pours home-made looking wine from a clear bottle. My plate's filled with coleslaw, green tomatoes, fried cornmeal balls. Hushpuppies, maybe.

"We make this muscadine wine here ourselves," she says picking up her own glass and raising it to me. I nod, gaping at her, I know it, and lift my own glass to her, to all of them. We drink. The stuff's cool and sweet and powerful. I gulp half the glass down, and the girls choke back a giggle. The woman smiles, leans over again like she's making a point of showing me and refills my glass, this time holding my gaze in her own shining eyes.

Blushing now, I bend my head to my plate, quickly stuffing the cornmeal things in my mouth. The fried taste is good, of peanut oil, I'm sure. But underneath the cornmeal, something else. Chewy, slick, smooth, it defies clean mastication, squirts between my teeth, nearly out my mouth. No, not hushpuppies. Calf-fries. Rocky mountain oysters. Country aphrodisiacs. Call them anything but what they are: fried testicles.

Trying to swallow quickly, I almost gag, but manage to get them down. I drink deeply; we all do. This stuff, like Jim Jones' own Kool-Aid, it rises up in me so quickly, I'm already floating. I can feel them watching me, trying not to laugh, and then I can't help myself, I have to laugh at it all. And the relief bursts out, and we're all laughing, and I pop some more of the things in my mouth and wash them down again, and I'm almost in tears with laughter; maybe I am in tears.

Before I know it, a fourth or fifth bottle of wine is gone, and I've eaten all my calf-fries; we're all sitting on the couch together, drinks in our hands, a girl on either side of me, and we're carousing deep into the dark of the night talking about everything and nothing at all, like the best of friends, like lovers, like I've never been able to talk to anyone before.

Something's snapped within me. I don't know when it happened, or how, but without ever having made a decision, I realize, I've crossed over now into something else, being someone else. Someone bold. The things coming out of my mouth: flirty, borderline raunchy. Their quiet laughter encourages me; I feel the softness of flesh pressed lovingly against me. I'm leaning into the eldest now, lips softly to her ear. She flushes crimson, the other girls shush, shrink away.

"John," she says so quietly I can hardly hear, "what are you doing?"

"Mother?" one of the girls says. "Mother, do you want us to leave?"

The shock hits me, sobers me up like a police siren. My hands are back to myself. The girls are looking at me strangely. She is looking at me. She looks scared, sad. In me, a sudden violent effect: a volcano wakes spastically in my stomach. I lurch up, scattering girls like fallen petals. Walls tilt, doorframes twist, the black hallway opens like a mouth. Stumbling, I run for it, heading for the bathroom in desperate recklessness.

I almost make it.

The mess issues forth in an angry spectacle of burning and stench, enveloping the toilet, the floor, the tiles, the walls. I retch for my loss, again for my embarrassment, again for the persistent thoughts that can't be suppressed, even now, and finally: for the thought of him and the image of him, down there in the emptiness again. Dead. And the look on his face: like a sepia of some granite pharaoh in my history books, eyes wide open and an all-knowing smirk on his lips, like he knew it all along. Like he'd always known: in the end, I'd come to nothing.

To see me now. Dad, if you could see me now.

I keep at it until there is nothing left but breathless wretched pain, and I sink into my own crimson spew, and I am barely aware of soft hands and soft voices with wet towels and a mother's forgiving touch.

# LAWMAN

"John. You want some pancakes and sausage?"

A voice booms in my ear. A big voice. My head splits, and my ears recoil. It's more of a demand than a question. But I know the voice. From somewhere. A large, slightly blurry man comes into focus, just for a moment.

Mirrored sunglasses and a huge, creased face under a big white Stetson look down upon me. It's the Sheriff. Our Sheriff. I've seen him a time or two before; he's an imposing and hard-to-forget man, but we've never formally met. My father does something for him. I forget what.

My father.

I sit up with a start; my head reels. My father did, dead. He doesn't do anything for anyone anymore. He's dead. Yesterday, it was real, all of it, every bit. My father is dead, the Sheriff is here. I know the voice, too. It's COM, the one who called off the cop.

I'm done for, oh God, the game's up, they gave me away.

But what did he just say?

I blink bleary eyes again. His expression: amusement and intense scrutiny. My eyes drift down the dun-clad presence to see the Silver Star and still further to rest on the .357 Magnum holstered at his waist. I see no sign of the girls.

Think. What all did I tell them?

Moron, Dad says, irritatingly answering my own question, you told them everything.

But not about you. You know I didn't tell them that.

Least I don't think so.

The Sheriff's watching curiously. He either doesn't know or isn't sure. Not yet.

I'm sitting up on a sofa under a blanket with no shirt on. I look under the cover. I'm wearing gray boxers now, nothing else. I lay back down and pull the blanket up higher, tighter. Cottonmouth, stale muscadine, dragon-breath, I can't even speak. There's nothing in the world I want less than pancakes and sausage. My stomach geysers back into action, but I hold it down.

A new and horrifying thought. I sit up again with a start, aware only of that gun.

Oh, God, they're probably his wife and daughters.

In a flash I see the Smith and Wesson pressed to my forehead. The muzzle's scorching hot, and it grills a ring of pain between my brows. In the sunglasses, I see myself: dark lank hair, wide eyes, that blank look Dad hates. Gently, he squeezes the trigger, and...

I blink and blink and blink, and it is gone. Nothing.

The Sheriff moves over to the table, still the half-smile on his face, still watching me. He said my name. They must have told him my name. And this is clearly a meal I have to eat.

"Sure," my croak finally comes, barely audible, "I'd love some."

Somehow I manage to get up off the sofa. Every cut burns, every bruise throbs, a relentless pain wracks my whole body. On the floor beside me, I find the pair of shorts, the t-shirt, too, newly laundered and laid out on my racket. I put the clothes on, noticing something in my pocket as I do. My ten dollars, folded, and a small plastic card. Feels like an ID. I take it out and look it over quickly. It is an ID, a driver's license, and it is just as real looking as can be; the name says: John Fears. In the picture, I look different. Scared, happy, drunk, all at the same time. Warily, I move to the table where he waits, stuffing the card back in my pocket as I do.

The girls must have called him here, allright. But they didn't give me away. I stop by the chair and feel the card in my shorts again, vaguely remembering her words.

They called him here to help me.

Slowly, I sit. My place is marked by a steaming mug of coffee and a huge stack of hot-off-the-griddle flapjacks, smothered in butter. The Sheriff leans over a plate of sausage patties, his fork poised to stab.

John Fears. Calling the Sheriff. That's nice work, girls. Some help that was.

I struggle to put down the thoughts of spewing on the Sheriff's starched shirt, of how much it must hurt, being shot, of bleeding and bleeding, of the women, too.

Girls, rather. I clear my head with a violent shake.

"John. Here, have some of these sausages, too."

He spears two burned, greasy patties from the white china plate. I shake my head, no. No way. I sneak a glance up at the Sheriff who is watching me closely, looking through me behind those shiny, opaque sunglasses of his. X-rays boring into my brain.

He frowns as he puts them on my plate anyway.

I focus all my will to just putting down one small bite of pancake at a time. I try not to speak to or to look up at the man again. He seems to take an intense interest in my labored chasing of each tiny morsel by gulps of scalding hot coffee. There's no milk, and it seems best not to ask for it. I still don't see any sign of the girls, and I don't ask about them. Eventually, the Sheriff breaks our uncomfortable silence.

"Heard you had some car trouble, somewhere?"

His question is more of a statement. It seems to be the way the man speaks. I look at the Sheriff. Surely, he suspects me already. And when he sees my car, he will know me instantly, fake ID or no. But I don't know what the girls may have said to him already. I can only hope.

"Yeah," I finally manage to say, wincing, "that's right..."

The Sheriff waits, expecting more explanation.

"I came here in the dark," I blurt out the words. "My car's wrecked. After, I was lost. Got even more lost when I was running. Walking. The girls, ah –" Psychobabble. I wave my hand vaguely in the direction of the path that had brought me to this house. "– My car's way back that way." Just shut up.

Saying nothing, he sits there, scrutinizing me.

Squirming in my chair. Stop it.

"Well, we better find it and get you taken care of," the Sheriff finally says.

He stands abruptly and pushes back his chair, instantly ready to go. He doesn't stop watching me, and I don't have any choice but to go with him.

"Okay, sure." I stand too quickly, my stomach roiling.

What does he mean by "taken care of"?

I follow him out into the hot morning light. His white County Sheriff Bronco is there. It is spotlessly clean. He points for me to ride up front, and I hesitate, feeling like I should run away all over again. I look wildly all around me, not seeing the forest path from last night, not knowing which direction I even came from.

Can't do it. Not here, not now.

I get in, and he turns to look at me.

"Don't be scared, boy," he says, not unkindly. "Just show me where."

I nod and point. The way I came, or not, I don't even know.

In the dim morning light, from the seat of the SUV, the forest doesn't seem so threatening, though it's much the same as I remember it. He navigates the truck slowly and expertly, and it submarines through the monotonous greenery in an easy grind.

"You a tennis player?" He asks, glancing at the racket beside me. Surprised, I look at him, staring, and nod yes, but he is focused on the path before him. "I always wanted to play some," the Sheriff continues. "Used to watch Borg and McEnroe go at it. Looks pretty fun."

I glance down at his .357 and his silver-trimmed snakeskin boots. What's he getting at? Is he trying to be nice? I study his face a bit. It's hard to read, but he doesn't seem to be toying with me. The words don't fit this man.

"Yeah," I venture, "tennis is great." No reaction from the Sheriff now, his expression remains enigmatic. Damn shades he's wearing. "And I can make some good money off it since I teach a little bit." I stop abruptly, feeling the fool, and something else grips me now: a constriction of my chest, a cold sweat. Why are we rambling on about tennis of all things? He's probably just trying to get me comfortable and talking so I'll confess my real name, my address, maybe that I killed my father only yesterday, and I ran and left him just lying there, like roadkill.

Something like a small smile disturbs his upper lip, as if he knows he's close to getting my confession, and all he has to do now is wait for me to blurt it out. The fact is, he is close. I do want to tell this man the truth. It would be so easy, just to tell him everything right now. But in my mind, Dad advises: The truth? Always tell them the truth, he says, just don't tell them the whole truth.

"Yeah, those matches with Borg were great," I forge on, and the moment passes, and I play the Sheriff's game. "I loved watching those old replays, too. Wish I could've played at Wimbledon." The Sheriff gives a slight nod—could mean anything—probably that I'm the biggest loser he's ever had in his truck. And maybe I do have him figured all wrong. Could be the Sheriff really is just making small talk, and maybe he really does feel the pull of getting out of here, of leaving this backwater behind, of being on that sunken stage and seeing your name lit up there on that green and white marquis; and your parents, they would be there, and...

Maybe not.

Through an opening in the dense East Texas thicket, I see a stream bed cutting through the trees. A trickle of water in the mud-gravel bed. It looks like it could be the one I'd sped through in last night's tar black. It's close enough to the truth.

"Through there," I point the way. "Through there is the field where I wiped out and this big... sound. Well, I heard something mighty weird."

The Sheriff shoots me his sideways quizzical look again, but says nothing. He just engages his four-wheel drive and plunges in, wincing a little when the rear wheels slide down the muddy bank.

For a while the branches and brush close in even more, and I think that we'll not be able to make it through, but we do. Finally, to my right and through some undergrowth: a wide, bright field.

"There it is!" I say, trying to temper the relief and the anxiety flooding through me.

The Sheriff forges up the bank and through the tough shrubs. We come up into the field and onto a four-wheeler path cut around the perimeter of the field. Glorious sunlight shines from the high blue dome of sky. A lone oak tree stands majestically near the middle.

Yeah, this is going to work, Dad says to me now, this'll work great. Good one, John. He'll know that yellow piece of crap in about one second, and then what are you going to do, huh? You think you can outrun that .357 he's toting? Do you?

"No," I shake my head; can't get him out of my head. "Stop it."

"What?" asks the Sheriff. "Stop what? Is this the right place"

"I mean, stop the truck. Please. Please stop. My car should be here. Somewhere."

But he's already stopped; he's looking intently at the clearing. My car is nowhere to be seen, but this really does feel like the place. This field is just a big, round opening in the forest, but these are no normal weeds. More like some crop. The plants are almost man-height, big weedy green plants, iridescent in the glaring sun. For the first time, the Sheriff's face registers a noticeable change. He looks more agitated than I've seen him yet. An obvious frown erodes the creases of his face. Looking all about him, he fingers the big Magnum revolver, muttering.

"What sort of crop is this?" I ask, nervous as hell, as he starts back up and pulls onto a wide path, cutting across the field. "I've never seen anything like it."

The Sheriff pulls to a halt again, turns to look at me, and holds my gaze uncomfortably long with his inscrutable face and big shiny glasses. Judging me, it seems. Mesmerized, I stare back, wondering what I'm in for now.

"Boy, you really don't know what this is, do you?" He says with his usual finality.

"No, ah, my Granpa had a farm out in East Texas, and I used to go out there. But I never saw anything like this. What is it? Some kind of cattle feed?"

"Cattle feed!" The Sheriff guffaws with a start. "Ha! Them's some happy cattle that eat this here feed!"

He's in tears with laughter, and I, well, I feel the shit-eating grin come over me. I can't seem to wipe it away. Why the hell won't he explain? What's so funny?

"Cattle feed!" He says again, shaking his head. He actually takes off his glasses now.

Disconcertingly, it seems as if he's removing part of his face. But as he shakes his head side to side in disbelief and wipes his eyes, I see them for the first time. Surprisingly, they are kind and brown when I had imagined them to be steely gray and grim. Maybe that's why he wears the glasses—to cover those kindly, bright eyes.

"Well, where's this car of yours? Let's go find it before the cattle get to it." He chuckles to himself and puts his glasses back on. The glimmer of kindness fades, and he gets back to business. "And by the way, Son, it's marijuana. A whole field of pot. You crashed into a multi-million dollar crop last night."

I feel even more the fool, if possible. Of course, marijuana. How could I be so stupid? I slap my forehead unconsciously and immediately regret doing so as the pain throbs in my head. But it soon changes to panic. Dad was right. When the Sheriff sees my car, he'll know it for the one his cops were chasing all over the county yesterday. No choice now. I think of opening the door, of leaping out and running away. I eye another gap in the trees across the field, too small for the Bronco; then I see the path making its way towards the solitary tree in the clearing.

Maybe. If I can just get him over there and away from the truck. Maybe, he won't shoot.

"I don't see it," I tell him. "Can we get out and look around?"

He hesitates. "Allright," he says, "but let's hurry it up. This here's one place we don't wanna have us a picnic. Not unless we want to invite the Texas National Guard, that is."

I nod and hop out of the SUV and jog down the path. He follows. But near the tree, I find the scene of my accident. Any idiot could see it. The long, deep furrows made by my wheels are clearly visible cutting across the field and through the flattened cannabis. There is no sign of my car. Suddenly, I recall my flight from this place in vivid, sickening detail, and I eye the small gap in the trees again; but curiosity is overcoming me, and, somehow, I don't want to try for it now.

In the corner of my eye, a bit of yellow sheet metal; I jog up the tracks a little, finding a nut here, a bolt there, one of the engine mounts, half buried. But still no car. The tracks simply stop at the tree, and there's nothing else here but mud and crushed weed. It's as if the Porsche has been swallowed whole, consumed into the gullet of the earth. In me, an overwhelming relief and a sadness, too; I can't breathe. I sink to my knees in the moist dirt. Dad is pounding on me from inside my skull. He says, you think you got out of this? Think again. Where do you think he's going to want to take you? Home, that's where. You'll be just another failure arriving in the back of a cop's car. I've been betting on it all along.

The Sheriff is right behind me, now beside me.

"It's gone," I whisper. "It was here, right here, but my car... it's gone."

The Sheriff says nothing and I blink up at him, sensing his nervousness as he just stands there, panning his head side to side in constant motion, his hand held lightly on the hilt of his weapon, the strap of his holster unbuttoned. He freezes, awestruck, staring not at me, but down at the ground. I see them now, too. At his feet are the largest footprints ever. Someone of immense proportions. Some *Thing*. It has trampled the ground all around here. The prints are deep and filled with wet seepage, and they are full of purpose. I get up and follow their progress. I find the nest I'd made. The gargantuan footprints are there, right beside the impression of my own body. I see, too, my own prints, running away. His follow. They are twice as big as mine. Twice as big at least. In a terrible vision, I see the scene and I am he. I am The Colossus, monstrous and angry, and I'm watching my own flight and stepping after myself in a darkness turned to day. I am making three yards to a stride, and I am catching up.

"Well, Boy," the sheriff breaks in with a pat on my back. I blink up at him again; he's still looking down at the footprints. The forest is quiet, and he seems to have forgotten what he wanted to say. What I expect him to say: here be monsters. But he doesn't. Instead, he says, "There's nothing for it now. I'll send some of my deputies back here to look for your car. We better get out of here muy A-SAP. I don't want no trouble here."

He pulls me quickly to my feet by the scruff of my t-shirt like a child and practically drags me back towards his truck. I'm reluctant to leave, despite the oddness, the fear of the place. I stumble almost blindly in his grasp, looking back the whole time.

Out of the woods and on the pavement of a blacktop, the Sheriff begins to breathe more easily; he seems, oddly, almost happy now, although my own mood doesn't improve. Gets worse, in fact. I know what's coming. I just stare at the floorboard, barely noting the passage of time or the movement of the vehicle.

I'm not telling him. No way.

I think of the look on Dad's face. I close my eyes and put my hand to my face; tears are coming up, and I fight them back, pinching my busted lip to feel the pain.

Not here, not now. Not another tear shed for him.

I glance up at the Sheriff, driving implacably along.

The Sheriff is looking at me now, about to speak. I'm waiting for him to ask me where I live. I don't know what I'm going to say. But what else can he do? No way he'll just drop me off by the side of the road somewhere.

"Boy," he says, then stops and considers his words.

Here it comes.

"You've done me a great service just now," he continues, "and I'm sorry your car is gone. I know you don't got much left."

I nod. That's for sure.

"But I been thinking... and you don't have to tell me or nothing, but I figure you up and run off from home, and that's why you been acting kinda' strange..."

Here he looks up at me for confirmation of his thoughts, and I barely manage to nod again, so stunned am I. Now the Sheriff picks something out of his front shirt pocket; it's a small plastic card. He hands it to me, and I look at it. Unbelievably, it's my ID, my very own driver's license, the one I'd left with the cop. Hardship rating and all, the picture like a lost, mute child. I gape at him open mouthed. Can't help it.

"...Now, see here," he starts again, more sternly now, "giving this back to you is against my better judgment." He looks me up and down, like he's reconsidering, but then he continues. "But you seem like a good kid who wasn't thinking too clearly. So, boy, the next time some officer pulls you over for a traffic violation, you better cooperate with him, and don't you go running off, you hear me? Because if you do it again, you'll get a free trip to the County Jail, and you can believe me, that ain't a nice place. Nosirree, not nice at all."

Somehow, I manage to nod.

"Anyhow," he says, relaxing a little, "it's like I said: you done me a favor, and now I'm gonna do you one. I got a place for you to go, and a good job for you. I know you probably had other plans, but this'll get you on your feet." He glances over at me and shakes his head a little, reconsidering again, perhaps. "If you want the job, that is."

I stare back at him dumbly for a moment.

Did he just offer me a job and a place to stay? He did, and I start to say, yes, hell yes, but I'm not sure this is a great idea. He's looking down the road again, like a man who has just spoken words already regretted, like he never spoke at all.

"Well. You mean?" I stop again, remembering the line I gave the girls about being a struggling tennis pro on the Challenger circuit, just living out of my car and heading down to Galveston to play the next tournament. Or something like that. Not a bad line really.

Except that there's no Challenger in Galveston.

"I mean... well, I don't have much work experience."

At this, he looks me over a little, but he doesn't take back the offer.

"And I was heading down to Galveston, hoping to play a pro tournament and get a job teaching tennis or something. Somewhere."

He doesn't even nod, just sits there like a statue.

"But. But I can't, I can't do that now, I guess." I think of the Porsche again. The way I felt driving it home that first day. I do need some money. To do something. To do anything. "So. If you've got a job for me and a place to go, I guess. I guess I don't have much choice. I mean, yes, thanks, I appreciate it. I'll take it."

Whatever it is.

He smiles a little.

"Hopefully there's no commute," I think to add.

He smiles broadly this time, finally looking at me, and confirms the deal with a quick handshake. "Nope, no commute," the Sheriff says. "No commute at all."

Whatever is he talking about? For that matter, whatever am I doing? But I guess it doesn't matter. Galveston sounded good, actually, but I'm not going to make a go of it there on thirty bucks.

"Well, then, it's all settled," the Sheriff says, interpreting my silence. "I got a buddy over in New Boston. He runs the highway department there, and I know he needs a hand."

"Oh. Okay."

The Highway Department. Well, isn't that just great. Better not tell him my own father didn't even trust me to mow the lawn, or that I don't know the first thing about highway work. We pull onto Highway 59, and the Sheriff points his truck down towards New Boston. Towards my new job. And still a free man.

Imagine that. Me, a highwayman.

Wouldn't he just be laughing his ass off right now.

$\lambda$

# A SPLENDID GAME

"Jesus, why didn't they just go ahead and put smiley faces on the damn thing," Chip says, wriggling his fingers, and looking at the cheery blue cast encasing his forearm, wrist, and most of his hand. He looks out of the big picture-frame window on his seventh floor office with some satisfaction, but he's not cheery, and he's not pleased with his work this morning. It's not that things have gone wrong, necessarily. And it's not the pain in his wrist that throbs through the bandages every time he touches something. That's nothing. It's just that he got no pleasure from work, and he's been so distracted, so unfocused; he's been day-dreaming for God's sake. Of some things... things he hasn't thought of, not in years.

John had turned up all right.

Chip had come home from the hospital late last night and turned his phone back on. There had been messages. A couple of callbacks from Dodgen, an obligatory one from Diane. Then there was the one from the woman people call "The Priestess."

Chip puts his phone on speaker and listens to the message again.

"Now ain't this ironic," she laughs softly. "Little, lost bird turns up on our doorstep, and who do you think it could be? That's right, I do believe we got your boy out here, Chip Sharpe, and, my, but he's a chip of the old block, so to speak. I ain't seen him since you sent that pretty, young pregnant thing out here to my mother to deliver him all those years ago.

"Anyway, your boy come running out of the woods, all lost and scared, totin' a tennis racket of all things, and carrying on about being chased by our old fairy-tale Fouke Monster. Pretty cute, if you ask me. But don't you worry now, we'll fix his broken wings and set him free." A pause while she says something to someone with her hand over the receiver. "Ah, but here he comes again, all spic and span, gotta run. Don't you stay a stranger any longer." She kisses the phone softly, hangs up.

"To repeat, press four," the she-computer voice blares out. "To –"

Chip quickly presses the button and listens to the message all the way through, two more times. Then he deletes it and puts his phone carefully back on his desk; he turns back to the big window, fingering his cast, thinking grimly of his own past. All these secrets, all these years. His mind snaps back to John.

How could he have possibly found his way there by accident? Did he know about them?

And still, Chip hadn't called her back. He'd called the Sheriff instead.

Chip's admin sticks her head in the door and points to the blinking light on his desk phone. "Sheriff Dodgen for you?" she says.

He nods his head and moves to pick up the desk phone as she closes the door.

"Bill," he says tersely, "was it him?"

"Yeah, Chip, it was him. He sure has grown. Hell, I hadn't seen him in ten years, except for his picture in the local sports page a couple of times."

"And the Maurys? Were they there?"

"They were. Those are some strange acting girls, Chip, but pretty as pictures, that's for sure. When I come up to the house, all three of them came out on the porch, and the two younger ones looked kinda' worried, for some reason, but the older one, she just smiled like she know'd I was coming and said, 'There's a boy in there's had some car trouble. Breakfast's on the table. Help yourself Sheriff,' and then all three of them just took off. Like I said: strange. Now, Chip, what are three girls like that doing out there all by themselves? And just how do you know them?"

Chip grins, feeling much more like himself. Just as he thought.

"Bill, don't worry about those girls, they're harmless. I want to know what John said, and what did he do? Did he have anything to say for himself?"

"Chip, you are a piece-of-work. First you tell me to let him go, then you tell me to go pick him up. I ain't your damn call-boy, you know. Now what is it that he's done? Why don't you just tell me what's on your mind?"

Chip says nothing.

"Allright, be that way. No, he didn't have much to say. He was all beat to hell and scared looking, real scared looking, and I'm pretty sure he had a hangover about the size of the county jail. Anyway, he just said something about how he wrecked his car, and then he showed me where. But you know, Chip, it don't take a genius—and Lord knows, I'm not—to figure out that you two got into it, and he run away from home."

"Yeah," Chip says, slowly, tapping his cast.

"Well, anyhow, that's what he said, too, and don't worry, I didn't say anything to him about you, like you *told* me. But get this: he led me straight to a huge field of marijuana. Never seen anything like it. His car, if that's really where he wrecked it, wasn't there, but I'd say it couldn't of been too far away, and it's a good bet he nearly got into some very serious trouble out there last night."

"What, marijuana? You mean there's a big growing operation out there?"

"Yeah, Chip, hell, it's gonna be the bust of the decade. And John led me right to it."

"Why, that's great. Bill, that's just the thing we needed. That'll—"

"Chip, don't you want to know about John first?"

"Well, yes, Bill, yeah. What'd you do with him?"

"What'd you think I'd do with him? Just drop him off beside the road?"

"Yeah, well, no, actually. I thought he would... but never mind that. Just tell me."

"I took him over to New Boston to the Highway Department. The foreman there, Herbert Long, he can always use a good hand, and I thought to myself, well, this kid, looks like he might need a hand, but more of the helping variety."

"Bill, are you telling me you got him a job? At the Highway Department?"

"Yeah, Chip, hell, that kid had nothing but the clothes on his back, and for all the chase he led us on yesterday, he seems like a good kid. Doesn't say much, but you can tell a good kid when you see one, and he's one of 'em. He sure as hell did *me* a favor."

For a moment, Chip almost laughs, thinking of John working on a road crew. But then he thinks of John as a good kid, and it starts to make him angry again. Yeah, he thinks, the good kid who pushed me down the stairwell and doesn't even call an ambulance. The good kid who never even makes a pretense of trying to perform the jobs he's given. Not even a little bit.

"No, he does not say much. Well, I'm not sure about this, Bill. What's Herbert like?"

"Herbert? Why, he don't say much neither, but he's a good man, Chip. He's kind of a stern man, it's true, but he's one of the very best. You can bet on that."

And, now that Chip considers it, he decides that Dodgen's act might be the perfect thing for John. It'll serve him right; it'll be like a prison camp. Scared of being found out, no tennis courts, no car, nowhere to go. He'll have no choice but to stay right there and do what he's told.

"Well," Chip says, feeling better and better about this, "I'm guessing John will get run out of there pretty quick, because I don't think he's going to do much work. What have you got on Herbert? Is he going to give you some kind of trouble, if John screws up?"

"I don't got nothing on Herbert. Hell, Chip, he's just a friend. You know, friends? Those are the guys who help you out, because they like you, not because you got something on them. Jesus, Mary, and Joseph, Chip. What's wrong with you?"

Chip snorts. Dodgen, he thinks, gullible fool trusts everyone. "Oh, I know about friends," he says. And I can get something on Herbert, he tells himself, just see that I can't. "And don't you talk to me about friends, *Sheriff*, when you're going off and coddling my law-breaking kid without even asking me about it."

"Chip, sometimes you scare me, you really do. But don't worry about John working out there, if that is what you're worried about; he'll do fine, and Herbert'll take care of him. What does worry me about your boy is that he looked mighty shook up. He was scared as hell of something. But maybe it was them pot growers, 'cause I was scared, too. Them kind of guys mighta' come storming out of the sticks, firing M16s at us or something. And there I was alone with your kid in the car. Anyway, so you're sure you want me to go through with this? Or should I just turn around and bring him back home so you two can sort things out?"

"No, you're right Bill. You did fine, come to think of it. John's damn near, what, eighteen years old? Believe me, he's barely done a real day's work in his whole life. Some structure will be good for him and he's got some thinking to do before he comes back here."

"Well, I guess you know best," Dodgen concedes, "and boy, when we get this thing with these pot growers wrapped, that'll be the absolute shit. The Gazette-ateers over there will finally have some big news to print in their little 'ol paper. I could just hug the kid for leading me straight to 'em. He's going to be a goddamn hero, and you won't have to worry much about my re-election. It'll be in the bag."

Chip doesn't like the thought of John being portrayed as a hero. Screw that, Chip almost says, but stops himself and has a brief moment of introspection. He thinks of Father: national hero in war and in civilian life, small town icon, extraordinarily kind to every stranger and loved by everyone, especially John. Gave everything away to the Church he saved. Died mean and poor as dirt.

"Yeah, well, I don't know about the hero stuff, Bill," Chip ends up saying. "Nearly getting yourself killed is not too heroic, you know? Besides, we don't want John's name out there in the papers. Those goons might come after him. And hey, listen, we still need to get your campaign financing going." And don't you try to tell me you don't need me to raise your money, Bill Dodgen, Chip's now thinking, back on his game. You'd be nowhere without me. "You are absolutely right," he says, "we'll raise more than ever. This pot bust will be just the thing we need."

⅄

# Highway Department

Herbert, the lead foreman and department manager, isn't in when we get there, so the Sheriff goes off looking for him and leaves me sitting in the office. Looking around me, I'm impressed by the brownness of the Highway Department building. It is constructed in some energy-efficient sixties style of brown brick: a blocky single-story with a brown roof, brown trim, and a brown metal entry door. The form-molded fiberglass chairs are brown. The metal desks are brown with brown fake wood-grain tops. The highlights in the terrazzo floor glint brown in the fluorescent lights. Even the crusty old office lady has a brown tint to her, though she's a whitish-looking Anglo like me. Oddly, the place doesn't strike me as drab. It's surgically clean and tidy, but lived in, comfortable.

The Sheriff walks back in, his snakeskins clicking.

"Herbert'll be back soon," he says.

I stand at his approach, stuffing my hands in my pockets, ready to do anything besides sit here and feel miserable but not knowing where to start. "What am I supposed to do?"

He stops directly in front of me, assesses me again briefly and then thrusts out his hand. I take it and he clasps me in his grip-of-death handshake.

"No problemos, don't worry about that. It's all been worked out."

And just like that, he releases my now nearly lifeless hand, turns on a well-polished heel like some military commander, and steps out. He's gone before I remember that I forgot to thank him.

A steel grate drags across concrete.

I wince at the sound. I realize then that the brown office lady is speaking to me. Jesus, it's her voice. I am never, ever going to smoke.

"I'm sorry, what did you say?"

The grate drags again.

"My name?" I interpret.

My name. Crap, yes, I have a new name, if I want it. But do I need to use it? It's hard to get my mouth around it. And what name did the Sheriff give? He knew my first name, but he got that from the girls, I bet. Did he remember who I am? I don't know.

"Yes, your name," the office lady says, getting impatient.

"John... Sharpe. No address at present."

Christ, I didn't think of this. I'll be found out in a week. There are quite a few John Sharpes out there, but when they find my Dad, and the Sheriff finds out about that, he'll know exactly where to find me. I eye the door, thinking of just running out of here right now.

"Okay, Honey, that's all I need," the metal grate says, laughing like a rusty spring. "You come pre-approved by The Powers That Be." She rolls her eyes up to the ceiling, "The Powers That Be, however, did not trouble themselves to tell me your name."

"That's it?" Pre-approved, what's she mean? The Sheriff, I guess.

"Yep, that's it." She smiles a nicotine-brown smile kindly, but her voice annoys me so much I can hardly think straight. Damn muscadine wine last night. I just want to get outside, but I can tell she's about to speak to me again.

Just don't ask about my family.

"But, Lordy, you can't work here in those poor things."

She's looking down at the gray gym shorts I'm wearing and studying them. I restrain the urge to cover my crotch with my hands. "Ah, well, these are all I got." I start to explain why, but stop.

"Really? Well, hold on. Maybe we got something back in the lost and found." She makes a curious sound I can't interpret and bustles off. I don't want some crap from the lost and found. But now she's back, and she has a pair of jeans in her hands. "You just try these," she says, handing me a faded pair of Wranglers with black spatters all over them.

The two-way radio crackles to life in the back office, and she snaps-to, leaving me abruptly so she can answer it. That must be Herbert's voice on the radio, though I can hardly hear it from here. Some instructions are issued, and she returns. Her metal-grate voice drags again and tells me I'm supposed to go weed-eat the fence line of the grounds.

"Okay, sounds good."

I go in the bathroom and hurriedly put the jeans on. They're too loose for my skinny frame. I'll have to find something for a belt. But no matter, right now I'm ready to just get outside and be by myself.

The yard's a big ten-acre or so place, fenced entirely by chain link topped with razor wire coils. Like a prison. I try to imagine how guys get over something like that, but can't. On my way to get the weed-eater out of the garage, I see huge piles of road building materials. Asphalt, gravel, some lime looking stuff, stacks of black plastic barrels. Enormous machines are parked in proud rows like some museum display. The huge road graders, front-end loaders, Gradall excavators with giant shovel booms, forklifts, I can make out, but there are trucks of all sorts and specializations and many other machines about which I can only guess. Nobody else is about. I climb up to peer in at the levers and switches of some of the equipment, but can't fathom how to use them. Keys are in none of them. It's a while before I remember the weed-eater.

Eventually I find it and I gas it up after struggling to decide which gas container to use. The mixed oil and gas fuel, I hope. I give the rip cord a pull. It doesn't even sputter.

I try to remember the last time Dad made me do yard work. Been awhile. I try the machine again, this time pulling harder, and nothing, not even a spark.

The last time was a punishment of some sort, wasn't it?

If you want some exercise, get out there and mow the yard, he'd scolded me. Just the sight of me getting ready to go play tennis made him mad. And I tried to do it the way he liked it. I did. But he couldn't stand it. He didn't like the way I cut it or something.

I give the thing another futile yank, and I feel a strain in my right arm, my playing arm.

Dad must've been watching me from the second floor window, and he just hadn't been able to take it. Before I'd even finished half the front, the yard-guy showed up in his beat-up old double cab with four of his workers, and they pulled out their own mowers and sprinted past me and mowed around me without even looking at me, like I was a piece of yard statuary. I watched them for a while and couldn't believe how fast they were and how willing. They didn't want some gringo kid taking the food off of their families' plates, did they?

Another hard pull, and it sputters a little like it's going to start but dies. I think I'm doing this right. Why won't the damn thing start?

I start pulling furiously now.

"C'mon, damnit."

I pull the thing a thousand times, sweat's running in rivulets now, my arm's definitely strained, my back is aching.

"C'mon, you piece of crap!"

Pull now.

"C'mon, you piece of shit!"

Pull.

"C'mon," pull, "c'mon," pull, "c'mon!"

Yank, a thousand more times.

"Goddamnit!"

I'm screaming at a machine, thrashing on a piece of metal and plastic. Standing and staring down at the yard tool, I think about getting help. No. I am not going back in there. Who'd help me anyway? The office lady?

"You idiot, John. This is just great."

I kick it.

Suddenly, rough strong hands brush me aside the way you'd brush aside a tall weed or a small branch in your way, like I'm nothing at all. A big man picks-up the weed-eater and starts it with a single smooth motion, and in the simple movement: confidence, strength, knowledge, the perfectionist.

I stare at the stuttering, fuming thing that has already been thrust back into my hands. It runs perfectly. Looking up now at the man incredulously, I see a disappointed, stern look on a roughly weathered face. It's an in-charge face, and I know that look, know it all too well. He's probably pushing sixty, but he's tall and ram-rod straight. Green eyes, faded and watery, somehow manage to pierce me through the bottle thick lenses of black old-fashioned glasses. Embarrassed, I try not to shrink from him a little, but fail.

Damnit. At least I manage to hold onto the weed-eater. Of course. This is Herbert. Herbert, the head-man. The lead guy. The head honcho.

This is just great. You're just real slick.

I can't hold the look in those eyes, so I focus on his starched blue button-up work shirt, waiting for the yelling to start. The shirt's immaculately clean, well-worn but spotless. But he doesn't say anything. He just points to the fence with a poker-look on his face. I know he wants me to get on with it.

"Don't kick the equipment," the man says.

I nod, "Yessir,"

Still not able to look at him directly, I take to examining his matte black work boots, also clean and worn, comfortable looking. And within them: legs of oak, like roughly hewn beams, the sense of massive solidity.

And just like that, the boots, the shirt, the man like an oak tree—they're gone. By the time I look up, he's already five yards away, striding purposely back to the office. He doesn't even look back to see that I'm doing my job. He knows I'll do it. I'm nothing more than an irritant to him, an obstruction to be removed from his well-oiled machine, a small problem in a day filled with more important things.

What have I gotten myself into?

I survey the entire long expanse of fencing already hot in the morning sun. It's more of a glimmering, silver mirage, like it's no barrier at all. But it is. I look back to the office just as the door bangs shut.

"Well, nice to meet you too, Herbert."

I turn back to the job before me. The perimeter fence alone must be two mile's worth of weed-eating. Not to mention the mowing.

I get on it. I'm a man possessed now, I'm getting every stray weed, every patch of errant grass. Dad is laughing. I can feel him pointing, jabbing that finger like a spear behind me.

Missed a place, missed a place, he says. What the hell's this? You, working? You?

"Shut up. Just shut up."

The fence done, no break now. Time's getting on. On to the interior, the whole damn yard. This is worse. Dust and stray gravel kick up in my face, my unprotected eyes. This thing reeks of gasoil. Fumes are in my lungs. I'm coughing. Thoughts of cancers, diseases, they come unbidden. I suppress them.

A couple of hours into it, the task seems utterly pointless. The dialogue of the disgruntled nags in my head.

"What's the point?"

I stop and rest, then look back at the office, barely visible across the yard. I keep going.

"Ha, now you are a waste of taxpayer's dollars."

I'm around the other side of a big gravel heap now, the sunny side, sitting down where I can't be seen from the office. This gravel's not comfortable, though. The rocks are like embers, burning my back, my ass. I'm sweating like a pig just sitting here.

"Who gives a crap if there's weeds in a yard full of rocks?"

Herbert does.

I get up and get on with it.

I'm resting at lunch in the grass, eating junk from the vending machine, and keeping an eye on the idling weed-eater, not having dared turn the thing off. It's shadier in the shadow of this asphalt, but the material radiates heat like an oven. I can see the office windows from here, completely opaque and reflective, intensifying the sunlight. I wish I could tell if he is still in there. I'm sure the office lady is watching. I push the thoughts away. Nothing eases the monotony.

Finally, I get it all done. Well, done enough, I suppose. Standing there in the late-afternoon sun, surveying the lot with thumbs hooked into my pockets, it does look pretty good. I'd even managed to refuel the weed-eater and get it to fire up again in ten or twelve pulls.

It's something, I guess.

I look around me. Nobody's near. The yard is hot and empty, except for a big truck loaded with road signs and steel poles. I look in it, but the keys aren't there. Wouldn't know how to drive the thing anyway. A fine grit blows off of the sand piles, like banners streaming in the wind. It's close enough to five now I hope, and I go into the office, wondering what to do. Nobody seems to be back from the roads yet. Herbert's not here either. The office lady is in the back typing on an antiquated blue IBM Selectric, filling out stacks and stacks of forms with machine-gun bursts of typing. She ignores me when I stick my head in there. Back in the break room, I look around.

Do I fill out a time card?

I go to the window looking out at the highway, the air-conditioned cool raising goose pimples through my sweat-soaked shirt. I hope I don't cramp. It hits me then with a force. I hadn't even thought of it.

Where am I supposed to stay tonight?

How am I going to eat?

When the Sheriff said he had a place for me to go, did that mean a place to sleep? I've no money, no clothes, and no friends here. I worry by myself in the empty, cold office, now sitting, now pacing with hands stuffed deep in my pockets.

What am I going to do? Will Herbert give me an advance on my pay?

I can't ask him that. Or can I?

As I'm fretting over this, the door from the yard pops open, caroms off the stop with a bang and is sent bouncing back again by a jarring Heisman trophy stiff-arm. Before the door can come back and hit the guy, he jumps across the sill.

"Hi!"

The greeting booms out of the short, powerful figure; a big chuckle follows. A sound like heavy chopping, it comes up from the depths of a gut shaped like a wooden barrel and barely concealed by a faded red t-shirt. Crazy, piercing blue eyes beam out at me from a tanned face with chubby red cheeks and a walrus mustache shot with grey. The guy is like some demented jack-in-the-box Santa Claus. His whole attitude is one of familiarity.

Is he talking to me?

I look around me. No one else here. "Ah, hi," I reply, looking around me again uncomfortably as he continues to stare right at me with a smile on his face. I don't think he's blinked yet. Maybe he can't.

"You must be the new guy," Jack-in-the-box says.

"Yeah... yeah, that's right." I back a little further away from the crazy blue eyes until I bump into one of the fiberglass chairs banked-up against the cinderblock wall. I want to get out of here, but there's no easy escape. "Yeah, I just started today."

Suddenly, he lunges. And as he lunges, he barks a guttural utterance; his face is a distorted predatory grimace; he throws up his sausage fingered hands like claws, going for my neck. He moves like lightening.

I'm yelling and I fall back into the chair behind me, throwing up my hands in a worthless self-defense against this maniac.

"Aha! Gotcha!" Jack-in-the-box yells, checking himself right over me.

He wraps his belly with his arms and laughs hysterically.

"Shit man! What the Hell!" Cautiously, I uncurl myself from the fetal position I've found myself in, sit up in the chair, and put my feet back on the floor. He thrusts a meaty hand out to me.

"Ron's my name. Ron Smithson. Nice to meet you!" He's still chuckling so hard he can barely get his name out.

Yeah, real nice to meet you Ron. Christ, you nearly scared me shitless.

"John," I offer, crossing my legs like girl in a skirt and extending a tentative hand, half-expecting him to grab it and put me in some wrestling move. "Good to meet you too, Ron." We shake. "Thanks for not, you know, killing me there."

Ron booms an appreciative laugh and plops down next to me, producing some sort of paperwork from his back pocket in the process and laying it aside without looking at it. He's so close, I can smell him. And it's not good. A rotten smell coming off him, like I don't know, like something dead and swollen in the sun and ready to burst. Strange stains fixed in his shirt. Red and black clods clinging to his jeans. He's looking at me earnestly now, an idiot's half-grin on his face, beaming his crazy blue eyes at me.

"You know, John, the Lord is in me. It's the Spirit of Him that guides me."

He says this and stares at me uncomfortably, expecting some sort of response.

Oh God, he's one of those. What, does He tell you to scare the shit out of people?

"Oh." It's all I can manage. "Ah. Well, that's cool."

"Yeah! It's very cool. Super-duper cool. That's what it is!"

He gesticulates wildly at the super-duper cool thought of being possessed by the Holy Spirit, and he almost hits me in the face with one of his paws.

"The Lord brought me back to the shop early today. I know it. I know it. He wanted me here to meet you!"

"Oh." I realize I'm shrinking away from him as much as is possible without getting up and running for the door. He's still staring at me intently. He has this piercing kind of stare, but it's not the look of intelligence. Nor is it the look of someone who's sizing you up, assessing you, evaluating you. No, it's a frightening look, a vacuous empty look, and I can't help but gape at him. He doesn't seem to notice. "Well, uh, yeah, maybe so," I say.

"You go to college?" Ron blurts it out.

What? What's he talking about now? "Excuse me?"

"You look smart, like you go to college."

"Ah. Well, I took some summer classes last year."

"So, you can read?"

Is he kidding? I stare back at him, his idiot's grin still lights up his face. No, I guess he's not kidding. "Yeah," I respond, wondering what he's after. "I can read." Yeah, and do arithmetic too.

"Great! I knew He would provide. The Good Lord always provides!"

And with those words, he grabs his paperwork, glances furtively around the room, and thrusts it into my hands. I'm thinking he's going to try to sign me up for some church donation or maybe for some Amway or something like that.

"I'll give you ten dollars to help me with this."

"Really?"

He nods. Yes, really. "The Regional Office has these new papers," he says, pointing.

I look through the few simple highway-sign manifest forms.

"Well, I don't know much about highway signs," I say, figuring he'll be disappointed, "but what do you need help with here exactly?"

A face already lit from within lights up even brighter.

"Ha, ha!"

He thrusts his finger up, emphatically making the 'I'm number one' sign and looks up, presumably in gratitude, to Heaven. I flinch at the finger darting around so near my face. I can't help myself.

"I knew I had the right guy! Ha! You knew in twenty seconds what this was for!"

I stare at him incredulously. It's hard to believe he's not screwing with me.

He grabs a pen from his sagging shirt pocket and points it at the papers in my hands again, this time searching them very intently. I see a blankness descend like a fog, clouding his face. He hesitates, as if waiting on me to figure something out. Then it dawns on me.

Can this really be true?

This guy can't read. He doesn't know how to fill out the simple standardized forms.

"See," Ron says, pen dancing over all the wrong places, "I used five of the medium orange warning signs, and one custom four by six sign for the Liberty Eylau turn-off, and–"

"–It's cool, let me see," I say, gently as possible, and I hold out my hand for the pen.

And that's all it takes for him. In a relieved rush, he hands it over to me and continues rattling off the stuff he used for the week. It takes me all of five minutes to finish.

Just as the door starts banging open and I see tired, hot and dusty men begin filing through it, Ron slips me a twenty dollar bill, casts me a quick glance that somehow says at once "thanks" and "keep quiet," and shifts off casually to the water dispenser, as if he'd never been speaking to me.

I don't want his money, and he's overpaid me from what he promised earlier, but I obviously can't give it back to him now and, truth be told, I do need the money.

Ron, I'll pay you back later, you crazy joker. I promise.

So, I'm sitting there at the end of my first day of work with my twenty dollar tip, and I'd be feeling pretty good about it, if I wasn't worried about cops flooding the place every time the door opens. I can't help but wonder about all these guys coming in now: if they're good guys or if they're all crazy like Ron. They're starting to notice me now where I sit on the far side of the room, and I get a few courteous nods and a couple of times a "hey" when a group of four young guys shows up, all surrounding a familiar-looking young dude who acts like he owns the place. They cozy up to him, fawning over him, but he takes no notice of his hangers-on. He scans the room like a man looking for trouble. Dirty blond hair falls nearly to his shoulder; his fat lips are blue and chapped, a blood shot look to his eye.

"Hey Jesus Freak, how's it hangin'?" he says to Ron as he walks by him. Ron catches my eye a brief moment, then he looks up at the guy and grins ear to ear.

"Blessed, Bobby, just blessed. And how are you doing this fine day?"

But Bobby doesn't answer, because now he's seen me. He sits down opposite of me and stares across the breakroom. I do know him. At least from pictures. And I was at that game. Our big school vs. his little school, and we lost. He's barely recognizable, but it's him: the quarterback, Bobby "the Lone Ranger" Granger. He was a senior when I was just a sophomore, and they held him back a year just to make a run at the 3A State title. He was worshiped like a god. Twenty thousand people came to see his games in a town that had fewer than two-thousand residents. Girls hanging off his arms, a deep-throated hot-rod, adults and kids alike practically kissing his cleats. He had it all until he got two of his ACLs snapped on the very first play of the title game. His coach simply replaced him with the backup quarterback, a kid who could do more than just run the ball. The team won big behind that new kid, and nobody thought about Bobby Granger anymore. Damaged goods and too stupid to pass his college entrance exams. Now look at him: puffy face, thirty pounds over his playing weight, maybe more.

"Look here, boys" Bobby drawls, still looking at me. "If it ain't the new one we heard about. The one the Sheriff brought in." Then he addresses me curtly. "Where you come from?"

"Texarkana," I reply after some hesitation. "John's my name."

"Texarkana," he mocks me, adding a whine to his voice, "John's my name." His cronies laugh. Suddenly everyone is watching, some with interest; others shake their heads and look away. The room goes quiet, and the guy stands up, never having taken his eyes off me. An attitude of aggression. "You know that Sheriff is a piece of shit." He looks at me, as if he expects me to agree with him. Maybe he does. I just look down at the floor, shrinking into my seat. "So what does that make you?"

Suddenly, the Office Lady is here, standing right beside me with her fists on her hips.

"Bobby," she screeches, and even he cringes at the sound, "behave yourself." She looks down at me now and say more quietly, "Honey, do you need a place to stay tonight?"

Holy crap, what is she asking me? She must be fifty at least. And that voice of hers.

"Uh, well," I stammer, not quite sure how to respond.

"Ha! Boys, Darlene's gonna take this young pup home with her!"

The cretin has overheard and pounced on the comment.

"Whew, Darlene, ain't he kinda young for you!?"

This from yet another of Bobby's smelly guys. I can feel myself turning three shades of red. I sit on my hands and examine my feet. The Office Lady wheels on them and unleashes her metallic screeching voice: "Boys, you can all just shut it right now!" She turns to me and says more softly, "Don't pay them any mind Darlin'. Herbert said you could stay here in one of the spare lab trailers out back 'till you get on your feet."

"Oh." I'm incredibly relieved. "Well, yeah, thanks. Yeah, that'd be great."

She shows me out the back of the building and behind the warehouses where there are several small white portable trailers lined up neatly in a row. She selects a key from a massive key ring, detaches it, and hands it to me.

"This used to be a mobile labs for testing road materials. They don't use it now; Herbert ought to get rid of it," she shakes her head. "That man don't get rid of nuthin' though, if he figures he's got some use for it."

"Oh, yeah," I nod in agreement, though I'm guessing Herbert knows what he's doing.

"Well," she says smiling, "I guess he's got a use for it now though, don't he?"

I nod. At least until he or the Sheriff figures out I'm a murderer, that is.

"Okay," she concludes, "don't have too much fun back here." She turns and walks back to the office. "Thanks!" I remember to call back to her. She raises a hand in a sort of wave for response and keeps on going. I'm still surprised by this turn of events. I doubt the state would approve of felons on the lam living in their lab trailers, but I'm grateful, and it's free, and you won't catch me complaining.

The door creaks open at the turn of the key and a push. Inside, it's nearly bare except for a metal table running the length of the front wall. There are a couple of Bunsen burners still on it and a few metal plates stacked next to them. The plates are flat and broad with a two-inch metal rim around the edge, like a dog bowl, sort of. They must be for heating road materials, or whatever, and they fit neatly into a steel wire hoop that tops the cylindrical wire structure also encircling the burner. It's a custom fit. The plates look hospital-clean, like they've never been used, though I'm a little suspicious of them.

I leave the trailer and slip into the back warehouse on a scavenging expedition where I turn up a couple of spare TxDOT issue protective coveralls and a shipping blanket or two. Then I sneak back into the front office to find my tennis racket where I'd hidden it under the reception desk. The one and only reminder of my former life; it's the last of my tennis rackets. I look around, both arms wrapped around my plunder, and find some plastic forks and knives from the breakroom, a roll of paper towels. Everyone's already gone home now, except for Herbert, but his office door is closed, and I can hear a muffled conversation going on in there. I feel guilty with all the stuff in my hands.

Get used to it.

All the same, I'm relieved he can't see me. Slipping back out to my trailer, I decorate the wall with my racket, hanging it on the one rusty nail in the paneling; then I arrange the utensils and paper towel neatly on the table, make a pallet on the floor with the blankets, and stand back to assess my homemaking.

Well, this will do, I suppose: used lab trailer, fake wood grain paneling, Bunsen burners for stoves and all. Not exactly what I would envision, but I can't help feeling a little pride. It's certainly unique.

Sure beats a prison cell.

⚔

# THE PERFECT TOOL

These lab trailers are smaller even than mobile homes, nothing more than a rectangle about half the size of my old room. Plastic fork in hand, I spear a ravioli from where a can of them bubbles over the flame and swallow it whole. I look out the window on the darkening empty yard, chewing the fabricated food I bought at the gas station down the road.

Here I am, first Friday night on my own, first real payday of my life—all two hundred one dollars of it—and I'm celebrating by eating junk-food from cans that I've heated up over a Bunsen burner.

Some celebration.

But tomorrow I'll walk the three miles into town, go to the bank, and cash this. Assuming they *will* cash it without opening an account. I'm sure not going to do that, but I smile at the irony of getting paid by the very state that must be out there, right now, looking for me.

It's a wonder, making it this far without being caught. I throw the hot, empty can in my garbage bag and watch it shape the black plastic around itself. That was the last can and Ron's twenty is already gone. I count the dollars left to me. Just six bucks and some change.

"Well, it's going to be a mighty lean weekend if they don't cash it."

I examine the check again closely. My name's printed right there in incriminatingly bold letters. I sure had to work for this little slip of paper though. Today, I had to mow all ten acres like a madman. Again. With a push-mower. Herbert just can't get enough of having a neat and tidy yard, can he? A neat and tidy yard full of gravel and dirt and asphalt and trucks I'm not allowed to drive.

"John Sharpe, you're a teenager with no plan."

I take out my fake ID and examine it closely. Could the girls have actually known? John Fears really is a tennis pro. Was, that is. A good one, too from Dallas. I hit with him one time at the club. A nice guy, maybe too nice, he broke through the qualies at Wimbledon and the US Open a couple of times, but didn't quite have the grit to make it big. Then he quit and moved off somewhere. Haven't heard of him in years.

"John Fears, you're a man who needs a new plan."

And three days here is already too much. I can't stand these feelings I'm having. I jump every time the front door opens, expecting the cops to come storming in. I'm defenseless, and I got no wheels, and I feel like everyone's watching me all the time. But I can't leave on foot, that wouldn't last too long, and two hundred bucks is not going to buy a running car, not even around here. My mind keeps coming back to the highway trucks.

"John, you can't steal a truck."

Or can't I?

Looking out again, I wonder what became of the last yard boy. Did he live here, too?

I move to the little window in the door and peer out past the tar-splatters on the glass.

This view's no better. My stomach growls menacingly. Probably, he got canned.

"Gotta get off this yard work detail."

"The trucks, the trucks, get a truck, or you're..."

Yeah, the trucks. Gotta get myself assigned to one of those trucks.

A bright warm Saturday. A first Saturday, isn't it? I'm in the town's only diner, sitting half-sprawled in a red vinyl booth-seat for an early lunch. I eye the approaching waitress in her miniskirt and take a sip of the strong black coffee. She's not bad. Not bad at all. Under the table, I idly run a finger over the hundred dollar roll in my pocket. The bank had cashed it, no problem at all. Just threw Herbert's name out there and it was like gold in that place. I got it all in fives just to feel the weight of it. I pull the money-roll out and put it on the table. Maybe she's a little older than me. Maybe not. I'm starving in more ways than one.

Surprisingly, it works; she sits down in the booth right beside me, her bare legs brushing my legs, her body half-turned to me, a small hand with brightly painted nails is somehow on my shoulder.

"You know what you want?"

What I want? What I want? What is she asking me? I'm speechless for a moment.

"Huh?"

She smiles a beguiling smile. There's laughter in her rich, brown eyes as she places her order pad perkily on the table, fishes out a pen from where it is tucked in her cleavage, and prepares to take my order.

"What'll you be having to eat?" She's smiling still. It's a nice smile.

"Oh. Steak and eggs, please. With the hashbrowns."

"I bet you take 'em sunny-side up?"

I stare a moment. "Oh, the eggs? Yeah, sunny-side up's good. Please."

"Okay, coming right up," and she rises from beside me, somehow keeping her legs together in her tiny, short skirt and using a delicate hand on my shoulder for balance.

"Oh, I'll have a beer too."

"Sure thing," she says, and starts to turn. But then she stops and her fingers touch my shoulder again. She says, "I'm real sorry, but I have to ask. Are you really twenty-one?"

I nod and get out my new license, swallowing hard. "See for yourself," I say, handing it to her. "Twenty-two, in fact." She looks at my fake ID, smiles sweetly and hands it back to me, looking pleased. Very pleased.

"John Fears, huh? I'm only twenty-one myself, and I thought I knew all the cute boys from New Boston, but I don't seem to recall you."

"I'm from Galveston," I say quickly, blushing. "I'm new here."

"Galveston? Galveston's a nice place I hear. I always did want to go there," she says, turning slowly and letting her finger drag across my shoulder before she walks off to place my order. Her hips are mesmerizing.

Galveston. I wonder if she'd come with me.

I stay in that booth a long time. I order some toast. I have another beer. I have the chocolate pie and another coffee. I eat until I feel queasy and the beer goes to my head. But I can't work up the nerve to ask her, and I can't think of any excuse to stay any longer. She sits by me again to take my money and watches expectantly as I count out the bills. I blow thirty bucks on the meal, and I tip her a ten. It seems like a good deal. She takes the cash with another of her smiles and walks off slowly, letting me see her, to help another table.

"Come back now," she says over her shoulder. "I'm here nearly every day."

I nod. Oh, you know I will.

Outside the road is burning and the heat rises in shimmering mirages, as if the road itself is dissipating into the pale blue sky. I walk the slow walk back to the yard on the shoulder, still feeling the touch of her legs, the touch of her hand.

I stop, frowning. Don't think a stolen highway truck's gonna impress her. Nice, John.

Monday morning, and I'm sweeping again. Another endless day of yard maintenance staring me in the face. Nothing to do but think, and that's just what I don't want to do. The pretty waitress down at the diner quit her job. I'd gone back the very next day, intending to ask her to come away with me. She was gone, gone, gone. Left town with a customer she just met, they said, laughing and shaking their heads.

I lean on the broom and look at the brown building. This seems to be all that Herbert has in store for me: sweeping, mowing, weed-eating. I'm no closer to getting near the keys of one of those trucks. Darlene sits on them like a hen while I stalk the empty yard by day like some furtive illegal itinerant. Everything's locked up in Herbert's office at night.

I start sweeping again, unenthusiastically. All the men are already out working the roads and won't return until the end of the day, except for brief re-fills or for equipment changes and maintenance. Maybe then. Maybe someone will leave the keys in the truck. And then... but, I don't know. How long would I have? Not more than thirty minutes. No, Herbert will have to give me a truck for some assignment. I'll need at least a whole day before I'm expected back.

But how?

The gate opens, and I step out of the way of a shiny, white quad-cab from the regional office. The words "TxDOT Engineering" are stenciled on the driver's side door, underneath the Department of Transportation's 'flying T' logo. The truck stops, and four young dudes in work khakis, polo-shirts, and clean boots climb out of the pickup laughing about something that could have only been an insult and put on their hard hats. One of them puts his on backwards.

I think of Bobby as I catch something like "bunch of dumbasses" spouting from his mouth. He shuts-up at the sight of me standing here with my broom. But these guys are more like prep school Bobbys in the way they bunch together in a familiar, intimate way behind one guy, their unofficial leader. They look me over while I smile broadly at them.

That's right, that's real smart, guys. Yeah, follow a dude wearing his hardhat, like, backwards, man; like that's so totally cool, man.

I barely stop myself from laughing, and they stare back at me like I'm a psycho, not knowing what to make of me. I'd heard about these guys. They're college kids in summer jobs with the engineering division of the Highway Department. Bet the backward-hat knows someone big at the State.

"Hey," he says to me, full of his own self-importance, keeping an eye on the broom I'm holding as if I might hit him with it. "Where's Herbert? Where's the lab trailers?"

I shrug. "Well, I don't know about Herbert. I expect he'll turn up when there's someone important to see."

This comment earns me a scowling frown. Backward-hat is puffed up now, indignant. And I'm ridiculously pleased with it.

"And the lab trailers? Show me where they're at. We got materials tests to run, orders of the State Office."

Oh, sure you do.

"Right over here."

I reluctantly lead them back to the trailers, still clutching my broom like a weapon. They stay behind me by just about the length of the handle, not speaking. I try to shake the feeling that showing them back here—where I live—is a violation of my space.

But this isn't mine. Not for long, anyway.

Using the master key Darlene gave me for the trailers, I unlock the new one furthest away from mine, and stand aside as they file in. The leader sticks his head back out the door.

"Thanks," he grunts and shuts the door hard.

The slam has barely stopped echoing before the retorts come, muffled but meant to be heard. I catch the words "prick" and "loser" hurled through the closed door. I stand there looking at it. Gotta shake my head. That's so stupid, it's not even insulting. But then there's resounding laughter from his groupies within.

Asshole. Man, what an asshole.

I amble back to the sweeping and see Herbert pull up in his white Olds sedan, get out, and walk straight back to the trailer where the four prepboys are presumably working. He shuts the thin aluminum door behind him. He doesn't even look at me.

Losing what little interest I had in sweeping altogether now, I go sit on the gravel pile in the full sun, thinking strange fell thoughts and letting the heat soak deep into my bones.

This evening in the breakroom, the road-guys know the young engineers have been here today, and it's all they speak of. I sit and listen, sipping burned, stale coffee, a bitter offering to the end of a bitter day. The invectives are amazing. It's the contempt from the anger of exclusion, of opportunity never offered, of expectations unfulfilled. That part I can understand.

"Those little shits don't know nothing," one of the guys, named Jim, is saying with the surety of his years' experience mixing asphalt using the sweat-soaked alchemy of on-the-job experimentation.

"Tried to tell me to mix some fuckin' rubber in the asphalt." Heads shake in derisive disbelief. "Rubber. Shit. No-way, I says, you can take your rubber and –"

"– And, yeah, and Christ almighty, they told Bill he was mixin' the concrete wrong," another guy interrupts. Bill! I mean, he's been mixin' for twenty years and never a blow-out."

Bill says nothing but is clearly appreciative of the support. I notice that they glance over at me a lot when they speak, more often than usual. I realize then that they're not sure where I might stand on this matter. It's known that I've attended some college, and that links me to these young Turks who think they can tell the old hands what to do. But here I am, sitting here, wearing my black t-shirt for the fourth straight working day, and I'm the lowest of the low in this place, the yard-boy who doesn't know squat. Who doesn't say squat either, for that matter.

"Yeah, they were a bunch of assholes," I interject.

Conversation stops, heads turn to look at the new development of me speaking.

I hesitate, continue. "...marched right in here and demanded to see Herbert, like they could order him around or something. Unbelievable."

And the pure bald outrageousness of the idea of ordering Herbert around really gets them going again. New and ever lower invectives are created and hurled into open space, and there's no way that the ears of these presumptuous young engineers, wherever they may be ensconced in the overlarge houses of their well-connected parents in Texarkana, aren't burning red with fire. And though no one actually comes to sit nearer to me, I'm closer to these guys now. They're more relaxed around me. I'm on their side.

But not Bobby's.

He is sitting there watching me with his bloody eyes, a malingering hate emanating from him, almost visibly. And it's all focused on me. A new thought has been working its way through me since this afternoon, and now it crystallizes into action. I catch the eye of Victor, the thin, pale fork-lift operator, who, when he speaks at all, speaks of chaos: automatic weapons, knives, ways to maim, all the perfect tools for the arts of death. He plays the part with relish, too, his hair dyed jet black, disturbing red contact lenses in his wide eyes, always wearing the black Nazi boots. He may rarely speak, but he's a damn good fork-lift operator and he's always there, hanging on the fringe of every group with those bizarre eyes of his darting around, taking everyone and everything in. Sometimes they whisper that his eyes really are red and that those are no lenses. They laugh then, but there's a nervousness in it. Hesitantly, I sidle over to him as he watches me greedily, red eyes boring into me. His skin is shiny, polished and lacquered shiny, like he's got a glass coating. It sparkles in my eyes so that I have to blink and look away. He stands and we shake. He's got a broad hand with long, delicate musician's fingers.

"Hey Victor," I say quietly, "I was wondering if you could help me?"

He licks his shining lips and he grins with a disarming sincerity. "Now that just depends, don't it?"

Two in the morning. The wind blows hard and hot and blustering, like a Sirocco wind, picking streams of sand off the material piles and pelting the metal sides of my trailer in gritty waves. The aluminum door rattles in its frame and tremors shiver through the trailer floor in strange cadences. The clacking of the window-unit fan can't drown out a whispering and groaning. Out in the yard. In here. Everywhere. A home of thin metal and thin wood and even thinner plastic, pre-fabricated and insecure. The permanent feel of complete impermanence. Push a hand on a wall anywhere, inside or outside, and it'll yield like a paper sack; it is so very little of nothing between me and anything out there that might yearn to tear its way in.

I rise from my pallet to stand at the window, gazing into the desolate yard, a hand on the door handle, thinking of going out. In the stark moonlight, material piles like dunes. Large equipment hulks ominously in giant reptilian silhouettes. Retaining walls loom like crumbling ruins. The artifacts of a long dead race long gone, and I the only one left behind. Stop. Wait. Something large out there. I check the door: locked. In the shadows between the shadows, moving quickly. A dark, long-limbed shade picks its way between walls, piles, machines, gliding in liquid shifting bursts. I stand and watch and wait. I reach for the pistol and look again. Sweat breaking out on my brow. But it all seems to move, and there is nothing out there.

What kind of boy is afraid of goddamn monsters, he'd said, so long ago.

I remind myself: just the wind.

But I am not afraid, no. At least not like he would have said. Another sleepless night, true, empty and haunted. Mine, a life in a void, so unreal, but something new grows in me. I feel it. Maybe the meanness of meals and the meanness of my marginal existence. Maybe there is an effect. A brute physicality, a bodily confidence that I've never experienced from tennis alone. For the first time in my life, I feel strong. And now this. I heft the small pistol and sight down the barrel, aiming at my forehead in the window reflection. It's a short, brutal thing: black matte, metal-on-plastic, a dense and top heavy weapon; it's a .40

caliber compact semi-automatic with the etchings of a bull on it. "Taurus," it says, beside the bull, in big block letters. It'll blow a hole in you, for sure, Victor had croaked when I bought it from him in a daze, feeling strange and empty, like I was someone else. We'd furtively done the deal after work, sitting in his bright red truck in the parking lot. He showed me how it works, how to service it, too, in loving parental detail. I'd handed over most of my remaining cash then and stuffed the thing in my pants and shuffled off quickly, glancing all around me, feeling thrilled and sick and scared. But I got it, and it's mine now.

"Just you come and get some," I say, peering out at the darkness. Then I drop the magazine and put it and the gun under my pillow and lie my head down upon it, feeling the solidity of the weapon and the sharpness of metal edges. A backup magazine is close at hand. The wind rattles on, and the trailer sways with it. I close my eyes, and my father's death mask greets me. His bulging sightless eyes are wide open, just like every time. Only this time: they are glowing red. I try to fall into sleep.

⋏

# SnakeRoot

"Hey, Slick, you missed a spot."

It's Bobby on his way into the office for the morning roll call, pushing Herbert's boundaries of when to show up for work. Looks hung over on a Wednesday morning. And still he has time to screw with me out here, cleaning up some spilled lime I've found on the drive.

"Yeah, Bobby, good morning to you, too," I say, just before the office door bangs shut behind him. "Idiot." Well, if I seem to be more accepted by these guys, then it's only by the older men. Something about me bothers the younger ones. Not that I should blame them.

Probably none of them killed their father.

I don't know, maybe I'm just being paranoid.

I sweep up the last of the lime and shake it into the dumpster. Yesterday came and went and still no opportunity to leave. I wipe my hands on the back of my jeans. The pistol is there. Damnit, speaking of idiots. When did I put it there? Talk about getting arrested. Should run back to my trailer right this second. But now I'm late for the call, and Herbert won't like that.

Shaking my head, I shove the gun further down into my jeans and pull my shirt down and walk into the office, feeling sick. I'm the last one in now. Herbert stands ready to address us with today's work detail. A few heads nod in greeting at my entry.

Bobby and some of the younger guys are grouped together in a pack at the back of the room, not paying any attention to Herbert. A whispered "Hey, lookee there, it's Slick" floats over. They know I can hear it.

Most of these guys already like to call me 'Slick'—as in city slicker—because I'm from Texarkana. And when one of them recalled that I'd played tennis in school, they'd all laughed like it was the funniest thing they'd ever heard.

I sigh and don't look at them, trying to understand. Maybe harassing the new guy makes them feel better about themselves. I guess they are a little nervous about me. If they could even articulate what bothers them, they'd probably say that they're worried that, one day, they'll walk into the office to find that I'll have gotten my college degree and then I'll be the manager, the big cheese. John Sharpe, Highway Department foreman. It does have a nice ring. And, for a moment, the thought of that makes me smile up at them bitterly where the huddle together in the corner, sizing me up like a pack of hyenas. I'd like to see their faces then, especially Bobby's.

Dad probably could've made that happen.

But he's not going to make anything happen, and I sure as hell won't be finishing college.

Now Herbert is calling out the work details from his clipboard, and we all pay attention. So far, he's always called me last, like an afterthought. He goes through the roll, assigning everyone to various work and maintenance details. Looks like today is no different.

"Sharpe," he finally calls. I flinch.

As he hesitates there on my name, hope rises in my throat, catches there with my breath. I cross my fingers. Maybe he'll send me out today too, or, better yet, on some errand in one of the trucks, as I've seen him do. Anything besides being trapped here mowing or sweeping and waiting for the police to show up.

"Yard maintenance. Sweep the warehouses and the main drives."

He moves on, and my hopes crumble back to nothing.

Not again. I can't take this any longer. I'm running out of time here.

"Allright get on outta here and get to work," Herbert says to us, the work assignments now complete. Immediately everyone crowds for the door. Somehow I find myself surrounded by Bobby's pack as we jostle towards the door.

"Hey, Slick! Now don't you forget to mow that ditch today!" Jim, the dump truck guy, startles me with an elbow to the ribs as we shove out into the yard together.

"Ho! McEnroe," Joe, the Gradall guy calls, "you get Herbert's Olds real clean today. He told me you missed a spot yesterday." They all laugh riotously.

No way would Herbert tell something like that to this guy. Herbert doesn't talk to any of these jokers.

Bobby chimes in last of all, "Well, if it isn't tennis-boy. Hey, I heard you went to college? That true?"

I look up at him, wondering what he's up to, feeling my shit-eating grin spread all across my face. Finally, I nod.

"I bet them sweeping classes was hard, huh?" Bobby mimes a broom sweep to the men's increasingly nervous laughter. "But I guess you didn't do so good, huh?"

Quiet now, quiet. Don't rise to it. I stare at the ground, just wanting them to leave now.

But they don't.

"'Cause, why else you come out here? Didn't they have no 'sanitation engineer' jobs in Texarkana? Or were all the nigs and spics up there more qualified?"

Knowing that he's pushing for my breaking point, doesn't make it any better, doesn't make it any easier. I think of the gun.

My breaking point. If he only knew about my breaking point.

Look up at Bobby. Smile's gone. Hate in my eye and in my thought. Former quarterback, huh? That what makes you so cocky? I size him up. I'm taller. He's older, but four years is nothing now. Idiot's already let himself go to pot, but those arms, look at those arms. I bet he's still strong and dirty as a snake. But you think you're strong? You're not half the man my father was.

Let's go, right now.

I see my own fists: flying, connecting, with Bobby's swollen head, with his fat, sneering lips until blood spurts from them, gushes from them. A beating, a beating. I could do it. I don't even need the gun.

No.

They come swarming. Sirens, badges and guns, young trigger-happys one and all, yelling, let's get 'im. Handcuffs. Can't do it. Won't do it. No. Control yourself. I'll get outta' here soon. Forget about these losers.

I take a step back.

"Hey, slick where you goin'? Now don't be gettin' scared," Bobby says in mock sympathy. He turns to his cronies, but his hand reaches out to grab my t-shirt. "I know. Fellers, how 'bout we make Slick eat some tobacca'?" No one says anything, laughter's gone.

"Slick," he pulls me back by the scruff of my shirt, and speaks to me directly now with the sneer he makes heard in everything he says, "hadn't you never had no Red Man?"

"No, I don't do that stuff," I say, fighting to control my voice.

He leans forward to speak right into my ear, "Well, how 'bout you startin' now?" He whispers it loudly, like some foul-mouth lover. His whisky-and-tobacco breath is stunning.

Bobby, Bobby, Bobby, brush your Goddamn teeth.

I shake my head.

"No? What about some Copenhagen?" Bobby presses even closer, his reeking breath like a corpse. "We start the pussies and the little babies off with dip. That might just be your speed, Slick." He laughs in my face and then turns to the men to laugh at me.

Somehow, I can't let this go. Not this time.

"Bobby," I whisper. He glances back at me, unsure I said something. Go on. Say it like you mean it. I do. "It's time to shut your face before someone shuts it for you." Bobby snaps back to look at me, incredulous and angry, coiling like a snake. Shouldn't be doing this, shouldn't. I do it anyway. "What?" I go on, forcibly removing his hand from my shirt. "Nothing to say, Bobby? That's what I thought. Now, you take your oral fixation and go find someone else to blow."

Bobby hesitates. Out of the corner of my eye, I notice Victor. At some point in this, he's appeared on the fringe of the group, saying nothing. Come from nowhere. But when? Red eyes watch me intently. Scientific interest is written on his blindingly shiny face. He knows I have it on me. He must.

"What?" says Jim while Bobby stares at me. "You going to take that from some city turd, Bobby? He called you a faggot. That right, Bobby? You queer as a three dollar bill?"

A quick image of nights out with him, these guys: always goading their young star, always challenging him like this. Someday he'll wind up laid out in a ditch, dead and cold, and they'll be gone boy gone, whew nice to know ye, weren't that a close call fellers?

Time to stop this.

"Look, Bobby," I say, "I —"

"— what," Jim hisses in Bobby's ear, glaring at me. "You afraid of this pussy?"

Suddenly, we go at it furiously. Two bodies hurtling together. We're a single mass: grasping, cursing, rolling. Can't believe I'm doing this. Fighting this guy. What the hell? Goddamnit, he's biting me. Get out of this hold. Shit, that's my playing arm. Little shit. Don't let him pin you. Gravel's in my face; dirt is in my eyes. Grab for his arm. Roll him over. Goddamn, dude's strong. I'm quicker. I can beat him. Get that arm down. Get it behind him. Stay on top of him. Can't. Yes. He connects somewhere. I don't even feel it. A thousand thoughts speeding, speeding. Fists in his face in quick, quick beat, pummeling raw meat. His nose blooms snot and blood. A fat lip opens like a pale, hooked grub. Milliseconds pass. Underneath it all: the undercurrent of the ludicrous. Apes grapple one another in the dust. A show of dominance. The impression of folly. He's not fighting, he's beating his chest. Not I. I'm someone else now. I'm for real, Bobby, you fucker. And wouldn't he just be real proud? But he's dead, dead, dead. Got you now, Bobby, I got you now. I find myself on top of a prone and writhing form. Face in the gravel, Bobby is screaming. I see his arm twisted back in unnatural angles and I see myself holding it there with one hand. With the other, I start to reach back behind me for the gun, like a magnet, pulling.

A strong rough hand grasps me by the scruff of the neck. It has reached in from the sky, from above, from somewhere out of the blue. It squeezes painfully. Another one descends, falling like a thunderbolt. It's got Bobby by the shirt collar. I'm wrenched to my feet with surprising ease. Bobby, too. I don't resist. Puppets in the thrall. I laugh. I got no strings to hold me up. I don't even have to look to know. Of course: they are Herbert's hands.

We are both fish limp in this terrible grip. Heads hang down now. Bobby's vacant eyes, looking at nothing. Silence hangs in the air and dust; men look uncomfortably around them, nervously separating themselves from the scene. Victor looks at me and smiles and walks away.

Of course, Herbert had probably seen it all with that way of his. Just where's he needed, just like they said. Did he see what I was doing, there at the end? Had he seen the bulge in the back of my pants? Something tells me he'd been waiting to see what was going to happen. Either way, this is it. Well, come on, here I am, I won't run. Look where I've gone with this. I realize I'm shivering.

Herbert says, "You boys got enough to do without wrestlin' in the dirt." He lets us go. Disgust is written in his every motion. "Bobby, get in that truck, and get on to work."

Bobby slouches off quickly with Jim pulling him along. He leaves a trail of spattered blood. Herbert looks at me now, his face unreadable.

"Sharpe," he says with rock-like calm and restraint, "I expect more out of you. Everybody does. Go on now, get on with your work and leave that boy alone."

"Yessir."

With one last look, he walks off. His body moves like a piston. I pick up my broom and stand there, trying to stop trembling. Finally, I force myself to get to work, and this time there's a calmness in the simple act. I work patterns in the dust. Shapes form in the mounds. Bobby's blood is covered over, buried, gone.

I take an inventory of myself: there's a throbbing in my nose; dust, blood, and sweat-encrusted scratches down my right arm sting like fire, bruises somewhere on my back and thighs—must've been his knees. I remember his face. Pretty bad. He got it pretty bad.

Stupid bastard will think twice next time.

The day drags on. I've put the gun up. Hidden it under my pillow. But I can't stop thinking about it. I want to be clean; I want to shower, but I don't. Should change my clothes, but I'm not going to. I don't even wash my wounds. I want to feel them there. And I want everyone to see them, and remember: I kicked his ass. And I'll do it again.

I feel the small of my back where the weapon had been.

Feels like it should still be there, like it belongs there.

The evening closing. I've already helped Ron with his paperwork, and all the men are back and getting ready to head home for the day. Nothing is said of the fight this morning, but it hangs heavy in the air. Maybe it's my imagination, but to me, it seems there is a new respect. Guys are friendlier than normal. No one ribs me. A few jokes, a few nods from people who seldom notice me. Maybe I have surprised them. And maybe no one noticed my, ah, little peacemaker. Or they're not saying. Bobby comes in last, his purpled face throbbing almost visibly with shame. I watch him as he hurries home without a word, and then I notice Victor. He is sitting by himself against the far wall. Red eyes follow me in everything I do, and watch me still as I hurry out the door.

Retiring to my trailer, I'm tired and sore and self-satisfied, but I am not sure whether I am happy or not. I'm scared, that's what it is. Almost, almost, look at what I almost went and did again. Should I be pleased? Did I win, or did I fail, or was it both? The Bunsen burner warms my can of meat. It tastes great, better than normal somehow. I wolf the meal down and turn out the lights and take off all of my clothes.

This strange weariness now, stretched out on my pallet on the floor. In the darkening sky, stars appear when I'm not looking. And the planet like a red eye, too, smiling and shiny. But no peering out dirty windows tonight. I know I won't be up. No monsters in the yard, not tonight. Yes, strangely, it is something like pride that I feel. Guilty pride, perhaps, because there is loss in this feeling, too. As if I had anything else to lose, as if I had any right to feel proud. Pride and loss. How odd. How sad. Protect yourself from yourself now.

That was too close, too close.

I get up and unload the gun and put it in my bag. I remove all the bullets from both the clips and hide those in the bag, too. Then I pack my few things and zip it up. That's better.

John, how could you? What were you thinking?

Next morning, everything feels different. Something is going to happen. I don't know what, I've just got that feeling. Herbert hands out assignments in the break room where most of us are drinking coffee. Last of all, he comes to me.

"Sharpe," Herbert looks at me hard over his glasses and hesitates.

I feel the worst coming on. "Yessir," I finally manage to whisper.

"You gonna behave yourself today?"

"Yessir, I will."

"Allright," he says with just an edge of softness. "Road detail. You know Henry?"

Road detail. Finally. Tomorrow, it will be ten days since I pushed him. Ten days too long. They must've found him already and Sheriff Dodgen is sure to get wind of it. Tomorrow is my eighteenth birthday, too. I am not going to be here on my birthday. Today then. If I can just get the truck away for a few unnoticed hours, it'll be enough. Has to be.

"John?"

"Oh, yessir. Thanks. I know Henry"

"Report to Henry," Herbert says, looking at me a long last moment, then he walks away.

I should tell him goodbye. Thanks and goodbye Herbert, it's been nice knowing you.


Driving to the work site in the back seat of Henry's dually, a beautiful blue summer morning pours into the white pickup, illuminating me, the interior, giving a shine even to the sullen Bobby where he slouches in the corner opposite me. Tomorrow. Look at what I've done with these eighteen years. Another washed out kid, heading for oblivion. And I wanted so much more. I reach my arm far out the window, grabbing slowly at the onrushing air, as if I could hold onto it and let it sweep me along to leave this life for another. If only I could.

If only, if only, is this what my life has become? A wish for what could've been?

If only I hadn't pushed him.

"You boys is a real party this morning," Henry, the sub-foreman, says. "But you better cheer up 'cause this here's the good part." He looks at us in the rear-view mirror, but he gets no reply from either of us. He laughs happily. "Yessir, the best part of all."


"Roots," Henry, says. We're at the job site. He's pointing down at an object in the red-dirt of the site. He's been telling me what to do.

"Roots?" I repeat dumbly, not understanding. "Now what do I do with the roots again?"

"Just toss 'em in the ditch. Pick 'em outta' the base material and just toss 'em," he repeats patiently and without the least trace of sarcasm.

He's not kidding. I can't believe this. "Don't we have some kind of machine for this?" I say. I know we don't have a machine for this. Henry just laughs and walks back to his idling pick-up truck, shaking his head. I eye the open door. No. Can't make it. Then I look back down the road dubiously. Or rather, it's not so much a road as it is the makings of a road. All powdery dry and mixed with red clay, it's the substrate of another lonely country road in the making. No asphalt has been laid yet, of course, but the giant heavy rollers have already been through to smooth the material down. It's packed tight, but it leaves little clouds of fine red dust with every step you take. I imagine it's like walking on Mars. It's almost two miles long right here. A red tongue trailing into the distance, I can already barely see the other end, even straight as it is on this clear bright day.

Maybe this is what they do to juvenile murderers. Maybe I've already been caught.

"Roots. Okay, well, roots." I catch myself talking out loud. Just shut-up.

Bobby stands next to me, still silent. Looks like he stayed up drinking all night. He's staring glumly down the red ribbon with forlorn blood-shot eyes and a bloated pout. His bloody lip and smashed nose carry scabs that have not even been cleaned. I can't look much better.

Bobby and I—without exchanging a single word—simply move together out onto the road bed and stop almost simultaneously a couple of feet away to stoop to our first roots of the day. Almost simultaneously we pick the two-inch pieces out of the dirt and give them a little pitch off to the side of the road. Repeat. Another two steps. Stoop. Toss. Stoop. Toss. Repeat a thousand times, a million times. We're automatons with aching backs, and it's not even 9:30 AM yet. Almost three hours until lunch. I'm aware of every second. Every single one. And with the passing of each second, I lose a little bit of hope. I'm averaging twenty roots a minute until I lose count.

Herbert. This is crazy. That crazy old man.

I'm mad at him, and I'm mad at the Sheriff, and I am mad at my father. Somehow I suspect that they're all in this together, that they're doing this just to punish me.

But that's impossible, and my father is dead.

The day of roots and watching for someone to leave a vehicle long enough for me to sneak off with it drags on, one second at a time. Roots, and roots, and roots, and roots. One at a time, I litter the bar ditch with them in thick layers. I form mounds of roots, middens of them, a landfill-mountain of roots reaching to the sky. I see them growing and multiplying. Roots, short and thick, they wriggle through the dust of an endless road through a Martian landscape. There's nowhere else to go. No shade or trees or water; just plains full of red powdery dirt, shot through with millions of living roots. Entire bleak prairies devoid of anything but red base material. The roots live and grow back as quickly as I throw them off. I can't leave the road because everything is a road. Roots grow back all around me; snakes of roots writhe towards me from all sides of the infinite dirt prairie, right up to my feet. I pick them up and throw them over and over again for days. I'm exhausted and hopeless now.

One gets to my ankle.

It's curling around it, grasping and strong; it leaves stinging red burns.

I don't care. I don't resist.

Another and another curls around me until they have me down in the soft, red dust. It fills my lungs, stings my eyes, covers me over. I'm pulled down into the powdered earth by a thousand woody tendrils, a million of them.

Strong rough hands lift me up to stand me on my feet.

The whole thing repeats.

I gotta' get out of here. I gotta' get outta here.

Bobby never says a word and keeps his distance from me by twenty yards or more. The road grows longer as the men prepare more of it in front of us and the men of the asphalt team behind us pave it all over. We live in a slow moving, never varying buffer zone of powdery dirt and roots. A moving prison. Hour after hour after hour.

When someone does drive by in a dump truck or a grader, they are merciless.

"How's them roots coming," shouts one moron from his cab.

That wasn't funny the first time.

"You got all them roots up yet?" Another joker says, as he rumbles by.

Just shut-up.

"Hey, Slick, I think you missed some roots back there."

There are endless variations, but they're all the same.

Just shut-up, you idiots.

I say nothing. I can see no way out of this. Somehow I figure I must deserve this.

I try to amuse myself by imagining Herbert sitting there in his office saying: by God I'll show those boys to go jackin' around in my department. But he'd never say that, and he probably hasn't thought about me all day. But it is, has to be: my punishment.

Absentmindedly, I pick another root from the red dirt.

This one moves.

What the hell?

I bring the dirt encrusted thing up to my face.

This waking nightmare is getting too real. It really is moving.

And it hisses.

I recoil suddenly at the realization and drop it in the dirt with a red puff. I examine it again. Not a moccasin, not a rattler. The little snake seems disoriented. It's just a small, scared, helpless snake. I pick it up again, and it wriggles impotently in my grasp. Bobby, like a zombie, doesn't notice. He's just staring down the road.

Close by, Henry begins turning the giant diesel motor grader smoothly. I look up at him, holding up the snake, but he's not looking at me. I don't know how he can see what he's doing past the long, long nose of the thing, much less handle it like a scalpel. Operates the complicated control array by feel alone. He raises the steel-carbide claws of the ripper and lowers the big fourteen-foot blade in the middle of the turn, never taking his eyes off the run he's about to make. His cabin door is tied open against the afternoon heat.

For the first time all day, I grin.

Henry powers the grader to within ten yards of me.

In slow motion, end over end, the little snake arcs lazily, writhing in the nothingness of air. It's a perfect toss. As if by ultimate design, the hissing, scared reptile sails through the open cabin door and lands squarely in Henry's lap.

All six wheels of the fifty-one-thousand, three-hundred and twenty-six pound behemoth lock in unison. The rig skids sideways in a cloud of red dust and screeching groaning yellow metal. A loud metallic thunk sounds in a sickeningly familiar way as a control arm fails in slow motion. The right front wheel buckles.

This is not good.

Henry, sub-foreman of the crew, master of the motor grader, and incessant maker of jokes about roots, leaps from the cabin with an inhuman shriek.

This is so not good.

With a growing sickness, I watch the whole thing. He's a cursing beer gut with stick limbs and work boots flailing everywhere. His jump must've cleared a good ten feet.

"Boy! You get! You get! Snake! Goddamn, Boy! Goddamn snake outta' there!" He screams, running, apparently nowhere in particular, for his very life. I watch as he runs and flails and cusses some more. "Get that snake outta' there!" he screams at me again, a little more coherently this time.

I amble as casually as possible over to the machine and find the frightened little grass snake. He's curled up under the seat now in a tight little ball, barely moving at all. I toss him in the grass. I hope he gets away before Henry comes to his senses.

This really can't be very good at all. What was I thinking?

Wish I'd known Henry's got a snake phobia. But, having been reduced to an incoherent fool at the sight of the harmless reptile, he calms down immediately after the snake is gone. What's even more astonishing is that he is actually grateful to me for having removed it. It's as if suddenly a ten-foot rattler had appeared in his lap and I had been there to save his life. It is that kind of grateful.

Very strange.

I'm both hero and villain, and I don't know what to say to him. I notice the broken wheel again, but don't point it out. I'm not sure how long his gratitude is going to last.

I wasn't the only one watching the whole thing. From hundreds of yards away the men have converged on the scene. There is laughing and jeering as Henry composes himself and makes his way back to inspect the grader, watching nervously for snakes all the while.

The laughter stops.

Herbert's here; he has materialized again.

How does he do that?

He's already out of his car inspecting the broken control arm. No one has to tell him what's happened. He knows already. He looks at the broken metal and shoots me a single, frowning glance. There's nothing to say. That one glance is enough. I envy the snake in the grass. Hebert gets back in his car and drives off, leaving us all there open-mouthed and cowed, wondering what to do. I should just leave. On foot. Right now. With everyone watching me.

Tonight, there are the stories. In boisterous tellings, my snake has already become three feet long and poisonous. I don't correct, and I don't participate. I just listen and watch, knowing my chance for escape has come and gone. When Herbert is not around, one of the guys capers around, re-enacting Henry's brush with death. Everyone laughs riotously. But not me and not Bobby. He sits by himself glowering at me with an unconcealed hate. Then he gets up and storms out. The laughter goes silent, and we all hear his aging Camaro burn rubber out of the parking lot. Men exchange knowing glances.

Henry slides over and says, "You'll wanna watch out for that'un, John."

I look up at him and ask, "Why?"

"Bobby ain't real nice, that's all," he shrugs and smiles. "And you ain't exactly endeared yourself to him, if you know what I mean."

A long night in the trailer. My fears magnified a thousand times. I am unprotected, vulnerable. I don't know what to do. I just sit on the floor with my back against the wall, facing the door, holding the loaded gun in my hand, not even looking out the windows. Just waiting. Thinking I better get the hell out of here. Now. But I can't seem to move and can't decide what to do. Assuming Herbert doesn't fire me first, they'll file a report tomorrow, and then they'll connect me to my father's murder. And no telling what Bobby's going to do.

Escape scenarios in my head, none good.

And Dad's back, back in my head; he's making shooting noises. Bang, bang, he laughs. Bang, bang. That's what you're in for, John Sharpe. Yeah, go ahead and break into Herbert's office, grab the keys, and steal a truck. Run away in a five ton vehicle with State markings and the alarms blaring, that's a good one. Just see how long you last.

"Shut up," I whisper to the ceiling. "Just shut up."

But he's right; he's always right. I've got nowhere to run, no way to hide. I replay the sound of breaking metal over and over in my mind. It sounds like the breaking of a bone. Or, more: like the breaking of a skull.

⋏

# Signs

I wake with a start to a loud bang.

I'm slumped against the wall. The gun has slipped out of my hand and lies on the ground beside me. A gray and indistinct morning light streams through the small window. Today, is my birthday. Today, I am eighteen. Today, there will be no parties, no cake, not even a card. No one will know. No one will remember. But today, things are going to happen.

The shocking, screeching sound of bending metal. Shouts outside the door.

The blade of an absurdly large tire-iron is working its way between frame and door. With a crunch it penetrates and thrusts violently through, all the way to its handle. Now it flails around, a predatory, metallic arm, reaching for me. It pulls back, and the blade gropes for purchase, finds it, wrenches the corner of the door outward. Through the opening, I see one of Bobby's blood-shot eyes. The look of an animal, drunk and malicious.

He is screaming for me to come out.

The gun finds my hand; I'm on my feet. I grab my bag and kick the door open in one motion. The sharp twisted edge slams full into Bobby's face and sends him sprawling with a howl of pain and rage. Stepping into the open space, my gun levels on human beings, my head ringing, ringing again. Three men with crowbars, not humans, visages of death I've never seen. Bobby's on his feet in an instant; blood pours out of his nose, his lip. They see my gun and freeze. Slowly, I descend the steps, and slowly they back away, keeping an even space, just about the length of a crowbar. Turn away for an instant, and I'm dead. The song ditties in my head, unstoppable: *Happy birthday to me, happy birthday to me, happy birthday, dear John...* I try to shake it away, can't.

Bobby says, "You don't have the balls to—"

"—Don't I?" my gun's leveled right between his eyes. He believes me.

Not a word, not a sound from anyone now. I point my gun from chest to chest.

The main gate begins to opens automatically as a truck pulls up. It is Ron. Ron and his sign truck, getting an early start on things. His windows are open and he is literally bouncing in his seat. God's perpetually happy clown, so eager to get to work, he doesn't even notice us.

I run for it.

Keep the gun pointed, keep it on them.

Nobody follows.

Stuffing the pistol in my pants, I sling my bag into the bed, throw open Ron's passenger door and jump in. Ron's so startled, he nearly hits the roof.

"John!" he says, "what are you doing here?"

Looking out the window, I see Bobby wipe his bloody mouth with a sleeve. He takes his tire-iron and stabs it into the wall of my trailer and leaves it there, buried to the hilt. His three goons look from him to me, undecided.

"I'm with you today, Ron," I say to him. "Let's go. Now."

"Super-duper!" he says, still bouncing, and pulls through the gate and out onto the road, singing, "*Onward Christian soldiers, marching out to work, with the cross of Jesus, going on before...*" Then he laughs insanely, and I laugh with him, just as insanely, as he meanders down the highway and turns onto a little ranch road, and together we pass singing into the morning of a countryside that is wet with sparkling dew and has wild cannas bursting out in orange along the fence lines and open spaces of bucolic grandeur with cows and horses browsing peacefully on the long, brown grasses of the fields.

And as we pass further and further down the road, I relax a little and slump into my seat in relief, taking stock. Just look at me. Drenched in sweat and shivering. Hands that will not stop shaking. Rhymes in my brain. *Today's the day, the day for change, the day for leaving, gone's this short life, full of grieving.*

"Today's the day," says Ron.

"For what?" his comment's a surprise to me; was I speaking out loud?

"For delineators," he laughs his big belly laugh. "Praise the Lord that you're with me!"

"Yeah, whoo-hoo, praise the Lord, delineators. I can hardly wait." I look at him, still bouncing, ludicrously happy, the comment totally lost on him. Today's the day allright. The day I better get out of here. Unless I want to be killed. I look Ron's truck over with interest, studying how he works the gears. Looks complicated. Better wait and watch a little. "What are delineators?" I ask, and, oh, does he tell me.

It's ten in the morning and there's a hundred-degree heat coming off the road we're on. My wakeup call this morning is already a bad nightmare. Only I know it was real. I think I can drive this truck now, but Ron hasn't given me any opportunities; no easy escape has been possible. We're hammering delineator bases into the red brick-hard East Texas clay, and if I thought I was sweating before, it was nothing compared to this. It pours off of me in a steady stream, my clothes so wet with it, wiping my face on my sleeve just makes me all the wetter.

These things are just plastic poles with a reflective sticker on them. Never once gave a thought for them, but they are everywhere out here: demarcating curves, ditches, culverts, any and all obstructions on the side of the road. Ron loves them, makes them all "straight as God's word." Crazy bastard. And they are, all of them, within ten measly yards of the roadway. The feeling of exposure is awful; I flinch every time a car comes around, expecting it to be Bobby, flying out to run me down. I almost hope for the Police to come pick me up.

At least I have the gun. And this sledgehammer.

Hefting the thing again, I resume pounding on the metal wedge. Remarkable how like my tennis serve this swing is. Fifteen strokes this time, already down from twenty. Tennis, yeah, tennis. That's what I used to do. Seems like a different life. And it was.

"Hey, not bad," Ron says, "not bad at all. The Lord gave you a good swing there."

"Serving up a million tennis balls gave me a good swing, Ron."

Ron laughs, pontificates in the name of the Lord. Best just to be quiet around him, too.

We move on to the next markers in the row and Ron explains everything to me all over again. I watch his lips move. They just move and move, even while he pounds away, and I stand there, delineator in hand, analyzing his brutal chopping swing.

Ron drones on. Hot sun beats down all around me. Glimmers of old visions rise up in the hazy fields of blond grass. I see it then—The Court—stretched before me, shimmering in the heat, and there is nothing, nothing but the feel of the ball on my strings at the instant of impact on the last shot. The winning shot.

Match point at the U.S. Open.

The ball stays on the sweet spot, caught there an eternity. The defining ball of an entire life-time otherwise wasted chasing little yellow balls. Just one more ball. So easy, so loose; my arm registers the impact, flows through it. The satisfying crack of the graphite sounds at the edge of consciousness. And, in a breathless millisecond, it hurtles across the net, warped by the speed, just where I want it to go. My opponent stands there, frozen by the unreachable shot; his eyes track the missile, knowing, as I knew even before I made contact.

I sink to my knees, and tears of joy well in my eyes.

The vision's brief spark fades into the bright orange reflector I hold. The sound of Ron's sledge-hammer rings. A future with no hope and I'm an adult today? Some birthday this is. Eighteen. Jesus, I've done nothing. Nothing, except... Now I'm running, will always be running. I'm less than nobody, I'm nothing. Never was. I inhale the rising heat of the day. Now I'm going to have to steal Ron's truck. But I don't want to. I really don't.

Should've just left on foot. Days ago.

Down, down, down the rabbit hole...

"John? John?" Ron's stopped his talking. He's looking at me, the smile gone for once. Concern shows on his simple face. "Hey, you allright there? What's wrong?"

"Yeah, it's nothing."

"Something's wrong."

"Nothing's wrong Goddamnit! Nothing's fucking wrong!"

He's shocked. I'm shocked. Anger from nothing. Not his fault. What an asshole, what an *asshole*, I have become. Me, the murderer. Me, the brawler, loser, malcontent. Here's the one guy in this whole damn place who looks out for you. Bite his head off why don't you? *Asshole*. I look up at him again, holding a hand out, but his head is down now. His eyes are closed. Oh, he is. Oh Jesus, Ron, Jesus Christ. He is praying for me. I feel stupid and embarrassed and superficial all at once. And how could I've even been thinking of tennis? In my situation. Of all things. A stupid sport. But the thought won't go away and the vision burns in my head again, despite it all.

We're back in the truck, cruising slowly, looking for any delineator even slightly out of alignment. Ron's happy and grinning and singing again. Somehow I couldn't bring myself to steal his truck. The chance had been right there. He'd been down on his knees in a ditch, fooling with a crooked base as I'd gone to the cab to get a drink of water. The keys were in the ignition. Wouldn't have been a problem at all. But I couldn't take it. Maybe I should just call Dodgen. Bobby'll stay away from him. But what then? Prison, that's what.

On foot then. When we stop for lunch, I'll just take off. Yes, that's really all there is to it. Just take off. Now's the time. Smiling, I turn to my first and last friend at the Highway Department and say, "Today's my birthday, Ron. Today, I'm twenty-three."

"Praise the Lord!" Ron exclaims, just as excited for me as can be. "Happy Birthday John! This calls for a special prayer!" He beams his joker eyes at me and squeezes my shoulder with a grimy hand. "Oh Lord!" he wails, "Watch over thy child John, as he begins another year; bless and guide him wherever he may be. Give him strength when he stands; raise him up if he falls; and in his heart –"

"– what the hell is that!" I yell.

Turning out of a neglected county road amid a cloud of gravel dust: a bright yellow Porsche 914. Mine. It is mine. Driving the car is the biggest, the hairiest, the ugliest *Thing* I have ever seen. He's even bigger than I'd imagined from my brief glimpses.

Emerging from his interrupted prayer-rapture, Ron notices him, too, the fear of something besides God coming over his face. Full-length hunting coveralls erupt from the 914, a riot of orange. Body-hair streams out pell-mell in long, wild dreads—from the collar; from the arm sleeves; it's all matted and thick, even on the backs of his hands. Those hands. Frying pans smothering the wheel of the car. Enormous. His head sticks a full foot above the windshield; he's had to ditch the tops just to fit in. His legs are so long that the left knee actually angles out of the car crazily. He must be better than seven feet tall. I imagine size twenty boots, wondering how they could possibly fit the pedals.

"Ron, do you see what I..." But my car is pulling quickly away. "After him! After him! That's my car!" I'm shouting at Ron. He's too stunned for immediate reaction.

"What?" He finally stammers, gazes dumbly at me, doubt and fear on his face.

"After him! Now!" I'm screaming and pointing, completely out of my seat, "guy's got my car!" He snaps to it this time, rams the stick in first, drops the gas pedal hard. He understands a command. The modified dump-cum-sign-truck spasms forward and groans up to the turn. Ron works all sixteen gears in furious, metal grinding succession; revs the 6.0 liter V8 right up to the red-line before each wrench of the stick. The Porsche's overburdened with the Mt. Everest of a creature, but he's pulling away anyway.

"Turn on the sirens!" I yell. "Turn on the sirens!"

Ron obeys. He flips the switch. The yellow warning lights of our truck strobe to life, clicking rhythmically above us. They're not really sirens; they don't make a sound. Flashing lights are flashing lights though, even to this guy.

He's driving erratically, veering around; now speeding up; now slowing down. I'm half out the window, gesticulating wildly. "Pull over! Pull off the road! That's my car!" Choking into the on-rushing wind; I'm clutching the rear-view mirror with my left-hand while flailing away with my right. In front of us, the hairy giant locks up the brakes, careens off the road, and skids to a halt halfway in the ditch. Ron slams the sign truck to a stop right in the middle of the road with a force so hard I fly out the window. But it's nothing. The momentum of the halt just helps me hit the ground running, running wildly for my car.

I stop dead in my tracks as all seven feet of the *Thing* simply elevates through the open targa tops. In an otherworldly graceful display of pure power, the behemoth levitates clear of the car and lands in a crouch by the fence line, a low bass rumble emitting from somewhere deep inside him.

What in the hell was I thinking?

I turn back and run for the truck. "Forget the Porsche! Forget it!" I'm yelling and waving both arms at Ron as I run. Stumbling, I clamber back into the safety of the truck, scrunching down in the floorboard as I do so, and slamming the door shut. Locking it, too. "Just get outta' here!"

But Ron doesn't do anything. He's not moving even a single muscle; slack-jawed, he's just gaping, like he's beyond being scared. I rise up and take a peek, my eyes following Ron's gaze. The *Thing* is gone. A seven foot beast has simply vanished. I think I catch the sound of something big running away through the undergrowth of the encroached woods, but I can't be sure. It's silent now; silent except for the clicking of our warning lights.

I remember to grab my bag from the back of Ron's truck before cautiously returning to the Porsche. It's still idling. There's hair everywhere in the seat—long, course strands of it, matted clumps of it. Otherwise the car looks good. Great, in fact. I reach in to run my hand over the newly polished dash. I feel the smooth curve of freshly waxed yellow fenders. The VW mid-engine, four-cylinder idles perfectly. It sounds even better than it had before I wrecked it.

I open the hood. My other two rackets are still here. The cans of meat from the old gas station, too. Even the engine's been cleaned. Something like guilt creeps into my wonder.

It was him, the *Thing*. And he was helping me.

I stare into the forest, close and tangled and capable of hiding even him, but there is no sound or feel of him nearby. A birthday like no other, this one.

Turning back to the car, my hand slips easily into the door handle, and I am down and in the seat. The feeling of the old car wrapped around me again, cradling me, it's good and secure. A moment of wonder and reunion. I look back at Ron, then at the steering wheel again. The dash, the gauges, the feel of the stick in my hand, all like old friends. The tank's even full.

Forget John Sharpe, I'm John Fears the tennis player now. And I'll make my own way.

I back my car up and turn it around, waving at Ron as I pass, but he just sits there following me with wide eyes, and disbelief is written all over him. I'd have to laugh if it wasn't so sad, seeing him like that. I know how he feels.

Goodbye, Ron, and don't say a thing because they'll never believe you.

They never do.

⅄

# Ghosts, White

It feels good to be in my car again. It feels good to have my own money in my pocket, even if it isn't much, just a hundred and thirty dollars. But it is mine. Earned with my sweat. Nobody helped me.

A movement, a presence, flickers at the edge of my vision. I peer into the deeply forested piney woods enveloping Highway 59 on both sides of me, looking, hoping for a glimpse, straining to penetrate the greenish darkness.

But nothing's there at all. Just the trees standing silently in the breathless heat.

Suddenly, something large in the road. Unthinkingly, I swerve to avoid it; bloated and grotesque, the thing flies by. A roadkill deer. Just a deer. Poor thing. A glimpse in the rearview mirror: rear legs broken in strange skewed angles, burst guts glistening redly in the harsh light. But I'm around the curve now, and it is gone.

Nothing dangerous here now. Nothing except me in my car, this black road before me.

Herbert sure wouldn't have allowed a roadkill like that to stay out here so long.

I look at my watch. Noon already. Must be out of the district now. I let out a sigh. Glad I didn't see anyone on the way, but then, I knew I wouldn't. Going out through Maud like that and cutting back to 59 again let me avoid the crews working the I30 access road today. I hadn't seen Herbert or the cops or Bobby or any of those guys. Just heading south again and leaving the past all behind me now. All except this car.

A road sign flashes. 'Jefferson, pop. 2024.'

That's the old place on the bayou. We used to go there sometimes for my birthdays. But Dad also went there to meet this idiot client of his for some kind of business deal. It was always about the deals, deals, deals; money and deals, that's what he was all about. The antiques are good here, he'd told me, which is why his client's wife loves the place. The place is actually kind of cool. The old town is on a big slow bayou where they used to run barges. They've restored a few buildings and homes from the mid-eighteen hundreds, I believe, when the place was happening.

How many birthdays was it, here in this place, just me and Dad and his clients? Two or three, at least. And where had Mom been? Lord knows. My birthdays, and she hadn't even come. It seems strange to me only now. But it'd been over between Mom and Dad, even then, I guess.

Last time, we had a nice meal at the hotel where we used to stay. Now what's the name of the place? It's right there on the old main street, the place of places to stay in Jefferson, of course. And a meal would be good; my appetite's returned with a vengeance and I'm utterly exhausted. Still got plenty of money left, and it is a long drive down to Galveston.

Yeah, why not?

I turn left at a marker for Historic Downtown. A right at another marker, and buildings from another century rise up. The Oldtown comes into view. This looks about like what I remember, better even. They must've kept working at it.

Surely, I won't miss the restaurant, though I've never driven here on my own.

I don't. The Excelsior Hotel, that's the one—white painted brick, an elegant two-story box with its mullioned windows stretching floor to ceiling. A black-iron balcony wraps a double porch in ornate stacks, like a wedding cake. More like something from New Orleans than Texas. The whole town is, really.

I pull into a parking space right in front and unfold myself from the low seat to stand there looking at the clean white respectability of the building. It's famous for being haunted, too. A ghost woman in a white dress floats through walls. Furniture moves around where there is no furniture. Doors slam on windless nights. A confederate specter in dress uniform comes to stand over you in the night, just watching you, bayonet in hand. I was scared, but Dad wouldn't let me sleep in his room, even after I'd heard creaking footsteps and soft wailings in the middle of the night. Wouldn't even open his door, when I knocked, crying.

Just told me to quit being a baby and get the hell back to my own room.

I hesitate before the place and look down at myself. It's really too nice a restaurant for me to go in there like this: wrecked jeans, ruined sweaty shirt, dirt clods and cement clinging to my destroyed tennis shoes. Haven't even bathed but twice since I ran for it, and those times it was in an emergency shower with industrial cleaner that abraded like wildfire. Never want to do that again. I brush myself off a little and run a hand down my t-shirt. It doesn't help much.

Well, what the hell, I am a working man—or was. Here goes nothing.

The hostess at the stand hesitates and looks me over with a frown while I shift from foot to foot. She considers, relents, and shows me to a four-seat table near the back. A few guys in open-necked dress shirts huddle together; they take no notice of me. There's not much else going on here today.

My order comes quickly. Veal and Crab Lamache and a glass of wine—all the most expensive things on the menu. Nothing but the best for me today. I sip the wine and chew the food slowly; it's rich and heavy after my spartan days in the trailer eating canned crap. The hasty retreat from the Highway Department looms in my mind. Shouldn't have just left like that. Herbert deserves more. The least I could've done is go back and quit formally. Said goodbye to him and Darlene, or something. Bobby wouldn't have done anything, not with them around.

At least, I don't think so.

"Oh well," I whisper, tipping my wine glass to myself and draining it, "Happy Birthday, John, you loser." Eighteen, and I'm old enough to drink this thanks only to having killed my father and gotten a fake ID from three lonely women in the woods. I have to laugh a little. Not the proudest moments of my life, these. No, not really the proudest. Could be worse I suppose.

I could be lying dead by a trailer with a tire-iron stuck in my brain.

"John Sharpe, what is your skinny young ass doing here?" A man's friendly familiar voice whispers whiskeybreath in my ear, a big hand claps down hard on my shoulder.

Startled, I turn and look up from my meal, feel the blood drain from my face. My fork drops to my plate. My teeth clamp down. Gobs of my un-chewed meal still in my mouth. Him. She is there beside him. They know me. They will know what I've done. I stand abruptly, looking, flicking my eyes from face to face—his is still friendly, hers', stony. She's wearing dark sunglasses, her expression unreadable.

I start to say her name.

I gag, choking down veal. I feel it lodge deep in my throat.

The expressions before me show concern, now horror.

I'm gasping, ragged and painful, but the breath won't come. I reach for her and see my own hands before me, detached and distant things morphing into dark claws, grasping at nothing. I'm dimly aware of sinking to my knees. Her. She is here. Can't take my eyes off of her.

She fades into stark whiteness.

The fantasy of her returns.

The feel of her, the smell of her, it's like the gardens she keeps, gardens filled with Tyler roses, azaleas, magnolias. I see her over me, on top of me, her arms thrown back behind her, leaning back, sharp nails dig deep, deep. Her dark hair flows, let down her face like a veil, it sways with her rhythmic weaving.

Knowing I shouldn't be doing this, that we shouldn't be doing this. We're doing it anyway, powerless to stop. She leans forward, our mouths come together wet, open, urgent; they part. I follow, raising my head, reaching for her again with my mouth, my hands, my body...

"Whoa, John, what the fu...! Now don't get excited!"

It is his voice. His loathsome, loathsome voice.

There is relieved laughter, applause.

I tear sweet breath from the air around me. Everywhere, there is precious air. For a while I do nothing but fill my lungs with it. I'm just breathing and darkness is before me. I can't seem to open my eyes. Don't want to open my eyes. The taste rises in my throat: of bile, of whiskey, of things far worse.

My eyes snap open. I'm on the ground, looking wildly around. I'm encircled by service staff, random people, the business men in pressed dress shirts; they're all clapping.

She stands, hands on her bent knees looking down at me. Her face shows concern, she's leaning in behind him. The scent of her, it's still the same. I try to breathe it in, but his cologne overpowers my senses. He is on his knees beside me. No, he is right on top of me. His hands are on my chest, and his big head's thrown back, laughing drunkenly.

He is my savior.

"Robert? Gloria?" I croak their names; pain sears my chest.

"Now that's a greeting John, shit! That is a fine hello!"

He yanks me bodily to my feet. I am limp, helpless in the embrace of Robert Baker, Dad's old client, hated husband. I have no will to stand. I want to sink back down and die. I look at him just long enough for him to wink at me and I want to puke.

"Course I'd of preferred to use this stuff on one of the ladies."

I lurch free of his grasp, stop myself woozily, and double over.

Please let me puke.

"Yeah..." I say before bending over and coughing again violently, as if my ribs will crack, and my guts will come out. I notice a mouthful of my un-chewed veal on the carpet. "...good thing you're here," I gasp.

My eyes are closed again, I'm not wanting to see what is right before me. Instead I see her as she'd come to me that one night back in Tahoe as I sprawled alone on the balcony of my dark resort room, watching casino lights pierce the sky and illuminate low clouds, like the old-fashioned reel projection of some surrealist auteur. A soft knock on the door, and I'd cracked it open to an apparition in white. And this had been no dream, it was really her. She slipped in quickly and put a finger to my lips. Don't say anything, she'd whispered then, taking my hand and leading me toward the bed, our fingers softly intertwined. Just don't say anything.

I didn't. I haven't.

"John," Gloria says. She is here, this is now. Her fingers; there's a tentative touch on my shoulder. A trembling response. "John, are you okay?" It's her first words since those words, the first touch since that night. That strange night when nothing really happened and everything got so confused. When the fantasies began. I can't stop my trembling.

"He's okay," Robert bawls, stepping in. Her hand departs, the touch lingering on until a whack on the back jolts it brutally away. "He'll be fine. John, eh? Whaddayasay? You're allright."

I can only nod. Slowly, I gather myself and straighten up, not wanting to open my eyes. There is no other choice but to face them though, and they don't seem to know what I've done.

"Shit, give him space," he says, though he's thrown a suffocating arm around me as he steers me back to my chair. "A man nearly buys it, it's perfectly normal to be upset."

He snaps his fingers, and I wince at the sound.

"Hey! Hey, waiter! Bring us a couple of Scotches—Balvenie twelve, neat. Make it snappy!" They sit down on either side of me, her hand lights on my left forearm, while his grasps my right. I can't bear to meet either of their eyes. "Hell, John. Been a long time since we've seen you. What—since that crappy resort your Dad took us all to back in Vegas?"

I can't believe this is the guy who saved my life; that this guy, of all guys in the whole world, has to be the one to take me in his hands, place his foul lips on mine and bestow his breathe upon me. The gift of life blown from an asshole.

"Tahoe," I manage to say quietly, "it was Tahoe. But yeah," I nod my head, glancing up at him. "That was the last time." His frat-boy haircut bobs, sweeping nearly over his right eye. It looks even more stupid now that he's nearly forty. The starched white dress shirt fit perfectly to accommodate his round, expanding belly, the brazen golden cufflinks, the dark dress pants of finest wool; it's all there. It's the stockbroker's thousand dollar "casual" uniform, all pressed to perfection, all wrapping the body of the simpleton toad who dresses like those he admires most. It's all vintage Robert.

"Shit, how long ago was that," he says.

"Two years ago," I mumble quickly.

The waiter brings our whiskeys and we all straighten in our chairs, regarding each other. Her hand leaves my arm, his grabs desperately for his drink. I take a long pull on my own. The whiskey is smooth and strong and good. The same kind Dad drinks.

Was it a present from Robert? Probably.

Robert the multi-millionaire. Robert the drinker, gambler, and partier. Robert, the inheritor of an old family oil fortune. Never worked a real day in his life. Gone to pot before he even left UT.

I glance up at Gloria; she is watching me curiously. She's dressed demurely, expensively, of course, in a long sleeved blouse and jacket, despite the heat outside. Money makes up for a lot doesn't it, Gloria? Is it worth it? Is it worth the desperate nights? Is it worth the nights being groped by a drunken sod, the nights you're left alone and stranded in all the cities of the world; left wondering if this is it, if this is all that's out there, if this is all you have to give? Or do you even wonder about it—or anything? Besides the money, that is, besides The Life? I look at him again; he's about to speak. The danger's already forgotten. He's seemingly happy, completely carefree. He really seems not to have heard about Dad. Not any of it.

"Yeah, that's right," Robert says. "Good memory. Well, I was drunk off my ass every night." He laughs. "Your old man does show you a good time." A question troubles his prominent brow. "Gloria, you were with me on that trip, weren't you?"

Oh yes, dumbass, she was there.

But just who am I to talk—big success that I am?

"Yes," she says, watching him carefully now.

"Yeah?" He looks at her a confused moment, clearly not recalling her even being there. He looks back to me. "Yeah, well, John, your Dad hasn't been to Tyler to see us in some time." He laughs, takes another big drink of whiskey. "Maybe it's because I fired his ass! Bad move that, the fund hasn't done as well as when he managed it." No one knows what to say to that. Robert considers something with what passes for seriousness in his wasted face. "Maybe you two should come over some time and talk," Robert finally continues. "You could play some tennis with Gloria here." He extends his glass toward her. She smiles, says nothing. "She's still crazy for it, judging from all the lessons she takes out at the goddamn tennis club."

I look at her. The sunglasses have finally come off. Her lean, angular face still looks good, despite some kind of meanness about it, hovering there, even when she smiles. Or is it wariness? Maybe the latter. I don't know, but I notice a new look. The drawn, tight look; the plastic surgery look. Christ, she must be what? Nearly thirty-five now? Still, she's beautiful, and it's hard not to stare at her and wonder. Why me? I shake my head. "I think he's out of private fund management these days, but I'm not sure." I glance at her again. "Not that I wouldn't mind hitting a few balls with Gloria."

"But Christ, John, you look like shit. What've you been up to?" Robert's got a swollen paw grabbing onto my shirt. "You look like some homeless headbanger. Does Chip know where you're at?"

I look at him in alarm.

"No." I almost shriek it. Keep calm now: stay close to the truth. "No, he doesn't. Know where I am. I'm out on my own now. Haven't heard from him in a... few months."

Her hand lights softly on my left arm again, barely there at all; it's electric.

"Robert, he looks fine. Better shape than ever, John," she says and pats my arm soothingly. Looking back to her, I immediately soften, wanting more than ever to be wrapped in her embrace. Just one more time. She's about to speak again when Robert interrupts.

"– Well, what the hell are you doing, man," he spots my cement encrusted shoe sticking out, "road work or something?"

"Well, ah, actually..." I say, quickly tucking the shoe back under the table.

"You are, aren't you?" He laughs over loudly, triumphantly. "Oh man, you're like a road Mexican. You want me to get you some refried beans, Señorita? How 'bout some nachos with that whiskey?" He throws back his head and laughs again, not noticing that he's the only one doing so. A swoop of hair comes loose and bounces there in front of his face like some blond greased ganglion.

I force a half-smile and look down at my drink; her hand gives me a soft, quick squeeze.

"Well, why don't you blow this dump?" Robert says, "come to Tyler, and I'll get you a decent job. We'll be there through the winter." Robert drains his drink, then gives Gloria a hard look. "Once we buy every goddamn antique in this little burg that is. Gloria's about –"

"– Uh, well," I say. "I'll think about it."

I look up at Gloria. She smiles. Robert loses interest in her again.

"Well, my job is done here," he says. "Gotta go save another life somewhere."

He laughs to himself and fishes out a fat money clip and thumbs four twenties on the table, expertly with one hand, like a professional gambler.

"That ought to cover it. Gloria, you checked us out already?"

She nods yes to him without taking her eyes, or her hand, off of me.

"Yeah? Well, let's go my little queen," Robert says. "Adios, John."

He's already standing, ready to go; he's beating me on the back again with a meaty hand.

"Think about it."

I nod. She rises from her chair, still fit I see, taut curves show beneath the loose pants.

"You should," she says and squeezes my arm one last time before letting it go.

He's already walking towards the door, not looking back. She holds my gaze in her own a moment, and I nod yes at her, though I'm not sure why. It's too dangerous. She looks at me still, and I can't perceive what she's really thinking. Perhaps she knows. Perhaps she doesn't care. I break off first, and look down into my drink.

She puts on her sunglasses, turns and goes. I look up again to watch her hips move, swaying with that walk of hers, feeling her again in my hand, like it was yesterday. Just like it was yesterday. I'm sure she knows what I'm thinking.

Robert's money has paid for the drinks and my meal. I pocket the change and wander out to sit on the front porch bench, staring out across the nearly empty street. I look at the renovated buildings, the clean streets, the idyllic little place.

Galveston. Well, that was the plan. But Tyler—could it work? The cops have gotta be close. And now that I have this car back, I'm a rolling advertisement that says, 'John Sharpe is here.' But no, it'd never work. Tyler's too close, and the Bakers won't hide me. Not when they find out what I've done. Or would they?

Gloria might, she just might.

A new, black Cadillac with darkly tinted windows pulls into a parking space in front of me. For a moment, I think the Bakers have returned. But, no, an old man steps out. He's hunchbacked and flaccid and yellow-white as a rumpled old sheet. The old man frowns at me disapprovingly.

Reminds me of those old guys in the VA hospital, the one they took Granpa to after he fell sick and wouldn't let Dad put him up in decent hospital in Dallas. I shudder a little.

Walking those long halls to his little room, the whole place smelling sweet and sickly rotten at the same time like that giant carrion flower I'd read about out in Africa, or so I imagined. I remember, too, how I'd clung to Dad, and he was embarrassed by that and practically shoved me through the corridors. But I couldn't help it; I was afraid. All those old men up there, they gave me the creeps, shuffling along on their walkers or sitting nearly insensate in the sun below the clerestory windows. Old withered lizards, they'd all stop what they were doing when you passed, and they'd goggle at you, and some would even reach out with bony claws and jointless fingers to try and grab you, and some were drooling. They were all barely with us in this present world, as if they lived mostly in the memory. And because the little they still perceived of this reality was all bad, they seemed to disapprove of your very presence. They'd whisper amongst one another in your passing, as if they were saying: see, will you look at that little shit? This is who we saved the country for? It gets worse and worse with every generation. Nobody's quite up to snuff these days. And I couldn't help but feel like they were right about it all. Even then.

The old man ambles off down the street.

And that was the last time I ever saw Granpa alive, wasn't it? By then, he'd grown mean and bitter and he'd accused Dad of all sorts of things. Nasty things. Nothing more than a criminal, he'd whispered, lying in his rickety iron bed, wrinkled eyes shut tight to the sight of us. Then he'd stretched his head up from his husk of a body like a turtle and looked at us with absolute clarity and snapped the words at us: never come back. The doctor said dementia; that's what they do when they get dementia, but I don't know. I couldn't shake the feeling that Granpa knew what he was doing. After he gave everything to the church, he wanted to be shed of us once and for all. Both of us. I wasn't after your money, I wanted to cry out to him. Don't throw me away, don't do this, don't do this. But I didn't. No one said anything after that. Granpa just closed himself back up in his sheets then, and I stood there in shock, like a desecrated wooden icon, broken and cast away to be sold for pennies. But Dad wasn't stunned for long. His face set grimly, he turned and gathered me up and hurried us out of there. What I should have said, no, what I should've screamed: I love you, Granpa. I love you, no matter what you say. And what I should have done: go back and just sit with him. Go back and just be with him.

Never did. And look at me now. He was right.

I get up off the rigid bench and stretch a little. Look back to the hot brick streets, the timeless solidity of these buildings. It's not much different from my first time here, all those years ago with my father. After the birthday meal, Pop just sat there, opened up his briefcase, and started preparing for a meeting, leaving me to to wander around the place by myself like the stolen child. Until Gloria showed up and took me by the hand.

The first time I was alone with her.

She was so beautiful then, so young.

I liked Gloria right away, and she liked me, and I was glad to have her there. She had that bright look in her eye. She seemed happy to be with me. Interested in me, and what I'd been doing. She'd sat right here beside me, maybe it was on this very same bench.

It's your tenth birthday, she said, what do you want to do? It was startling, her question, and it'd been the first time anybody asked me what I wanted to do. Dad just told me what we were going to do, pure and simple. There'd never been a choice.

Nothing. It's all I could think of.

Nothing? She was looking at a brochure, smiling. This nice little town and nothing?

Is there anything to do?

I smile a little. And she had shown me what a nice little town it was.

We went out and saw the trains. They were these old steam engines with huge black boilers, and we saw some oldtimey railroad tycoon's personal railcar, too. If he lived a hundred years ago, Robert would have had something like the railcar. Its insides were fitted with gold and brass and lined with private curtained alcoves. Carpets of rich purple. In the middle, an intricately burled dining table reared up on its feet of harpyclaw, like some unknown fantasy beast that lived to serve you rare wines poured in crystal glasses, dainties from trays of Tiffany silver, exotic dishes heaped on priceless Meissen china of the most vibrant blue.

Gloria had loved the railcar—the silver and china and the purple carpets especially: all the symbols of wealth, all the trappings of royalty. American royalty. I shake my head.

Don't want to see the railcar.

We rode the steamship through the bayou too, eating ice-cream bars for fifty cents. It burned real wood—small logs and scrap wood, surprisingly little. The big paddlewheels slowly slapping water, the soft pleasant chugging, she'd held my hand as we looked through portholes into the green and brown depths of water and trees. She had such small pretty hands, soft and tanned, holding onto me, as if she'd never let me go again.

I cross the street and stroll down the sidewalk, picking up tourist pamphlets and peering in stores shaded by verandas from times even before Granpa. It's all still the same: the railcar, the shops, the steamboat. This is the way we'd walked, too, wandering around in the hot sun, reading rusty old historical plaques written like textbooks.

I stop and read one. Yeah, boring as ever.

Another official acknowledgment of a once great family around here.

Oh most ancient name of Sharpe, and just where might I raise your historical marker?

But that name's for better men than I.

I stop at the end of sidewalk, shading my eyes against the lowering sun and peering towards the docks down by the bayou. It looks forgotten and desolate in the afternoon sun, but the boat's just visible. Maybe I can catch the last ride of the day.

Really, I should just get going though. Quit hanging around here. But Tyler or Galveston? John Sharpe or John Fears? It really shouldn't be much of a choice. But still, seeing her again today. Now the thought won't go away. Surely, she'd take me in, but what about him?

The Big Cypress Bayou, a dirtlot canopied by trees. There's almost no one here, just a minivan, two pickups, some banged-up car. The boat's tethered to a narrow wooden shack out on piers over the water; inside the building, there are books of local history, of folklore, and of ghost tales, too. I scan through a couple of them; they all look bad. Another pamphlet catches my eye: Caddo mounds. The picture is of a tall grassy hill and strange beehive huts; the Indians are nearly naked. Yeah, that always gets them in—the topless native women. But I went there with her, too; the second time I saw her here.

The steamboat whistles for departure. I pocket the pamphlet and walk out and board the boat across a gangplank that sags under my weight. The boat looks good though. White and crisp, it's smaller than I remember, almost like a toy. The prow is stenciled with the ship's name: The Graceful Ghost.

Up top, I choose a wooden bench by the back rail. Two kids are up here play-fighting, pushing each other hard against the railing, laughing like fiends. No parents in sight and none come running as the Ghost slides off and traverses a channel so narrow its sides shear brown mud from the bank in long, greasy curls. A Great Blue Heron startles up with an ugly discordant squawk that seems at odds with the beauty of the thing. The enormous bird flies alongside the boat with great slow-motion wing beats, like some pterodactyl raised from the primordial depths.

Something interesting about the Indians and the symbology of the bird. Can't quite recall it, and I look to the kids. Intent on their game, they take no notice of the huge thing flying right beside them, and they chase one another downstairs, laughing. The heron wheels away and labors off into the bluegreen distance, leaving me alone in the afternoon heat.

So very alone this time. With an arm thrown over the rail, I watch the steady passing of the cypress and the strangely translucent brown water and the lily pads and the small black bog islands rising up between sentinel trees. A landscape unchanged for a thousand years. And even in this bright light, the mystery of the place lulls me into thought and reflection, and I look for some universal meaning in all the things I see, answers in the low moss-hung branches, portents in the rafts of floating plants, whispered reason in the rhythmic steaming of the engine.

I find none.

∧

# Good for Business

Retirement. Chip contemplates the word, thinks about it as a past event, tries out the sound of it on a parched tongue. It leaves a bad taste. "Never retire," he whispers between rhythmed breaths. He runs on, checking his watch at the point. Mile five. Three to go. The humidity and heat, even at five AM, is oppressive, all-enveloping. The worried cast on his wrist itches miserably, but he ignores it. No hint of daylight yet. Pine boughs reach across the neighborhood streets, like the darkened arcades of abandoned skyscrapers. Abandoned cities, dead and forgotten. Not the whisper of the wind though he's heard there's a storm coming. A strangely claustrophobic tightness all around. In the black tunnel before him, a jogger. Another soul, plodding and heavy in the pre-dawn, he comes in direct opposition to Chip's own path. The sweat bloom on the man's shirt is oddly visible, the white socks too, churning in place almost. The wraith comes on slowly, never deviating, and Chip arcs around him at the last moment, watching as he passes. The man does not speak nor look up and cannot be heard.

Showered at the building's locker room and dressed in a suit sent directly from the cleaners to his office, Chip starts his day. Things have been much slower these last couple of years. With the financial crisis and the recession and the general malaise affecting the markets worldwide, people pulled out of his private equity fund at an alarming rate and it hasn't shown any new growth in over a year. No matter that he's still doing well short-selling and buying T-bills and hustling the portfolio he does have.

Madoff and all those assholes in New York rankle in his mind. He trusted them, too, and why? Because everyone did. Because it made money. Lots and lots of money. Because it was Wall Street. Chip is disturbed by what he doesn't know about his own industry. An industry built on trusting people you never see, don't know, and don't ever want to know. And what kind of business is that? He's not sure he wants to go there. "Lemmings, all of us," he says. But what really irritates him: how could he have not seen it coming? Look at the graphs. Nobody gets returns like that for so long. An idiot could have seen it coming. "Some expert I am," he says to the empty office.

But still, for some reason, the last few days have seemed even worse to him. Not even two weeks since John pushed him down the stairwell and yet it seems like years, and his interest in his own work has waned again to the point that he's thinking about retirement for God's sake. Not even forty and now this. He can't put words to how he feels about John. But the word that comes closest: regret.

"Regret nothing," he tells himself, thinking of Father's treasured maxims, "Always move forward." Then he stops, just a small moment, and thinks, not for the first time, what his true father might have said about this, where his true father really is, if he's even alive. Why Father never talked about his own son, Chip will never know now. John Griffith, "J.G." Sharpe, the great man, acted as if his own son never even existed, as if there was simply a generational gap and the old man had sired Chip on his own. And such was the legend of the man in that little town, that people were willing to let it go, never even mentioning the son in J.G.'s presence. But Chip had heard enough and done the research on his own when he came of age. Philip Charles Sharpe, that had been his father's name. His very own father. The young man had been a golden child in Daingerfield. Already thought of as a worthy successor to his war hero father, they'd even whispered that something else had been in store for the young man, something greater. Tall as a young tree, Chip had heard, and fast and strong, a pure, natural athlete and a nice guy to boot. He was the kind of guy who people always called by his full name Philip Charles, never Phil or even Philip; no, it was always Philip Charles, like he was royalty or something. He was a young man who needed two full names not because he demanded it for himself, but because the popular consensus demanded it of themselves. Philip Charles, that's what they always called him, and people still remembered him, just as he'd been in High School.

His senior year, he'd taken four puny little scrubs from the basketball team, put them on his broad shoulders, and carried them all the way to the state final, and, in the process, he'd turned a rabid football town into a basketball crazy town singlehandedly.

The pictures are still there in the high school, hanging right behind all the trophies. Chip had seen them over and over growing up. His biological father had been a man among boys, towering over the rest of them like a god, and never smiling, this relentless look in his eye as he drove toward the basket. But in the state final, he hadn't really shown up. He played, but it just wasn't there for him and he'd only scored a few points, gathered up a few rebounds. The team had been destroyed. Some people still made excuses for him. Sick, some told Chip, he'd been sick. But others said, no, something else had been wrong with him. It was like he was already gone, they'd said, like his body was there, but not his mind. Like he was far, far away and all the basketball stuff was of no concern to him. And still some others hinted at darker reasons, as if the state final hadn't really mattered for him because the basketball scholarship offers had already been piling up and he'd already written off his little Daingerfield team. UT, Houston, Rice, even UCLA had got wind of him somehow, and the mean spirited people said that Philip Charles was already thinking about the bigger glory. But that couldn't be right, Chips thinks, as he has always thought, because his father hadn't taken any of those schools up on it, not any of them. He went to war instead. Philip Charles wasn't drafted either, he'd volunteered for service. He joined the Marines, asking for combat duty on the front line, and they'd given it to him. He'd gone to Vietnam.

And that's when his story had simply ceased to exist for the people of Daingerfield. The way Chip had heard it, most people thought Philip Charles died there in the Far East, and that Chip had been born either beforehand or while his father was over there. Nobody mentioned it, but Chip knows that his father did return, if only briefly, looking strangely wild and speaking to no one. That's all Father had ever told him, too, and Chip knew, even back then, that it'd be all he'd ever get out of him. But apparently Philip Charles had come back home. He'd come to the front doorstep like a stranger and handed his father a new born child and said, "Here, Father, his name is Chip. He's more like you than he is me, anyway."

And the way J.G. told it, he'd asked, "and you can tell that from a baby?" And Philip Charles had replied, "Yes. Can't you?" And then the son had simply walked off and that was the last J.G. saw of him. The last anybody saw of him.

Chip likes to imagine Philip Charles there among the Vietnamese. Most of those people wouldn't have even come up to his waist. What a terror a guy like that must've been. Probably was, Chip knows. A true terror. Chip knows too what J.G. had never told him: that his father had been dishonorably discharged for insubordination to a commanding officer. There weren't too many details in the official records, but Chip had dug up what he could, and he'd found it. There had been a massacre. He's seen some photos the pentagon had tried to cover up, but couldn't: women killed, children murdered, even their animals; an entire village had been utterly annihilated. And those people weren't just shot, they were shot hundreds of times: in the head, in the body, everywhere. Those villagers had been gunned down and they'd been raped and they'd had their genitals mutilated and their limbs hacked to pieces, and then they'd been napalmed and bombed—hundreds of them, piled up, tangled in pools of their own blood by the doors of their own burned huts, in the dirt of their only road, and in the furrows of their own razed fields.

And something had happened there between Philip Charles Sharpe and his fellow soldiers, and the war had been over for him, and he'd pulled secrecy around his young, bright life, and he became a mystery, disappearing from the face of the earth and leaving nothing but an infant son in the hands of an aging, single father whose own wife had passed away during the birth of his only child.

Philip Charles, Philip Charles, the name echoes now in the son's mind. It was Philip Charles that had driven Chip away from Daingerfield. Driven him away and driven Father to be a remote and distant parent, who set the bar high but barely even noticed you while he wrapped himself in the glory of a past before his son or his grandson even existed.

Until John had been born.

And Chip thinks of how the old man had taken to his little great-grandson, and he'd gone out of the way to be with John, loving him as a son should be loved. How John loved him back, too. And how excluded Chip had felt then and had always felt around them. Still does, even though Father's long dead and John's gone for good.

Philip Charles, you coward. You worthless son-of-a-bitch.

Chip bangs the window with the palm of his hand. He worries with the itching cast. He bangs the window again and again, and he gets mad at Philip Charles and at Father all over again. And he thought he *had* put all this behind him. But here it is again, surfacing in his mind like a monstrous, ugly stain. All because of John. All because of a fall and a crack on the head.

And look at John now. Running away. Like Philip Charles himself.

"Regret nothing. Father was right about that. No regrets now."

But, still, it is there: the feeling that leaves him empty. Chip wrenches his thought away with an effort. Back to his business. His business. His salvation. Can't retire now, not ever. Not until he dies, because he is not a quitter. He will never be a quitter.

"I'll get it back," he says to his own reflection. "It'll all come back."

And besides, he thinks, still trying to make himself feel better, he's still got Simon, the magical money machine with his million dollar monthly income. The superstar preacher has sure been killing it lately. No small wonder, Chip reflects, in times like these, God's got work to do. Keep the donations rolling and Amen for that brother, and you can kiss my ass IRS because it is, all of it, tax free. Non-profit indeed.

Chip has had the sense to take care of himself, too, having parked his own reserves in very safe places. Untraceable places. Again, he loses himself in the modern treasure hunt, working the numbers, calculating his personal burn rate against the amount stashed in what he calls his "little war chest." Even accounting for the most conservative of returns on the chest funds, it should easily be enough to last him the rest of his life, and in style. Not Simon kind of style—that would be too conspicuous anyway—but very nice nonetheless. The rest of John's life too, should he ever come back and apologize. Should he ever give it to him. Chip thinks of what his own father left him: a legacy of unspoken expectations, some broken junk, and nothing else. Not a red cent.

He moves to the window overlooking Texarkana and stands there with his nose pressed to the glass, looking straight down to the street below. It feels again like his town, as it always does to him. Like he owns the place. How much time, he muses, have I spent here in this office, working to become what I've become.

Another voice in his head comes to him now, an unfamiliar voice, a new voice: and what is it that you've become? It mocks. And for what? He shakes it off, but he can't help wondering about John's choice to stay with him during the custody battle with Diane. Chip had argued for it, of course, because you don't just let your only son go live with your cheating ex-wife and some flake in Ohio, but the Judge had let it come down to John's choice. Chip thought it had been lost then, that he'd spend the rest of his days alone with his wealth and his infertility. But surprisingly John had chosen to stay with his father. I'll stay with Dad, John had said to the judge quietly and quickly, and then clammed up again. A rare instance where he seems to have already known what he wanted.

The phone rings. Chip strides over and snaps it up.

"Sharpe," he says.

"Is the Lady of the house present!" A sunshine voice.

"This is she," Chip says gruffly. The voice stutters, goes cold, and Chip smiles, feeling better now. "What idiot is selling you my contact info?" He yells, and the sunshine voice is abruptly gone.

Then he thinks of making a call of his own, but decides not to. He hangs up, missing his recently laid-off admin now and wondering why he fired her last week.

The phone rings again. This time, it's his cell phone, buzzing with the personalized tone of someone Chip knows. A client. Opportunity ringing. He looks at the display and his pulse quickens: Robert Baker. Robert, the career alcoholic whose only good business sense is in his infallible picking of trustworthy people to manage his money, to give him an allowance, and to steer him away from day-to-day business troubles. And trust Robert does, as implicitly and naively as a babe. And somehow—at least where his money is concerned—it has always worked for him; and this too: he is the man who inexplicably dumped Chip for another fund manager in Houston. But someone put him up to the switch, Chip feels sure of that. Robert wouldn't have done it on his own. Perhaps Gloria, perhaps not. But if so, she could be forgiven for it. How could he not? Thinking of her, Chip's palms begin to sweat. A stirring, even now, after all that's happened and all these years. There was once a time where he thought of her every day. And she knew it.

He lets the phone ring a couple of more rings, and then he answers.

"Robert Baker, now there's a name I'd hoped to forget."

"Chip?" The wavering braggadocio voice answers. "Is that Chip Sharpe? Damn, I dialed the wrong number! I meant to dial someone relevant."

"Robert, always good to hear from you, too. How are you, and how's Gloria? To what do I owe this dubious honor?"

"Hey, Chip, long time no see. Well, Gloria's shopping and I'm paying so we're good, we're good, same as always. But listen, you'll never guess who we just saw? And in Jefferson, Texas, of all the shitty little places."

"Who? Not Ross Perot out slumming antique stores?"

Robert laughs appreciatively. "No, they wouldn't let him in here, 'cause he never pays for his shit! But really, we just saw your boy... John. He was mighty surprised to see us, too. Choked on his goddamn lunch and I had to give him the old Heimlich and then fuckin' mouth-to-mouth! You owe me big boy."

"What? Robert, you're kidding. Is he allright?"

"Yeah, scout's honor, it was John, and I saved his little life. He's fine though. Nothing a stiff whiskey and me buying him lunch couldn't fix. Looked like he *needed* for someone to buy him lunch, too. Chip, he looked like a vagrant and he 'bout jumped out of his seat when we asked him about you. So, what's the story? He said he's out on his own, but Gloria thinks he must've run away from home or something?"

Chip holds the phone away from his head a moment, just looking at it.

"Chip?"

"Yeah, it's just a big surprise, Robert. Let me get this straight. You're telling me you saw John in Jefferson Texas and that *you saved his life*? Now Robert, no bullshitting me on this one."

"Chip, yeah, fuck! I am not bullshitting you. So what's the deal? Inquiring minds want to know."

"Well, you see," Chip says cautiously, "John is out on his own. I did throw him out; it's true. And he's not allowed back here until... he makes something out of himself. But listen, Robert, I would like to know what John was up to? Where was he going?"

There is silence on the phone for a moment, then laughter. "Chip, you are one tough son of a bitch, man! You just tossed him out with nothing but the clothes on his back? What for, just to get rid of him?"

"Not exactly."

"Not exactly? Goddamn, Chip."

"Look, Robert, it's for his own good. And I don't need anyone telling me how to help my son, not even an upstanding citizen like yourself. Now, just tell me what he was doing."

"Well," Robert laughs, "strange way to help your son, Chip. But I guess I see your point. My old man was never so hard as all that and look how well I turned out!"

Chip shakes his head, thinking, yeah, my point exactly.

"Anyway," Robert continues, "I don't think he even knew what he was doing. Kid looked like a lost puppy. So I told him to come up to Tyler, and I'd give him a job, no problem, but—"

"—Did he come?" Chip interrupts, catching his breath on the questions, "What did Gloria have to say about it?"

"Gloria? Christ, Chip I don't know. Gloria won't care. She's not even here. Went off to the beach house in Galveston or someplace. But, as I was trying to tell you, no, John didn't come, and I doubt he'll show up. But listen, seeing him again did get me thinking—"

"—That must've been difficult for you," Chip says, relieved at the news.

"—Oh, shut up, Chip. Listen, I'm serious here. I got a proposition for you..."

And, suddenly, old friends, finding that nothing has really changed between them, are reunited around the commonality of the Great Game, and, in the matter of an hour, Robert is acting on the thought that has been working its steady way through the whiskies and the leisurely pastimes of his idle richness. Before the call is over, a gentleman's agreement is made; it's a done deal. Plans are made and, once again, the entire speculative fortune of Robert Baker is entrusted into the steady guiding hands of his good friend, the self-made man, Chip Sharpe.

Chip hangs up the phone, and from where he keeps it hidden on his laptop, he pulls up the photo of her, looking at it for a time with renewed interest. Inarticulate feelings define themselves and more plans known only unto himself are made. The unspoken name on his lips: Gloria. And on into the waning hours of the night he works, planning the investments, setting up the accounts, assiduously checking the tortured red-lined and blue-lined and green-lined peaks and valleys of global market trends. Furiously written emails are sent to all and sundry. "Hey, I've got a deal..." he writes, and "check the price..." and the list of professional, legitimized gamblers he contacts—aka: brokers and fund managers and investment advisors—grows. They are cronies all, united in the patriotic, money-for-nothing grailquest of economic growth. And if there's some personal enrichment to be had in the process; yeah, well, what's the harm in that?

No harm at all, he tells himself. It's all the cost of doing business.

# Run and Hide

Night in the Excelsior hotel room. Still undecided, I lay on the pressed sheets, staring at the beadboard ceiling. Soft light leaks in from streetlamps; the old building creaks in the quiet night though there is no wind. I close my eyes, but I can't bring the sleep; can't bring anything: no answers, no direction, no nothing except for the memory of her on that last night in Tahoe.

She'd appeared at my door wearing a robe over white and gauzy short pajamas, see-through enough to know there was nothing on beneath them. She'd let the robe fall to the floor, and then she'd put her arms around me and kissed me softly on my cheeks and on my lips. I couldn't look, couldn't even respond; I watched the robe there on the floor and couldn't make myself look up, hadn't even been able to move. And then she'd taken me and guided me to the bed. I'd looked then, drunk her in, and God was she beautiful and then we'd lain down and she'd just held me, nearly the whole night, her arms wrapped around me, embracing me with a fervor like I was the last man on the face of this earth. How I yearned for her, desperately, utterly. And yet I could not act and some strangeness of being kept us locked together there an eternity, neither moving nor yet sleeping at all. I just stared out into the night and into space, trembling to feel her body wrapped around mine, wondering what to do, trying not to think those thoughts, to have those wakeful pornographic dreams. She got up sometime before the dawn and she was weeping and the back of my shirt was wet with her tears, and she didn't say anything. She just hurried off, wrapped in her shame, leaving me there by myself, and I could not come out for the whole day thereafter. Two years and nothing but the secret loneliness of that night.

She won't come tonight.

I clutch sheets, listening, hoping for the same soft knock, and looking for the glimpse of her small pale feet, bare and shadowed in the gap beneath the door. Willing them to come.

I gasp and freeze. Something is there.

A shadow, dark and wide, light creeps in from around its edges. It moves nearer to the door, and the light is blotted out altogether. The knob twists; the door rattles softly against the deadbolt, but it is locked and does not yield. At first I sit up on the bed, watching, listening for her voice, but then the sounds come: a desperate call, full of longing, the breaking of glass or china or both. I thrash to get under the sheets. Covering up, I curl into a fetal position, watching the doorcrack, horrified. Feeling at the same time like the scared child all over again and wishing I hadn't left my gun in the car. Wondering if I will ever be completely shed of this.

The doorknob is not tried again. There are no more sounds. But whatever is there stays there an eternity. Then it moves on, disappearing in the span of a blink and making no noise. I spend the rest of the night staring at the thin bar of hall-light under the door, wondering if something was ever there at all.

Seven in the morning, and I don't think I've slept a wink. A headache rages at my temples, as if every single blood vessel in there will burst open at any second now. I'm standing by the check-out desk in the hotel lobby and looking out the front door at the new wind in the tops of the trees, just turning my car key in my hand, wondering what to do.

Should I really go on to Tyler? No. I should just go away. Far away. In the complete opposite direction. Galveston. Stick with the plan. But somehow, I can't.

"Sir?"

I'm dead tired. This could be bad. I need to leave this, just let it go.

"Sir?"

I start and stare. The woman is talking to me.

"Yes?" She's mid-forties, perhaps, with soft brown hair; she's plump and kind-looking in a featureless sort of way. She looks tired, like she's been up all night, like me, but she wears her good attitude like a uniform. She comes out from around the desk holding a coffee pot and a porcelain mug with flowers on it. Brown nurse's shoes on her short, wide feet. Calf muscles built for endless standing. Timeless waiting. She looks like she owns the place.

"I just made some fresh coffee." She holds the mug out to me. "Would you like a cup?"

"Coffee? Oh, yeah. I'll take some before I go. Please."

She pours me the coffee in the flower mug and then tops off her own cup. She looks me up and down, and I realize that I probably don't look like much this morning, wearing the same old beaten clothes from yesterday, as I am. At least I showered

"Are you visiting with us because of the hurricane?"

"Hurricane?"

The woman smiles at me with her nice smile, and says, "Yes, there were several families coming up from the coast to stay with us, evacuating before the hurricane got there."

I give away a dubious look out the front door. It's just as sunny a morning as it can be out there, except for the wind. The wind is blowing hard now.

The woman notices and laughs. "Yes, looks like Hurricane Jenny turned into tropical storm Jenny. And now they're saying it's not even going to make landfall. Until everyone cancelled last night, I was worried sick. I was afraid it'd be the Big One all over again."

"You had evacuees from hurricane Katrina all the way up here?"

"Oh yes, the whole town did. For weeks and weeks. Those poor people, they had nowhere else to go."

"Well, that must've been good for business."

"Oh no, it wasn't like that. We didn't even charge them after a couple of days. No one did. It was just a miracle, a real miracle. The whole town came together and we fed and housed those people and it was like one big family here. It was wonderful. We had one elderly gentleman who stayed for months because his whole house got destroyed and he had no family left. He was just completely destitute and God told me to take him in, and I did."

I don't quite know what to say to this so I don't say anything. I try to imagine the harmony of the scene, but I can't. And all I'd ever heard about hurricane

Katrina evacuees were bad things—like how all the homeless from New Orleans had descended on Houston and Dallas and over-run the place like vermin, stealing everything in sight. That's the kind of thing I heard. But not here. Here, it was a miracle. Here, God had spoken to this lady directly, and He told her to take these people in and she did, she did.

And who will tell me what to do, where to go, how to survive?

Certainly not Him. For me, just the voices, just the things that never were.

"Well, anyway," the owner-woman says, "I thought you might have evacuated. I saw on the weather channel that the storm is still coming, and I thought you might be wondering whether or not to go back home."

"Oh, well, my home, no... anyway, it's okay. I was just staying the one night."

"Okay, that's fine. I hope you had a nice stay?"

"A nice stay? Well, I don't know. Didn't sleep much. By the way, last night. Did you... no, never mind; it was fine. I was just about to leave." She smiles vacantly while I fish the room key out of my pocket, stare at it a while, and then hand it to over.

She rings me up quickly. "A hundred and twenty-one dollars and sixty-three cents," the lady says, handing me the room bill.

"A hundred and twenty bucks?"

"Yes," she says happily, "I gave you our special discounted rate."

"Oh, really? Thanks." I get out the money, trying to do it smoothly, like Robert had done, but drop the wad of bills on the floor where it explodes all over the place, like confetti. The nice lady quickly finds something to busy herself with and pretends not to notice me fumbling around down on the floor. Finally, I gather the money in a crumpled heap on the desk and pay out the twenties one by one. It's nearly everything I have.

"Thanks again," I say, stuffing what's left in my pockets and hurrying for the exit.

"Thank you! Have a safe trip," the hotel-lady calls after me, "and watch out for —"

I shut the door behind me quickly, feeling like an ass, not waiting to find out what I'm supposed to watch out for.

I climb in my car, turn it on, and put it in reverse. But now I just sit here with my foot on the clutch and the brake. The engine idles. Gloria is nowhere to be seen, and I know they've left already. For Tyler.

You should. She'd said it.

Dad fights his way into my brain. Go, go, he jeers. Yeah, go. She's really interested in you, John. Filthy rich older women always go for run-away teenagers. Just flash your cash at her, and she's all yours. Do it. Just see what happens.

He's right. She's not interested in me.

But Robert's an asshole.

He is an asshole, laughs Dad. You're right about that. A stinking rich asshole.

I shake my head clear, violently, spastically. Pulling out, I drive slowly, not knowing where I'm going; brick streets rumble underneath, a rhythmic jarring. I think of Gloria and how she'd talked about these streets. Like the cobblestones of Europe, she'd told me. I can't even remember what country she'd visited. Germany? France? Switzerland? All of them.

Time. Still need some more time.

In my pocket, the Caddo Mounds pamphlet. It's not far at all.

A big dome of grass rises up from the clearing. I can just make out a little knoll on its top, like a banded green crown. The clearing is maybe ten, twenty acres, and it's surrounded by thick growths of pine trees, oaks, some other kinds I don't know. The interpretive center in front is a low, brown, rectangular cinderblock building, barely noticeable in the open landscape.

I don't even remember it being here the last time.

My eleventh birthday, was it? Yes, it was. Just before our family broke up for good.

Dad just left me with Gloria in Jefferson, and she drove me out here by herself.

I get out to go to the center, but I look again at the mound. One small tree grows about halfway up, like it's standing guard; probably got roots into the tomb. Cotton candy clouds with dark centers scud above in the blue nothingness, and a dank cool wind disturbs my hair. It is peaceful here, relaxing. A good place to think.

It's just after the nine o' clock opening time, but no one seems to be here. I try both doors and one rattles open to admit me, yawning and scratching into the warm, stale air of the center and wondering if someone forgot to lock the place. Someone is here. Behind the front desk, a plump old white lady peers at me over half-glasses as she turns on a computer. Her mouth, like a dry withered lemon, puckers at me sourly.

This one's no Caddo Indian.

Though, if she were, I guess they wouldn't have her sitting here in a deerskin skirt.

She catches me ogling her, looks over her glasses again suspiciously, saying nothing, and watches me like an old buzzard. I must look like the perv I'm feeling like right now.

"Uh, hi..." I say, trying to compose a nicer look. She purses her lemon lips to speak but does not. "...Uh, so, is there an entry fee, or something?"

"Two dollars."

"It isn't free?"

"No," she responds, with a false little smile. "It's just two dollars."

Reluctantly, I hand the two bills over, and she tucks then into a metal box in her desk, although she's got a cash register. She gets back to her work without a further word and I hurry through the small museum. Painted images of the Caddoan city everywhere. Beehive huts cluster around the central mound, small plots of corn grow around them, naked brown children play on packed dirt, and topless women in skin skirts till the red East Texas earth with stone hoes, hafted in pinewood. Atop the mound, a larger beehive hut looms over the village. A shaman stands outside the structure, his back to a small dark door and arms spread wide to the face of the yellow sun, entreating some inscrutable god for rain, mercy, perhaps the death of his enemies. I look out the window at the solitary mound and back at the painting.

Guess it didn't work.

Passing out and into that open field is like reliving a memory, like Gloria herself should be here now, walking with me. She'd brought a picnic: cold chicken salad, homemade white bread, cookies, cokes, all spread out on a green cloth at the base of the grassy mound. After lunch, Gloria had lain down and sunned herself while I stole around the side of the mound and climbed up to the top where I sat on the crown, cross-legged, like an Indian, and looked down at her laying there elegantly, her hands clasped in her lap.

I think that's when I'd fallen in love with her.

I lie down where she had lain, and look up. Clouds of blue and gray and white feathering out above me. The frantic passing of small birds, pushed by the winds at high speed. A piercing hawk keen. My eyes search the edge of the forest, but the raptor is nowhere to be seen. My stomach rumbles, and I know it's from hunger, but it has no urgency. I close my eyes and pass into a daydream, or something else, on the edge of my awareness.

I am a child and she sits across from me with the lunch spread out between us.

"What do you want to be when you grow up?" Gloria says, studying me amusedly.

I look down at the green picnic blanket, averting my eyes from hers. "I don't know."

"You don't know?"

I look at her again. She looks back kindly now, waiting for me to say something.

"I guess, maybe... a tennis player."

"A tennis player? Good. I like tennis... I heard you've got a lot of talent, John."

A shrug from me.

"Chip doesn't like that idea so much though does he?"

I shake my head, looking away.

"Well, don't listen to him," she protests brightly. "You can be anything you want to be."

I look up at her in surprise but she's got laughter in her eyes. None of them takes me seriously, not even her. "He just thinks I'm dumb."

She nods, the smile fades a little. "You don't speak much. It's sometimes hard to see, but alot goes on in this head, I'll bet." She raps me playfully on the skull with a knuckle. "So, you don't want to go into your father's business?"

I shake my head quickly. No, not that.

A different sort of thought comes to her. She is still smiling, but I see sadness in her lovely green eyes. "But you're just eleven years old. You have time to decide."

I shake my head again. No. You can't understand. "He doesn't even care."

"And your... Diane? What does she think?"

"I don't know. She wouldn't tell him anything anyway."

We sit there for a minute, sandwiches in our hands, uneaten.

"It'll get better, John," she says at last, "you'll see."

I look at my own sandwich and take a bite, but I can't chew it.

Maybe. And maybe it won't ever get better.


I open my eyes. Inky clouds roll through gray twilight; they tumble over one another in gray waves, chewing up the sky in their advance. I am lying in the grass, my back to some embankment.

The mound. My headache still roars, but I must've slept—the whole afternoon's gone.

An electric pulse illuminates jet black clouds in the distance and I'm left with the nightmare image of something alien swimming in the blackness, like monstrous incandescent things, freakishly glowing. Now fingers of lightening begin to stab down, reaching for the ground. In the throbbing light, strangely silhouetted trees stand out from the ragged edge of the forest, like a child's Halloween cutouts.

Dancing up from the grassy field are small yellow points of light, beautiful and ethereal and oblivious to the coming chaos, perhaps excited by it. They are everywhere, hundreds of them, thousands. Pixies or fairies, bobbing, weaving in and out, appearing and disappearing in the sky, in the grass; they are fireflies. I lay back again mesmerized by them and watching them in wonder, even as the approaching storm sucks the turbid air into the coolness of its black vacuum. And suddenly all the lights simply cease to exist.

A thunderous crack sounds. I'm reeling. The sound of boulders breaking, of whole mountains ripped asunder. I am jolted to my feet, looking around wildly. The mound looms black and ominous behind me. I turn away to face the storm wind. An unnaturally large rain drop the size of my thumb stings my face. Now a whole wall of the rain drops advance on me, a hail of seeker arrows. Thunder claps again, and something else comes: the smell of cooking sulfur. Unimaginable voltage sizzles the air. The heat of the sun. I drop to a squat, hugging my knees, breath's gone. Panic, don't panic; I am panicking. A gob of hail the size of a tennis ball thuds down, like a meteor from space. Nowhere to hide. It rolls to my feet just as the rainwall hits me. I am soaked in a millisecond, and the hail balls begin to thud around me like mortars. Spring up, sprint away. This is death, death all around me. Running, witless running, I know not where. Pitch dark forest looms before me, a black mass of trees. A giant hail ball grazes my shoulder, just missing my head. More, thousands more, thumping down behind me, coming this way. Dead, out here.

Plunging in, plunging forward, stumbling into the void of the woods. Bursts of lightening illuminate a surreal scene: dead cities shocked out of the dark, all tumbledown and broken, there just for an instant. Gone another. Another flashing burst. Now a tangle of fallen pines is before me: ripped out, roots reaching skyward. Forward, I stumble, forward I lurch, hands outstretched, grasping blindly. Another burst of light. A hole appears, an opening in the roots of the tangle. Salvation. Crawling now, I clamber into a pit of darkness, groping muddy roots, pushing myself forward frantically on all fours. A wounded animal sliding down, down.

In this womb-like blackness, water streams down my back, into my pants, over my mud-caked shoes. I am soaked and shivering and cold and dumb with disbelief.

The roar of pelting rain. Close my eyes. Focus my will. On the storm. Pass, pass, I command it: pass on. But it does not. The onslaught of water, of hailstones, of wind. It finds its way into my refuge. I think of the possible forms of death: by lightning strike, by snake bite, by exposure, more trees might fall, trapping me in this hole; the tons of mud and dirt in these roots could collapse, burying me alive.

I whisper uncomfortable prayers, begging the Almighty for deliverance. It doesn't work. Now come the promises, many promises to Him I can't keep. There is no response, and the storm like chaos rages on unabated. A cold sludge streams down my face, into my mouth, all around me. Surely there is no hell worse than this. A prayer of apology spills out of me, like a chant, but it is filled with a choking grit and the wretchedness of the un-repentant, and it doesn't work. Nothing works. Now the pictures come: of the shaman, of the long abandoned mound and the long-dead people; all flashes through my mind in a quick, quick pulse.

Nothing has ever worked. He does not care. He never has.

I close my eyes again, gripped by the feeling that this is the end of it all, that nothing is out there, that nothing has ever cared, and nothing has ever mattered in the end. But then a new chant rises, simple and close and believable. It's okay, I tell myself; it'll be okay. Just listen, just wait. As all things pass, this too must pass.

I close my eyes and shut them tight, saying the words over and over and over.

And it does work.


Somehow, I have slept, but I do not feel better. How long? Fifteen minutes? An hour? Complete darkness shrouds me. No sound but the sound of the wind rushing heavily through the pines, like the crashing of a storm surf, expending itself angrily. Slowly, I realize that the downpour has lightened. There are no more hailstones. Irregular spatters of rain find their way in; a drop, drop of water on my neck begins to calm me. I remember my car; it's not far away.

Pushing through inky blackness, I grope for a way out by feel alone, reaching for the lightness of the air, and I find it; breezes touch my skin, the feel of empty free space before me. Like a fetus emergent, I lift my head up towards the opening to cry aloud.

The sound of an animal movement freezes me.

Something large, trundling outside my refuge. Carefully, I back down, back into the tangle. Could there still be bears in this forest? Wolves? Mountain lions? But, no, not those, and they've been hunted out for years and years.

Drawing my knees up to my chest, I will myself into inconspicuousness. The thing moves and squelches in the mud, mumbling to itself in a deeply troubled and indistinct voice, as if searching for something.

Is it looking for me? Am I in its lair?

The thing pauses, seemingly right outside the opening, and then it goes absolutely quiet. If anything, the dark in this trap is now darker, as if the opening is obscured by something immense and dangerous, something looking in. Still I hear nothing, nothing at all, and madness creeps in, starts to take over. Each second is an eternity. Sweat beads on my skin, despite the cold and wet. There is nothing now, nothing except this presence and this sensation, the very same sensation. I've felt it before.

But this time, as I sit and listen, forehead bent to my knees, focusing on the passing of each second, I begin to feel that I will not be harmed. And yet, I dare not come out. Cannot. But, somehow, I am moved to speak.

"Is it you?" My voice cracks on the question in barely a whisper. Louder now. "Is it you? Have you come for me? Did you help me?"

Questions asked of no one, met with silence. This is it: I have gone crazy. There is nothing out there. I am speaking into thin air. But then, like a miracle, a resonance like words tumbles down to me in the gloom.

Is it me? the voice asks in its rumbling sigh, Is it me? What, who, no. There is no me anymore. But I know you. Yes, I have helped. Don't know why? Am, is, was, you. You are.

I look up. "I am what?"

Silence.

"I am what?" louder now.

I raise my head up higher now, my whole body. I'm out and into the fresh, resinous air. A glimmer of gray in the tree tops. Complete darkness before me.

"I am what?" I'm shouting now, shouting and stepping forward recklessly. "I am what?" I scream it, "Tell me what I am. Tell me."

I trip and I am down, sprawling; my face is in the water, mud is in my mouth, my nose; a soaking, miserable wetness courses through my whole body.

There is nothing out here. Nothing at all, and I am alone, and I will always be alone.

I raise my head, sobbing now, choking, crying out, "come back. Why don't you let me see you? Come back. Come with me."

But there is no one here, and my voice is lost in the restless sweeping of the pines.

A voice heard by no one, lost even to me.

# Tennis Bum

**M**oscow, five miles. Highway 59 South. The two road signs flash by, and a little gravel drive appears. It looks good, and I pull all the way up to where the drive terminates in a thicket of scrub growth. Looking both ways first, I slip out and pull my clothes on quickly, remembering how I came all the way through Lufkin in my birthday suit, slouching down at the stoplights, speeding through without looking at anyone, just wanting to get far, far away from there. All because the old museum worker lady had shown up early, just as I was wringing out my soaked clothes in the parking lot. The look on her face as I'd stood there naked, covering myself with my hands. Pretty excited. I'd barely had time to grab my keys, before she'd whipped out a pistol and started waving it around insanely. I do believe she would've shot me.

A darkly comic thought in my mind: behold now the ruthless killer, the wanted fugitive of the law, speeding away in his German sports car. "And nearly taken out by a fat museum worker in her sixties." What a screw-up I am. Not even a good criminal.

But my mind's been made up at least. Not going back now.

Moscow, population 170, emerges from monotonous rows of farmed trees on both sides of the road. I'm starving. About ninety miles left to Houston and forty more or so down to Galveston after that. Need to stop and eat somewhere. There's a convenience store here, and an abandoned drive-in, too. Not much else. I'm disappointed. I don't know what I was expecting, but with a name like

Moscow, well, an onion-dome church or something, maybe a mini red-square with a putt-putt course in it? Something crazy silly at least.

Something large catches my eye. I veer off the road towards it and stop the car, pulling right up to a green metal fencewall. I am staring at a giant T-Rex. He looks over the wall at me; his mouth is open, and his teeth are bared, but somehow he's happy looking, sorta like a playful dog. The horns of a Triceratops, just visible above the fence line, seem to be poised at the Tyrannosaur's belly. I see the triangular fins of a Stegosaurus sticking up nearby as well. The things look like they're made from concrete or fiberglass; they're enormous, cartoonish. Reading the sign for Dinosaur Gardens on the fence makes me smile with pure childish delight.

Life-sized dinosaurs. Right here in Moscow. Now here's a monster I can deal with.

I get out, get one of my cans of meat, and eat it right there, lying on the hood of my car and looking up at the T-Rex grinning down on me goofily. He's totally unaware of the malcontent herbivore sneaking up on him, using the fence for cover. Stegosaur looks like he might want to join the fray.

"Not too bright there, are you big fella? Better watch it, or you'll catch one in the gut."

My meal long gone, I sit there a long while and debate with myself about going in, but I really should get going. Caked in drying mud, only got ten soggy bucks in my pocket and there's a foul smell coming off of me that'd scare even T-Rex away. With a long look over my shoulder at the smiling dinosaur, I head on down south.

Nearing the outskirts of Houston, and I'm thinking too much about what I'm doing. My mood sours darkly again. Don't know what I'm doing. Got hardly any plan, no money and still just running away. I look off into the velvet green on either side of the road, trying to remember what I know about Galveston. Dad had a beach house there once, but it was so long ago, I can barely remember what it looked like. Think I only went there a couple of times, and I'm not even sure there is a tennis club on the place. Must be though. Has to be.

And something else drawing me there.

Hah! My father says, gloating. Your kicked ass is drawing you down there. You're going to Galveston 'cause it's the end of the road, John; the last place to run to. Oh wait, sorry, he says. It's the end of the road, *John Fears*. Either way, you'll be hightailing it out of there in five days, tops. The quiet quitter, quits again. Quite so! Like always. Only, this time, you won't be running, you'll be swimming.

He seems to think this is funny. I don't.

On my left, the first strip mall appears. Miles yet to Houston.

"Let the sprawl begin," I fling at a passing four-thousand square foot McMansion squatting, not a hundred yards from the road. Another pops up behind a fried chicken joint. And all of sudden I'm surrounded by an exurbia like no other. Seedy looking gas stations and adult bookstores mingle with insurance agencies, real-estate agencies, aluminum drive-through liquor stores, and car dealers by the dozen. A church like an afterthought with a cross of plastic. Shrines of shame and shrines of sin and shrines of consumption. The laissez faire flotsam of the human tide.

I feel myself tensing.

"Welcome to lovely Houston."

Yeah, he interjects, yeah, keep on driving. Just drive right on through Houston. Wouldn't want to stop there. It's only the largest city on the gulf seaboard. The one place around that'd actually be a good place to hide.

"No. Shut up. I'm not stopping here." I want to see the waters of the Gulf of Mexico. Shallow and brown though they be. At least it's the ocean, and I'm not up for all this.

I45 comes up. The VW engine is running smoothly, and I gun it up the on-ramp and onto the Interstate, nervous about being in this tiny car amongst the hurtling morass of trucks, SUVs, fancy foreigns, and old beaters, all flying by at high speeds. It's a life or death experience every second. Never driven in traffic like this. A place as crazy as this. I look up at a grimed, dark sky; it is unrelenting, unhelpful. Not gonna get into the speed-racer stuff this time. Both hands death-gripped to the steering wheel, I motor right on through, sticking to the middle lane, feeling the shudder of enormous machines blowing by me.

The I45 bay bridge looms ahead of me, rising from an endless field of marsh grass; the Texas City refinery lies off to my left. Interesting contrasts here. Not a city, but a strange and gigantic apparatus built of twisting pipe, enormous tanks, smokestacks of steel. Blinking rows of lights by the thousand and shiny tubes spouting naked flame, floating on a wasteland. It could be the ruin of a gigantic alien artifact just sitting there in its enigmatic magnificence. I slow to look, but the rest of the traffic speeds on by, and no-one else seems to notice it.

What did it look like in the 1520's when Cabeza de Vaca passed through here, escaping from Indian captivity on Galveston; the first of the European conquerors who lived? Take away the refinery, and the bridge, and the spindly dock cranes now poking up across the bay like a scene from a tiny play set, and it's probably pretty close to the same landscape, even now. There had been huge oyster reefs then, so thick you could walk across them, if you had tough enough feet. He wrote, too, of snakes. So many snakes, that to walk across the island, he had to beat the path in front of him with a thick oak club to ward them off. There were billions and trillions of mosquitoes, too. De Vaca described them vividly; how he groveled naked on the beach with his giant, tattooed Karankawa masters, his body smeared with grease, the firesmoke burning his eyes, his skin an agony of thousands of burning welts. Eight years. Eight lonely, scared years, wondering if he was going to live to see another sunrise. Not only did he live, he prospered; he rose from Karankawa slave to some sort of traveling shaman, moving among Indian tribes, almost like a god.

Or so he said.

Before I know it, I'm across the bridge and into Galveston. Curious looking historical places stand-out, like gingerbread houses, like confections made of wood with windows that used to open out to the sea and to the bay.

The homes of the victorious. Spoils of the American conquest.

Not stopping at any of them, not at the strand either, though it looks inviting. It's newly sophisticated these days, better than I remember. The shops look cleaned up, they're restored and full of new merchandise. It's all tourist stuff though. A sham of t-shirts and trinkets and seashells from places other than this.

Past the seawall, too. The seawall's for tourists and for tourist traps, for crowds and for drunken beach parties. Not for me. I drive on by, following my whim to go bathe in the ocean itself, to cleanse myself finally of this itching East Texas earth that has glommed onto me like a red cement. Finally, the beach houses start to falter and the island dwindles to a half-mile wide strip of scrubby oaks and waving green grass.

Much better. This is more like it. Now I smell the ocean, the sand, the cool brine wind. But there's been no sign of a tennis club. Nothing looks familiar. Through the dune line, a relatively secluded beach clips in and out of view between low mounds of sand. A sign for a public area comes up. I slow to a crawl and pull in.

This will do.

There are some beach houses near here, but this place is some kind of protected beach habitat, and it's un-crowded today, on the heels of the storm. Waves are up, way more than I ever remember seeing, and the surfers are out cutting them up, dreaming of days like this every day, no doubt. Some guys fly enormous, colorful kites, and beach-combers walk the shoreline with dogs. A monster truck whines by on balloon tires, music blaring, and in the distance: oil platforms float on the gray arc of the horizon, like tiny insects, reminders of where I am, what Texas is. It's a peaceful enough place, though. The parking lot is more than half-empty.

I pull the Porsche up to the edge of the parking lot, eyeing the sand, still hearing the truck out there. Other cars have obviously been through here to get out to the beach too. I feel guilty for even thinking of driving there, but it's a powerful compulsion just to pull all the way up to the water's edge and sit there, listening to the sound of the waves. So much like the sound of those pines. The trees in the storm.

A sign states: Motorized vehicles strictly forbidden.

But there's no grass between those two dunes here and that rule is surely for the idiots on ATVs. I don't guess it'll hurt anything so I edge the car off the pavement and onto the soft sand.

Keep it moving. Don't let it sink.

From nowhere a kid runs directly across my path, and I slam on the brakes, sliding to a halt. The car settles down, sinking quickly into the softest part of the beach. The kid's gone. Anger wells up in me hotly. This is bad. Very, very bad.

I get out for a look, leaving the car idling. The wheels are already half-way buried in the sand. Looking back, I see I've gone ten, fifteen yards off the pavement. There's no packed sand for at least twenty more yards in front of me.

John, you idiot, you're screwed.

There's nothing to do but try to back it up to the pavement. I get in and put it in reverse. Feather the clutch and easy on the accelerator. The car tires spin— and dig. The smell of burning rubber on burning sand. More gas. The wheels burrow furiously, buzz sawing through the sand. I'm going nowhere but down.

I cannot believe this. Wild anger takes over me and I gun it, digging the wheels even deeper, revving it to the limit. No good, no good. Stop it, you fool, stop it. I do.

Pulling on the handle and pushing hard, all I can do is crack open the door. The weight of the entire beach presses against it. Sand bleeds into the floorboard and fans out in neat piles. The door won't shut again, either. I yank it and push it, and yank it again, until there's nothing for it but to climb out through the roof.

Squatting by the car, I see what I already knew. Like it's been cut off at the knees. Sand all the way past the wheel wells. I climb back in and just sit in the driver's seat.

Try to think.

But I have the submarine sensation of riding under the sand. Or of being buried alive. My racket rests on the passenger floorboard. I pick it up to straighten the strings. Seagulls wheel and dive excitedly as if challenging the low, roiling clouds. The tide's advance makes it feel as if the whole horizon is closing in on me. Nobody's near me and the beach seems suddenly devoid of activity. This sinking feeling threatens to overwhelm me.

"Loser, don't just sit here."

Jumping out of the car a second time, I stare out to sea. I inhale deeply. Smell the tangy salt odor of the Texas Gulf Coast, the warm humidity of seawater and Mississippi River water, of rotting fish and of seeping oil. It's rich and organic and not at all unpleasant. The sound of the gulf and the cooler wind begin to calm me, though I don't know why.

I have to call her to come get me. But him. No, I can't call her.

Not gonna let that asshole lord a job over me.

From the depths of my thought, Dad gleefully forces his way forward again. Funny how the man was never happy when alive. Now he can't stop laughing, and I can't shut him up. You're a homeless and penniless murderer, John, he's mocking. You don't have a job. You've screwed up your car again. In record time. This is some escape you're pulling off here, Killer. I'll tell you what, go ahead and look Gloria up; yeah, call her right up. You think a bored, rich, married woman like her cares about you? You've seen her, what? Five times tops? And now you want her to just fly down and pick you up and take you home for some cuddling and some snuggling? That's a doozy, John, a real doozy, even for you.

Can't do that. No, he's right; I'm on my own here.

I feel like swimming out to the oil platforms in the distance, on out to where the container ships crawl in almost imperceptible movement. Like I should just keep going south.

You could almost wade out there.

I think of the sailors on the vessels and the oil workers on the rigs living their whole working lives on some vast machine on the heaving sea. Living out there, that'd be different.

So it would. Maybe they have offices at the port.

Yeah, right, John, you got a lotta experience working oil rigs. That'd go over well. You'd be lucky if the roughnecks don't kick your ass and throw you off the dock over at the port.

But there's gotta be some sort of job for me around here. Somewhere.

I look at the racket in my hand.

That was the plan, Mr. John Fears. That was your story. You have to make it work, and there's no reason it shouldn't. I have taught tennis before. Yeah, well, more like babysitting on a tennis court. But if I can just pick up a few hours at a club, I can make it. They probably won't even make me sign a contract, much less do a background check.

The story will work. It has to.

Opening the trunk, I look at my other two rackets. Miraculous that they're still there, after all this car's been through. I hesitate, wanting to take them all, but feeling like I'll look stupid carrying tennis rackets around. But how else am I going to look like a pro? I don't even have any shorts, and even a teaching pro should carry his sticks. The bag with the gun, all that ammo. Can't leave that either. Can't take it into a tennis club though.

I'm startled by the sudden presence of a man.

Spin around, quick. The racket's in my hand; my arm's cocked.

Crap. This guy, will you look at this guy.

He is tall—a good three inches above my six foot one—and muscular. Ripped, in fact; a beast of a dude. He stands with the sun behind him so that I can hardly see him, but he's dusky and tanned an even darker shade of brown. His shirtless chest and arms are stained by the ink of barbaric tattoos: a flaming Spanish cross covers his chest, a wreath of thorns encircles the left bicep. Some tribal designs ring the right. Ceramic plugs gleam from both ears, and silver stakes pierce his nipples.

Jesus Christ Almighty.

"Hi!" I say, voice cracking. Stupid, what did you say that for?

"You gonna hit me with that?" A rolling voice, deep and measured.

"No!" I throw the racket back in the trunk and slam the lid. "I just–"

"–You're stuck," the man cuts me off.

He steps closer, much too close, until he uncomfortably invades my personal space. I back up until my legs make contact with the car. No way can I get to my gun in time. I feel like he could dismember me and stuff me in the trunk and throw me, car and all, out in the Gulf. And there's not a damn thing I could do about it.

"Yeah, I guess so," I say. "I was just about to dig it out." Liar.

"I got a Jeep," he says.

I nod over at his Jeep. Even I can tell that it's been heavily modified. It looks capable enough to tow a house. "You really think you can pull me out with that rig?"

He looks down at me for several hard seconds and, for the first time, I see the color of his eyes. I've never seen anything like them; they're an unfathomable dark slate blue, and I get the unsettling sensation of staring up into the eyes of some feral, predatory creature.

Is he going to help me or beat the crap out of me? I'm still not really sure.

"Sure," he finally says.

With a quickness belying his size, the guy turns and lopes back to his SUV, and I'm struck by the impression that he did all the work on it himself. He pulls out an impossibly long, thick steel-link chain and heaves it to his shoulder.

I couldn't even lift that thing.

He hooks his chain around the re-enforced bumper of the Jeep and is already digging down to the Porsche's frame before I realize that I'm just standing around. Jumping down to help him, we dig with our hands. Finally, he reaches in and attaches the chain.

"Put her in neutral," he says, as I clamber back in the driver's seat. I do as I'm told.

"Ready," I call back to him.

Back at the Jeep, he engages the four-wheel drive and backs up. The chain snakes through the sand and snaps taught, throwing off a shower of grit. The SUV skitters for purchase a moment, grabs, jerks, and then pulls hard. I hear sand bleeding from every cavity as my car is inexorably and unceremoniously wrenched from the beach and back onto the pavement. Rubber tires firmly back on pavement, I leap out, fists raised in triumph.

"Yes! Thanks, man. Thanks a lot."

He's come back to meet me, having smoothly collected his chain as he walked. Muscles bulge effortlessly under the weight of the steel coils. We shake hands.

"No prob. Sixty-nine 914—cool car," he nods again in the Porsche's direction.

"Yeah, well, thanks. Not as useful as a Jeep though, I guess."

He smiles something like a brief smile—the first emotion of any kind he's shown. Nope, it sure isn't, he seems to agree. But he's done with me now. He nods a farewell and turns back to his Jeep.

Off to find some more idiot tourists to pull out of the sand, I suppose.

A new thought comes to my head. "Hey! I forgot. Is there a tennis club around here?"

He turns back and takes his time answering. "Yeah. Back on the main road," he indicates the direction with a small hike of his free thumb, "towards town. Turn left on Buccaneer. Can't miss it."

This guy is efficient with his words. "Really?" I ask, pushing my luck with him. "I was thinking of seeing if they need a tennis-pro."

He hesitates. "Maybe. Last one just left."

"Really? Why?"

He just shrugs one little shrug.

"Okay, thanks. Thanks again, man. I'll go check it out." Then I look him up and down again and, couldn't be, but still... "You're not, you know, by any chance, a Kara..." The word chokes in my throat as his tattoos seems to smolder and writhe in the bright sunlight. No, couldn't be. The last one died over a hundred years ago, killed in a final battle against Lafitte's pirates. Still and stolid as a bronze sculpture, he just stands, watching me, as if I haven't just spoken. Hopefully I haven't. "Anyway," I mumble, "never mind. See you. Thanks."

He nods in response, barely moving his head. Or not. I hurry away.

The old Galveston Country Club is tucked inconspicuously beneath imported palms trees, and ancient black live-oaks that are permanently bowed from the wind, like old mendicants. I sit in the car and check it out for a while, screwing up my nerve to go in. Like most private clubs, it looks to be an exclusive sort of place, but it's not as pretentious as I'd expected, and I kind of like it. A white, faux Spanish stucco affair. Has to have been there for years. Weather-beaten but proud. Like the island itself.

Like me, too, I guess. Too proud to go in there. Looking like this. Feeling like this.

How is there anything left of this island anyway? How is it that such an insignificant purchase of land as Galveston weathered all those hurricanes, all that wind and blinding, sheeting rain? All that sun? It's nothing more than a sandbar, furred with a few trees, tangles of undergrowth and grass. Just a few feet of sand, it's barely even here at all. I wonder if any one grain of sand on this living island is the same as when Cabeza de Vaca's bare foot made its first watery imprint, or even when Jean Lafitte ruled as a pirate lord—or has it all been replaced, churned up again and again from the depths of the Gulf in everlasting renewal?

It's not pride. It's fear. You're stalling. It's Dad. I can almost feel his prodding finger.

"No, I'm not."

Walking by the well-manicured golf course with all three rackets in my hand, trying to adopt the swagger of a world-class player and not doing a very good job, I see the tennis courts. They're a bit of a lonely afterthought over there by themselves, barely rising above a field of grass on the other side of the club drive. Golf seems to be the thing to play here.

Coming up to the building, I take in the arcade of stuccoed arches shading the front side, and stop at the glass door, cautiously looking in.

Well. C'mon.

Golfers have wives like Gloria, who'd rather be playing tennis. Like Mom, too.

And, for the first time in a long while, I think of her, and a creeping guilt rises. Wives like Mom. I've barely even thought of her, and here I've been gone for days now. Should I call her? Did she even cry when she got the news about Dad? Did she go to the funeral? Did she try to call me and talk to me? Probably. But not too hard. I bet she was mostly just relieved.

Finally shed of us both.

She'll still be going out to her club in Ohio, I guess. I went up to visit her once and the strangeness of it; I just couldn't handle it. Her world up there was one she'd improved upon, proudly made better. We didn't have much to say to one another, and she was clearly happier without me. Her new husband, James, he was nice enough. Even offered to take me in, if that's what I wanted. I didn't. She'd quit the job she'd spent so much time doing when she was around me and fallen into a daily routine of nothingness: tennis lessons, shopping, social clubs of all description. But she still had the new kid, James Jr., in daycare full-time, just like she did with me. Because that's how she and her friends handle parenting. She went from having every professional ambition in the world to none at all—all it took was a baby she really wanted.

But it was ambition, too, wasn't it? A kind of competitive ambition to better those women she called friends. A game of who had the most: the prettiest clothes, the best servants, the most accomplished husband, the most vibrant socialite life. The cutest kid. The thought starts to make me sick. It's demented. Those aren't friends she has. They are her opponents in some depraved game of leisure. That's what it was all about. And I'd been there, all along, just waiting for her to pay attention, but never more than a quiet afterthought in her busy life.

Yeah, wives like Mom, oh yeah, that's great.

I stand there at the threshold of the club and think of just going back to my car and driving away again. The valets are standing there patiently, uniforms dark and crisp, even in this heat, casting sideways glances at me.

But these people pay, don't they? They do pay, a lot. And I've got less than ten bucks, three rackets, and an old car to my false name. Poor little rich boy, and look what I've done with it. I smooth my reeking, mud-scabbed clothes. Damn it. Forgot to wash off in the Gulf.

Well, here goes nothing.

A pro-shop attached to the main clubhouse looks like a good place to start. Inside's a sweeping view through big glass windows to the number one tee box. A couple of old hackers at the bar prepare to tee off by fortifying themselves with a cold cocktail. There's a big golf shop here and a dark hall leading back to a sunken restaurant in the main clubhouse.

Despite the Southwestern exterior of the whole place, the interior's all done up with the trappings of the wannabe European establishment: plush carpets worked with ornate medieval designs; a row of Roman columns demarcates the hallway; black iron sconces from a Parisian street scene dot the walls—but they're electric and throwing off a garish yellow glow.

I smile.

Well, only child of rich parents, you know this place don't you? It's almost like coming home. A girl talking on a telephone peeps up from behind a raised wooden desk.

Why, hello there.

She's got clear cinnamon skin and warm brown eyes. She wears a green V-necked, slim-fitting shirt. I try not to look down it when she leans over to replace the handset.

"I heard ya'll are looking for a tennis pro?" I say to her, nervously, my tennis pro persona evaporating instantly. She looks me over for a tense moment. I can see her taking in my get-up. A skeptic look. If I were her, I'd think of calling security, too. But instead of turning and running back out the door, like I feel like doing, I surprise myself. I straighten up, stride a step closer, and extend my hand.

"My name's John Fears, former touring pro. I came right over," I say, making a hand gesture towards my clothes, as if to say, just as is, "when I was told of your opening."

"I think so," she says, relaxing just a bit, "but Zingleman's the guy you need to speak to."

Zingleman, really? I try not to laugh.

She notices my snicker and smiles a little, encouragingly. She thinks it's a funny name too. "Here," she says, "He's a real nice guy. We'll just use my phone and give him a call." She leans over in front of me again to make the call to the man. The V-neck sags low.

"Yes, Mr. Zingleman," she's saying, "Yes, John Fears, that's what he said." She pauses a long moment, listening. "Yes, he's right here. Yes, I'll tell him to wait." She replaces the receiver, and I just manage to meet her eyes in time. "Mr. Zingleman will be right out."

Only now do I notice her name tag. Adela, it says. A pretty name. A pretty girl.

Zingleman is all smiles and fawning grins, the personal, touchy-feely type. He shows me back to his office, and it's only two minutes into the conversation, before I've tuned him out. I can't help it. His hair glistens and shines in waves of polished ebony, and I'm reminded of Victor. A sort of anti-Victor, rather. So bright, so perfect, that hair, it's a helmet carved of wax in frozen waves. I blink and blink, trying to focus. Zingleman doesn't seem to be saying anything important, anyway. I search my mind for the word to describe him, intent on just watching his lips move, nodding and smiling in agreement—trying to pay attention.

Obsequious. That's it.

Zingleman, why are you pandering to me, when I don't even know you?

He's saying something of relevance now.

"...it turns out I just happen to be looking for a tennis pro."

"Really?" I say, trying to act surprised.

"Yep, the last one just left. Didn't even give me two-week's notice."

"Man, that's too bad." That guy with the Jeep was right. My timing is perfect.

"Yes," Zingleman says, "I have to say, I had no idea what I was going to do, to be honest." He smiles widely at me. His hair sparkles and glows. "And then you just walked in the door." He snaps his fingers. "Presto, just like that! What good luck! Like it was meant to be!"

Well, Zingleman, if that's how you make decisions, I guess.

"Yeah, must be," I respond and attempt to return his false smile. Now he remembers something abruptly and starts fishing around in his desk.

"Ah, ha!" He hands me a one-page job application form. "Here you go. Just fill this out and we'll be ready." I examine the form. It's just a standard job application form like you'd use for the wait staff or the receptionist or something. My hands are shaking.

This is never going to work.

But I think of Adela back at the counter, plunging V-neck and all, and I grab the pen, and I fill out the form right there in front of him. Zingleman taps his fingers annoyingly on his desk. He seems to be humming under his breath—a song vaguely like the Texas A&M Aggie fight song. Yes, that would be the mega-university who bought our little Texarkana College. Gobbled us up and changed our name: *Texas A&M University, Texarkana.* Hey presto, instant University. We still just called it TC.

But the Aggies, well, the Aggies are nothing if not *loyal*.

I guess Zingleman would've gone to the main campus in College Station.

Zingleman hums fight songs. *Hullabaloo, Caneck, Caneck...*

In the education line, I fill in: BA Sociology, Texas A&M University.

No harm in leaving off the Texarkana part.

Sweating profusely now and feeling dirty, I write the name, John Fears.

There, I did it. Not much else to fill out here. No, a few things. For address I simply put "Galveston." In the experience lines, I write: "College Tennis, two years," and "Touring Pro." No names, no social security, no places, no telephone numbers, no nothing.

*Hullabaloo, Caneck, Caneck. Goodbye to Texas University...*

Something moves me to write in a job reference: "Gloria Baker," I scribble and include the phone number I'd looked up as being hers and memorized, but never called.

Finished, I hand the form back to him tentatively, the already spare document nearly empty. So empty, it's beyond embarrassing.

Can't do this; this is ridiculous.

I reach out to pull it back away from him. But Zingleman is already looking it over with a puzzled look on his face, and I retract my hand slowly.

Less than two seconds later, he looks up at me. I place my hands on the arms of my chair, ready to jump up and run, hoping he doesn't call security right now.

"Perfect!" he practically whoops, yanking up an enormous smile. "You're hired!"

A huge sigh, a hugely relieved feeling. I relax a little.

But, what the hell? He's really not going to ask me for more details—nothing at all?

"Ah... well, do you, you know...?"

"Whatcha' need, John?" He's glowing in my direction.

"Ah, nothing. That's great... When do I start?"

He turns his computer monitor towards me, and I catch my breath, afraid of what information he may have on me there. On his screen: the name John Fears and a few of his accomplishments googled up on the internet. There's also some kind of schedule app. "Adela set this plan up online," he exclaims, happily pointing it out, "very cool!"

"Yeah, very cool," I say tentatively.

"You start today by the way!" He runs a finger down the schedule. He finds a colored rectangle with a name on it, and looks up at me. "How about at two o'clock?"

"Ah, okay," I say looking down at my clothes and wondering what I'm going to do about them, "sure. Why not?"

"These lessons were already set-up by the last pro, so you can just take them over. Adela has the schedule, too. So just go check in with her and we can go from there."

"Okay."

"Okay, then. Oh, by the way, you get twenty dollars an hour for groups and privates; the club gets the rest."

"Works for me," I say, standing and shrugging, but I'm ecstatically happy about this and can barely keep from hugging the guy now. It's more than twice my Highway Department wage.

He stands, too, and shakes my hand once, firmly.

"Welcome to the Galveston Country Club!" he says, his smile widening even more, his hair pulsing light like a halo, the man glowing brighter than should be humanly possible.

Guy looks like a well-oiled robot. But I like him already. Or at least I have to try.

Back in reception area, I'm still a little stunned and just standing there not knowing exactly what to do with myself.

"How'd it go?" It's Adela. She must have seen me just standing there, for she's materialized in front of me. A lovely smile lights upon her lovely face.

"Huh?"

"How'd your job interview go?" She's asking me something with a quizzical look.

"You know, with Zingleman?"

She's close enough for me to smell her; it's an exotic smell, an aroma of spices.

"Oh... I got the job, I guess."

"You guess?"

"Yeah, well, I mean, yeah, I got the job. Somehow."

She smiles again, reaches out to shake hands, and I take hers in mine; it's soft and small and warm. "Well, welcome then," she says, "I guess that makes us co-workers."

"Yeah, I guess so." I grin back at her. "Thanks," I say, reluctantly letting her hand go. We stand there awkwardly a moment, not knowing what else to do, and I break the impasse. Something in me wants to flee the scene now. "Well, see you later," I mumble, turning quickly and pushing hard at the glass door without looking.

My face smacks into glass with a crack.

Crap, crap, crap.

A spider web fractures the glass of the locked door. One of my hands is on my painfully skinned cheek, another gropes for the other door. "Stupid door," I mumble, feeling her wince and listening to her barely suppressed giggle.

The sign clearly says: Please Use Other Door. I hustle through it and outside and smack myself on the forehead. "Idiot." I bang my head again. "What an idiot."

The valet stands there, looking at me strangely from across the walk, and I hurry back to my car where I open the trunk, and throw my rackets in, looking at my pilfered Highway Department bag. Nothing in there. Except a gun.

Great. Idiot. How could you've forgotten that?

A lesson in an hour, and I need some clothes.

Turning back to the club, I try hard to compose myself. The valets are still staring at me.

Forget about them. Don't even look at them.

Inside the pro shop, there are racks of expensive tennis clothes at terrible prices. Adela looks up at me with surprise, amusement.

"You know," I say to her, holding up a pair of shorts, "I've got this small problem..."

Back at the beach after giving my first lesson as a tennis pro, and there's no sign that a storm ever passed this way. I'm standing ankle deep in the now gentle surf, wearing new tennis clothes bought on a promise, and I see her smiling, brown face again; possibilities open up before me. The lesson had gone surprisingly well, too. Easy, in fact. It'd been some guy—a pretty good one—and we'd just worked out, hitting ball after ball after ball.

Well, it's a job I can do.

Now I find myself hoping to see the savage-looking guy again. Didn't even get his name. Barely even thanked him. But his Jeep is nowhere to be seen, and I retreat to a dune to sit and wait, and for the first time in what seems like years: just relax. No monsters. No Dad. A new life wearing the skin of a man I only met once.

And it seems to fit. Yes, this is what I came for. Here it is at last.

Now the late afternoon Texas sun shows her colors through a windblown veil of clouds, and it makes that special kind of magic light that washes the whole horizon in an orange glow. The kind of light that makes even a murky old Texas beach the prettiest place you've ever seen or ever will see, like the coming of the first evening of the world. A different place. A perfect place. Remote and beautiful and unreachable. I get up and just walk the saltwater soaked sand, letting the sea-foam lap my feet. Dreams flood back. Pro tennis, love, friends, it all seems possible again in this light. But then churned up in the brown curds of waves, a fleeting mirage appears: my father. His face is drawn and mean and pitiless. His lips don't move. His voice can't be heard. But he speaks.

You can hide, but not from me, he says. You can't ever hide from me.

# Reacquaintance

Sitting there alone on the beach after my long walk, I watch it grow dark. The few beachcombers still out are quiet and reverential, speaking as lovers might, in hushed tones. A fisherman casts into the surf, catching nothing. Stars, and ship lights, and the little Christmas tree lights of the oil derricks all wink into existence. Sometimes I can't tell them apart, even with my keen eyes. I'm thrilled a little to spot a satellite speeding over, a tiny pinprick of light, so far away. It's all a wonder. I feel again like I could stay here forever, in Galveston, in this place. I look down the beach and wish I owned one of the stilted houses down there rising behind the dunes.

A new thought occurs to me.

Where the hell am I going to stay tonight?

There's no way I can rent an apartment now, even if I had the money. I sure don't want to spend the night in the cramped car seat.

Better get going.

With no definite plan, I find myself driving back to the club. Something in me is hoping Adela will just be leaving, closing up for the night.

And what would you say to her? You'd probably just creep her out.

The silent beach houses glide by. Only a few have lights on, and even those look like security lights; they're probably on a timer. The thought of these huge houses standing empty most of the year alternately appalls and appeals to me. I imagine that I could break into one of these and live there. No one would ever know it.

Something in me wishes I had money, but then I think of Dad and of Robert. I wonder which one of these was Dad's. He and Mom met down here occasionally by themselves, leaving me with Granpa. Used to think they bought the place just to get away from me. Maybe they did. But they'd only been down once or twice themselves, at best.

On the club drive, the gravel crunches loudly, even under my slow cruise. I stop the car and leave it idling; security lights make an artificial halo of brightness around the darkened clubhouse. Adela's long gone, along with everyone else on this Saturday night. The golf course looks unnaturally smooth, a black carpet in this flowing silvery light. Tall palms rise randomly from around the fairways, dark obelisks catching moonlight oddly in their crowns.

This won't work.

I drive slowly out the back way, looking for what, I can't even say. Behind a green fence and a screen of palms I come upon a metal storage building of some sort. There are garage doors. It's about the size of a small house. I'm reminded of some of the warehouses at the highway department, and the thought appeals to me. I pull my car up in the small empty parking lot behind the structure and scout the place. It must be a storage and maintenance building for the grounds crew, and right now a pile of mulch bags seem like as good a place to sleep as any.

The world's most incompetent felon, I try to lift the garage-door, but it's locked and it rattles shockingly. The Sheriff's frowning countenance is a disapproving presence in my mind.

I am an employee now.

Small comfort, that.

I work my way around the shed, my fingertips feeling out the corrugated metal. Somehow, I don't think the cops would believe me. I discover a regular sized door. It's sheet-metal like the rest of the shed, a cutout panel. I'm reminded of childhood playhouses, like those Granpa made with me, sawed out from old refrigerator boxes.

A twisted piece of baling wire is worked into the door; it's punched through, as if on purpose. A door handle. I pull the wire. The door shudders and catches. I pull again, harder. A metallic screech pierces the gravequiet, makes me jump back cringing. But it has given way and creaks open now.

Shit, that was loud.

My skin crawls, and I look all around me before going in.

Groping the wall by the door, good fortune strikes. There's a light switch crudely bolted on here, and I throw it on. A single bulb snaps into existence, dangling from steel rafters by an extension cord. Soft yellowness dimly illuminates a breakroom of sorts. There's a plastic folding table with metal folding chairs. A refrigerator stands next to some crude, home-made cabinetry against the right wall. There's even a microwave on the counter.

On my left, a wall of plastic mulch bags rises to about my height, creating the partition. A darkened garage beyond the wall of stuffed plastic sacks. Stores of materials. Tools. I step further in and notice a mattress on the floor in a corner of the mulch wall. The thing seems to be made of old pool furniture pads, but it's got some rumpled blankets on it and looks comfortable enough. I grin.

Perfect. This will do nicely.

Just to be safe, I creep back and move my car out to the parking lot of the main club house, hoping it'll look less suspicious parked there next to the couple of other cars left there. I hurry back to the shed past a sentinel row of moonlit palms, trying to walk casual, like I belong here. I probe the black shadows of the trees with my eyes, thinking I see movement, feeling followed. Half-way there I decide to give up the cool act and just run.

Safely back in the building, leaning against the shut door to catch my breath, I feel silly. I search the room further, and I'm amused to find beer in the fridge. No wonder there's a napping spot here. I like these guys already. I'm tired, tired now and sore everywhere. I leave the beer, drink some water and set my watch alarm for four.

Best to get out of here early.

I turn out the lights and strip down to my mud-browned underwear, groping for the bed in the pitch black; it's not as moldy as I suspected. Hands behind my head, stretched out, I look up in the dark nothingness and let sleep come to me.

A good ending to a good day.

I try not to think of Adela. Or Gloria.

My eyes open to darkness, and the feel of the girl fades away.

Where the hell am I?

Someone is moving in the pitch black of the room.

Galveston Country Club, maintenance building.

Holy shit, someone's here.

Soft footsteps approach my pallet.

This can't be good.

Softly, I pull the blankets up past my head, then freeze, not moving a muscle. The someone is getting down on the bed beside me.

Please, God, just make him go away.

A strong hand feels my stomach from above the covers. I hear a soft grunt of surprise.

"Adela?"

What? Do something. Say something, you fool.

I can't. I don't know what to do, don't know what to say; I'm frozen. The hand makes it way stealthily under the covers. It's running lightly down to my underwear, both thrilling and revolting.

Oh my God.

The hand stops.

I'm dead.

A grunt of outraged surprise. Covers are torn away.

I think I shout.

A tremendous impact. Light and pain searing my brain. My nose feels broken. I know I scream before the second blow comes. Lightening shoots through me in a blinding white light.

I'm awake, lying down, on my back. An ice pack is on my face. I'm not sure if it's light or dark outside. Everything comes back to me. Everything hurts even more.

A pitiful groan escapes me.

My face: an agony of throbbing. Eyes still closed, I assess the damage with my hand. My cheek and nose are swollen and painful to the slightest touch. This pain goes beyond hurt.

I take the ice pack off and look around.

I see him.

I jump up with a wild start, think of running, and then catch myself. He's just sitting there in one of the metal chairs, eyeing me curiously from across the room with those unmistakable and disturbingly blue eyes.

Shit, the guy with the Jeep. From the beach.

He's got a shirt on now at least, but arm tattoos glower at the edge of his sleeve-line. I glance down at myself. In nothing but my underwear. I sit quickly down on the bed and scramble to put my pants back on while staring back at him, feeling awkward, tense, revolted. What do you say to a guy about all this?

Stone-faced, he's examining me, probably wondering what I'll say, and what I'll do. Several times I start to voice the thoughts and questions speeding through my mind, and each time I leave them unspoken, the words hanging in my throat. I can't read his face. It's completely impassive. He doesn't twitch so much as a single facial muscle. I can't be sure that I've even seen him blink.

"You beat the crap out of me, man."

"Thought you were somebody else at first."

Our eyes connect. The whole scene replays itself.

We burst out in laughter together.

It's relieved, embarrassed laughter, the laughter of camaraderie. The first such laughter for me in months—or more? It all just releases, so that there's nothing more for us to discuss; there' nothing else to say. It was all very stupid anyway.

What an idiot I am.

"My name's John... ah, John Fears."

"My friends call me Bal."

We get up and shake hands in the middle of the room, smiling. This is a guy I can trust, a guy I can hang out with.

"You need a place to stay," Bal says.

It's more of a fact that he's re-affirming.

I nod my head, yes, hoping he can set me up. "Well. As a matter of fact, I do." I look around me hopefully.

"We can make another wall," Bal says, indicating the one behind him. "Make your own room. We got plenty of bags."

And it is true. A mountain of mulch-bags is there in the semi-darkness behind him.

"I can stay here?"

Bal nods yes, and without a further word starts tossing bags around to make my room. Before I can lift a finger, he has a neat cubicle outlined directly off of the main room. I jump in and help then, but I hardly get five bags placed before he has it all done. My new room is snug and private, and I'm intensely pleased.

Bal surveys the effort a little, apparently satisfied.

"Just need a mattress," he says. "Let's go to the pool."

I follow him as we make our way stealthily back across the dark golf course. I try to match the silence of his footfall, but fail. At the pool, we climb over the chest-high iron fence, and Bal gets to work. He quickly removes a few pads from a couple of chaise lounges and hands them to me before going off to the club side of the pool to rummage around again. I look at the pads I've found myself holding.

What the hell am I doing?

Standing there dumbly, I wonder what Zingleman would do if he caught me here, at 2:00 AM, holding stolen pool-chair padding, all bruised and encrusted in two days' worth of mud and brine? I'm not sure I want to have that conversation.

But before I can think about it any further, Bal comes storming by, holding an entire potted palm in his arms and bodily leaps the fence, hitting the ground in stride, whooping crazily, and running like hell for our metal-sided home through the pitch black dark.

Guy's an animal.

Overcoming awe and laughter, I quickly throw the pads over the fence and clamber after them, hustling to catch up to my rapidly departing new room-mate.

Oh well; sorry, Zingleman.

Back in the shed, with the pads duct-taped together for a bed and a potted palm in the corner for color, I forget all about Zingleman and whatever might be right and wrong about this. It's been one of the longest but oddly satisfying days of my life, and I'm incredibly exhausted, not to mention sore. Bal crawls up under his covers with hardly a word, and I throw myself into my own, new bed, knowing I'll sleep the sleep of the dead.

# NEW BARATARIANS

The sound of cars pulling in behind the building filters into my sleep. I wake with a start, wondering if the whole thing really happened last night. Doubt is quickly removed by the throb of my nose and the sight of a potted palm standing there in the corner of a room constructed entirely of mulch-bags, like the antechamber of some landscaping cult's shrine.

It was real all right.

And I'm probably not supposed to be here.

I look for Bal, but he's already gone. My watch shows Sunday, 7:00 AM.

Crap, must be the course crew. Sunday's a big day for golf. Now where'd he get off to?

Quickly as I can in the gray light, I spring up, rummaging through my bag. But my old highway stuff won't do. Nothing's clean. On go the new black shorts and the new collared, red shirt, already stained with sweat and saltwater. Gotta pay Adela for these. Quickly now, the broken tennis shoes. No time for socks. I hear Spanish outside, spoken quietly but familiarly. I stop, standing, and catch something of the talk of grass and lawns and the tortillas for lunch. It's barely understood, coming up somewhere from the deep well of my childhood, the first language I remember spoken; there's the feeling of a nanny's warm embrace.

Don't just stand here.

Just as the groundsmen are opening the garage, I step out of the shed door, hoping I look like I belong. Like a tennis-pro, just having a coffee out at the break room, or something. But I know I don't look the part.

I don't even have any coffee.

Feelings of guilt and strangeness inarticulate are rising in me—and for what? But, if they notice me at all, they don't show it. I'm sure they do, though. Heads are down in a studied inobservance.

Question not the strange ways of thé gringo.

But I wonder. Are they used to people coming and going from Bal's hideout like this in the early hours of the morning?

I stroll towards the little convenience store down the road to kill time before my first lesson of the day, passing the weedy overgrown patch of land, noticing something rising above the weeds. A lonely granite marker. I read it.

Here is Jean Lafitte's grove?

Right here?

Here is the place where his pirate fortress stood? Where he and his men terrorized the Spanish Main and killed off the last of the ferocious Karankawa? Where he housed cannons and ships' stores and fought Indian, Spanish, English—anybody and everybody—for a profit?

Why, this is a crime.

The three oaks that famously used to mark the place appear to be gone, too. Those things were five-hundred years old—they survived the entire recorded history of the island—but not my generation. Those are really gone?

I step a few paces into the lot, trying to imagine the scene. It's now vacant, indistinguishable from any other vacant lot around here, overgrown with weedy brambles—waiting, no doubt, to be developed into more unused beach houses. I get visions of some pushy money guy developer over in Austin saying to some obscure state historical official: hey, can I have that grove yet? Can I have that worthless weedy spot that no one ever visits? That no one's visited for fifty years and never will? It's nothing, nothing at all and, well, here's a little something to help you make up your mind...

I shake my head, turn away, and resume my walk.

I hope not.

It's not until I walk into the store and see the frightened reaction of the teenage girl behind the coffee counter that I realize it. I haven't washed the dried blood off my face.

I must look pretty rough.

She serves me coffee, but she can't stop staring and can't help herself from shrinking away from me as I pass over my crumpled money.

Sitting there at the single laminate table in that convenience store, blood on my face, salt-brine on my clothes, drinking my coffee and eating a pop-tart, I laugh out loud at the absurdity of it all, like some demented homeless guy. I've got a hideout not two hundred yards from the site of Jean Lafitte's old fort, a savage for a friend, a pilfered plant, a stolen bed, and the wrecked face of a pirate after a fight. All I need to do now—like Lafitte, the wild Baratarian himself—is rape the woman, rob the cash register, and torch the store.

Hail the reign of the New Baratarians!

I get up from the booth smiling a wicked smile and approach the counter with the girl leaning away behind it. I stuff a dollar in her tip jar.

"See ya' later, my pretty."

Surprised and more than a little scared, she smiles nervously, says nothing, and I leave the store feeling her eyes on me. Walking slowly back to the club, sipping my coffee and enjoying the deepening blueness of the morning, I feel like I've come home.

Still with plenty of time before the lesson, I walk to the pro shop. Adela's just opened it up this morning. The cracked door hasn't been replaced yet. We smile and nod a brief greeting, and then we both look at the door at the same time. She giggles pleasantly, and I'm sure I'm turning four shades of red. I can see, too, that she notices my face is in bad shape today, but she doesn't say anything about it.

I remember what he said in the dark. That one name, the way it was spoken. Adela, he'd said. Adela. It has to be her.

Perhaps she's already spoken with Bal, but she's busy opening the shop and the reception area now, and I don't exactly know how to ask her about him.

You don't need to go there, anyway.

I shop a little in a pro-shop mostly catering to the stupid golfers. Not that I can hit her up for anything more, but I like glancing over at Adela, interrupting her by asking questions about the price of these shorts, or this shirt, though they're clearly marked. I pick out a few more clothes. I tell her to hold them for me. I like placing the clothes in her small, brown hands.

"Thanks, Adela," I say.

"Good luck today." She smiles a genuine smile.

Lucky, lucky Bal.

I go to the men's locker room to shower and get ready for my lesson. The bruises don't look so bad once the blood's gone. Still, it's pretty ugly. With not much time now, I go back in the shop and wait; just standing there and wondering about Bal and Adela, despite myself.

She's been smiling at me in a sideways kind of way. Surreptitious little smiles, beguiling little smiles.

Damnit, it's driving me crazy.

I feel the bruises on my face, and look over at Adela again. And that was only a couple of punches he threw. I'm imagining a really and truly angry Bal when Zingleman sweeps in, almost prissily, with a quick-stepped gait and his undulating helmet-hair bouncing up and down. It's possible he smiles like this and looks like this all the time, even in his sleep.

Would Bal really would kill me?

"Well, well, good morning there, John!" Zingleman starts in with his super-happy-nice routine, "and just how are you doing this, ah, this..." He's noticed my purpled face now. For a couple of seconds, even his perma-smile disappears, "... this beautiful morning?"

I just stand there staring back at him, trying to act stoic, like Bal would, waiting for him to make a comment. He doesn't. He just cocks a fist on his hip and asks me what happened without actually asking anything.

No way am I telling you, Zingleman.

No way I'm telling anybody.

Presently, he gives it up and gets back to business, ratcheting the perma-smile back onto his face with some visible effort. "Okay then. Your first lesson today is already out on court."

"Really?" I say, looking at my watch. It reads 9:45 AM. "He is?"

Looking past Zingleman, out the window and over towards the tennis courts, I wonder how I've missed him checking in and getting out there.

"Yes, *she* is," Zingleman, says, correcting me. "It's your friend, Gloria Baker."

My mind recoils, I stagger bodily. Can't be. "Who, did you say?"

"Gloria Baker," Zingleman replies happily.

"Gloria Baker?"

He looks at me strangely.

"Yes...John." He grins now. A Cheshire grin. "I thought you knew her?"

"Huh?"

"Don't you know Ms. Baker?"

I compose myself with effort, try to straighten up, and stop the room from spinning.

"Yes, yes... 'course I do. Sorry. Just surprised. You know... expecting a guy and all."

Zingleman relaxes, gets happy again.

"Yes, she's a very prominent member, John."

"Ah, of course."

"Just don't run her too much! Okay?"

"Okay."

"Okay then, Tennis Pro, knock 'em dead!"

Zingleman actually punches me playfully in the arm.

"Yeah, I do knock 'em dead, that's for sure."

He's not too sure what to make of this comment. I try to smile back at him, but it doesn't come off, and I just walk away, the pit in my stomach growing larger and larger, as if I'll fall into it, disappear into it, die in it. But can't run now. Somehow, I must've known this all along, and now I've got to go and face her. She's the one person who might understand... or not.

Try not to puke.

I find the teaching cart; this one's just a grocery cart filled with old tennis balls. I push it over to the courts, numbly, trying to force my mind onto the problem of handling this.

There she is.

I walk on the court, pushing the rickety cart. Her back is turned to me. She's wearing a skin tight white tennis skirt with a tight red stretch tanktop. The outfit shows her entire figure. All of it. She's still very shapely, trim, curvaceous.

She dressed up for me.

I stop. I try to put my finger on something new in my mind, something strange, a new thought. In some way, she's different. Something. She's not quite as athletic, like I remember. Or is it something else? I start pushing the cart again. She seems thinner, yes, that's it. Thinner. Skinnier, like how you get from starving yourself. For years.

Gloria tosses her hair, looks over her shoulder at me, a hand on her hip, then turns to face me slowly. And, as she turns, like she's some supermodel, the memories flood back to me all over again: of playing tennis with her back in Tahoe, of seeing her in the casino, hanging onto Robert, of how beautiful she looked then, of how I've thought of her for such a long time.

A long time.

And as she looks at me, expectantly, she doesn't smile. Words escape me entirely.

"Well, aren't you going to introduce yourself?" Gloria says.

I'm completely taken aback by this.

Now she smiles. I can do nothing but stand there, dumbstruck, and look at her. And now that I see her, revealed here in the bright morning light, wearing, really, nothing very much, I'm somehow completely underwhelmed, now utterly deflated. It's strange; it's disturbing. She's at once very familiar and a complete stranger. Familiar to my memories, yes, but in those she's something else, she's a dream perhaps, a vision, something completely unreal. But she is a stranger now. A stranger who knows me.

And I'm going to have to trust her.

Gloria's smile turns to a frown. She senses something's not quite right with me.

"Well?" Gloria says, tensing up.

"Oh, uh, good morning, Mrs. Baker, I'm John Fears."

We stand there looking at each other for a moment.

I smile. I am John Fears.

And in some strange way, I've suddenly started to feel light now, like I'm totally carefree. For some reason, I feel happy, really happy. And seeing me smile a genuine smile, Gloria relaxes again. She smiles back at me tentatively.

"I found you," she says quietly.

"No, you didn't."

And we just stand there again a moment, looking at one another, and then, something seems to pass for both of us, and we relax, both smiling, and it's all good again, and I don't really know why or how.

"Uh, well, ready to go?"

"Fears? Your name is John Fears? I seem to remember knowing a boy named John. He looked a lot like you." She smiles again, a happy smile.

"Oh?" I say, "that couldn't have been me."

She laughs a little. "Well," she says, "that John was a boy. The one I've got here seems to be a man..." she smiles a wicked smile. "But Zingleman says you're good, so I'll have to take his word for it. Personally, I'm sorry he fired the last guy, just as my forehand was starting to improve, too."

What? I'm stunned all over again. Zingleman fired the last guy? No one told me that.

It's hard to imagine him firing anyone.

Is she kidding?

But she's not. That knowing smile of hers, sparkling. The smile says it all.

"Oh. Well. So... so, you want to work on your forehand, do you?"

"Yes, among other things," she says.

"Okay then, well, let's just have a look at... your strokes. If you'll just go over behind the baseline," I gesture to the far side of the court with my racket, feeling incredibly awkward. And suddenly I'm ready to just get on with this.

"Okay," Gloria says walking over, now in a hurry herself.

"We'll pay special attention to your forehand."

Positioning my cart at the net opposite her, I then feed her a few balls. She sprays them all over the place. She starts frowning.

I forgot how bad she is; she can barely hit the ball.

"It's allright, you're just getting warmed up."

A few more balls, a few more shanks and mishits. Nothing goes in. I fall back to the refrain of every tennis-pro I've ever heard (which is very few).

"Keep your eye on the ball now, Ms. Baker!"

"Okay," she says, as she mishits one groundstroke after the other. Now, I actually think about trying to improve her game. It's not like last time, when I had just hit her a few balls, played around for a half-hour, laughing. I'm supposed to be a tennis pro now, not some shy teenager dragged along on his father's business trip.

Quickly though, I see I don't know how to help her game. She's not doing anything right. Bad footwork. Wrong grip, I think.

A disturbing thought.

How the hell do I hit the ball anyway?

I don't really know.

She's becoming very unhappy, not liking this turn of events at all. I stop feeding and step over the net to her.

"Let's try this."

I place her hand on the grip, just the way I hold the racket myself. I'm close to her, reaching my arm lightly around her, holding her hand in position with my own. She relaxes a little. She likes the contact. She seems to move closer to me, almost into a cuddle. We're so close I can smell her, and it's good. She's wearing the same perfume I think, the very same one she wore that night. It's disturbing. It's making me dizzy. I release her hand with relief and step in front of her, shadowing a few forehands like some sugar-hyped kid.

"Okay, Ms. Baker, just stroke it like this."

"Okay, enough with the Ms. Baker, John."

"Gloria, okay, sorry, just go through the stroke with me. Imagine what it's like to hit it."

She tries to mime my own. She does it all wrong.

I decide to just let it go. "Just don't think about it too much."

"Okay, I'll try," she says, smiling again, a genuine smile this time.

I show her how all the strokes work like this: her hand in mine, with me positioned behind her, wrapping my arm around her, like a light embrace, swinging through the strokes together in some strange slow dance. But it works much better, and I like just holding onto her, just touching her. And this is, all of it: very, very weird.

"Let's try some volleys then," I say.

Escorting her up to net with me, I step over the netcord again and back by my cart. We're opposite each other, only a few feet away. We dink a few volleys back and forth, lightly, like some beach game played with large inflatable balls, like last time. Soon, we start relaxing again; this is better.

"Nice shooting Gloria. I can see you're a doubles player... it's good to have a partner."

Another smile, a little shake of her head.

I stay away from all instruction now. I go across the net often to show her little things, we make contact sometimes, I feel her body brushing up against mine, and strangely, now there is nothing between us. Now it is gone.

Finally, one of the most awkward hours of my life is up. Relief and regret and happiness surge through me, all conflicted. She comes up to me tentatively, wiping her sweat self-consciously.

"Great job, Gloria."

And now I feel obligated to say something more, something nice, all kinds of crazy things. I want to say thank you, and I want to say I used to want you, and now I don't. I feel like saying I don't know what I was thinking, and also: I've never stopped thinking about you.

But I can't. I can't say any of those things.

She smiles slightly, perhaps sadly, perhaps not.

"Thanks, dear. That was fun."

She gently lifts my hand and places a neatly printed business card in it, but she doesn't let go. She holds the card there in my palm with a slender thumb, her hand cupping mine, her body touching my arm. She's writing a number on the card. I shoot her what must be a surprised glance but turn my attention to her card while she finishes. I almost shrink away from her. I don't know what to do. The card is embossed with some gold curlicue-things. All it has is her name, a Galveston address, a phone number. No title or business, just her name, not Robert's.

"My personal cell phone," she indicates the newly scrawled number with a tap of her pen.

"Call me, if you need anything. Anything at all."

I don't know what to say. I stare dumbly at the card.

She turns her head away, looks in a new direction though she's still pressed up close to me, poised, as if to write something else on the card. "I'm going to have to go back soon," she finally says quietly, "but you can call me anytime you want."

"Gloria," a woman's voice says lightly, "are you hogging the new pro already?"

Gloria releases my hand slowly, lets her finger tips lightly brush down my forearm, looks at this new woman over her shoulder. I know I'm turning an embarrassed red. I quickly look down and bounce a tennis ball on my racket.

"Oh, hi Cynthia. Well, of course I'm hogging the new pro. He's sensational. But, I'm sorry, you can have him now. He's all yours."

She looks at me one last time in a way I can't interpret and then stoops to gather her stuff. Quickly, I pocket the card and move over to the cart. I can't even watch her departure. I don't think she looks back.

I'm hardly even present for Cynthia's lesson. I am there on the court, mumbling instructions, but I cannot concentrate on this woman. She's older than Gloria, kind of dumpy with puckered, full lips, like a fish mouth, but the rest of her is: all dried up. Her game's much the same as Gloria's, but I just stand there feeding balls, and I don't go over to her. I don't know if she's pleased with my coaching or not.

Probably not.

But, nothing much matters to me any more today. Cynthia is followed by Jane, Susie, someone else. I don't take a lunch break before the group lesson. The time passes in a haze until there are no more women to feed balls to, and the afternoon sun is getting low. Of all these women, only Gloria has left her card. I take it out of my sweaty pocket and smell it. But all I can smell is myself, and the memory is all spoiled.

I put the cart up. Adela's not in the pro-shop, just some pudgy girl named Mary with acne and unkempt hair. Zingleman's gone too. Thank God there aren't any more lessons today, because that was a beating.

Wandering back towards the hide-out, I don't know what to do with the rest of the day. I kind of want to work-out myself, just to get my legs moving again after the hours of standing and feeding, but I've got no one good to hit with. Strolling across the twelfth fairway, I get Gloria's card out once again. It's wet with my sweat and the ink of her looping writing has run and pooled on the thick paper. There's a blue stain on my new shorts. But the number's still legible, and the words are still in my mind. Call me, she'd said.

Nearby, the low diesel rumble of large machinery. Looking up, I see Bal working only a few yards away, digging with a shovel. A big backhoe sits idling. "It's Sunday," I say to him, "what are you up to?"

"Workin'," he says, not even stopping his digging. "Gotta set up the course."

"Oh," I eye the backhoe, the widening pit. A grounds-guy runs up to Bal from behind me. The man asks him how to do a fertilizer application of some sort or the other. There's a complicated discussion of treatments. The man nods, and I hear Bal addressed as "Boss."

"Boss?" I ask when the guy runs off again.

He just glances at me.

"Head Groundsman," Bal says with what could be irony, but I'm not sure.

He's already started digging again. I can't say why I'm surprised to find out that Bal is the head Groundsman, but I feel bad about being surprised by it. I watch him expertly excavating the new trap a while and crumple up Gloria's card into a tight ball.

I throw it in the pit.

Bal stops and probes me with those eyes of his for a moment.

"A girl's calling card," I say. "I'm not interested."

He looks at me stoically for a moment, slips me a sly wink, curls his lip in a half-smile.

"Need some help?" I ask. "I'm an old hand from the Highway Department."

"Allright, he says, handing me the shovel, "you're hired. You keep the edge of the line sharp," he points to a neatly spray-painted line demarcating a new trap, "I'll run the backhoe."

"Yes, Boss," I say, and he smiles. "Anything you need."


We work hard into the evening, Bal urging on the machine, and I digging steadily around the edges of each new pit, smoothing and finishing the lines. A course of greens and fairways and traps, all changing overnight. I'm tired, but it's a good tired, and there's a comfortable camaraderie in the work. It's almost enough to make me forget. Almost, but not quite.

I found you, she'd said.

No. No, you didn't. That boy you knew was not me. That boy was never me.

# A Confusion of Place

I n Clear Lake, the rain on the golf course comes down slowly and quietly, in big measured drops, not that the players sitting inside the club bar would know it. Except for Chip. He looks at the gray patch of the window far away and small in the dimly lit interior and grimaces slightly. He'd rather be out there, playing in the rain and the cool. Not that he has any great love of golf. It's a bit tedious to him: hit the ball, see the ball disappear, watch the other guys hack it out of sight too, do it eighteen times and on to the bar. But it's good to walk the course and get out of the office and talk somewhere else for a change. J.G. would have never dreamed of playing such a thing as this game. Never held no truck with this kind of deal, Father might have said. Neither with pastimes such as golf, nor with anyone who would waste their time in such a fashion. No, not Father, not when there was a big field of potatoes and corn and collard greens and cauliflowers and okra needing to be harvested in an Indian summer such as this. Not when there were trotlines to run in every lake within thirty miles of the house. Not when there was real work to do—useful work, Godly work—not this game you use to take other people's money, which you also like to call doing business. Not that. Father had actually said as much, and the way he'd looked at Chip when he first saw the golf clubs had said it all.

Chip looks over at Robert, laughing and sucking on the ice cubes of his fifth or sixth whiskey of the day and talking about his frat days at UT again, and decides he better get this on track before it totally devolves into the drunken waste of time it is becoming. But abruptly and uncharacteristically, he changes his mind and sits back to sip his drink and simply observe the people he is here with. Around a circular granite bar table sit Zingleman, Robert, and two brothers down from Houston who Chip thinks of as Dumbass One and Dumbass Two. Scott and Tom, Scott and Tom, he repeats the names to himself to make sure he doesn't make the mistake.

The brothers are third generation owners of an oil and gas distribution network run by their uncle. Chip doubts either one of them could even find half of their holdings on a map. Possibly they don't even know where their own offices are. Only one of them, Scott, who is a former frat brother of Robert's, has managed to get a degree.

"I was at that kickoff party," Dumbass Two is saying, "down at Moody Gardens, remember? The one where both John Denver and JFK Jr. were there and it was the last time either one of them partied because they both went down in plane crashes, BOOM!" here Tom's hands work up the image of airplanes crashing into the ocean.

"Yeah, crap, am I glad *we* didn't fly down there for that," says Dumbass Two. "I don't think we flew our plane for months after Jr. dumped it in the drink."

Robert flings a joking insult at the brothers and sticks his tongue out at them in a grotesque lapping motion. "You guys better watch out," he says, "or Zingleman here will come over and lick you up."

Zingleman laughs and plays along, but for a fleeting moment, he makes eye contact with Chip as if to say, what is it with these guys, this stuff wasn't funny, even in high school. Chip smiles and shakes his head slightly. Indeed. What is it with these guys? None of them are tennis players or even very interested in tennis, but here they all are, doing the deals to fund, market, and sell the inaugural challenger tournament of Galveston. Using Robert, Zingleman and Chip have already hit Scott and Tom up for the major corporate sponsorship of the tournament, convincing them that a pro tennis tournament will be just the thing to fit into the company's brilliant marketing plan to build a "brand." They'd met at the new club in Clear Lake, to formalize the deal. Although the brothers are investors in the club and members, they'd really met here instead of in Galveston so Chip wouldn't have to risk seeing John. Zingleman, much to his delight, has been let in on the secret of Chip's assumed death and Chip isn't too happy with that, but he has to admire Zingleman's use of it. Signed him right up for a sizable personal sponsorship. But Chip has also got a piece of the pie since he's managing the fund development on an on-going basis, and he's reasonably happy with it all. Curiously, the whole tournament had been Robert's idea in the first place and he'd called Zingleman and Chip together to make it happen.

But Chip thinks he knows where the plan really came from.

And where is she, he thinks, looking around him, as if she might be hiding somewhere. He'd like to see Gloria again. He'd even jumped at the chance to come to the meeting in person on the hope that she'd be here. But she isn't. You're the dumbass, he admonishes himself, ran down here like a highschooler on his first date.

"... no way should we have national healthcare," Scott is saying, somehow having managed to seamlessly move from parties to politics, "we'd be paying for every Mexican in Mexico."

"Excuse me," Chip says getting up, "gotta take a leak." These doubts, they are a poison. He leaves the barroom, just walking the halls of the club. It's a sprawling red brick colonial mansion sort of job with Doric columns that look as if they're made of plastic. There's a Spa and hotel and conference center as well as the Golf Course. Uniformed porters, Mexicans all, stand in every doorway, at every counter.

The modern day plantation and no real black guys in sight.

In the bathroom, however, the shoe-shine man is a black man about Chip's age with baggy, red eyes and a proud disposition. He has a niche of sorts set up in a corner of the bathroom by the door where you can't miss him when you enter.

"Them shoes sure are shining, sir," the man says from where he sits in one of the booth chairs. He indicates Chip's well glossed and buffed black dress shoes with a crooked finger, "looks like something I woulda' done myself."

"I'm sure," Chip says and smiles at the man, "but they could use a little more, anyway." He climbs up on the shoe-shine booth as the man climbs down and kneels on a board. Chip sits down in the throne-like black leather chair, and places his feet firmly upon black iron treadles. The bootblack kneels before him, places his rough handled wooden box upon the footboard, and methodically lays out the tools of his trade: a worn piece of chammy that looks like the real thing, greasy tins smelling of wax and soap, a glossy horsehair blacking-brush. The man goes to work with care. Calloused hands anoint patent leather shoes with the gravity of a sacred rite. Unctions applied in hypnotic circling rhythms. Soft rubbing sounds echo in the silence of the room.

"So, tell me how it is," Chip ventures at last.

"It's all good, sir," the man says cheerfully. "This recession, she's going to end soon and then we'll be there, sittin' pretty."

"You hanging in there, then?"

"Yes, sir, doing pretty well. My portfolio's only dropped a little bit, sir, but I think it'll be right back up there again."

"Your portfolio?" Chip asks dubiously.

"Yes, sir," the man says, not in the least affronted, and then goes on for half an hour knowledgeably discussing financial strategies with Chip. His own course is a balance of stocks, bonds, mutual funds. Chip's advice on these matters is gratefully received. Then on to the bootblack's two sons: both are in college, making good grades; one is into a business degree, the other pre-med. Chip learns the boys' names, their ages, their interests. On this subject Chip has no stories of his own to relate. Not a word about John. The man stands and steps back, examining his own handiwork. The shoes are absolutely and perfectly like new.

"Thanks, I needed that," Chip says, handing the man a five and getting up and going back out and walking slowly back to the bar.

She is there when he gets there. Her back turned towards him, her perfect shape practically hums from inside a short fall dress. He wants to run to her, to take her in his arms, to rip off the clothes deliciously. She turns towards the sound of his carefully measured steps.

"Hey there," Chip says.

"Hey Chip," she says and hugs him tightly and he can feel all of her body and she rubs him on the back in that familiar and intimate way she has with people, holding him until he pulls out of the embrace, still touching her elbows lightly. And when he does, he looks her in the eyes, and in there is the memory of himself, and his body breaks into a cold chill, and for a moment he feels as if he'll faint. But he doesn't.

"Will you come stay with us?" she asks.

"Sure," Chip says. "Thanks, that'd be great."

He lets her go with an effort and forces himself back into the group of men. But by this time, they are bored with this venue and ready to go somewhere else and they ask him to go with, but he declines and Zingleman says he's got to get back to Galveston. Chip says his goodbyes with relief, and goes back to his room to lay on the bed a while, but doesn't undress. Then he goes back down to the now empty bar to sit by himself.

The man behind the bar is tousled and wiry with wildly curled hair, shaggy and streaked in gray. A leathery face straight from a Scottish farmyard, as indeed it is, smiles warmly. He recognizes Chip and limps over to him, bottle of Balvenie in hand, two glasses readied with two cubes each.

"Back for more?"

"Back for more," answers Chip.

"Don't mind if I have a wee one myself," says the man. He sets the glasses on the black and shining granite bar and carefully pours out two measures of the twenty-four year old whiskey.

"Thanks," Chip says and they clink glasses and throw back their drinks. The barman pours two more.

"Looks like you could use a dram or two," he says.

Chip doesn't look up as he nods and tips his glass. Then he says: "I know a man whose son doesn't even know the face of his own true mother."

"Now there's a wee bastard," says the barman.

"Ah, but he carried two burdens that never mix. In the one hand he had the love of woman and an unborn son, and in the other hand: poverty, hopelessness, youth."

The barman nods. "So what happened?"

"Well," Chip says, "the father met a woman and the mother met a man."

"So let me finish the story, the barman says. "He married the bitch for her money, and she married the bastard for his."

"More or less," Chip concedes. "And who's the bigger bastard?"

"These drinks are on the house," says the barman, shaking his head. Chip nods and sips his drink and the barman leaves him and moves off to the corner of the shiny bar to polish his already clean glasses and sip his drink by himself.

Three or four whiskeys later, a few people have trickled in and sit in huddled private groups. She comes into the bar and makes a slow circle in it but doesn't look at him. Then she leaves. Chip finishes his drink and leaves a hundred on the bar and gets up and walks slowly in the direction she has gone.

She is there at the elevators down the hall, just getting on, and she glances up at him briefly before she enters the lift. The doors shut. He walks up and studies the stainless steel panel of numbers for a moment, noting the floors and the endless and nearly random machinations of the lifts. He presses the up arrow and the doors open and he steps in and presses the button for the floor. In the long lit halls, the quiet drone of banks of neon lights, a diminishing single point perspective of closed doors. One is ajar. Chip touches the door handle a moment with a finger. The bent cylinder of steel is cool and grainy. Then he pushes open the door and slips in the room and from without the sound of the door locks being thrown is the sound of finality, but there is no one there to hear, and within, the years slip away in the nothingness of the moment.

# BELIAL'S CHILDREN

We're drinking Beer at the hideout, not saying much, sitting in pool-chairs leaned up against the cold sheetmetal, looking off across the golf course. Witnesses to a slowly expanding horizon moon. Stars pop out from the inkblue above the palms. The petroleum laced tang of bay water insinuates itself into the dense, humid air. I've never had a brother or sister; maybe it's something like this. Two months into this, and I still don't know him all that well. Still; feels like I've known him all my life. It's been enjoyable helping him out, especially with tennis lessons already tapering off this Fall. There were never that many of them anyway.

Gloria again. Her comely figure pauses in the far distance at the end of a blinding white hallway. The door stands open. Is she coming in or going out? The tattered shreds of her memory mingle with others, with newer ones. The touch of her, the smell of her, the imprint of those feelings now inform the desire for others: Adela, some of the women I teach, random acquaintances of random encounters throughout a life spent hoping, waiting, wanting. Gloria never came to another lesson. Haven't even seen her since that first day here, but I guess she didn't talk because I haven't heard anything about Dad either. Not that I would, I guess. It's not like the cops are going to give me advance notice, if they come here looking for me.

John Sharpe? If he came here, that kid is gone. Never knew him.

I did hear from one of the women that Gloria's gone off to Bali or something, somewhere exotic, getting away from that cold Galveston winter. I shake my head, smirking a little, but creeping and unaccountable feelings of guilt worm away within.

Just what I don't need: more guilt.

And if she had come back what would I have say to her anyway?

Let's be friends? Come to my metal shack and hang out?

I take a drink of beer, ponder the can, shaking my head again, and then drain it. With my head tilted back, I catch sight of Bal out of the corner of my eye. He's looking right into me, watching me.

"Forget about her," he says.

"What? What're you babbling about?"

"Ten dollars says you were thinking about the woman."

"Yeah? Well, deduct it from my paycheck."

He smiles and slowly turns his gaze back to the horizon, reaching for another beer.

"Here," he grunts, handing me the beer. "Lot more reliable."

I think of Adela. Don't think of Adela. Thinking of her anyway. A mumble: "Yeah, man, easy enough for you to say."

Taking the fresh beer, I toss the empty in the cardboard carton. Sighs escape me. Well, I can't begrudge him that relationship. Yes, I can. But I won't. They're both really nice; they seem happy together. I've often wondered why they don't marry. Though why do people marry at all? It sure doesn't seem to be about love.

The silvery new can sweats chilled rivulets from a crust of frost. An entire icy world in my hand. With the lightest touch of my godly finger, I obliterate whole river systems, entire glaciers. Pop the top and geysers erupt. Licking foam like a cat. Ah, the joys of illegal, cold, hard-earned, beer. Where every man's a god.

I rub an aching shoulder. Helping out Bal, I'm going to be a good digger, if nothing else. He can shovel it out like an armadillo, and I try to keep up with him, but I'm never even close. But he's been paying me to help him with the grounds anyway. Not that I ever asked him for it. He just started paying me. And it has been satisfying—cleaner than teaching tennis somehow—though it's dirty and back-breaking.

'Cause there's nothing like good cash money, earned the manly way.

Really, I should be saving to buy another car. Something more generic, something easier to maintain. Instead there are more rackets leaning against the wall; new pairs of tennis shoes lined up neatly beside the bed. Settling in here, though, the old dream's come back with a vengeance. The dream of playing pro tennis. I started working on my serve again and it's coming down hard, like I'm getting stronger somehow though there hasn't been too much opportunity to train properly. Surprisingly, there just aren't that many good players around here. Last night, I drove all the way up to Clear Lake to hit with some guy. What a hack he was. This morning, it was just a bucket of serves before lessons. It's not much practice, but I'm getting better somehow; I can feel it. I'm starting to believe in it. I imagine pummeling a forehand, swinging my beer into the stroke.

"Challenger's coming up, isn't it?"

Bal's seen me. He knows what I'm thinking. Again. Scary.

"Yeah, in November." I pop the top on a new can and take a long drink. "I don't know man. I don't know about that."

Yes, the Challenger is coming. Except for the Masters Invitational in Houston, it's the only pro tournament in the whole region—coming right here to our club, an inaugural event on the circuit and brought here by Zingleman of all people. It's just one step below the big leagues of the ATP and a perfect venue to make my start.

"You're playing," Bal says.

I look over at him as I lean over to see how many beers we have left in the cooler. I don't know if he's asking me or telling me. He hasn't moved or even taken his unblinking gaze off the horizon.

"Nah, I don't know. It's not that easy."

"Qualify."

"Yeah, maybe; it's almost impossible to do anything as a qualifier. And I'll have to win a pre-qualifying tournament, just to *get* to the qualifier. The odds of that... not too good."

Making the faintest of grunts, he drinks deeply. Not sure what this means from Bal—sounds accusatory though, like I'm wimping out on him. Maybe I am.

"I mean, maybe Zingleman'll give me a wildcard... but nah, no way. They'll save it for some dude from Houston, like Brasington or Tommy Ho or somebody like that."

Washed up former touring pros with local attraction, that's who, not somebody with no credentials, no real name, nothing. No, there'll be no wildcard for me. Bal doesn't understand. And for the first time in a while, I am able to think of Dad without his actual voice clamoring for my thought. An improvement, true, but not much help, because he was probably right about one thing. This dream of mine, it is delusional.

And Bal'd known about it somehow. Known, even though I'd only ever told one person. I never told Dad, or Mom, or even any of my friends. And in our final blow-up he had known and he told me exactly what he thought about it, scorn in his every word.

You actually think you can go pro, he'd said. You do, don't you? You really want to go off and tour the world playing that goddamn tennis. That's what this is about, right? I got one word for that, John: delusion. You didn't even win State. And now you think you can go pro? Christ, you are delusional, just like always. Now, you get off your ass and you go...

What I should've done is go to him earlier, when I was fourteen or something. When all my friends went off to the academies, but I stayed in Texarkana. Hoping, dreaming. Hoping for what, exactly? For Dad to support my fantasy? Did I expect him to just come ask me? Like he was going to come knock on my door and say, John, you've got talent, talent in spades. Whaddya' think? Let's get you off to Bolletieri's and get you some real training.

Yeah, right, that was Pop, always going on about my talent. But, for once, why hadn't I just marched in and told him what I wanted?

Because.

I point a finger at my temple and pull the trigger. Bang, bang, you're dead, what a shoot-down that'd have been. You want what!? He'd have said, Tennis school!? What a complete waste of money, John! Look at me. LOOK at me when I'm talking to you! Capital N-O, NO.

I know he thought like that. I know it.

Pro tennis does seem like such a stupid notion now. Grew up in the wrong place. Never could've gotten good enough in T-Town anyway. It's the place where everyone stops, but no one ever stays. Except the psychos. Let's see: Ross Perot, The Phantom Killer, The Boggy Creek Monster, The Texas Chainsaw Massacre guy. Yeah, John, not a lot of tennis pros hailing from Texarkana, are there? Lots of killers though.

But still.

Hell, it's stupid to still be thinking about this. I'm old. Way, way too old. Should've given this dream up back when I was sixteen. Back when I'd confessed it to my high school coach, right there on the practice court, and he'd just looked off across the boiling hot asphalt, off into the distance somewhere, anywhere but in my eyes.

I don't think so.

That's all he'd said.

I don't think so.

I guess my results proved it. And Dad was right, I didn't even manage to win State.

Not that he was there to see it. In the state final, and he doesn't even come.

What the hell do they know, anyway? Nothing. To hell with him and all of them. They never gave me a chance. It's not too late. I just need my confidence. I just need to find it.

"You're killing yourself over there," Bal says, looking at me now. "Waste of energy."

I say nothing. But Bal's right—I do want to play—and I do feel hope, despite myself. I can't make the dream go away, no matter what doubts I have—not lately. Fifty thousand dollars, ATP points; that's a pretty good start. It's a small chance, but it is a chance.

I really ought to try.

Bal offers no more commentary or encouragement, or whatever he's driving at. He'd make a hell of a player with that poker face of his, that inhuman endurance. We both pull from our beers again, sitting silent some more in the waning day.

I steal a glance at Bal, this wild-looking friend of mine, and wonder at what I don't know about him. But confidence? Man, I know he's got that. He never says much for sure, but something big goes on in that stoic head. Always up to something, he comes and goes at all hours, and he performs odd jobs for all sorts of people, including working on people's cars down at a guy's shop off Harborside. And those are just the things I know about. Even living here with him in his pad, I still don't know all that he does. He never seems to sleep.

Sometimes I go with him on his deals though I never quite know if I'm being a nuisance, like some pesky kid brother. But I figure if he tells me about it, then he wants me to come along, and I'm always happy to go; the man's a curiosity beyond anyone I've ever known.

I trace my initials in the sweat of the beer can. Goin' to the beach, he'll say, and then he'll look at me in that way of his, like a big panther trancing you to sleep before he pounces.

I laugh a little out loud and glance over at him where he seems to be contemplating the mysteries of life, or maybe he's just thinking of Adela, or maybe he's just sitting there spotting animals in the clouds, like I do. Who knows? He'd never tell.

The first time he said he was going to the beach, I got out a towel and put on my shorts and flip-flops, ready to go swimming. But Bal just shook his unsmiling head, no, and said: for tourists. And we'd gone and helped stupid tourists out for hours: pulling them out of the sand, helping change flats, whatever help could be offered, as if he's some barbaric ambassador of Galveston. I guess he is. He'd been there for me.

"Goin' fishin'," he says now, unmoving, still looking off in the distance.

"What, you're going fishing?"

I drain the beer can, toss the empty and look up. Somehow, he's already standing beside me, and I never even saw him move. He looks down at me until I rise, too. Guess I am going.

"Won't be needing that gun," Bal says.

Embarrassed that he even knows about it, I do not take it out, but I reach behind me to touch the cold metal there in my waistband and I run inside the shack, feeling stupid.

Some killer I am. Never even fired it.

Eventually, I hide the thing between the mulch bags of my walls and come back out to find him waiting on me. We walk to his Jeep, and he rummages around in the back, producing an old metal pail of what looks like putrid chicken meat and some tackle. No rod and reels, nothing else. He hands me the pail and jumps in the Jeep, and I get in beside him, holding a rising stink between my legs. I venture a look inside the bucket and wish I hadn't. Some of it is a sickly shade of green, some of it a fecal dark brown. All of it is slimy and shining and jiggling. I'm not sure I want any fish that eats this, but then I remember that I like to eat catfish, the buzzard of the lakes, and so hold my tongue.

We drive only to the other side of the club and pull through the gates of a solid fence wall right on the edge of Lake Como. Inside, just a gravel lot, but all kinds of small boats are stored here, haphazardly. Bal parks between two ski boats on rusty trailers and stops the engine, getting out quickly.

"You've got a motor boat?"

Bal considers the sleek looking craft.

"Nah, useless," he says. "Just hiding the Jeep."

Now Bal pulls out some thin corded rope on a spool, a scratched and yellowed plastic box of hooks. He starts walking back towards the entrance. I stand there a second looking at the two boats, kind of hoping that one of these really is his. He keeps walking. I snatch up my bucket of putrescence and hustle after him. He walks so fast I have to break into a jog just to catch up to him; the meat in the bucket oozes around as I jog, nearly sloshing out.

"Hey, man, slow down," I call to Bal.

But he just turns his head enough for me to see him put his index finger to his lips for quiet and keeps on moving. We cross the short Lake Como causeway and walk up another gravel drive. This one brings us into a big parking lot, also entirely invisible from the road, but because it's hidden in the long grasses and salt cedars, not because it's fenced.

Seems to be some kind of service lot for the State Park.

Bal moves, if anything, even faster through this lot and plunges directly into the grasses and shrubs on the other side, wading through them almost silently. I crash after him, getting a sinking feeling that we're not supposed to be here. We come to a road. Bal squats down in the grass beside it and uses a hand signal for me to do the same. In the dusk, I see the receding taillights of a green pickup, a State Park vehicle. I look down the road and see a sign for the State Park road. I grin over at Bal and whisper to him.

"We wouldn't be fishing illegally tonight, now would we?"

Bal turns his head slightly, gives me the briefest of winks, and then dashes across the road, right into the underbrush. It swallows him whole. I plunge in after him, becoming worried that I'll lose him altogether, and I almost do lose him. But here in the cover of grass, like some animal, he's crouched to wait on me. We continue on, creeping through the heavy grasses and over increasingly wet ground deep into a thicket. Finally, we come to a halt and I see a glistening tongue of darkness through the vegetation; it is the brown water of a narrow bayou hidden among the reeds.

"Where the hell are we?"

"Butterowe Bayou. Goes out to the bay. Some good fish in here."

Bal puts his tackle down and moves quickly to uncover from the brown and broken grass an old fiberglass canoe, stained and dirty as the muck itself. So concealed was the boat that I never would've seen it—even standing right beside it in broad daylight. Now he's got his stuff in it, and he's already got it in the water. Bal shows me the front of the boat with a hand.

"Ladies first," Bal says, quietly, smiling evilly.

"Yeah, right."

The pail, the paddle, sitting down in the narrow seat all at once: it's hard not to tump the damn thing right over. I remember that I really hate canoes. I'm sitting here like a weeble-wobble, and I think of bailing out of this enterprise while I'm still ahead. But, before I can back out, Bal is in the boat, and in a heartbeat he has expertly pushed us off and started paddling in smooth quiet strokes.

We haven't gone far when he backpaddles softly, stops the boat, reaches down in the water, and pulls up a trotline from the murky brown waters. I pivot in my seat unsteadily to face him. The canoe teeters crazily in the water at my movement, but Bal isn't bothered by it.

"Bait," he says, holding out a hand.

I pass him the bucket, clinging to the gunwale with my one free hand. He puts the bucket between his feet, squats on his haunches and runs the line deftly, pulling cord up from the depths hand over hand. He reaches the first of the clamps, and the drop-line comes into view, magnified strangely and at odd angles in the water. For a moment the line is loose, then it jerks back down with a snap. Bal holds firmly, and labors at wrenching up the drop-line slowly. He's got something for sure. I catch my breath, craning my neck perilously out over the water, hoping to see some monster fish, some fabled leviathan.

It's about a five pound catfish.

Whiskers trailing back, wide mouth agape, dark curious eyes, and smooth skin glistening silver and black in the rising moon, the fish comes straight up. It is watching us. Bal lifts its shovel shaped head just out of the water. The fish opens and closes its mouth, talking to us in a strange barking and clicking language and looking like some wizened piscine Chinaman, lecturing us harshly. But the philosopher catfish can't get his point across, and whatever advice he might impart is lost forever, because Bal quickly unhooks it with a pair of pliers and releases it skillfully, never touching it. The catfish drops like a stone, spiraling down tail first and talking to us in a mute dialogue all the way out of sight. We're silent for a moment, both of us still watching the spot where it uttered its last words.

"Hate it when they do that," Bal says.

He's peering even more closely into the spot where he released the fish, as if he might follow it down himself. A ray of moonlight illuminates him strangely.

"That one had somethin' to say."

"What was he saying?" I ask, jokingly bemused.

Bal turns his head towards me, looks at me hard, and studies me seriously.

"He talked about you."

The smile fades from my face.

"About me?"

Bal nods yes, still stone-faced and deadly serious.

"Well," I say, getting nervous now, "what'd he tell you?"

"Catfish say: swim your own path, little hatchling, or you come to bad end."

I stare at him, and something like a half-smile twitches into his passive face.

I grin. "That was wrong. You had me going there."

Bal shakes his head.

"He also says: thanks for the chicken."

I can't help it; I bust out laughing and throw a piece of rancid chicken at him. He ducks it easily, and it splats in the water behind him.

"Okay, okay," Bal says, holding up his hands in peace.

Bal re-baits the hook now and moves on already.

"Quiet now or Rangerman will come get you."

I settle down and watch him working his way down the line again, his hand-over-hand technique grooved into machine rhythm. "That was a pretty good catfish, why'd you let him go, anyway?"

"Hardhead," Bal answers as he works his way down the line hand over hand, "they got a nasty taste."

"What's a catfish doing in this saltwater anyway?"

"It's brackish," Bal corrects, re-baiting an empty hook. "We get all kinds of catfish here: Blues, channels, muds, sailcats, hardheads."

I watch him silently again, ashamed not to know of the existence of these fish. Presently he comes to another taut leader. A big one, maybe twenty pounds, maybe more, but this time it fights like a maniac, doing a strange death-roll and twist that I have never seen any fish do before; then it cuts sharply just below the surface and flares a dorsal sail fin, like some miniature marlin imitator.

"Whoa, what the hell's that?"

"Sailcat," Bal answers, not pausing.

He heaves the thrashing fish out of the water, grabs it by the mouth, snaps out the hook, and tosses the big silver-bellied fish in the bottom of the boat where it writhes grotesquely in its own shining slime, craps all over the place, and flares its sail as if it would fly out of here.

"That thing is sick." I can't take my eyes from it. I'm mesmerized.

Bal watches it thoughtfully. He says, "watch those fins. Needle-sharp. Poisonous."

And just as the words are out of Bal's mouth, the catfish flops over on its belly, sticks its sail fin up erectly, and goes straight for me—no matter that his medium is air and fiberglass boat and he a fish out of water—coursing like a killer whale after a seal pup. In a slowmo horror-movie sequence, I'm attacked by a barking, stabbing, shitting, slime trailing thing.

"Shit! Shit! Shit!" I panic, screaming.

Going over backwards. Legs and arms flailing. Flailing at air, at nothing. The canoe rocks crazily. Stays upright. Somehow I am still in it. Looking up through my legs. Where? How? The night sky. The moon bounces between my own dirty tennis shoes with the heaving of the canoe. I struggle to free myself.

"Stuck! I'm stuck!"

Just calm down.

But that sound again, it's coming. That barking. That watery, gurgling, horrible bark. I'm sweating profusely. The back of my head and neck are lodged painfully in the prow of the boat. Cutting into the back of my thighs is the leading edge of the front seat. Jesus, how this? Bal, what the hell? I am wedged butt down between my seat and the front of the boat. Out of my sight, coming from somewhere under my seat, the demented catfish is at it again: barking and slashing at my me with his poisonous barbs.

"Bal! Bal! Bal! Get me outta here! Get that damn thing away from me!"

I hear the loud whack of wooden paddle on fish, a soft chuckle. The barking sound stops. Bal's strong hands pull me out of my death trap and back onto my seat. I can't bring myself even to look at him. He sits now, studying me from the canoe's center bar.

Trying not to laugh, I'm sure.

What a fool, John. What a stupid moron.

I kick the stunned catfish childishly, and the fish shoots between Bal's legs on a trail of its own slime, splats against the far seat post, and comes to a rest twisted and nearly insensate. The killer's mouth gulps for water that isn't there, suffering in a slow asphyxiating death.

"Keep that thing away from me."

"You'll like him better when he's on your plate," Bal says, not unkindly.

He returns quietly and quickly to his seat and paddles us swiftly out of the bayou and out into the darkened bay. I don't even help paddle. Sulking in the front of the boat, just listening to wake being churned up by the canoe, just looking out at the blackglass bay water, the Christmas tree lights of refineries across the bay, the bottom of the boat. Trying not to act this way, but can't stop. Wanting nothing to do with any of this anymore, but not wanting to be anywhere else, either. Wanting, perhaps, to be anyone else but me.

We pull up beside the wooden docks of some darkened vacation houses on tall piers. There's a covered berth with a large powerboat in it and suspended out of the water, poised as if in mid-jump, as if ready to fly up into the yard, but it's covered with the dust and lichen of years of storage and disuse.

Bal lifts something large and rectangular a little ways out of the water. It bobs on floats made of thick black painted PVC fastened to a cage of black hog-wire. Curiosity overcomes me. I turn to see what he's doing now.

Some sort of trap.

He leans over and opens a wirecage door at the top, reaches in. With some effort, he breaks off something like rocks from inside the cage and tosses them in the boat with loud thumps. A pile of the rough oblong shapes accumulates. He doesn't look at me. He keeps working, moves to another trap, and another one, until he has many dozens of the things in the boat.

"Oysters?" I ask, finally.

"Yep."

"You're growing them?"

"Yep."

Bal rows the boat to another dock. I look up at the docks, the boats in storage, all the darkened houses, unused, nearly identical. I imagine the guys who own them.

Probably they're at a party right now in Dallas or Houston or somewhere, bragging to someone that they have a beach house on Galveston Island and a sweet boat and saying, why don't we go down there sometime and go fishing. And the other guy will say, You too? I got a three-thousand square footer on the bayside and two boats and a little Rover in the garage; why don't we have a big party down there?

They never will. I know.

"Uh, do you even know these people Bal?"

"Nope."

"Ah, I see."

I grin and grab a piling to hold the canoe steady. Another of Bal's mysteries explained. I help him lift the cage with my free hand, holding it out of the water while he harvests more oysters. And the pile grows until the boat sits low in the water and the night starts getting on, and the stars shine through the light pollution and the haze of the coast-side cities. And I am now strangely contented by this all again, just sitting silently in a dirty canoe with this strange friend of mine, this Karankawa re-incarnate.

I watch Bal working steadily, efficiently, quietly; his shirt is off now and his tattoos seem to suck in the darkness in strange black voids that move and change, as if in their movements, one might discern the future or the past or some mystic secret, if only you look hard enough, think clearly enough.

I blink.

The cross on his chest flares, burning, goes out.

The man himself is still a mystery. What is he always doing these nights? Sure, he brings a little fresh-caught fish back to the hideout at times, but nothing like the bounty in this boat. Where does it all go?

And it can't just be fishing and oystering he does. Sometimes he comes back covered in dirt and sand at two or three in the morning, hoses off outside, turns in only a couple hours sleep, and goes right back out to his course job without even looking tired or saying a word about it.

"Goin' to Grandma's now," Bal says, picking his paddle up and moving us out away from the docks.

"What? Your Grandma's?"

"Yeah, Grandma B's got us dinner."

He's got a Grandma? "Okay," I say, picking up my paddle, and putting my back into it.

We paddle around a jetty and left into a narrow straight channel between rows of beach houses, all raised up on black-tarred pilings. Many of these are actually lit-up here and in use, as if lived in permanently. Presently, we come to the end of the channel where a neighborhood boat ramp of sorts is lit by a single stark light, swarming with bugs. There are flat bottom boats and empty trailers and forgotten looking buoys tied with fraying brown rope. The place smells of salt and seaweed and old dried fish. A sign rises up on a metal post from a con-crete retaining wall. It reads: Jamaica Beach.

Bal runs the boat right up on the shore and leaps out splashing. Carefully avoid the still-alive catfish, I help Bal bring the catch up to his Grandma's house; it's illuminated by a row of strange treble hooked chandeliers supporting balls of yellowed light. The white, sprawling affair has big decks and crouches about fifteen feet up in the air on spindly wooden stilts, like some crazy giant spider.

I look up the long, broad stair of the place. It's tiled in a puzzle of stones and ceramics and there is no handrail. The whole contraption seems to sway in the dark. But somehow, Bal's signature is on the construction of the entire home.

Must be solid enough.

We come through a wood-framed screen door directly into a darkened living room. Stained glass lamps shine dimly from oaken tables. Deep red couches arranged in a U-shape face a couple of cubbyholes opening about a third of the way up a bright blue wall. I can't see into these openings; they're curtained in a dark green cloth like velour or velvet. Thick gold embroidery traces the curtains with floral and animal designs in a single long strand. I'm reminded of elaborate miniature stages for midgets or puppets.

Bal is no longer here. I'm alone in this dimly lit room. As I turn back to the doorway, I sense someone near and hesitate.

"Sit. Sit," an old woman's pleasant voice.

I turn again to see an aged and wrinkled hand beckoning me to the sofa, an old woman standing there. She smiles and waves a hand quickly.

"Grandma B?"

She's maybe in her eighties. Hard to tell. A pure black lock of her otherwise gray hair obscures one eye. In the halo of lamplight, her rich brown skin glows almost from within. Oddly, given the still fairly warm weather, she's bundled up in an assortment of colorful clothes. A dark green shawl of a material like the curtains is decorated with silver spangles of incongruent shapes; it wraps thin angular shoulders and tinkles with her movements. Under it, a harlequin shirt, pleated horizontally like ribs, and below, a thickly ruffled skirt in patchwork patterns hangs all the way to the floor, obscuring any sight of her feet. I imagine them to be bare.

"Yes, yes, have a seat, John, dear, have a seat."

Again, she waves a hand, impatient but not unkind, more like a bird. I catch the quick gleam of hypnotic dark-blue eyes, now clouding with age, and an odd feeling come over me.

Like she knows me.

I sit, open my mouth to speak, but she's already parted a glimmering curtain, moved through its doorway, and is gone. Just as quickly as she appeared. As the curtain ruffles shut, I just catch sight of a kitchen, and in it: Bal, his back to me. He works at cleaning our fish.

Five or six children come running through the kitchen curtain. Another child springs out of a curtained alcove. A glimpse of small beds. At first, the kids seem completely oblivious to my presence, as if I'm some sort of inanimate object on their couch. They whirl around the square of the sofas jumping and babbling and talking and laughing, hands and legs flying everywhere, pushing and prodding and chasing: the rustle of small dresses and t-shirts and shorts, the slapping of flip-flops; it's a twister of youth, a hurricane of island urchins.

It's hard to make them out individually, but from what I can see, they all appear to be related to Bal and his grandma. How exactly, I'd like to know.

What a wonder how very little you know of people.

Looking around through the whirlwind: photographs, everywhere. Among them hangs a big shadowbox holding a gleaming silver platter, ornate and anti-quated, its years beyond figuring. The pictures are everywhere: on the shelves, on all of the walls, set in frames on the tables. And hung within the pattern of the photographs are some sculptural objects of varying small sizes; they appear to be cut from wrinkled plates of the thinnest china in forms like the petals of a flower, or like rays of light from the sun, and rising up from those is a central cross, shaped like a sword.

As I look around me, the flock of children comes gradually to my sides, like butterflies coming to rest. One or two kids perch on the sofa beside me.

"Whatcha' doin'?" One says, a little girl.

"Just sittin' here. What're you doing?"

But she laughs and flies away again.

"Whatsyourname?" This time an olive skinned boy.

"John Fears, and you?"

"I'm Indian Joe," he says and up and whoops a war chant.

Another child now leans to the sofa by my side, legs bouncing to a chaos beat, looking up at me with recognizable blue eyes, Bal's eyes.

"You Belial's roommate?" A strange high voice, questions me.

"Belial?"

"Belial! Belial! Bal! Bal! Bal!"

He's sing-songing more strange words, now he's pogoing up and down. From nowhere, he's tackled by another boy, and the flock scatters around them, picks them up, flutters and fusses, swirls again with them.

Watching them makes me almost nauseous. I rise and part the storm of children, walking to the wall to examine the strange objects. Now I see that a figure is cut into the cross; a figure in agony, in long robes, crucified on a cross of bone, eclipsing a sun made of bone.

It's a crucifix.

But it's not carved by any human hand. Can't be.

The object makes me uneasy. It's like no religious artifact I've ever seen. I move away to inspect an old black and white picture, large and framed in gold gilt. In it, I see houses splintered like matchsticks in vast mounds, the frame ribs of some structures still standing. A church steeple with no church. An oldtimey carriage upturned, wheels spinning at the sky. The bloated corpse of a horse broken over a wood piling. A house, resting on its eaves, like some child's Lego construction cast aside. In the scene are acres of bare mud, pools of water. The detritus of floods and high wind. The remains of an unimaginable storm. In the foreground, crawling over the devastation, is a ragged line of men wielding axes and picks and shovels. The men's actions are frozen in time: the swing of an axe, the thrust of a shovel. One lifts a huge timber, but one stands still for the camera and stares straight at me through the years, accusatorily. His strength and defiance and that same penetrating unknowable gaze are captured in perfect clarity. His impatience too. He doesn't lean on his broad rusty shovel. He holds it at arm's length, the tip just touching ground, as if handing it to me. He's ready to get back to work, to repair this broken mess, to rebuild his life. He frowns in judgment of me.

You are worthless, he says. You are worthless, homeless, a destroyer. You are useless.

I look away.

You're right, Old Man, you're so right.

"John, John, John, John Fears" a girlchild chants happily at my side, slaps at my hand, skips in place. Happy, happy, joy, joy. Don't be morbid, she says with her every graceful move. And I am not.

"Who's this, what's this," I ask her pointing back at the big photograph.

"Great, great, great, great, great grandpa Belial,"

She giggles, grabs my hand, pirouettes, flinging back long dark hair, and runs off again.

"The Storm," a small boy's voice continues loudly.

The boy jumps up and comes down with all his force on both feet, making loud, wet storm noises as he does. He jumps back into the fray of kids with both feet hopping, thrashing out with his arms and spinning into the others, re-enacting total destruction.

I turn my attention back to the photograph, avoiding the man's stare. The Storm. Must be the great hurricane of 1900. Bal's family rebuilt and stayed here, is still here.

Moving down the wall, I bend to look at the other photos. There are several of Bal at various stages of his life; he's rarely captured smiling. And here's another slightly older man that could be his uncle and another person, a pretty woman.

Could be his mother.

The strange slate blue eyes grace all of them. The most recent photos hang by the kitchen doorway. Now it seems that there is just Grandma B, Bal, and these children here in this house. I look around me at the strangely magical room and the playing children, and I sense that here's where most of Bal's hard-earned dollars go.

Might these be his kids? Some of them, anyway?

"To bed. Now!"

It's the sing-song command of Grandma B. She appears right beside me, parting thick curtains to the kitchen with her curious looking hands. She looks at each and every one of the kids in turn, like she's casting a spell. And off they scatter. Startled birds running to get behind curtains, jumping into hidden beds, retreating to hidden rooms. There is the soft sound of children's muffled laughter. She looks at me now.

"Supper's ready, John, if you'd like some."

I stare a moment, almost compelled to find myself a bed and get in it.

"I would like supper, yeah. Thanks."

Grandma B steps aside, holding one curtain open, and beckons me in the kitchen. I walk into a small room, full but organized. Strange looking implements I can't identify sit on the blue-tile counters; copper pots and pans hang, ordered by size, above a deep porcelain sink. A big iron pot steams over a green gas flame; the fire blasts up from an old white and blue enameled stove like an acetylene torch.

Bal leans on his elbows on a butcher-block table, arms crossed, bemusedly watching me.

"Met the kids I hear," he says.

I look at him quickly. I can't hide from him the question in my eyes.

"Relatives," he answers quickly.

"Oh, I see," I say.

But of course I don't see. I don't understand anything about this family or about the mysterious pictures or this unusual place, right here under my nose for months. And I'm not sure I should ask. Perhaps they will tell me.

"Okay, kids, tuck in," Grandma B says as she places big blue crockery bowls in front of each of us. The bowls have designs of circles and lines worked in them in unusual patterns. Warmth, steam, the smell of seafood and broth and spices unidentifiable wash over my face. I inhale deeply and take a bite. The gumbo is delicious—a peppered savory mélange of seafood with rice and vegetables and some kind of meat resembling duck.

I hold a piece of the meat up in my spoon, grinning, and looking at Bal.

State Park too? I mouth the question at him silently.

Bal breaks out a mischievous smile, nods yes, and turns back to his food.

Guess we won't be inviting the Park Rangers to dinner.

After a steady diet of Pop-tarts, canned spaghetti, and assorted microwavable stuff, this meal is incredibly good. I down the bowl of gumbo, ask for another, not speaking while Grandma B busies herself in the kitchen. Regular meals like this would do wonders. Pushing into the third helping, my curiosity gets the better of me.

"I saw from the pictures that ya'll have lived here a real long time?"

Grandma B laughs, comes to sit at the table with us.

"Longer'n any of us remembers. Longer than's good for us. But we like it here. Belial's mother says we should've left a long time ago, like she did."

Bal looks at her sharply, gives a quick glance at me, and returns to eating with a grunt.

"Belial?" I ask, going for a safer topic. "I heard the kids use that name too. What sort of name is that?"

"Bal's real name," she smiles kindly at Bal, "it's our traditional name for the oldest boy of every generation."

"It's from a family legend," she continues, looking a tad mischievous now. "Looks like you've never heard him use that name before?"

She's enjoying telling me, and I can see by his reaction that this may be what passes for embarrassment in Bal's limited repertoire of allowable facial responses. He's acting like he's ignoring the whole topic, still slowly eating his soup, looking only into his bowl.

Maybe this is why he brought me here.

"Nah, I never heard it before tonight."

I look over at him, let my lip curl up in a half grin.

"But do tell since Belial never told me."

Bal doesn't flinch; perhaps he even smiles a little.

"Well, John," Grandma B continues, "The Tamas..." she catches my surprise and embarrassment, realizes I didn't know the last name of my own roommate, and forgives with a kind look. "...that's our family, we've been here a very long time—though we don't show up in any family histories over at the Rosenberg library."

She brushes back a dark lock and props her two brown hands tent-like on the table and pauses a moment. I know why you won't find the Tamas—or any of those men I saw in the pictures—in any official historical record. I look at her in wonder and at Bal, expecting to see bitterness, but I do not. I see persistence; or is it a bond with this place that needs no record and requires no claim? They simply are, were, will be. She doesn't have to say why there is no recorded history of the Tamas, and I'm sure she won't, and suddenly I am envious in a way that I can't quite understand, but it is there, and it is perhaps because I know it may never be like this for me, and I might never have ties like this: this belonging, this sense of place. I'll never have family like this.

"But we endure here. My Grandfather, my great-grandfather, and all those first born male ancestors, they were all named Belial."

Suddenly a flood of questions comes, and I see the man staring back at me from the photograph. "The man in the photo. He was Belial right? Why Belial? What was that storm? Was it the Hurricane of 1900? Was that right here?"

Grandma B smiles, laughing easily and lightly.

"Yes, that is my father, Belial. Yes, that was after The Storm of 1900. There have always been storms, and we've survived just about everything this little island has to give and give it does—the bad with the good."

She gets up goes over to the counter, picks something up wrapped in blue cloth, and comes back to the table, sits down.

"Now, Belial's name, that's from an old story, so old we don't know when or who it was exactly, but the legend says it is from an old Spanish Priest named Morfi. Now this Father Morfi, he was a vile one, and he hated all people who weren't his people, his Church's people. We lived here, just as we do now; living it our own way and wanting to be left alone. And Morfi and his people kept coming here thinking they knew everything, bringing their churches, and trying to save us when they couldn't even save themselves. And we said to these men of the cloth, 'you just come here and you go again and we give but we get nothing in return. We didn't ask for your religion; why don't you just go back where you came from and stay this time?'"

"But I guess that didn't happen?" I ask with irony, knowing the answer already, starting to feel ashamed for my whole race, my whole history.

Grandma B laughs.

"Oh no, no, they just kept on coming and coming, that's for sure. Still do."

She pauses, looks at me a moment with some sadness or thoughtfulness, I'm not sure which. "So, this Morfi," Grandma B continues, "he heard that a first born son of our family was coming into this world, and up he came on his big stallion, and he said this was our last chance; that if we didn't baptize that child and come into his church, we'd be damned for all eternity. Well, of course, we just laughed at him and said 'no' and told him to get on back home. But no, oh no, he didn't just go home. He got mad and flew into a rage and he cursed us and our whole family and called us all sons of Belial and damned us forever. But we just laughed again, and right then and there we said 'well, we'll just name this son of ours Belial.' And Belial it was, and Belial it still is."

She looks straight at me and unwraps an object from the blue cloth without looking down at it. It is a bone crucifix, like the ones in the living room. She opens a palm flat, rests her elbow on the table, places the thing there with her other hand, as if to examine it. I stare at it. I want to ask about what or who Belial is, but clearly she thinks I should know it. Some demon or bad character out of the Bible, I guess.

"Did Morfi leave?" I ask, still looking curiously at the object, wondering what she's doing with it. Casting a spell? Grandma B points the thing at me. Cursing me? She shakes it. It rattles oddly. Cursing the whole human race? I don't know; she looks like she could do all that, if she wants. I'm starting to get nervous.

"Well, he did leave, but not before he threw one of these at us..." Grandma B says, now lowering the object down to the table on her open palm, almost ceremoniously.

She doesn't take her blue eyes off of me.

"...And they let us be for a while, a good long while. But others came, many others." She smiles now in a disturbingly mischievous way, and looks over at Bal. "And so do our Belials, they just keep on coming too, thank goodness."

She extends the object to me, as if for me to take it. As I reach for it she shakes it and it rattles again, and I withdraw my hand quickly.

"This one has a good set of Roman dice in it; good, good."

"What is that thing?" I squirm uncomfortably; I want to see it, but I don't reach for it again.

"It's yours."

"Mine?"

"Yes, John, this one is for you."

I stare at the thing.

"What do you think it is?" Grandma B asks.

"Well? How'd you make it? Isn't it a crucifix—Jesus on the cross or something?"

"I didn't make it; Bal cut it out of your catfish, John."

"My catfish?"

She smiles, amused. "Yes, it's the skull of the sailcat you and Bal caught tonight—a nice one too. Here, take it now."

Reluctantly, I take the skull from her hand and examine it, not sure of what to say.

"If you think it's a crucifix, then that's what it is."

"Oh." I look up at her. She's still watching me. "What do you think it is?"

Bal is watching us curiously.

"Well, John..." Grandma B laughs, leans back in her chair, relaxes, "...I think it's the skull of a sailcat."

I feel the fool.

"Well, yeah, but..."

I run my thumb down the cross, a cross so much like a sword. The figure does indeed look like a robed and bearded person in great pain. I shake it.

"What's that rattle?"

"Some say it's the sound of the Roman's dice."

"Huh?"

"The resurrection story says Roman soldiers threw dice; gambling for Jesus' robe at the crucifixion."

"Oh."

I shake it again. "This sure is strange. It looks more like somebody getting skewered by a sword than a typical crucifix though."

She watches me, waiting.

"I mean this can't be coincidence can it? This can't be chance?"

She considers, then asks: "You mean you think it's the presence of the divine, John? That God would put this creature on this earth so we can hang it on our walls, keep it in our curio cabinets, and, in its death, find divine inspiration as well as meat for our table?"

"Well, I don't know." I'm distinctly uncomfortable with this topic, feeling stupid. But still. "I mean...well... maybe."

"Would it look this way to a Buddhist? A Muslim? A pre-historic native?"

I don't know. I can't answer.

"But, say," she continues, "of all the millions of animal species that have ever lived, this one, by chance, happens to look to some cultures like something resembling the crucifix in a story from the Christian Bible? What then? Wouldn't there be a pretty good chance for something like that to happen?"

"Well, yeah, I suppose there's a chance."

"It's like the old cliché isn't it? Everything is chance and nothing is chance. But chance is really what you make it, John, what you see in it. What you do with it. Some things do have power, but only if you and everybody else believe that the object has power. If you see a crucifix set here just for you, then it is a crucifix set here just for you. I won't tell you otherwise."

Bal laughs, a long deep laugh.

I've almost forgotten about him over there, so absorbed am I in this thing, these new thoughts. I look over at him, and he's smiling for once, happy.

"No, you wouldn't tell him otherwise," Bal says. "Now, would you Grandma?"

"No, no I wouldn't," she says shaking her head, joining Bal in his laughter.

Bal looks over at me, still amused.

"That's because she sells them on eBay."

# Magic and Circumstance

**O**bsession. You don't always know when you become obsessed by something— thinking about it, dreaming about it, seeing it in your waking thoughts—but sometimes you do have moments of lucidity. Lying awake in my bed rolling my crucifix over and over in my hand, feeling its smooth undulations and edges and crannies with my eyes closed, I realize that you can get so completely enamored with something that you're rendered useless on almost anything else. It's never happened to me before—not once in my life that I can remember. But it is happening to me now. And my obsession is tennis. Sure, I've played all my life, and, having done so, it is odd to be experiencing this now. But with a shot at the pros coming up in the November Challenger, tennis is all I can think about. Store windows have become mirrors for shadowing my strokes; lessons become matches with Roddick or Federer. Of late, old losses have been replayed and the mistakes corrected, over and over in my sleep. All I want to do is practice, and if no one's available, I'll even pound balls on the backboard, or hit buckets of serves for hours.

It was never like this on the high school team.

There, I'd just wasted my chance.

And it's not just this Pro Challenger—it's all of this: teaching the sport, hanging out with Bal and the Tamas, doing jobs that I've gotten for myself—free from... Yes, "free from you," I whisper to the dark. There I've said, I've said it and I'm sorry for it, but it's there. It was always there. The constant plotting and prodding. The scorn. Everything your way or no way at all.

Now, it's not.

Yes, it's a stupid sport, that's what it is. A waste of time. Your words dad, your words. And what if it is? Because it's something I'm good at. That's what it was with you, wasn't it? Something you knew nothing about. Something that makes me feel good about myself.

But not this time.

No, this is truly different from all those years before. I am obsessed; I have a direction in life, and I like it. It takes my mind away from Gloria and Adela, away from the Fear, away from all those empty places. Mostly it takes my mind off of you. It does all of that. In me now: something sustaining, something that goes beyond mere sport; something I can't define.

But I like it.


I hear Bal preparing to leave again, and I check my watch. 11:30 PM. He's just getting started. I know he won't be back until three or perhaps four in the morning, dirty and exhausted again. Suddenly I realize that I'm not the only one with an obsession.

But what is it—Adela? Why would he hide it?

The soft screech of our metal door sounds as he leaves, and I leap out of bed, dress quickly in shorts and t-shirt, put the crucifix in my pocket, and grab my keys. I feel bad, I really shouldn't intrude. Perhaps I think I can help him. Or maybe I just want to know if he goes to her; I can't bring myself to ask him.

I make it out the door just in time to see him pulling away, Jeep taillights turning on Stewart. He's taking the old way into town. Firing up the Porsche, I leave the head-lights off and follow him, keeping to the middle of the dark tongue of road. Slowly, slowly now. In the stark moonlight, Lafitte's grove stands out in sharply contrasted lunar colors. Silver and black: the ancient light of silvery dry seas. The place is somehow greater; it is menacing. Nothing of daylight's overgrown brushy patch remains. Within the strangling mass of growth, claws of spiked timber grope skyward. Palisades form. A stronghold rises. A crude brooding structure, looming. Through it: eyeholes, loopholes, in malevolent lines. Chinked in gleaming black eyes. Blackpowder muskets, gaping. Waiting, watching. Slavering wolfhounds and swarthy men with black intentions lie ready to issue forth, to tear you limb from limb, to raise your grisly head upon a pike for all to see. And be warned.

I shudder. The car coasts almost to a stop, and so compelled am I to get out, so pulled in am I by the notion of this fastness and the reality of it that I hit the brakes and start to open the door of the still-moving car.

The scene vanishes. In my head all along.

Behind a barbwire fence and a rusty gate, I notice a sandy drive to the west of the grove; its two spurs shine almost white in the moonlight.

Odd, how could I've not seen this before? Has it been here all along? And as I follow the track with my eyes, it disappears into a clump of live oaks, like the dark and ragged shape of the mouth of a cave.

And It is standing there. Him. The Monster.

I recoil, sweat rises instantly on my skin and my mouth goes dry. Tongue swelling, I can't even cry out. There is nothing to protect me from him, nothing at all. No, something. I stop the car never taking my eyes away, even more compelled to get out. To confront him. I take the gun out and put the magazine in and pull the slide back. Darker than dark within that cave mouth, filling it, discernible from the void around him only by his huge glowering presence, he watches. He's found me. Again.

Bal's taillights wink in the corner of my eye, disappearing to the east. I shake my head violently. I look to the main road and think of Bal.

I look back. He is gone. Vanished in a heartbeat.

I try to see the fort but it is gone, too. There's nothing here but weeds and bushes and trees. The sound of night insects. Bright moonlight all around. I shut the door again, and place the gun in the passenger seat, still cocked and loaded. Hit the accelerator.

Catch him up, John.

Dark road unfurls before me; I'm relieved of the grove and the strange gloomy road.

These visions, again. But, no way was He really there. No way at all.

Or is there?

Bal heads clear on into town, driving past all the old pristine mansions floating like antique islands above the glowing wastelands of grim apartments and derelict homes. Falling houses with opened doors frown and sag in the night. Naked bulbs of electric lights shine from open doors. Guys wandering around in undershirts or with no shirts at all hold baggy pants up by their own piece and drink from paper bags—beer or whiskey or God knows what. Some sit on street corners doing nothing, wasted humans all, trapped on this island of doom.

Ashamed of my own thoughts, I look around me, feeling vulnerable and nervous in my little open car.

Not as uncomfortable as you would be living in one of these places, though. Just one small hurricane is all it'd take to destroy this again, wipe it away, cleanse the island of this, this, what is there to say?

Say it John, these worthless people? These worthless, broken places? Prejudiced ass.

And what are you?

One step away.

I look in the night sky and envision the wall of the hurricane, the raging dark beast of the storm. The destruction. A towering wall of seething brown water advances. A vortex of trash and garbage and refuse, the detritus of a billion lives gone before, it sucks within the monster. The houses, the cars, and the people are completely obliterated. All is washed away in a final accounting. And who will stand to weather that storm?

"Hey!"

The storm vision snaps out of existence. The gun is in my hand and I am pointing it at another human being and my finger is on a trigger, which I am close to pulling.

"Hey Man! You got a dollar? Fifty cents? You got fifty cents?"

An emaciated dirty old white man is staggering towards my open car, one hand palm-out, the other held straight out to his side as if in the rigor mortis of death—only his hand is clenching, releasing, clenching, releasing. Grasping at phantoms. He takes no notice at all that I'm threatening to kill him, and I'm entranced by the hand, until suddenly I look at his face and see some future version of myself there. I put the weapon down quickly and it is repulsive to me and a strong desire to rid myself of it overcomes me but there is nowhere to do so, and instead, I clutch it in my lap.

The sound of men's deep laughter from a darkened porch.

"There goes old Roger," a voice says.

Another one: "Get 'em with your grabber before he blows you away, Roger, get 'em with your grabber!"

The men on the porch laugh again, entertainment served.

Shivers in my spine. Bal's taillights turn on Harborside, heading east towards the old fort. I look at the old man one more time in pity and disgust and shake my head at him. Ashamed, I shut the gun in the glove box and stomp the accelerator. Through the squeal of the tires, laughter comes from the porch again. Above the wind and accelerating engine, I just catch the jeering.

"Missed 'im Roger, missed 'im!"

"Shaddup! Shaddup! Shaddup!" The old man's shrieking voice fades away as I round the corner and look up to envision the hurricane wall again. It's almost real in the passing night clouds, and I'm sure history will repeat itself.

Doesn't it always?

But we're close now. I can feel it. We're close to that something which must be Bal's objective. Looking in all directions, there's not much going on tonight though we're near the tourist district. Dockside cranes and looming empty container ships look grim and strange juxtaposed against a shining, luxury cruise-liner. Way up, the ship's top floor is full of dancers in formal wear moving slowly round a brilliantly lit ballroom. From this distance, the dancers are made surreal, like they're all tiny tuxedoed and sequined mannequins, magically animated.

Bal's Jeep stops for a few seconds in front of a darkened lot. He's spotted me, but no. Now he starts moving again. Pulls into a side street. The red glow of brake lights switching off. He's stopped there and parked. I keep driving on Harborside and park a block further down. Looking over as I pass Bal's position, I do a double take. He's stopped by the ruins of the Maison Rouge.

Jogging the block back to the ruins with the pistol back in my pants, I'd half expected that Bal was just going to his buddy's shop near here to work off-hours on some car. To see him pulled up here by the remains at the site of Lafitte's former headquarters begins to give me a new idea. I can't believe it, but it must be. Just like him, come to think of it. Intrigued by the pirate's fort near our hideout,

I'd done some research on this place one afternoon. This is the site of Lafitte's old house in town and, for over a hundred years since his downfall, a site of intense treasure-seeker interest.

But Bal? Didn't people quit doing this years ago?

Rounding the corner, I catch site of Bal crawling under the fence. I stop in the shadow of a scrubby bush in the alley and watch him reach back to re-cover his entry hole. I'm relieved he's got an easy way into the place, but I can't say I'm too happy. Had he climbed an eight foot fence topped with barbed wire, I wouldn't have tried to follow him. I would've just gone home like my common sense is now telling me to do before I get arrested, mugged, or worse.

You've gone this far; might as well keep going.

I eye the gap under the fence, and then look back to the Maison. I hesitate again. When I'd checked this out in broad daylight, I'd been vaguely disturbed at the sight of the ruins. I'd had no inclination to go in at all. And if I'd been disturbed during daylight, at night the ruin is something much more ominous. Daytime's gray crumbling walls are at night tinged red by the gleam of distant dock lights, so that the place is re-painted with its namesake color. "Red House," the Maison Rouge: fortress, absinthe house, and place of buried treasure. Known as a haunted ruin, it was said to have been painted red by the devil and ultimately destroyed by God in a hurricane. It's probably the most legendary place on the Island, and here it is all weedy and falling down, another decaying relic of a questionable past.

You'd think they'd at least clean the damn place up.

I hesitate in the back alley, fingering the pistol in my pants. I really ought to go home. Or at least pull my gun out. Then I see the old man again and I hate myself for that thought, too, and I hate myself also for my fear of staying here alone in the darkness of my hiding spot, which is really no hiding spot at all.

You are such a loser, John. Damnit.

The sudden shattering sound of breaking glass. It's not twenty yards behind me. Deep angry voices, swearing loudly.

They're coming this way.

Run for the hole. Now. At least my mind's been made up for me. Bal's inside the fence; who knows what drunken killers are back there in the alley?

Quickly crawling under the fence and hiding in the dark of the undergrowth, I try to calm my breathing and look around me, ashamed all over again. Nearly hyperventilating. I can just make out the high arched windows of the tilting walls overlooking that gloomy weed-choked yard. A treacherous stair stands alone, and hangs there by itself with no other structure around it, as if leading up to some hidden gateway in the sky, some netherworld or some incarnation of heaven that is only blackness. Or as if, perhaps, the way to heaven is shut eternally and forever, and should I ascend those stairs, I would come to the end and meet nothing except the precipice. And should I attempt to step across it, I would fall, fall forever into the pit of eternal blackness.

No, no, no, it's just a stair, just a ruined stair.

I start to pull the weapon out again but instead I go for my pocket where I find the crucifix. I clench it and am calmed by it.

Look around you, there's nothing here. Calm down.

Where's Bal?

I can't see anything of him. Creeping cautiously forward, I stumble in an unseen hole, stagger forward, catch my feet on undergrowth that seems to reach out and grasp me. I start to fall forward. I cry out.

A strong hand clamps my mouth, catches me.

I'm dead. I'm dead. I'm dead.

Panicking, I attempt to break free, but cannot. A strong arm tightens around my chest; it's an iron vise. I struggle to free myself in a wild mindless rage, but I'm as helpless as a child as a hand reaches down beneath my waistband and disarms me expertly, and I know that I am going to die.

"Shhh."

It's the hiss of a familiar voice in my ear. Thank God, it is Bal's.

"Guys in the alley might hear us," he whispers urgently.

I relax in relief, going limp as a rag doll in his grip, and he pulls me deeper into the darkness of the yard. We wait in silence, and after the quarreling drunks have gone on their way, I start to explain how I just want to help and didn't mean to sneak after him.

"Okay, okay, it's all right," he interrupts my blather. "Mind if I hold this a while?" He holds the weapon out to me.

I shake my head, looking at the dirty thing in his hand, and he quickly drops the magazine and ejects the shell, catching it on the fly, and tucks it all neatly in his pockets.

Creeping further back into the deeper shadows of the lot, we go through a stone doorway and stop in the lee of one of the crumbling old walls. There, protected from direct view in all directions save above: a strange sight.

"Stay quiet," Bal says, as if he's anticipated the questions now burgeoning my mind.

Grandma B and Adela sit at a small blue rectangular table bedecked with several bright candles and a clear bottle of some thick green liquor flanked by two shot glasses. Spread under the carefully arranged objects on the table is what appears to be a large map. They're sitting quietly across from one another and concentrating intently, deep in the middle of some unspoken communication.

But for what?

Suddenly, they both drain their glasses. From some deep pocket in her many layers of clothes, Grandma B pulls out a large silver medallion by its gleaming silver chain. She dangles it a long while in front of Adela, spinning it ever more rapidly. Until the candlelit silver is a bright orb of light. The old woman begins murmuring in low singsong tones. Adela stares back at it until her body visibly relaxes and her dark eyes lose focus. Until she's completely mesmerized by the spinning silver coin.

What the hell?

For some reason I don't like it. I start to cry out and go to her. Bal anticipates me.

"Don't break it," he says with authority.

I don't. I just watch, tensing up even more. The metal coin dances. My skin crawls as the muttering continues, now in soft, oily tones. I look over at Bal again questioningly.

This isn't right. This is real. You have to stop.

"It's okay," he whispers. "She likes to try."

He pours me a glass of the same green liquor from a backpack he's got at his feet. I take a sip. It's pungent and strong with a medicinal odor.

"Absinthe," he whispers again, "for this place."

I try to cast him a mocking glance, as if to say: this is all so stupid. But it comes out as more of a grimace.

Is it stupid? I wonder.

And now I know what he's up to; now I know what he's been doing all those nights, dragging himself home during the wee hours of the morning, all dirty and exhausted. He's hunting for Lafitte's buried treasure. I'd read of this. Read of how people had been trying for years to find it, but no one ever has; read also of some of the techniques for divining the location—hypnotism, séances and the like. One girl even died under the chloroform-induced hypnosis of a treasure-seeking doctor. I grin now and look at my absinthe. The idea of summoning the supernatural to find buried treasure is starting to be a little bit fun now, and absinthe must taste much better than chloroform.

Cheers, I mouth the word and tip the glass to Bal before I drain it.

He allows a small smile and pours me another.

"To the old way," he whispers and drains his own glass.

I wonder if he has ever—even for one moment—doubted himself.

"To the old way," I whisper back at him, draining my second.

I decide that possibly he hasn't.

The lucky bastard.

My attention is drawn back to the women. Adela's hand, index finger extended, is now moving ever so deliberately. It's hovering over the map, seemingly guided by some strange force, certainly not her own. Her softly unfocused eyes appear to see nothing but the hypnotic, sparkling orb. Seeing her vulnerable under hypnosis like this, it's perversely exciting.

I try intently to watch only the movement of her hand, but instead I'm drawn wholly to the coin; the spinning light fills my gaze now. I feel myself drifting against my will, begin to see something like visions of a sandy windswept isle and dark inscrutable eyes searching, searching for something long lost.

No, I shake my head, you're just imagining things.

Adela's finger stabs suddenly down with the rap of bone on wood, snapping me out of it. She points to a spot on the map, and Bal zooms in to mark it with a pencil.

Good Lord Bal, X marks the spot?

But he has the smug look of a man with the faith of absolute conviction. I can't help it; I'm swept up in his excitement now, too. There's a treasure out there, and suddenly, I believe.

"Bal," I whisper urgently as I sidle up beside him to see. "Bal, what do you think? You think we'll really find something?"

He glances up at me, nods, and returns his scrutiny to the map.

"Found the Spanish silver plate like this. Found that silver coin," he nods again in the direction of Grandma B, who is now slowing the spin of the coin, murmuring kind and soothing words to bring Adela out of her trance. "It's still out there," he says, and suddenly he smiles at me and claps me on the back. "You bring good luck."

I grin like an eternally happy idiot, or a loyal dog, or Zingleman or something. I know it, but I can't help it. And I don't care, I just don't care. Luck has been in short supply.

Adela's awake now. She seems to be exhausted and maybe a little scared. She just looks down at the ground, shivering. She doesn't even seem to know I'm there. Grandma B bundles her up with an old quilt and a comforting arm, despite the fairly muggy night. They go to stand in a corner of the walls, and drink another absinthe, waiting on us.

Bal's in a sudden rush. He blows out the candles, shoves the table up against the wall, and packs up the few things in his pack.

"Let's go," he says to me, rolling up the map and clutching it fiercely.

I follow along as he hustles the women back to Grandma B's, drops them off, and then cruises right back to our hideout, where we park our cars in the usual spots. But Bal doesn't go in. He's got other plans. Quickly grabbing a couple of shovels and a grubbing hoe out of the side storage, as if he knows I'm already thinking of abandoning this enterprise, he hands me the hoe, slings his own implements over his shoulder, and lopes off toward Stewart road on foot, like a giant hound. I hesitate, looking at the hoe in my hand and take off after him, struggling to catch up in the dark. I know where he is going, and I think of the figure in the trees, and I am filled with dread.

Before long we come to the grove and turn up the entry to the two-spur dirt road I'd noticed earlier tonight. The track shines only faintly now, but I stop in doubt and fear, watching Bal climb the fence without the least hesitation.

We're not supposed to be here.

What if he really is in there?

But that's impossible, you ass.

I stand there in the dark, completely frozen, my shovel hanging loosely by my side. I can't seem to move. Bal is over the fence now. My father is before me, his frowning face remembers the past: all the times I failed him.

What are you doing here, John? He says in a conversational tone.

I'm looking for a buried treasure that no one has ever found, or ever will find.

Fantasy Land, John, he says, looking at me stonily, his lips shut tight. It's Fantasy Land. He taps his head with a finger and looks at me ironically. His head is stove in. The finger tap, tap, taps at the wound and glistening black matter crawls around its shattered edges. A hole caves in, opens up, and in the hole: pulsing neon lights in red, now in blue, blinking and clicking like strobes. A waste, he says, you're a wasted life. You're going to get caught. I am coming for you. No one else would. No one.

I see the cops, the jail cells, the grim smiles of the grim perverts. They're coming for me, a whole gang of the hopelessly damned; they are all coming for me.

"No," I say to him. "Bal would come."

I feel for the pistol in my pants, but it is not there. The crucifix is there. Or is it a guy impaled on a sword? I rub it with my thumb. Either way, the vision of my father remains. He laughs. His damn laugh is piercing; it is triumphant.

"It's back in here," Bal says, coming back out of the darkness to the sound of my voice. "No worries, c'mon."

My father runs at me. His mouth opens in a gaping lightless maw; his arms are spread in a cold embrace. He passes through me and into me and cold chills tremble in my skin and he begins to pull me into his darkness from within.

But then a warm breeze catches my legs, and Bal gives one of his whoops, like this is the most fun thing in the whole world, and the trees seem like trees, not the entrance to an otherworld, and the thought of adventure seems just that like that—a harmless adventure. I am released and the vision passes as if it was never there at all. I grin shakily and step forward.

"Let's go," I say, "I'm ready. Lead the way, Cap'n."

Bal turns and melts into the darkness and I clamber after him into the impenetrable black. Shoving through the brush, I find I can see after all. The moon is still bright, and the silver light shows me Bal's path. Wish I'd worn jeans. Sawgrass, brambles, and other grasping things tear unmercifully at my bare arms and exposed legs. Think of what the ladies in my lessons will do when they see me tomorrow, half dead from fatigue, looking like I've been caned and whipped. With mischievous smiles, they'll talk amongst themselves in half-whispers and small giggles.

What does that John Fears get up to at night?

They'll whisper it to each other with hands over their mouths, and they'll look me up and down. Maybe one or two will smile, walk slowly away, look back at me over a shoulder in a fleetingly playful way. And I'll just smile back and be coy and let them use their imagination. Maybe Gloria will be there, too. Maybe she'll be back.

Bal stops and thrusts his shovel in the ground with one hand. It stands upright there, quivering. He consults his map one last time by the light of his shielded flashlight and drops it to the ground.

"Here we go," Bal says, and takes the hoe from me.

Bal's already clearing brush with the grubbing hoe, and in the stray beams of the light on the ground, I can make out the remnants of other trenches and pits, now overgrown. My hope sinks. "This isn't the first time someone's dug here, Bal."

"No kidding," he says.

And without a word more, he starts digging. By hand motions he indicates where I should do so as well.

The work is as back-breaking as anything I've ever done—maybe more. It's dark and dirty, but at least it's a little cooler here. I discover that DeVaca's mosquitoes have not left us—no, not at all. They've all come to live right here. There are millions of them, big ones, biting, biting, biting all the time and buzzing in my ear until I'm nearly driven insane by the sound of it.

An interminably long time. The sounds of mosquitoes and frantic digging, and Bal never seems to tire. I wonder how he can possibly do this all night long and then go right back to digging and planting the golf course on just a couple hours rest. Just watching him is exhausting. But I find he's as meticulous as any archaeologist and completely focused.

We work on. I constantly look up for the dawn, but it's still a long ways away. I have no hope that we'll find anything at all, nothing except sand, mud, billions of mosquitoes.

Our new trench is at least four feet deep, three feet wide, ten feet long. It's bisected at forty-five degree angles by smaller test trenches. Looking at the new excavations, I'm ashamed to note that I've only been able to do about a third of it. Bal doesn't seem to notice. But just when I think I'm about to completely lose it, Bal begins to talk to me. In low grunting tones while we work, he lets me in on the magnitude of his obsession.

"Been digging these areas for ten years now. Dug all over the island. Dug the Maison Rouge. Even got my scuba certification to work parts of the bay."

I stop and stare at him.

"Ten years? You've been doing this for ten years?" Incredible. How can he keep doing this when he finds nothing?

"Off and on," he nods. "Every other weekend or so. Sometimes weeknights. When I get a good feeling."

Man, you are one motivated son of a gun. I'm having trouble with just this one night.

"Do you have a good feeling now?"

He looks up at me briefly, nods.

"Yeah. Though I've been here before. Me and everyone else for the last hundred years."

"You've dug this before, and you're digging it again?"

"Yeah, several times," he says, and stops digging for a moment and sweeps the site with the beam of his flashlight. "Lafitte's stash's always been rumored to be here at the site of the old fort. This is exactly where the three oaks grove used to stand." His beam comes to rest at the center of our new trench. "Surprising how often she turns this spot up."

I guess he's referring to Adela, or maybe Grandma B. I wonder how many different people they've hypnotized, and then decide I don't want to know.

"I can't believe you keep coming back."

Then I think of the weird séance, or whatever it was, back at the Maison Rouge, and wonder if he really does believe in that stuff. What was it really? Was is it real and not just some cheap magic trick? Bal doesn't say anything, but he knows what I'm thinking. He waits for me to ask him about it. In the dark, I can feel the scrutiny of his eyes.

"Bal, you... you believe in that... all that junk?"

And I flinch at my own choice of words, knowing it's degrading to Bal. Who am I to be questioning someone else's fantasies? And I think, too, back to my own excitement and my own visions, and remember how I had so easily believed. I actually believed. But now I'm tired, and filthy, and this all seems like the futile pursuit of a superstitious hoax.

"Yeah," Bal says. I can't see him, but I know he shrugs. He resumes his digging, "it's as good a way as any to find the loot. The box may have decayed, the stuff inside might've scattered. This sand, maybe it shifted. Something like this would be easy to miss even if you've got the right spot."

Leaning there against my shovel, I stop to catch my breath again and just listen. Bal continues his story. He found the silver platter very near the spot he's digging right now. Grandma B's silver coin came from beneath the Maison Rouge, exactly where they'd placed the table tonight. There used to be a cabbage farm here, Bal tells me too. The farmer found a few coins one time, back in the fifties. Something is still out here, he is totally convinced. This is the most I've ever heard him speak, the most excited I've ever seen him.

"Dad used to think it was here," Bal says, catches himself, stops speaking.

What did he just say? He's never mentioned anything about his mother or father, not a thing, not a word. I hesitate, decide to go on and ask it.

"You mean your Dad used to look for the treasure too?"

Bal stops digging, almost in mid stroke, and he pauses a long moment. He starts digging again. "Yeah," he says, "yeah, Dad used to look for it."

"Oh..." I grope for words, unsurely. "Did he give up?"

The briefest pause in Bal's digging.

"Yeah, he gave up. He gave up on all of us, if that's what you're asking."

"What happened?"

"Divorce. He just... drifted." He pauses, goes on. "He left the island, got ambitious, got a new life. He's somewhere in the Northeast now."

"And the kids? Are they...?"

"Yeah, they're all his... different women." Bal digs a while longer, slowly, almost lazily for a change. "Mom couldn't handle it. She couldn't stand them all, seeing them all like that."

I can say nothing. For a long while there is only the sound of his shovel, but I can feel his bitterness and sadness, feel it with every bite of his shovel and with his every movement, like an aura around him that I'd never understood until now.

Maybe I've understood it all along.

"She's dead now." He hesitates, and I know what he will say next. Know it in my bones and in every part of me, and I don't want him to say it. "Killed herself a few years back."

He says it, not with the sound of pity or anger or any emotion I expected, but with the sound of relief. And I realize that, in me, he has confided one of his great secrets.

To me, of all people.

"My Dad... he's dead, too. I..." but I can't say it. I can't go that far. Instead: "Yeah, I know how you feel. I think I knew about her. Somehow. I'm sorry. I'm so sorry."

Bal says nothing. His shovel bites deeply.

I renew my digging now too, losing myself in the sound of our work. In the blankness of my mind, I feel in some small corner the spark of a new determination. I feel it there, nurture it. Quiet and strong and enduring. The mosquitoes still bite and the sweat still pours off me and sticks my clothes to me; it makes mini-rivulets of mud streaking down my limbs. But now it is all somehow inconsequential—of no matter at all—and there is only the thrust of the shovel and the fierce expectation of hearing the ring of my steel on old iron. The sound of lost treasure, found.

I think of my Dad again briefly, my own mother in her vacuous life, and there is the feeling of loss or anger, some irreconcilable confusion of emotion.

I don't know.

I think of Bal's mother now, and I see her happiness caught in one of the pictures, and that image fills my mind as a vision of beauty and suffering unimaginable. We dig on in silence. And I just don't know now. I'm not sure. Not about anything.

# TALISMAN

It's long past four in the morning. My determination's still there, but my strength is flagging. Through my weariness, I envision the sun coming up to show us the true folly of what we're doing. Bal seems to expect this failure though.

"Quitting time," he says.

They're his first words in an hour. I groan in relief but also in disappointment.

"But we've found nothing."

"The nature of the beast," he says.

I can't clearly see his expression. He doesn't sound the least bit dejected as he makes ready to go. We survey the work a bit in the beam of his flashlight; it's impressive. A whole team of grad school students couldn't have done this in a week. But we haven't struck so much as a rusty old nail—just roots and sand and dirt. I'm sick to death of roots and dirt, I know that for sure. Ground water is already seeping into our fresh trenches, and I wonder that any metal could survive nearly two-hundred years of this without completely corroding away—even Spanish silver in an iron clad chest. It all seems like a hopeless endeavor. But maybe that's the point. And Bal is, incredibly to me, happier. And somehow, I am too.

One thing's for sure, though. I will sleep well. Back at the shack, I barely manage to hose off and get into bed. Thank God I've got no lessons until noon.

I wake to the sound of men in the storeroom, and look at my watch—only a few hours of solid sleep. I can barely move. A bone-tiredness of the like I've never felt clamps me to my bed. Bal's already up and gone to work. I force myself to stand and look myself over.

How does he keep doing this?

As I'd feared, I look the worse for wear. Angry red welts cover my legs and arms, there are some slashes, too. It looks like someone's whipped me and punctured me with a thousand dull needles. I feel awful, but I drag myself up and dress. I find Bal has hidden my unloaded gun under my clothes. I hide it away and stumble over to the club.

What else can I do?

Zingleman sees me. He stops dead in his tracks; his mouth's open but he's unable to speak. His hair shines and bobs with the furiousness of his thinking. Adela's sitting there to witness the scene, and she suppresses a giggle. She casts me a sweet smile. She knows what I've been doing, and my pride swells. Where a moment before I had been cursing the morning, now I see myself as a heroic, tireless, Indiana Jones doing battle with elemental and mystical forces. I straighten my back. All it took was one little look from her. Then I feel like a toad.

Stop it, you idiot. Think of Bal.

Zingleman recovers himself without saying anything about my appearance, although I can tell he strongly disapproves.

Too bad for you, Zingleman.

He tells me that my lessons have been cancelled both for today and for the rest of this week since they're upgrading the courts to host the Challenger coming up next month. I'm overjoyed at the news. Not just because I can go back to bed now, but because I'd forgotten somehow.

Of course. The Challenger.

All feelings of weariness and thoughts of treasure and past failures are long gone. Yes, the Tournament. How could I've forgotten? It's coming here, to our very own club, for the first time. I have to find a way to play. I have to.

"Oh man, I forgot about that," I call to a retreating Zingleman. He stops, turns back to me. "It'd be awesome to play in it. I'd like to try it." I can barely sound casual. I don't know why I'm even suggesting this to him. What could he do about it anyway?

Zingleman nods and smiles enthusiastically.

"I'm sure you'd win it all!" he says.

Pandering fool.

I can never tell when he's actually sincere. He comes back over, claps me squarely on one of the long painful scratches on my back. "You should play, of course," he says. "It'd be great for our members to see the local hero win it all!"

"Nah, no way," I hedge, "no way could I even get in." Then I remember that I'm supposed to be John Fears, former pro. "I mean, I haven't played a tournament in so long, I'd have to win the qualifying first, and even so, getting into the main draw on my first go would be a good start. But to win it all, from the qualies? Not a chance."

Actually, considering it's really me, it'd be the most stupendous miracle ever. Look around you. Adela is beaming at me and believing in me. Zingleman is frozen in a clown-mask smile, waiting for me to speak again, hoping I will bolster his belief that he has a pro on his staff worthy of the tour, worthy of his tournament. They do believe. I take heart again.

"Well... but still. You never know. You just never know. Maybe I could at least make it into the main draw. I will try."

I look up at Adela, and she smiles even brighter. Zingleman claps me painfully on the back again. "Of course you can, John! Of course you can!"

He scurries off to his office; I watch his door close, and with it some of my confidence.

Oh what the hell does he know, anyway?

But I glance back at Adela again, and anything seems possible in the light of her radiant smile. With nothing else to do, I fairly skip back towards our hideout, all traces of weariness gone, envisioning glory: my triumph to come, every one of my strokes perfectly hit, the dejected faces of my fallen opponents, the adulation of the crowd. I even start working the words out to my victory speech—the quick modest speech of the local underdog hero who upset all the pros.

"Thanks. Thanks. Really, really; many thanks," I stop to tell the row of palms, quieting their cheering with my hands. "Really, my win here is just a bit of luck, and my opponent had an off day. But hard work and self-confidence is what it really takes to win this title. Hard work above all. You can do anything,

anything at all if you work at it hard enough and believe in yourself enough—even win as great a tournament as this."

It's an awesomely stupid speech.

Gracious. Humble. Stupid.

Federer might be able to pull that off, somehow, but not me.

I spy Bal, by himself, working with some large equipment back in the southeast corner of the golf course. He doesn't seem too happy about it, though his emotions are always hard to read. I stop myself and remember last night, feeling guilty now to see him, working there all alone. I jog over to him. He's got his backhoe rigged with some sort of giant four-pronged claw that holds a full sized palm tree in its pincer grips. It looks like he's already planted two more trees, but he's struggling a bit with this third one.

"Planting a palm?"

It's a question that obviously doesn't need answering, and he doesn't bother to even look at me, really. He just hands me a shovel.

"Ground crew's off working with the tennis courts."

Here he shoots me a somewhat accusatory look, I think. As if it's my fault that his crew's off wasting time with a tennis court, instead of manicuring the golf course as usual. I don't feel bad about that, though. The courts could use some work.

What I can't believe is this: fewer than eight hours after digging enough dirt for an entire lifetime, I'm digging again. I'm not going to complain, I'm not, but Bal is very particular about the holes he digs for trees, which is maddening to me still.

Somewhere, after the better part of an hour, the hole's now five foot deep, and I'm down at the very bottom cleaning out some debris.

Jesus Bal, I'm almost six feet under here.

Finally, Bal climbs back into the backhoe to position the tree while I do the final clean-up and shaping work. I make a last, exasperated thrust of the shovel at the very bottom of the hole. It hits something hard; I hear the sound of cracking ceramic.

Crap, crap, crap. That's just my luck. "Perfect! That's just perfect, John!" I'm whining now. I know it. "Bal," I call up to him, "I probably cracked a damn sewage pipe!"

Bal's down in the hole in a flash. "Shouldn't be one down here," he says, peering intently at the dirt where my shovel hit. "Dig it out some more—carefully."

I dig around some more. The cracked thing turns out to be a lid to a container. It's a brown ceramic disk, flat like a plate, and sealed with wax, blackened from age and a wet burial. I dig deeper around the sides of the vessel. It's some sort of huge amphora-shaped pot.

Just judging from the shape of the top of the thing, it'd be about four feet tall. We're both down on our knees now, digging with our hands. There's a large chunk broken out where my shovel hit home. I clean out the dirt with my finger. The noon sun slides out from behind a passing cloud, illuminating the hole. Through the crack, the light reveals the unmistakable tarnished glint of ancient silver.

The treasure.

We just stand there and look at the semi-excavated vessel for some time. There seems to be something of a forlorn look on Bal's face which I can't read. I expect to be incredibly overjoyed myself, but find that I don't quite know what to do. In the absence of his joy, a disquieting feeling now grows inside of me. Maybe Bal doesn't know what to do either. Maybe he never actually expected to find it. Not ever. Maybe it was the pursuit of the thing that mattered. The idea of the treasure. Or the thought of his father, his mother, certainly. Finding it is like finding them, knowing them, who he is; why she did what she did.

But what do I really know about another guy anyway?

Another cloud covers the sun. We're left with the view of a big cracked pot in a deep muddy hole. The feeling in me hardens, becomes more defined. It's the inexplicably sad feeling of loss, and now I understand. We have to bury this again, bury it in a spot where it will never be found and no one will ever know. Except us. This is to be a private commemoration, a monument to sacrifice and belief and memory.

"You found it," Bal says finally, reluctantly it seems.

It takes me a moment to realize what he means. I stare at him, but he's not looking back at me.

No, that's not the point Bal, that's not the point.

Suddenly, I envision removing the treasure and polishing it into a pile of gleaming silver. Ashamedly, I can see myself showing it off. I can hear myself saying: See what I found! See what I did! I think of taking the calls from the newspapers. Easily, I can imagine the interviews, the questions, the electric reaction around Galveston and all of Texas when the articles come out. We'll be crawling with tourists and academics and looters, too, and the long dormant mystery, the legend of the treasure that is now Bal's treasure, would be gone, trampled beneath the soles of thousands of strangers' feet.

And there's this, too: I'll be seen. Everywhere.

I look at Bal again then. He's squatting now, still just staring down at the treasure, lost in thought. He's unable to bring himself to touch the thing he's been looking for his entire life.

Think about that: an entire lifetime.

"No," I say. "You dug the hole. You... you've been looking for it for years. You found it. I just put in the final shovel." I hesitate again. Now it's my turn to be reluctant, though I hate myself for not wanting to say it. Finally, I get the last of it out. "Take it. It's yours. I stay out of this."

We look at each other for a while, each searching the other's face. And in Bal's face, I now see pride and fulfillment, and his pride is not only his own. It is pride for me, too. He is proud of me, and I am overcome by a quick joy I've never experienced, a foolish childish joy, and I don't care this time what others think. I grin like an idiot. Finally we nod at one other. We've come to a silent understanding. We each bend down to the treasure, and each of us takes a single coin. Not looking at it now, almost afraid to, we pocket the coins without a word. A sudden sad inspiration comes to me and I take my crucifix out and place it in the amphora. Bal looks at me quizzically.

"Live by the sword, die by the cross," I say, looking at the white bone object lying there, like some relic of lost ages itself.

"That's not how the saying goes."

"I know. It just seems appropriate somehow. Besides, well, maybe it'll help guard it or something." But what I don't say as I stand there looking at the odd crucifix is that this is for our fathers Bal, and our mothers, too. This is their burden. This is their grave. Thinking this threatens to bring tears to my eyes and, embarrassed, I turn away to put a dirty sleeve to my face, wiping mud and salt and sweat.

I will not cry for him. I will not.

Bal watches me for a while. I can feel it, but he says nothing. He seems to understand. He nods and climbs slowly out of the hole while I bend down and put the cracked pieces of ceramic back on the pot as best I can. I fill in dirt around the amphora with my shovel, climb out and stand off to the side to watch. Bal fires up the backhoe, raises the palm's root ball up high. With a smooth, quick motion, he sets the palm tree straight down in the hole while I fill in the edges with dirt. He releases the pincers and removes the metal claw. There's the sucking noise of displaced sodden earth. He comes down to help me with the rest. The job done, we stand there looking at the place in a reverential silence. Three palms mark the spot, and no one else will ever know.

In the next days, were it not for the silver constantly in my hand, the whole thing would have seemed a dream. I shine my big coin to a fine silvery sheen every few hours. The thing is beautiful and gleaming and perfect. I never tire of looking at it. As the days progress, Bal and I take to sitting in our lawn chairs in the evenings with our coins in our pockets, drinking a couple of beers and watching the three palms silhouette into the westering sun. Though we never actually speak of the treasure, it's clearly on our minds. Of all the living people in the world, only we know where it is, and it's satisfying to me to know that we'll be forever linked by this knowledge, this event.

It may be my imagination, for we never speak of this either, but Bal seems more contented now. He still disappears on occasion at night without a word, but I think I know where he goes, and I'm not inclined to follow. I can't bear to even think about that, though I'm glad for him, I am. He's got the air of a guy whose life's work is complete, as if he's accomplished his wildest dream, and now he's savoring this success, drinking it like a wine. He's even more confident, if that's possible, and the knowledge of our secret sits on him well, adding to his mysterious air.

I wonder. Will he find something else to go after—some other unattainable goal to strive for? I think he'd make an awesome archaeologist but I doubt he'll do something like that.

For my part, I'm not done. Not at all. I feel like I'm just beginning. I have a new confidence. I know what hard work is; I understand the achievement of a nearly impossible goal. After all, I'd helped attain one, if only in a small way. For me, the ancient silver coin becomes a good luck charm embodying all my hopes and dreams. What before was nothing more than a brief vision now seems certain.

I can win this Challenger.

Sitting there with my coin, drinking my beer, I feel like I've got it all figured out. For what is a charm after all, if not the manifestation of all your hopes and dreams? What I didn't understand before from Grandma B's words is that you have to create such an object. You have to pour yourself into it. Say a charm gives you strength, or gives you some power over someone. Well, you don't just grab hold of the thing and assume heroic strength. No, you grab hold of that rock, or coin, or whatever scrap it happens to be, and you focus on making yourself stronger. You've got to focus on it, believe in it, and make it a part of you. A true charm only represents your own abilities.

So I palm my silver good-luck charm, feeling the timeworn rounded edges of the heavy coin. I keep it with me constantly, either in my pocket or my bag. I dream of the Challenger. I'm working hard. I'm feeling better and better about my game—hitting balls every day, playing anyone and everyone I can, learning about my game even as I teach others. I wish I had more than a month to prepare, but I think it will be enough. I'll have to play against the toughest players I've ever faced. Even the qualifier will be filled with former world-ranked juniors and collegiate All-Americans. But it's just a few matches, that's all. Just a few matches, and the coin shows me the way. It's a risk I have to take.

# CHALLENGER

Zingleman asks to see me about the tournament. The message is relayed through Adela with excitement visible on her face. She knows, but she doesn't tell me what he wants. As I approach his office, I'm crazy with suspense. What could he possibly do? I try not to get my hopes up. Probably, he's just going to tell me that I can't play because I can't take off from teaching. I'd requested the tournament days off immediately upon hearing that lessons might continue at public courts in the city. I wonder if I'll have the nerve to tell him that I'll quit if he doesn't allow the vacation. I finger the talisman in my pocket as I knock on the door. He lets me in, bubbly and happy as ever. My optimism improves. Still, I'm cautious, waiting for the disappointment I know is coming, always comes.

Hell, Zingleman would look happy if he told you your dog just died. His happiness now doesn't mean anything.

Surprisingly, he gets up, comes around the desk, and man-hugs me before I can even sit down.

"You've been granted a wildcard!"

He holds me at arm's length now and beams up at me. I stand there, not comprehending for a moment. "What?"

"The Challenger, John, you've been granted a wildcard in the Galveston Challenger."

He laughs deliriously. Surely he's not serious. It's too good to be true.

"Seriously?" I say, still unbelieving. "A wildcard? Right in the main draw? You gotta' be kidding me."

"Nope, I'm not. Not, not, not!" He beams a megawatt smile.

"The tournament organizers told me I could award a local player with a spot, and I gave it to you. You're in the main draw! Congratulations, John! No need to tell you that you can have those days off, too."

I don't know what to say. I clinch my coin hard enough to leave scratch marks.

Damn thing works. It works, works, works.

The Court of my vision swims into view before me, the ball frozen in time again. I make the shot—just like I always make the shot. I see the defeated look of my opponent. I can almost feel the real tears of joy dripping onto the hot court and evaporating into the clear blue of the heavens, the witness of my great victory. It all seems possible now. I hug Zingleman quickly. Turn away now. Real tears are coming. I run from the room.

That very afternoon I step up my training to an even higher level, playing longer, harder, and with more focus. I arrange for two-a-day practices. Between lessons, I hit serves and run line drills by the dozen.

Tonight, tired but still exhilarated, I'm using a computer at the club to research the other players. Rising new stars, fading older greats; they'll all be here. The total prize money is only fifty-thousand dollars, but that's big for a satellite tournament. Enough, I see, for some of the top two-hundred pros to show up. Among them are all sorts of international playing sharks, hunting for the points and the dollars to play one more tournament, to qualify for one more tour-level event. Looking at the bios on the ATP web site, I'm amazed at who's entered. One guy was ranked in the top fifty in the world only a couple of years ago. Another is the number four junior in the nation. Two of them are former Division I champions.

My God, these guys are all great players—every single one a star where they're from. And they're coming from all over: The Czech Republic, Switzerland, Germany, Sweden—everywhere. Surprisingly, I'm the only Texan. The bios are fascinating and horrifying at the same time. Looking at the screen, I come to a new realization: a few of these guys will make it into a Grand Slam this year, but most of them will never make it on the tour at all. Probably none of them will ever win a major championship or even a minor tour level tournament, for that matter. I click through records and records of results. Some of these guys play qualifier after qualifier, occasionally getting to a main draw, but seldom winning a round after that. It's a sobering and shocking discovery. Even the best players fail at this over and over again. They're forever on the periphery of being a full-fledged professional. Like the real John Fears, they come and they go with startling rapidity. One year winning most of their matches—a challenger in Memphis or Dallas, a Futures tournament in Brownsville, scattered finals here and there, maybe even winning a round or two in the US Open. But the next year there are fewer wins, fewer qualifications for too few events, and something snaps, something gives. After a few years, most of these guys simply disappear from the records all together. And once this realization hits me, I'm awed even more by the top players in the world. In tennis, there's no team, there are no owners, and no home stadium where the fans all remember you. It's just you, all alone at the top of the world. And any day, at any tournament, one of the thousands below you can rise out of these nowhere events and beat you, bringing you down.

Year after year the whole thing starts over. Without ever having lived it, I can easily envision the constant stress of trying to find courts, trying to find the very few players in the world good enough to hit with you, or even harder: finding the ones good enough to make you better. And then there's the relentless travel between cities you don't know and don't have time to see, too. But I am undeterred. I feel the touch of a deeper destiny, one to trump them all, to send me to The Tour: the realization of my vision.

I push on with my research, and the deeper I get into these players' records, the more elaborate are the fantasy games I construct for each of them. This guy Ivo, he lost in the second round in Tampa last week, and one article mentions his booming serve and two-handed backhand. If I get him in the first round, I'll adapt a defensive strategy. He's probably a choker. Or this guy Lars, who has never won a Challenger but consistently gets through the first few rounds, he's got to be a pusher. I'll have to take it to him, aggressively attack. And so it goes until, in my mind, I know how I will play each of these guys, if I draw them. I prepare for them the only way I can without actual professional experiences to go on.

And each time I begin to doubt myself, I grip my talisman tightly. It feels good in my hand. I think regretfully of the near miss I'd had at State, and all the work that I'm doing now. This time it will be different. It has to be different. I'll make it so. Pulling out my coin, I put it on the desk. It glints even in this dim light. On the back it says PLVS VLTRA.

Further Beyond.

It is King Charles of Spain's own motto; I looked it up soon after we found it, and I'd felt even more that it was a sign of destiny. I examine it. This thing was old even when Lafitte's men stole it. I look closely at the Pillars of Hercules and the Spanish Coat of Arms still visible on either side of the coin. This thing is practically priceless. A twinge of regret comes over me.

We left a fortune under those palm trees. A damn fortune.

I spin the coin, watching it, remembering Adela under the hypnosis of another coin just like this. Further Beyond indeed, John. It means take risks and go further beyond, outside your comfort zone.

Well, here we are.

Nobody from my school has ever made it in the pros, even though we were one of the best in the State. Coach Ward was all about 'win now' and, hell, I was only a child. He didn't care about developing my game. The coin comes to rest, shows the motto again. A thought: we played for the glory of the school. I laugh.

Yeah, right.

For the most part, the rest of the school hadn't even cared about the sport. They were all about football, even though that team was terrible. My parents never came to my matches, and I'm not sure Mom even knew I was on the team. But I remember Gloria coming, once or twice. She tried to hide herself, but I knew she was there. And I did play better.

Another flick of the silver coin turns it back into a shining orb, weaving across the desk, like it has some purpose, as if it travels some path known only to itself. The coin comes to rest again, shows PLVS VLTRA again.

Wonder if this thing is weighted like that?

This time the tennis is different though, isn't it? I'm IN. Me, in a pro tournament, and of my own doing, because I'd wanted to. For the first time, I'm doing something on my own terms. Practicing because I want to, and teaching because I'm good at it. Here's the chance to prove that all my imaginings aren't just that—imagination. This time all my shots will just fall, because that's what I want them to do; because I have the will to make it so.

I pocket the coin and make my way back to the hideout alone, wondering where Bal and Adela are, what they are up to. Then I try not to think about it.

An important day comes: the draw is being released. I walk the golf course on the way to the clubhouse to check it out. Some old guys are out early playing a round. I see one of them get mad and throw a club in the pond.

"Goddamnit!" He screams at the top of his lungs.

I try not to laugh, but can't help it and laugh anyway, and it feels good. I must be taking this too seriously. I've been worried—literally sick at my stomach—that I'll have to play the number one seed in the first round. He's a former top fifty player, and it'd be way too tough to start out with him. I need to work my way through the draw and build up my confidence before facing someone like him.

I get to club and see the draw at the makeshift tournament desk in the club's barroom. The tournament director from Houston is there, working on it, even now. She's older, and it looks like she's been doing this for years. Her tag reads: "Jane Smith."

"Hi, Jane," I wave a hand at her. Then I stop, wondering if she might actually remember the real John Fears.

"Hi," she replies, barely looking up at me. There's no hint of recognition. She has the weary smile of someone who knows what the next question will be, because it has already been asked a thousand times.

I ask it anyway: "Do you have the draw?"

I try to muster a casual smile, but I'm sure it comes off weak and sickly. Just how I feel.

"Sure, here it is." She smiles kindly now and turns the large sheet of paper around so I can see. One hundred and twenty eight neatly printed names, all in intricate brackets; it looks more like some corporate ledger sheet. I can hardly look at it, but can't not look at it. "What's your name, honey."

"Fears," comes my quiet, guilty response.

"Let's see," Jane says. "I remember that you're here in the top half of the draw."

She runs her finger up the page. My stomach turns.

Damnit. The top half is where they always put the number one seed.

"Ah, here we are. You play Michael Clarke, the Lucky Loser."

Her finger comes to rest on my name in the middle of the top half. Thank God, thank you, thank you. I don't have to play a seed. Still, I don't quite understand.

"What's the Lucky Loser?" I ask her.

She's surprised by my question, but answers: "The Lucky Loser is the player who lost in the finals of qualifying but who gets to play in the main draw anyway. He's like an alternate."

"Oh, I see." I think so at least.

"In this case, Lindstrom," Jane continues, "the number three seed, pulled out of the tournament due to an injury, and we gave his spot to Clarke, who lost in the finals of qualifying."

"Really? That's pretty sweet. So I was supposed to play the number three seed, and, instead, I get the guy who lost in the qualies?"

"Yes, that's right, not bad, eh?"

"It's excellent! Thanks Jane. Thanks a lot!"

"Luck of the draw, Mr. Fears, luck of the draw."

And so it is. This is too good. I walk away twiddling the coin in my pocket. I can't believe my luck. Michael Clarke? I've never even heard of him; he wasn't one of the ones I'd researched. I guess we're both lucky losers, each in our own way. Both of us get a second shot at our dreams. The medallion is cool in my pocket, reassuringly solid.

There is no way can I lose now. No way.

The day before the tournament; I try to find out something about Clarke. It's easy enough to google up stuff about him. He played number two for Illinois a couple of years ago. They're a solid team, but not a great one, I think; they're no Stanford. The ITF site shows that he was a top junior, but he never got to the top spot. At Illinois, he was an All-American who'd gotten to the quarters of the NCAA tournament two straight years—but in doubles.

Now that was something. That's pretty damn good.

I read the articles on the school's website. Apparently, he left school early to try his luck on the tour. Well, he's never won anything major, but got close. He got very, very close. This guy is good. In the pros, he's qualified for the main draw once or twice before, but hasn't yet won enough points to get automatic entries. But yes, he will do nicely, I think.

Michael Clarke, you'll just have to try again. It's my turn now. It's my chance. No way am I going to lose this match to you, bud, because I want it more. I'm prepared to die trying. I laugh. That sounds idiotic, even in my newly confident mood. Okay, I'm prepared to try really, really hard.

The day is agonizingly long. It draws on, and I'm spending most of it just sitting in front of the computer surfing the internet. I should practice, I guess, but I don't know whether to practice hard, lightly, or not at all. I want to have fresh legs, but I also want to have a good feel for the ball.

I am worthless at everything right now. I sleepwalk through my two lessons. I can't bring myself to go help Bal, although I should; just don't want to get too tired.

I'm back at the computer until one of the pro-shop guys needs it, and I let him use it reluctantly. I wander back to the shack. Still don't know what to do. Mostly I just lie on my bed, staring at the wall of mulch with a racket in my hand, dreaming of playing, wondering if Adela will come or if Bal will come. I spend an hour just flipping my medallion in my hand, over and over again. I want them all to see this match, this moment. I think of my mother and father, of Gloria. She'd have wanted to be here.

I wonder: where is she now?

The day is here, the hour is nigh, and somehow I'm not ready. I'm at the shack and worried sick I might be late. I'd gone out early to hit against the backboard and bang a few serves around the court; spent way too much time debating with myself about going over to the player's lounge to ask one of the tournament guys to hit. That's what I should've done, but decided not to.

Idiot.

I told myself I didn't want to give my game away, but deep down I know otherwise. Well, the wall did just fine.

Now, all of a sudden, it is fifteen minutes before my noon start time. I grab all four of my rackets, each re-strung last night with crisp silver synthetics, the Big Bangers. They look good. I grab five or six shirts and a few pair of spare shorts, though I don't know why. I live only five minutes from the courts. I run for it. My overloaded bag creaks rhythmically as I make my way up the familiar golf-cart path. The golfers just stare at me, annoyed.

I get there just in time to check in. Michael Clarke stands there, waiting on me. I get my first look at him. He's shorter than me by a good deal; maybe he's five-nine. He's got blond hair and a medium-to-slight frame. He doesn't carry a lot of stuff. He's not wearing any fancy gear—just a collared cotton shirt and plain nylon shorts. He could've gotten this stuff at a department store. Maybe he did. I guess he's not got any kind of clothing contract yet.

He's just standing there, almost unobtrusively, with his three rackets and a towel, as if he's a club player who's come to hit, only to discover there is this pro tournament going on.

Damnit, I've forgotten my own towel.

At least I have plenty of shirts with which to dry my hands. Michael introduces himself cordially. He seems nice enough. I'm not sure what I expected, except that I hadn't expected anyone to be nice. These satellite tournaments were known as the most cutthroat of affairs. I guess I expected him to give me no more than a curt nod while he sized me up. But, no, he seems completely unconcerned, an open and honest look on his face, unassuming.

We walk through the opening between the bleachers. Clarke is just ahead of me. These stands were erected by Bal's grounds crew just for this event. They're only five or six rows high, not too impressive really. But even this limited seating capacity seems empty. There can't be more than ten or twelve people present, and I suspect some of them are other players out scouting. I see no one I know, except for Zingleman. He's running around, speaking on his cell phone. I know a noon match between the wild card and the Lucky Loser at a first time Challenger is no newsworthy event, but somehow I expected more than this.

Wonder if Adela and Bal will show.

If there are few people in the stands, there is no one at the courtside VIP tables. These are reserved especially for corporate sponsors and richos who are willing to shell out a few thousand for a fake wood grain table and vinyl chairs hauled over from the club's restaurant storage. Thousands of dollars in corporate largesse, and they don't even show.

I don't know why I look at the names on the tables as I pass, but I do. This empty one is sponsored by some Bank. Another one by an Insurance company, another by some guy named Smith. Looking over my shoulder, I stop dead. The world spins dizzily.

One is tagged "Sharpe." A man sits there and his back is to me.

For a wild moment, I think one of my relatives is here. I run back toward the table to see. But this is no relative. Turning towards me is the specter of my Father. He pivots slowly, looking at me with that look of his again. Now he's up on his feet, and he comes towards me, and he is smiling. A big, evil smile. A triumphant smile.

He slips; he falls hard.

His head hits concrete. The sound of a smashing melon.

And he's up again in an instant. Laughing now, laughing and coming towards me, with his sprung and broken head wobbling madly. His finger raps on his own crushed head.

Tap, tap, tap, goes the finger.

I cry out and turn and sprint for the court, right past Clarke, all the way over to the opposite side. A barrier's in the way. I'm about to spring over it, but the laughter of people in the stands stops me abruptly. I look behind me, expecting pursuit, but my father is gone. Michael Clarke glances up at me strangely as he steps onto the court after me.

Look again. Look, look again.

The table is empty. The specter is gone. There are no Sharpes here. It simply cannot be. He was never there. He was never ever there.

"Five minutes," calls the umpire. I stand there still. Then I see the cameras. Filming me. On TV, this event? Didn't think of that. Never even occurred to me before. What if someone recognizes me? The cameraman sees me staring right into the lens. He twirls a finger in the air. I'm rolling, says the finger impatiently, and quit staring at the camera, you moron.

We warm up. I can barely see the ball. Sweat streams down my body. My shirt is soaked. Five minutes goes by and I cannot have hit three balls in the court. I have no idea what Clarke's game is like. What his weaknesses may be. My strategy: none. I dare not look over there again. I dare not look at the camera. Thank God there's only one. I have to calm down.

"Time!"

The umpire's call startles me. He is down on the court and he has a coin in his hand. A coin almost like mine, big and silver. It spins in the air. "Heads," calls Clarke. The coin lands with a clatter.

It is tails.

From somewhere else I hear myself: "I'll serve."

"Ready," the ump calls down. He is back in his chair. Clarke crouches slightly on the other side, ready to receive.

I toss the ball.

I crush the first serve in the net.

The second serve, too. Double fault.

"Love-fifteen," announces the umpire.

I glance over at the table. It is empty. He is gone.

I look over at the camera man. He is still filming.

In my head. It's in my head. Get it together.

I toss the ball, going for the backhand. A solid serve. He calmly puts it back into play. Five, ten, fifteen balls, the rally grows longer; this guy does not miss. I decide to take a risk.

Go for the down the line winner.

I push the ball a little wide. An unforced error.

"Love-thirty," says the goddamn umpire.

Okay, John, okay, it's cool.

I toss the ball and find myself looking over at the empty table while the ball hangs in the air. Impossibly, the serve goes in. A winner.

"Fifteen-thirty," calls the guy. I'm on the board now. This is better.

I toss again, this time looking at the camera. An ace.

"Thirty-all."

I can win this. What if I win this?

I think of my picture in the paper, the headlines.

I go for an ace wide. I miss. Clarke pounces on my second serve—a clean winner: ad out. Another second serve, another twenty ball rally, I'm running balls down like a fiend. I see my false name in print in big black letters. I see myself in highlight reels. I leave a ball short, far too short. He crushes a winner.

"Game, Clarke. Clarke leads one game to love."

Walking over to change sides, I'm breathing hard, feeling tighter by the step. A strange nausea trembles through me. I am down already. It is only the first game, and he's already broken me. As I change my soaked shirt, I can't stop looking over at the table. Can't stop peeking at the camera. Dad was giving me a sign, that's what he was doing.

From the bench, Clarke speaks to me. "You're John Fears, right?"

I nod. My throat constricts, and the sweat pours out.

"I knew a John Fears," he goes on cordially, "played him once or twice. I was surprised to see someone else when we got out here. You guys related, by chance?"

"No," I whisper, trying to stop my eyes from bugging out. "No. Don't know him."

I get up off the bench and hustle over to my side. Clarke walks thoughtfully to his.

What am I doing out here?

He's winning his serve. I make all the returns and I'm moving well, side to side, side to side, working the point. He's hitting solid shots, but I reach them. I chase them all down. I can. I strike a winner and let out a scream.

He aces me with the very next serve.

Have to end this quick, one way or the other.

I'm down forty-fifteen, catching my breath. He makes another first serve, and I slice it back down the line, a laser. He's all over it. Goddamn he's quick. I can't seem to put a ball anywhere that stretches him. He's always there, almost waiting on it. I hit the ball harder and harder and harder. He gets them all. This is five or six more balls than I've ever had to hit against anyone before, but I can do it. Finally, I hit a winner and bend over, hands on my knees.

"Good shot Fears," Clarke calls, clapping his hand on his racket.

"Thanks," I gasp, looking not up at Clarke, but off to the side. The table is still empty. The camera clicks and whirrs.

What was I thinking, entering a pro tournament in someone else's name?

He closes out his first service game with an ace.

Down 0-two. I have to win this service game or this set is over. I cannot get down two breaks. Not against him.

C'mon John. Forget about all this stuff. C'mon, c'mon, just win it anyway.

My second service game's a war. I can't close it out. We're on our fifth or sixth deuce at least; I don't know exactly, I've lost count. Every time I get a game point, the guy comes up with a clean winner. I towel off behind the baseline, staring into space. My mind is wandering and I realize I still have no strategy here. I step up to the line and try to crush a first serve and miss. Second serve: the ball spins weakly into the net. Goddamnit. Another double-fault—couldn't have come at a worse time.

Shake it off.

Now it's his first ad of the game. I deliver a first serve right to his forehand, and he closes the game with a scud missile of a return.

"Three games to love, Clarke," the umpire calls promptly.

Just shut-up.

I stand and stare at the spot where Clarke drove the perfect winner right into the far corner. More serves like that last one and I won't have to worry about any headlines.

Sitting on the bench at the change-over, I pull my coin out of my bag and stare at it. I trace the PLVS VLTRA with a finger. Further beyond, John, further beyond. It's okay. I try to console myself, try to take my mind off of my father and the possibility of being recognized.

I cannot. I flip the coin, catch it; the motto turns up again.

"What's that?" Says Clarke

He's looking at the coin with interest.

"You mean this?"

I hold up my talisman to show him.

"Yeah, that's no normal silver dollar."

"No, no, it's a Spanish two-reales coin from the early fifteen-hundreds."

His eyes go a little wider. I don't know why I'm telling him this. I show him the coin and he examines it closely.

"Cool. I've never seen anything like this; must be pretty valuable."

"Yeah, I guess so. Not bringing me much luck though."

I look at him briefly and he smiles guilelessly and hands the coin back, and then I walk slowly over to receive serve again.

Nice guy, Clarke.

He goes and carves me up on his service game.

Now, I'm standing here, ready to serve, down O-four, and I can't stop thinking about that last game. I lost it at love. I got every single return back, every one. The rallies were long, but eventually, he won every single point—he hit it behind me, disguised a perfect drop shot, forced an error from me, or struck another winner. I have to face the fact that I'm being outclassed.

What the hell am I doing here?

Losing. Badly.

My third service game is briefly a battle, but I lose it, too, before I know it.

Sitting on the bench again, I can't even look at the coin. He's figured out my first serve already. All the returns came back—hard. I was scrambling from the very first ball. I'm no longer in control of the points and he seems to know where I'm going to hit it, even before I do. It's almost casual, the way his balls are all landing within inches of the baseline in long rally after long rally. I have to increase my risk level alarmingly to even win a point now. That'll escalate errors though. I've already got too many of those.

I pull out a new racket, hoping it will help.

It didn't. Sitting on the bench again, looking through the string of the new racket. The table is still empty. I'm still being filmed. I was hitting even my second serves as hard as I could in that last game. It surprised him for a bit, but not enough to win it. We went to deuce a couple of times, but he won it on a perfectly placed passing shot—a thing of beauty, marvelously timed and on the run. That point: he was gliding, working the court like a genius—here a deft drop, there a curling lob, another drop. I ran them down somehow, but he was toying with me, and he'd held that last stroke so long, I was forced to commit to one direction. But he saw me. Casually he'd just bent it behind me. One smooth cat, this one, so fabulously smooth. I had to applaud. I don't even have that shot.

Walking over to receive serve again, down O-five; this set is hopeless. I'm in serious trouble now. I almost don't care. I look at Clarke over there calmly waiting for me to get into position, so he can serve.

Maybe he is just that good. Maybe he really is toying with me.

Michael closes out the set with an easy service game.

I'm waiting to start the second set, serving again. Gonna have to get off to a good start now. Pros come back from bad sets like that all the time. I can do this. I can do this.

"C'mon, John. C'mon."

Even I don't believe it.

I pound a first serve as hard as I can. He crushes it for another winner. I manage to win a couple of points, but he's broken me in the blink of an eye. At the changeover, I don't even remember how I lost the points. I can't bring myself to sit on the bench. I just stand there looking at the ground, keeping my back to the stands and the camera, waiting on Clarke. I can't hold up to his level of play anymore. He's been winning these games more and more easily. He's rolling with a confidence that he hasn't displayed in any way other than his superlative shot-making.

He knows he's going to make those shots. He knows it. It's all I can do to even keep the ball in play. He's always in the right position. It really starts to sink in now. The double bagel looms. I've got absolutely nothing, nothing at all to hurt this guy with. Not today.

I walk slowly over to receive serve again. Embarrassment creeps into me, wraps itself around me. I see people pointing at me. I see people laughing at me. The table is empty, still empty, still empty.

Rally, John, rally. Right now.

I decide to switch to pure attack. I'll chip and charge on his service games, just try to have some fun. Serve and volley on mine. Disrupt him somehow, someway. Do something.

Just like that, I'm down 0-two. In less than five minutes. Standing there with two balls in my hand, examining the service line with a tennis shoe. The new strategy's been a quick disaster. I managed to chip a few returns and come in, but he passed me just as easily as a child, like I wasn't even there. Just like that. Down 0-two.

I can still serve and volley.

It doesn't work. He breaks me at love. He just calmly passed me, or flicked a topspin lob over my head, or I missed a volley. Walking over to the bench, I flip my racket and drop it. I'm only losing more quickly this way.

Quick's not such a bad thing. Just get out of here.

After the changeover, I decide to stay back again and go for bigger shots from the baseline. I make some, but they have no effect. He just raises his game higher, finds new gears.

It's all over in an hour. The score: 6-0, 6-0.

Didn't win a single game.

Standing at net after yet another failed approach on match point. There are tears coming? Oh Jesus, John, yes, hold them back. A stupid game, it's a stupid sport. Not for this. There are other failures far worse than this. Blinking back the disappointment, I watch him come up to shake hands. He's not even sweating, and I'm soaked.

My whole worthless life is summed up by this one match. Everything I ever thought about, everything I've always wanted is gone—gone in only 53 minutes and twelve futile games.

At net, Michael Clarke pats me on the back, and I look away, wanting to be far away from him, from everything. "Good match," he says, encouragingly. "You were just missing. Just an inch here and there, and it could've been different."

"Thanks man, but I don't think so." I choke out the words. "You played great… too good for me."

"Thanks," he says.

It was all just a stupid dream. Or was it?

Towel draped over my head, hiding my face, I go sit on the bench, and gather my stuff up, wondering what I'm going to do with the rest of my life, how I can even think about tennis, about my job or any of this anymore, and then, for some reason, I look into the bleachers. Between the edges of my towel, focused as if through a telescope, a realization: Adela and Bal are here, just sitting there quietly. And behind them—it can't be. My God, Gloria is here. And Robert, too. When had they come? They must've all seen this debacle. How could I have not noticed?

Adela looks sad, resigned. She's sitting there just fiddling with her hands. Gloria is already getting up and chatting with someone animatedly. She laughs and glances over her shoulder at me. Robert is on his cell phone, staring at me. A whispered conversation. I turn my head in alarm and see Bal, Bal, my only friend. He raises his eyes, looks straight through me and in me, and he knows what I am thinking. I can't meet his gaze; those eyes of his, I can't bear to look at them, to be seen by them. I can't breathe. I can feel myself flushing red.

*Goddamnit,* John.

I grab all my gear and run. Run past the bleachers and out the door, past the club; run all the way across the highway, all the way to the beach. I know I look stupid and obvious, running with my goddamn bag on my shoulder, weighing me down.

Why did I even bring the goddamn thing? Why?

It doesn't matter. Nothing matters.

I get to the edge of the surf and crash in, stop dead, water's up to my knees. An urge I've never had before. An urge to plunge. A thought. I stand there and stare across the blank ocean, feel the breeze; there's not even enough courage in me to do this: to go on in and end this.

Pointless. All so pointless.

Step back. Sea foam washes over my brand new tennis shoes. I look down at them. They'll be ruined, but I don't care. I never want to wear them again. The moment fades; the desire to sink, to let the bag and my gear and my fucking shoes, my fucking worthless rackets, and all this sink me, down to the bottom of this brown and ruined ocean.

It's not in me, never was.

No crying now. Not now, not ever. Not for anything.

It's an emptiness that comes over me then, standing there looking out to sea. It's the coldness of a void. I don't think this is anger or guilt or shame anymore—despair? No, it's just empty.

I'm done with this, done with this, done. I'll be caught soon anyway. It couldn't last.

Giving myself away like I have been, and now the name Fears has been exposed, too.

A new desire comes over me. I know it as surely as I've ever known anything. I drop my bag, squat down and unzip it slowly, remove one of my rackets. I examine it, closely. This is the one with the nick on the guard, where I'd hit it on a fence pole. Little details that only I'd know. Gives them a personality. Makes each one unique, treasured.

I throw it out to sea as far as I can.

It's beautiful really, how it arcs out over the water with a lazy spin, catches a gust, and lifts, as if it would fly. The racket becomes nothing more than a thin silhouette as it falls; it lands in a breaker, flips over once, and sinks in the vastness of the ocean.

Not even a splash.

I pull out the rest of the rackets and throw them far into the swells too, one at a time. When they're all gone I lie down, resting my head on my now empty racket bag, my feet still in the surf. I stare at the light blue sky until the sun sets and the tide recedes and the stars come out above me. I lie there not wanting to see anyone or anything except for the black void of space above me.

Within me.


The brief disturbing sound of police sirens hit once. Radio voices on loudspeaker babbling cop lingo. Flashlights panning the beach, moving this way. I'm wide awake now, feet planted in the encroaching surf, in a criminal crouch. I gather my bag and scurry for the dunes, staying low. I roll over the first of the barrier dunes and into a sward of sea oats. Back on my feet, crouching again, my eyes scan new surroundings. All is garishly illuminated in the unnatural orange of beach parking security lights.

The tinny cop speaker voices are on to me. They move this way.

My eyes adjust and a dark line of brush appears just beyond the grass.

Go for them. Now.

I dive in and crawl under a shrub and into a small protected clearing and pull up in shock. A headless beast of two naked, clutching bodies, groping at each other in an unnatural embrace. Oblivious to my intrusion, one is luminously pale, the other blacker than night, and they coil around each other and between each other, devouring one another greedily.

"Over here," one of the cop radios screams closely, "there's something over here!"

The feral thing near me shrieks and bursts apart, running. As I curl up under the bushes, I just make out their glistening bodies thrashing towards the parking lot. The police radios go mad with screeching and static and all the cops trail their new quarry in lustful, outraged pursuit, like the avenging angels of their own dreams. I am alone again.

Waiting. I begin to creep out of the bushes and stop abruptly again. A new presence approaches stealthily. But this is no cop. It is a large man, a quiet, stooping and crouching man, carefully tracking my footfall of minutes before. He pulls up on this side of the sea grass and stands to his full, formidable height. I stifle a cry. It is Bal. I cannot see his eyes, but I can feel them boring into my hiding place. I do not call to him, and he does not speak to me. In my mind, I think of the things I want to say to him. But it is all false, and I know he will not leave with me, if I ask. He will stay here. This is where he belongs.

He stands there for a long time, as if rooted to the very island, jutting up like a column of black granite. Then he moves on, and I look to the place where he so recently stood, and I seem to see him there still though I know he's gone and nothing's there but the windblown grass sighing with my ruined hopes.

I wake shivering to the feel of water lapping at my feet, a soft tapping sound nearby. The tide has come in again. The sun is just beginning to rise, and a lovely orange glow escapes above the horizon's thin low clouds. Again the tapping, not ten feet away; it's a great blue heron, huge and gray in the morning light. He's picking at something hard and black sticking out of the sand, playing with it.

It can't be. He's pecking at one of my tennis rackets.

Slowly I sit up, cold beyond even chills and craving the warmth of the sun. "That thing tastes bad, let me tell you."

The bird startles at my words, squawks reproachfully, lifts on prehistoric wings. Watching its flight, I think of Bal and then of the heron itself, and I remember then what I could not before. A symbol of wisdom, this bird. I crawl over and pick up the tennis racket. The irony in this. No one's around. No cops. No friends. No one. Just me. But I'm not even John Fears anymore either. Can't be.

What was I thinking coming here?

I hug my knees with my arms, the racket still in hand.

Sneaking into the hideout like the fugitive I am, I know Bal will not be here, and he is not. I snap on the light and quietly gather up my few things. It doesn't take long; there's still not much stuff to call my own. I grab my pistol and the box of shells and the two full magazines. I throw the tube sock full of money in the duffel bag. It's heavy but not so much; I could've saved more and bought less. Fewer rackets. The last racket is in my hand; I consider a moment how it came back to me. I decide to take it, too, and put it in the bag with the grip sticking out the zipper. The silver coin, my talisman, I put on the table; it's now utterly devoid of any kind of significance for me. I've failed it.

It was always yours, Bal. Not mine.

The Porsche fires up right away, and quietly I pull out, driving slowly past the grove. For a moment I think I see a movement in the thicket, something large, very large. I stop the car in the middle of the road, considering.

But that's impossible anyway, completely impossible.

Then, remembering our night digging there, I start to feel guilt, or humiliation, or something. All I know is I need desperately to run and leave and hide. I punch the pedal, speeding off. Look in the rearview mirror. I catch my breath. Something coming out of the bushes. Something huge and indistinct. Something I know. But it's rapidly diminishing now, and I can't be sure it is really there. Can't be.

And as I round the corner and my view changes, I breathe a little easier and laugh at myself and tell myself what an idiot I am for even thinking of it.

But still, I can't shake the feelings.

He was there. He is still standing there.

And he is watching me.

⋏

# GONE FOR GOOD

"The way he looked at me," Chip is saying, sitting with his chair turned away from one of the club's dining room tables. His elbows spike into his knees and his tortured head is in his hands, pounding. Gloria sits across from him and facing him, but they are careful not to touch each other. She leans forward with her fingers and palms pressed together and her hands tucked between her tightly pressed legs like a stifled prayer. Robert gets up and goes to fetch mimosas from the brunch bar. Gloria opens her mouth as if to speak, but then says nothing and falls back to examining him intently, inscrutably.

"I thought I knew him better," Chip says to her.

Robert comes back and hands them all the drinks. He pulls out a chair and sits down beside Gloria, slapping her playfully on a bare leg as he does. "Relax old bean," he says to Chip, "they'll find him. John's no suicidal loser. I mean, holy fuckups, man, the way you spooked him would freak out anybody. Why the hell didn't you just stay there and let him know you were alive?"

Chip shakes his head and puts the drink on the table behind him. For one of the few times in his life, he doesn't know. Or is afraid to think about it. Having envisioned a reunion of sorts, he'd meant to reveal himself to John well before the match. But John had been late, so late they'd almost defaulted him, and then, when he finally got there, he'd hurried onto the court and accidently seen his father, sitting there at the table. Chip got up and tried to go to him, to say something, he really had, but the look of horror on John's face, the way he'd run. There was nothing to say and Chip knew it had all been a mistake then, and he'd simply turned and left.

Zingleman comes in and over to Chip where he sits by the window. "Chip," he says, "no sign of John, the police have been looking for him all night, but there is some good news. When his roommate got back from his search this morning, John's car and clothes were gone. It looks like he's okay. I think he's just moved on."

"But to where?"

Zingleman shakes his head and places a hand on Chip's shoulder for a moment. Chip does not move or say a word and Zingleman looks at them all a moment and then leaves them alone again.

"Damn," Robert jumps up, laughing. "See, I told you! He's fine. You know, all things considered, John played like a fuckin' superstar. He's gotten to be a great player. Christ almighty those guys knock the piss out of the ball. If you hadn't screwed him up so bad, he mighta' beat that fast little fucker, Clarke whatshisname."

"Robert," Chip says quietly, "will you please shut up."

Robert does, and then he looks at Chip and then at Gloria and something seems to be clicking in him. But then he sees some people he knows sitting down to eat nearby and he gets up with a boisterous greeting, chugging his drink as he strides over to them.

Chip stands and looks down at Gloria in her neatly fitted cashmere skirt, still sitting there, watching him from the same exact pose, still saying nothing. He briefly wonders what she is wearing under there today and then he shakes the thought off and turns to look out the window at the golfers going through the motions on the balmy winter day.

"Well, he's gone then."

"And so are you," says Gloria.

Chip nods his head. "I knew it wouldn't work," he says, glancing back at Gloria. She has not moved. Then he looks over to the table where Robert sits in animated conversation and says, "Would you even leave him?"

She is looking at the tops of her hands, pulling the skin tight and watching it melt slowly back into place. She says nothing.

"Well, we did what we did," he says at last.

"Do you know what you're doing to John?"

"Doing to John?" Chip comes back, and sits down and snaps in urgent whispers: "Doing to John, Gloria, really? What about me? All I've ever done is help him, and what did he do? Push me away, that's what."

Now she looks at him. Now her anger rises and she meets his eyes and she tells him: "Chip, look at you. You act like you're an innocent, here. You're not innocent. You're the least innocent person I ever met. You always have a plan. But it's got to be your plan. And what harm's come to you out of all this besides a headache and a broken bone? Nothing, that's what. Nothing, but wounded pride. And that's really it, isn't it? That's the issue here. You and your pride. That's all that matters with you—and you know it."

"Gloria—" Chip stops his voice from rising. People glance up from their meals, frowning. Robert is still drowned in conversation, his back turned to them, away at the bar now.

He pauses. He listens. Her words reverberate with some truth. He thinks. He thinks of his father, his own real father, gone for a lifetime and living a life of sorrow. A father gone and forgotten and with a name that is never spoken, stained as it is by atrocities the man never committed. But he saw them, oh yes, he saw them. Chip knows he was there. And what did he do to stop them? Nothing. Not a goddamn thing. He ran, and he stumbled into the arms of some woman he barely even knew. And when he found no solace there, for there was none to be had, and there was no comfort, no consolation to be had anywhere, he kept on running and to hell with the consequences. To hell with the responsibilities. And then Chip thinks of his own son again. Of John. Out there, running away, and isn't it just like him?

"– Gloria," he says, under control now, calm, "you know, I tried. I tried to do it your way, and look what happened. Here we are sitting around wringing our hands and wondering if he's gone suicidal. But he's not suicidal. He's just run off again, and, look, it's about time he quit running away. It's true, you are absolutely right, my pride was wounded. But there's more to it than that. That's not all, and, by God, John will own up to his responsibilities, or I don't want him back. Do you understand?"

Gloria sits there, nearly defeated now, fidgeting with her hands again. She pulls, pulls the wrinkles of her hand, and looks into her lap, as if she's not heard him. But he knows she's heard him, and this is the only woman he's ever really loved. His face softens. "Besides," he says, "you know, I raised him. I think I know what's good for him, and, look, don't worry. I'll figure this out. You were right to try and help him, but I'll take it from here... and when I get that sorted out, maybe then we can—"

"—He's gone Chip. Gone!" Gloria bursts out, suddenly alert again. "Do you know what you do to people? Chip, it's over. You and your plans; it's always your plans. You don't know what you're doing to that boy, and you don't know what you did to me."

Now it's Chip's turn for silence. The drone of conversations. The formal, forced laughter of formal people dining together at a Sunday brunch. Chip turns his head away, gets up, and stands, looking out the window again. "Maybe," he says, "maybe you're right. But don't think I don't know what I did to you. I do know what I did to you. You think I don't regret things, don't you? Well, I do." Chip looks at her a long moment then. She is beautiful still, and radiant in the reflected, yellow sunlight, and regret does shiver through him. He can look at her no longer. "And yet some things don't seem to change between us," he whispers to the glass.

"Some things haven't," she says, remotely now. "Others have."

"So, you wouldn't leave him?"

"Chip, what would be the point of it? Did you really think it would work to put us all together as a family now? Do you think it would be the same between us, if you did."

Chip glances at her, shakes his head, looks out the window again.

"We can't," she says, "it won't."

"I'm going back to Texarkana."

She nods and looks away and Chip does not look back and does not look at Robert talking to his friends still, and he walks out and into the obscene brightness of the November morning, shading his eyes with a clenched hand.

# THE ROAD—AGAIN

L eaving Galveston Island behind, an incongruous feeling of carefree lightness comes over me. It's shaping up to be a fine clear morning, like so many here on the coast. The heater's going, and the Targa top's open. Warm air swirls up around my legs and out into the cool currents. I like the feel of it.

I find myself heading southwest across the San Luis pass, just letting the car pick a path. I've never been this way before, but it bypasses Houston. I have half a mind to go out to West Texas and feel the dry baking sun, to see the kind of sky and the kind of sunset you can only see out in those spaces this time of year. And the stars; I remember the stars out there. Cold and bright in skies so clear you can see the Milky Way unfurled across the black dome above you, and you sit in wonder at the world, and the vastness of the universe, and your own fate. All in a moment, all in a breath.

But I don't know.

What would I do out there?

Nothing.

Somewhere west of Angleton, I think I've gone far enough. I find myself caressing the dash, the custom chrome shifter knob. The engine is still running well, purring along.

Stop it. It's just a car. This has to be done.

I said I wouldn't cry, and I am not going to.

Cruising slowly now, I find a suitable gravel road to nowhere and follow it to the dead end I knew would be there. Around me, a tangle of live oaks and underbrush and grass taller than my car. I turn off from the little that remains of the road and feather the 914 into a thicket where it cannot be seen and may not be found for years. It is cold, just sitting here, and my resolve hardens. I wipe my face dry, and I get out my fake ID and throw it into the bushes. Then I grab my bag and crawl out through the open Targa top and head back out to the main road, and I do not look back.

Never look back. So they say. But that's not possible.

Walking on the shoulder, a car speeds by, and I make the mistake of looking at the passengers. All are in their Sunday finery, scrubbed and presentable to the unforgiving face of God. The little kids and the woman stare hatefully. The man driving does not look and his mouth is set.

Eyes on the road now, don't look. Keep walking west.

More cars full of Sunday schoolers shoot by without even slowing down. There's nothing around me here except forest and a muddy creek. Brazos river country. What town next? I don't remember. Another thought: surely a cop will come by and see me here. And what to do then? Run, I suppose. The woods, again. But it shouldn't be far to town. I jog.

It has become a fine fall, day and I breathe deeply in my rhythm and look at the oaks and forest on both sides of the road. What passes for fall and winter around here. Live oaks are just a duller shade of green. Depressing, except for the relief of cooler, drier weather. The wet and sandy tennis clothes from the day before chafe unmercifully. I should've changed, but this is no place for that.

Eighteen wheelers are practically blowing me off the road. Slowing to a walk, I think about hitching a thumb. Not sure now. Keep on? Or not. It feels good just to walk. Walk and think. And so, here I am, on another road, not knowing what I'm going to do. Again. It all comes down to the fork way back there, down in the river bottoms, almost half a year ago.

What if I'd taken the B fork?

Would it have led to this very same place, this very time, or would it have been a different life? Maybe I'd have gone back home and faced the consequences like a man. Maybe it would've been allright and we could both be at peace. But maybe I'd be right here, right now, walking to a destination I'm not sure I want to reach, wondering if I should just keep going west. Keep going west.

A realization: it was no decision. I don't make them; not any decisions. I don't, never did. Just leave it all to chance don't I—to whim and whimsy—to others? Like the poet wrote, I'd ended up taking the road less traveled—or, well, had I even done that? Surely I had. Perhaps the other one would have been worse, perhaps better, but I'd let convention make the choice, not me. I look down the corridor of trees. The asphalt bends away before me. No other roads. Well, there's no choice now, and there is no right or wrong here, just the path before me, and when the fork comes again, will I make the decision? Can I?

Just before I can see around the bend, someone does stop. Two people in a gray featureless sedan of some mass produced American sort pull over in front of me. I get a glimpse of a guy behind the wheel. I tense despite myself.

Probably a good Samaritan. Better than a cop.

But you can never tell. An uncomfortable feeling, seeing him stop, like something strange is about to happen. I catch myself thinking about pulling out my racket. No, not that: the gun. I resist the urges.

A young man, maybe a little older than me, steps out of the car and waves. He's wearing black wire frame glasses and appears to be dressed for church in khakis and a pressed blue collared shirt. He seems harmless enough.

"Hey!" he says, in a friendly Zingleman way. "Need a lift?"

Yes, but I'm uneasy about admitting it to some random guy. I don't know. And why? I'm wondering how to answer him when I am there before him and he extends his hand. He has shiny, shiny shoes. Dazzling. Even shinier than Dad's.

"I'm Mike Needham," says the man with brilliant shoes.

"John," I say, then shut my mouth realizing I have not yet come up with a new last name. Mike is looking at me expectantly and the chills come back over me. An alias comes, from out of nowhere. "John More," I say, "nice to meet you, Mike." We shake hands.

"Nice to meet you, too. So, you need a ride?"

"Well..."

I'm still not sure what to say and then I see the girl. She leans over from the passenger seat. She is speaking to me. Her lips are moving, I know it, she must be saying something. Good Lord, she's beautiful.

"We can take you! Hop on in!" she says.

This changes things. I hop in the car with embarrassing speed.

"Well, okay, if it's not too much trouble."

"It's no trouble," they both say, almost in unison.

They laugh while Mike fumbles with the keys. She turns in her seat.

"I'm Elizabeth," she says.

Elizabeth holds out her shapely delicate hand, and I take it, smiling at her. Smiling stupidly, I think. My first impression was not wrong; she's a beautiful, but a wholesome looking girl, too. Virtuous Sunday school clothes conceal a lithe and shapely form; she's that kind of girl. I feel guilty even noticing her body. Her hair is of a dark, coffee brown, falling just beyond her shoulders in a soft tumble. But it's her eyes I'm taken with. Her wonderful, pale blue eyes. They are pure, the pure crystalline color of a brightening morning sky just washed by rain. I try to keep from staring at her, but I can't quite manage it. She notices. A small rosy blush blossoms beneath translucent skin.

"... though we can't take you anywhere else right now."

The end of whatever Mike was saying breaks into my reverie. He pulls the car out onto the road, eyeing me jealously. Can't blame him.

"What?"

Forcing my thought away from her, I'm confused by his comment and suddenly suspicious. The doors lock automatically.

"We're headed to church," Mike says. "I thought you were coming with us?"

Yeah. Church, that's what he was saying.

I can stand any church, if she'll be there. I take a new look at the both of them. They're bubbly and nice, well-intentioned people looking forward to church and feeling better for doing their good deed for the day. I must seem like a safe one.

Little do they know.

I wonder—would they've picked me up if I'd been a black guy? A Mexican? Hell no, they wouldn't. But a white male wearing tennis clothes and carrying a gun?

Sure, why not, let's pick him up. He's only a murderer.

"Well, sure," I hear myself say, trying to match his enthusiasm. "Why not?"

On the way, we make small talk. Mike is the youth minister. Elizabeth teaches one of the Sunday school classes. Mike is married to someone else. A relief, and hope rises in me. Joy, even. Maybe Elizabeth is single; maybe there is no boyfriend, maybe, just maybe, she'll... But there's no way, not a girl like her.

"Are you single?" She asks the question suddenly, turning to look at me, smiling, her eyes like shining beacons, guiding me in.

I can't believe this. Is she asking me if I'm single, right here? In the car with this guy? All of a sudden I can't breathe so well.

"Um, yeah, yeah I guess so. Are...?" But I don't have the courage to finish the thought, and she interrupts with a laugh. It's a beautiful laugh, a songbird's song, easy and light, devoid of pretense or falseness, and I'm intensely embarrassed.

"Don't be embarrassed," she says misreading me, and she laughs again. "I also run the singles group at the Church. I just thought you might like to come to that, too, since you're single."

"Ah, okay," I say looking down at my lap.

Well, yeah. Yeah, Elizabeth, I am single and I will go to your class, to your group, to your house, to the ends of the earth to hear that laugh, to see those eyes.

"Thanks. Yeah, I'll come to your group, I guess."

"Good! That's great!"

Elizabeth turns back to face the road and she's genuinely excited: I look at the back of her head, and I smile, and I admire how she got that out of me, and think maybe she really is interested in me after all. Then again, maybe I'm just too desperate to notice the difference between friendly and interested. Then she makes eye contact with me in the rearview mirror, seems to penetrate my thought, and we both smile at each other.

Maybe there is hope. Maybe there is.

For some reason, I think of Zingleman. Snapping upright, I realize I'd better call him. It's the least I can do.

"Do you have a cell phone I can borrow? Just a quick call to Galveston, I promise."

"Sure, John, no problem," Mike says, and he hands me his phone out of the cup holder. "Do what you need to do."

"Thanks," I say, dialing Zingleman's office number.

The phone rings an eternity. Thankfully Zingleman doesn't pick up. Suddenly, I don't know what to say or why I'm even calling. Then I see her clear eyes looking at me again in the mirror, and I find the words.

"I won't be coming back," I tell the machine. "I'm fine though. I'm fine." I stammer, thinking of how I always made fun of him, though I shouldn't have. In the end, he's done nothing but help me. Abruptly I add: "thanks Mr. Zingleman. Thanks for everything, and I'm sorry... sorry I let you down, but I have to go. It wasn't my fault."

I hang up the phone and hand it back to Mike who's watching me in the mirror now. But he says nothing.

Going to church, who would've thought?

I'd gone as a kid, of course, everybody did in Texarkana, but I'd left off around junior high. Dad still went, but hell, for him the church was just another place to do business. He never brought religion home, and he'd never forced it on me either. Now I don't think about church anymore, or what I believe in, or if I do believe at all. The dark hair is serene in front of me, drawing my eye into its soft depths, and I wonder what she'd think about that. Maybe she already knows; maybe she can tell just by looking at me. I look out the window.

Well, I'll volunteer to be your project, if that's what you want.

Outside it's as fine a Sunday for church as I could have asked for, and the morning sky is just as clear as her eyes.

A

# THE WEALTH OF GOD

I can never get over how much water there is in these parts. I look through the car windows at it all as we pass by. Creeks and muddy brown pools and tanks and swampy forest bottoms are everywhere. This is the drainage for the whole state it seems. I wonder how much of the undergrowth and trees I see now was under sugar cane production in the days when it'd been big down here?

A lot of it, I guess. They'd had slaves to work it all, too. It's not a stretch to see those poor souls toiling in those fields, cutting the cane and singing some working song now long forgotten. I can see the machetes fall in unison to the beat, and see the cane fall in scything rhythm. See the women and children gathering it all up in great round bundles like top knots.

A truck blows by, and it all vanishes into nothingness again. It's just a rambling green mess, all overgrown or under the till of some huge mechanized farm.

Where did they all go? Houston?

Are their descendants out there still, living in the fifth ward, struggling in the ghettos? They didn't have a choice, did they? No, it was just a transition of form: from the slavery of the Whiteman to the slavery of being poor.

Either way, there wasn't much freedom to choose.

And how precious is choice?

"Here we are!" The beautiful eyes make the announcement in a mocking-bird voice.

Is she eternally happy like this? I wonder what it'd be like waking up next to her in the mornings. Does she sing? I shake away the thought, as the Wealth of God rolls into view. It is truly awesome—in size at least. A colossal arched roof forms a green half dome above the tree line. Manmade lakes and water features are everywhere. Fountains spring up pell-mell from the muddy depths of newly landscaped pools. Soaring limestone columns give way to immense steel poles that support the mighty roof. In front of the church, there's a pure white tapered cylinder of bleached concrete projecting a gigantic stainless steel cross skyward. Rising even higher than the dome, its knife-sharp edges cut the perfect blue sky. I consider the possibility that this thing could blast off and actually shoot up to the heavens.

Maybe they send cremations up in the thing.

Shoot 'em express—right up to God.

I start to laugh, but suppress it, thinking of Elizabeth. This is her church.

"Wow, you guys don't mess around!"

I can't really force myself to say something nicer. Part of the truth is still the truth.

"This place is mega-super-huge!"

Behold The Theme Park Of The Lord. The artificiality and size of it all is repelling me already. I start to regret coming with them. But both Mike and Elizabeth smile in their response to my commentary, oblivious to any irony in my words. They're proud to show it all to me. We round the final bend of the entry road.

"Oh, is that..."

The lion comes fully into view.

"...a lion?"

It is simply enormous. And it's green.

"Yes, beautiful, isn't it?" Mike says.

Elizabeth looks at me in the mirror.

"Wow!" I say.

It's not exactly bronze. It's not really patinaed. It's all a big fiberglass fake, even I can see that. I meet Elizabeth's eye in the mirror.

"Yeah, beautiful!"

But now I can't peel my eyes away from the monster lion. It rears up from a formed concrete boulder on muscular hind legs. Massive front paws as big as twenty inch spinners reach out in a clawless embrace. Green fiberglass locks worthy of Michelangelo's David tumble down about his head in a gloriously overdone mane. Gaping jaws bare six inch teeth in a mighty roar to the faithful. The boulder bears these words:

BE BOLD LIKE THE LION.

But somehow, despite the hugeness, and the dramatic muscular pose, the thing strikes me as benign and harmless. I try to figure out why as we drive slowly past the statue. It's mounted in the very center of the entry court. Kids are crawling around it, trying to scale the beast's mighty flanks when parents aren't watching. Mike is droning: about tens of thousands of members, the largest organ west of the Mississippi, thousands of young people, the sports facilities, the school. He's overpowered by largeness, in awe of the size of the Wealth of God.

I've got it. The lion's got no balls.

This time I can't stop myself; I laugh. Mike stops his speech, thinking I'm laughing at something he's said. Clear blue eyes search mine again in the rear view mirror. Mike's, too. They both show concern, they're looking for the joke, evidently Mike hadn't meant to be funny with whatever it was he was talking about. He forces a smile that prepares to be defensive, thinking I may be making fun of him. I can't help myself.

"What's with the maned lioness?" I indicate the feline colossus with a wide smile.

Mike's look changes to confusion. Elizabeth smiles and giggles, embarrassed. But amused. She looks back at me again and smiles mischievously, so that I'm wild with the desire to reach out right then and there and caress her. Now Mike gets my little joke and he starts laughing a weak forced laugh.

"Ah ha ha ha" he goes. It's more like the grinding of a gear. "Well, we had to do that! Ah ha ha ha! Gotta' think of the kids!"

Yeah, make sure they don't learn anything about sex 'til they're out of the house and going wild with hormones down at Baylor. That'll teach 'em.

"Yeah," I say lamely, "the kids sure do seem to like it."

"They sure do," Mike replies.

And then he's off again with the mega-church youth statistics: all the good the kids do, how they're serving Jesus in all the foreign ministries, away from the lap of luxury. In places like Scotland and Ireland.

Man, leaving the lap of luxury to go to Scotland and convert who? The Catholics? Is he kidding me? Doesn't seem to be. Thankfully, before he can babble on any more, he's parked the car in his specially marked spot for the Youth Minister. I spring out, ready to be relieved of both his talk and my own lecherous thoughts of the morning sky eyes.

Fortunately, the service proves distracting. It's not the words—for "Magic Simon," as Mike calls the reverend with the familiarity of a fan who daily speaks with his God here on earth—isn't really saying anything meaningful (just now he's going over his five points for self-improvement). It's the production of the whole thing that is fascinating.

"Point one..." Reverend Simon is admonishing the congregation, "...point one is you've got to diet! Diet brothers and sisters! And to diet—listen to this now—to diet, you've got to drink daily of the clear, calorie free waters of the Lord!" He raises both palms dramatically heavenward in a mighty entreaty for the Lord's Perrier. And lo and behold, water does gush up from both sides of the stage. It's a cavalcade of water rushing through the realistic man-made brook. The stage is suddenly transformed from a stony platform into an island in a mountain stream. The crowd oohs and ahhs. The children shriek with delight. They're eating this all up.

I don't listen much to the Reverend Simon's other four points. They say about as much of nothing as dieting on the waters of the Lord did. The special effects continue to amaze though. The stage raises and lowers, fog gushes from unseen pipes to place the good man in a cloud on cue.

A gargantuan choir materializes from behind the mist. Unbelievable. There are five hundred people in that thing. I know the number, because counting the members of the choir is better than listening to the sermon and much more amazing. Five hundred people in satin white are belting out—appropriately—Onward Christian Soldiers. Or rather, four hundred and ninety nine white people and one lonesome token black guy. Looking like a gnat in the milk, he stands towards the top row, his dark skin absorbing the low light. He is more like the absence of a white guy until, surprisingly, you hear him sing. A beautifully ominous voice, a rich baritone, rumbling from out of all that whiteness, like distant thunder on a sunny day.

And just when I think the show can't get any more Disney, the grand finale sends forth angels. Real women these, flying above the awed congregation on fluttering wings with extended open arms, chastely imploring heaven for admission of the faithful. Amazing. The angels are spinning, floating, dancing up there near the roof in intricate, kinetic formations. You can hardly tell there are cables. You'd swear there are not.

The angels have fluttered away, the lights come on. Show's over. Offering plates flow through the appreciative crowd. This guy, the Reverend, he's gotten an entire forty five minute sermon out of special effects and five points from a Gene Simmons exercise video.

Impressive, most impressive.

Now the good man tells us over and over again all the ways you can give money: automatic monthly withdrawal, on-line payment, credit cards, even PayPal. All forms accepted. Most amusing of all are the groups you can join. There's even a menu in the pews. You can be in "Simon's Army" (thirty dollars a month), or the "Simoniacs" (ninety-five dollars a month) or, best of all, the "Reverend's Inner Sanctum" (two hundred dollars a month).

I look over at Elizabeth, wondering what she really thinks of all this, but she doesn't notice me. She's still beaming at Magic Simon, enraptured with his words. I wonder how many used cars she's bought from guys like this. Hopefully, none.

I have to admit it though, the guy's got some kind of weird charisma. He doesn't sound cheesy, even as he fleeces the flock of their money. He sounds sincere despite the—to me at least—obvious insincerity of this whole crazy place.

I glance back at Elizabeth again, and I feel a sudden shock of guilt for my cynicism.

I don't even know the guy.

I do seem to recall something about him from grocery store tabloids—how his viral popularity tele-ministering to the suburbanites and the couch potatoes around the world is ever growing. How the newly re-faithful are flocking out here to the outskirts of Houston for his show. And, I have to say, it is quite a show.

And just what do I have to be cynical about anyway?

What have I done to help anyone?

Nothing.

These hands, look at these hands.

What pain and suffering have been relieved by my hands?

None.

Pain and suffering. My father's life. These are the hands of loss. In these palms: destruction. And in my thought and action are nothing but a constant rant against the world. A life of idleness. Thoughts of death. Maybe this Simon guy is helping feed the poor, educate the underprivileged, provide aid to the refugees of some war torn country. I'm certainly no one to say otherwise. I'm the goddamned antithesis of goodly action.

We file out of the sanctuary. Wonder where to go now. I start to follow the crowd out the front, but Elizabeth and Mike stop me and lead me towards a more discreet exit by the stage.

"C'mon!" Mike says, his shoes glowing like beacons in the bright lights, "time for youth ministry!" An inward groan. I must fall within his definition of youth.

Youth gone bad.

My tennis shoes are still damp. Faded black shorts and T-shirt are ringed with sweat and still shedding sand. Lord, what I must smell like. Just wanna get out of here. Church is no place for me. But Elizabeth. She seems to be coming with us. Can't leave, not yet. There is something here. Just stay. Stay and see it through the day.

Sitting in a circle of "young adults." All are pouring out their hearts one by one, in an ordered sequence of hand-wringing. It's a group confessional deal that I'm none too comfortable with. Not like any of these guys have any real troubles to worry about.

Trouble? Boy, let me tell you about trouble.

Amusing listening though. This one young guy with the sagging jowls and the hanging rolls of flab, he's talking about how he's been lusting after women.

Join the crowd, buddy.

"...anytime I feel the need to violate myself..."

Did he just say that? He did.

" ...I go to my Bible, the wooden covered one my G-Ma got me from Israel, and I read the Revelation of the Apocalypse, and I overcome the temptations of the flesh."

They ooh, and they ahh. They actually clap for the guy.

Well, that will put a damper on temptation, for sure.

Another now, a girl right next to me with the makeup of a hooker and the muffin-top tight blue-jeans. She went to a party and, though she wasn't drinking (yeah, right), she felt guilty "just being there." Now she's doubting her choice of friends.

" ...and, oh, like, I hated to, but I, like, looked into my heart, and I knew like, I couldn't party with them anymore. Now I have, like, you guys, and, oh, it's like so much cooler!"

More clapping. Shining eyes, near tears, all around.

Oh, so just ditch your friends. That will help them.

"John, what do you have to share with the group?"

Mike is looking at me. Everyone is looking at me.

"Share?" Damnit, he wants me to confess? Me? He nods and bobs at me. His shoes are shining at me. All these liquid eyes, all looking at me.

I am. I'm supposed to confess.

"Yes, John, I know this is difficult, but the path to heaven is difficult too, isn't it?"

There's a uniform nodding of heads. Everyone agreeing with his words. Elizabeth, I can tell, expects me to say something insightful and wonderful.

"The path to heaven is not something I've been thinking about too much lately, Mike."

"All the more reason to share your problems with the group, John" Mike encourages. "In so doing, you are sharing with the Lord himself."

"This group has problems the Lord needs to hear about? Hell, Mike, sounds like they better just tell their parents first."

A couple of people giggle. Mike is not amused.

"Jason," he says, turning to the guy next to me, as if I haven't just spoken. "Why don't *you* share with the group."

On cue, everyone turns to commiserate with Jason, ignoring me completely. Everyone except Elizabeth that is. I meet her eye, and she smiles a smile of sympathy that says she wants to know, and suddenly I want to fall into her arms and tell her everything. I want her to hold me, and I do want to confess, I do. But I want to tell her, only her. I have the feeling that all I need to do is to get up right now and walk out that door and she would follow. She would follow, and she would take my hands in hers, and I could pour myself into her and rid myself of this shroud of death I carry like it was my own skin.

But I cannot. I cannot move. Cannot speak.

And she turns away. Then, she gets up. She leaves.

The look on her face: disappointment. I do not follow.

An excruciatingly long hour. Staring at the door. Blinking up at the humming tubes of light. Imagining a purgatory where fools endlessly blather. An inane language of babble, understood by no one. Finally, the meeting grinds to a close. I could run to the sunlight, but for this strange inertia in me. I sit by myself. People rise and mill around me, talking, seeming to me like gilded icons shorn now of their thin veneer of godliness and emitting irritating noises. Mike seems to have forgotten me. Seems to have forgotten that he picked me up by the side of the road. He leaves the room with not a backward glance.

"C'mon, John, let's go shoot some hoop."

Looking down at me is, of all people, the apocalyptically restrained fat guy. What's his name? Thomas? Timothy?

"Hoop?"

"Yeah, you know, basketball. Looks like you're ready."

"Ready?"

"Yeah, I'm ready, too. Just gotta change real quick."

"Okay."

Forty minutes into the pick-up games, and I'm remembering how much I like to play basketball. The fat guy, who may be named Timothy or Thomas, sets a vicious pick. I roll. His elbows fly into opponents' necks. His knees thrust into opponents' groins. We are unstoppable.

Taking the ball out in Game five. Down by three, but needing five more points to go five and O. Five for five. Timothy or Thomas is getting tired. I should be dying, but I'm not. Feeling good. More than a match for these guys. A juke, a cut, my behind-the-back pass cuts through, find its mark. Fatboy scores. Jaws drop. Make it, take it. I take it. Take it strong to the hole with the double pump and scoop. Sharpe for two. Gameball, I take it out. Just need one, but why not the three? The guy can't believe I'm pulling up. He barely gets a hand up. From deep behind the line, Sharpe scores. Game over. I am high-fiving Timothy or Thomas or whoever he is. A whale of player, this guy. And I'm done. Quit while you're ahead. I wave a waiting guy in to replace me. Elizabeth is there, smiling at me with admiration in the glacial blue eyes. How long? Suddenly self-conscious, I'm breathless in more ways than one.

"Looks like you're having fun," she says.

"I am," I smile at her. "Yes, I am."

"So you need a place to stay tonight?"

My furiously beating heart thumps out to her, now raging even faster. Did she just ask me to stay the night? Can't be.

"You want me to come over... tonight?"

Now her face flushes beet red. A hand comes to her mouth. Total embarrassment and shock. "Oh No! I mean..." Now it's my turn. "...It's just that Reverend Simon wants to see you. He said he has a place for you to stay."

"Oh! Okay!" I reply, too quickly. "Thanks, that'd be great!"

Fool. Idiot. Moron. What were you thinking? Looking at the carpet awkwardly. Anywhere but at her. Eager to change the topic, I recover my wits.

"He wants to see me now?"

Look at these sweaty tennis clothes. Can't go in there like this. These threads are now going on thirty hours, two athletic events, and a dip in the putrid Gulf of Mexico.

"Oh, you can clean up a little bit first," Elizabeth says, reading my mind. She wrinkles her nose a bit. "I'll wait."

Showering nervously in the men's locker room, I wonder that the Reverend wants to see me. In a church this size there must be tens of thousands of members and hundreds of employees. What would he care about one wandering guy with no car? Maybe Elizabeth's a little closer to him than I want to know?

I shake the thoughts from my head.

No. Don't think so. Can't be.

Anyway, it was easy to see from the sermon that this is a guy who's on top of things. I expect he lives and breathes this church, micro-managing every detail. Seen enough of my father in action to know how these types operate. Only, I guess this guy possibly cares about every wayward soul.

Wayward soul. He's sure got that part right.

⋏

# AND BACK AGAIN

In the passenger seat of a jarringly decrepit taxi cab, Chip grabs the handle of the door with his right, the seatback with his left, and tries not to grimace. He's carefully watching the skeletally thin and dusky driver as they rocket towards the airport at nearly ninety miles an hour. The I45 and Highway 59 interchange passes in a blur of swerving insanity. Angry horn blasts fade away behind. The driver doesn't notice. The man has a bizarre way of guiding the overmatched car by rhythmically turning the steering wheel side to side, side to side. More like he's piloting a tiny wallowing boat—at top speed in a hurricane. Chip is not sure how he can keep it in the lane.

"I'm not in that big a hurry," Chip says.

The man looks back at him in the mirror and grins, nodding and showing two rows of perfect white teeth. But there is something wrong with them. Then Chip realizes that the front two incisors are sharpened to dagger points. Like a vampire.

"Yessir, hurry. I go," the man says enthusiastically.

"Jesus," Chip sighs, shaking his head and looking out the window. On second thought, he buckles his seatbelt up and returns to watching the jagged Houston skyline and the oddly turning angles of one black skyscraper, which, in his passing, appears disconcertingly as if it is being neatly sheared down the middle by an unseen blade of unearthly proportions.

In his pocket, the vibrator feel of his phone. Too loud in this bucket to hear the ringer. He angles the phone out and looks at it: Zingleman.

"Sharpe," he says, answering it. He listens with an expressionless face for a few moments, then he says, "Thanks, but just leave it. I'll handle it." Zingleman speaks some more, and Chip says, "yeah, it'll be okay, thanks again." He hangs up. The strange skyscraper is behind him and now to be seen: only featureless wastes of office buildings and houses and apartments.

Unbelievable. John showed up at The Wealth of God, picked up hitchhiking no less. A miracle? He asks himself the question seriously, but discounts it immediately. No, Chip should have known. Simon is a Charybdis of the lost and the vulnerable and the wayward, sucking them in for miles around.

And feeding on them.

Chip fingers the phone for a moment, debating and wondering at John's decision to call Zingleman. And who should he have called, he asks himself, you? He's got nobody and you're either dead to him or he wishes you were. Dead and gone and buried and what a wonderful parent you were. But maybe he does know, or senses it rather. Yes, he would call Zingleman.

Chip places the phone carefully on the seat next to himself and stares at it a time. Then he picks it up and dials Simon's number. No one answers, as he expected on a Sunday, a working day.

"Simon," Chip says after the beep, "Chip Sharpe here. There's a young man at your church today going by the name of John More..."

He stops a moment and looks up at a low airplane crawling in for a landing above him, hung there as if suspended in space, nearly matching the speed of their rushing taxi.

" ...he is my son."

On the other side, Simon picks up the receiver and shuts off the answering machine.

"Chip Sharpe," he says, "tell Us your problems."

⅄

# Simon Says

The good man sits behind an enormous mahogany desk and talks animatedly on the phone. I have an opportunity to observe him as I stand there uncomfortably waiting for him to finish his conversation. Still talking, he acknowledges me with a look and points a finger to a dark leather wingback chair. I sit, and the thing envelops me, eliminating my peripheral vision, forcing my focus onto the Reverend. His movements are quick, restless, and catlike. He seems to be doing two or three things at once: shuffling some papers, flipping through a spiral bound document of some sort. All sorts of things. His hands also never cease stroking back his hair. Distinguished waves of hair. Dark brown with a streak of steel-gray in just the right place. He's lean and probably toned beneath the white starched button-up. I realize he must work out pretty frequently, because you can see it in his athletic movements. Gold links gleam from French cuffs. The tailored silk suit fits his physique with European snug. The tie is bright and bold. Strong features, a sharp thin nose. He looks more CEO than pastor.

I'm startled. I was so lost in examining him, that I couldn't really say when he'd gotten off the phone, but he's sitting there observing me intently. Gray penetrating eyes, the color of his gray highlights, search me purposefully. His hands, still for the first time, rest clasped together on his battleship of a desk.

"John's a good name," he begins surprisingly. "A strong name."

"It is?"

"But what are We going to do with you, John? Or rather, what are you prepared to do for Us?" What the hell's he talking about? I lean over and peer around the wingback. No one else here; Elizabeth's long since slipped out. A look back, and he's still peering at me, questioningly. Guess he's wanting me to tell him something about my skills. Or lack thereof. It's sure been a hell of a day for confessions.

"Well... I can do lots of things..." I struggle to think of what those things are. Like what?

Swing a sledgehammer?

Teach bad tennis to old housewives?

Maybe I shouldn't elaborate any further. I remember that I don't even have all my rackets any more. What kind of pro has only one stick? Briefly, I see the rackets' slow shimmering arc into the water. I wince.

"We're sure you can."

He looks right at me for a while longer.

"You are?"

"We're confident of it."

Suddenly, he springs from his big black chair. He's around the desk and beside me before I know it.

"Walk with Us John."

I'm not sure he means literally or figuratively until he beckons me to come with him as he holds open his office door. I rise hesitantly and follow. He wraps one long arm around my shoulders, pulling me with him as we walk. Despite having showered, I worry about getting sweat and god knows what else on his thousand dollar suit. He's a couple of inches taller than I am and ramrod straight, so that he seems even taller. I feel insignificant in his presence, but somehow larger than my surroundings, larger than everyone else. Everyone else, that is, but him. I notice every one of the staff looking up at us as we pass in the corridor. He has that kind of charisma.

But what's with this royal We?

"What do you believe in, John?"

Gray eyes examine me again.

Oh no, not again. I don't know for Chrissake.

I remember the cops looking for me, my ditched car. I remember that I've saved less than a thousand dollars, and I've run away again. I remember that I've left my only friend in the whole world and the only place I felt good about anything. I remember the push, the thudding of his head. That sightless staring. I've failed everyone, and I've failed at everything, and I know nothing about what I want to do, where I want to go, who I am. Other than a murderer. I see a big dark figure the size of a mountain grasping for me; I hear a deafening roar in my head. I want to cry and cry and cry but cannot, and I want people to stop asking me things I don't want to think about and don't want to know. I gather myself to run, just run. But then I see smiling clear blue eyes, shining dark hair, a mockingbird's voice; and somehow I have to stay to see it through.

Just give him what he wants, just give it to him.

"Jesus?"

I hear myself say it, as if through thick oil.

I'm a liar.

Simon says nothing. I try again.

"Salvation?"

Obviously insincere.

What do you want me to say, for God's sake?

I just need a job. I just need her, somebody.

He nods with a look of inner wisdom; he seems to know my true thoughts, my innermost secrets, and he seems to forgive them. A beatific and handsome smile lights his face. With both hands he bangs open the double doors to the garage, puts his arm back around me, and guides me smoothly through.

The car is beautiful.

It is long, more racing yacht than car. It is muscular and smoothly refined all at once, clad in shining black and silver, so polished it gleams with an inner light. I'm stunned.

"Is that a Maybach?"

Of course, it is. I know it is. But, until now, I've only seen this car in magazine pictures, whiling away my hours in the convenience store.

There's a cool three hundred grand.

"That's right, John, salvation, salvation at the end of a long day." He strokes the gleaming vehicle lightly as he speaks. "The Maybach 62. Ah, John, yes, yes. The Lord, he does provide Us. He does provide the faithful well."

A uniformed chauffeur offers him the back door, and he glides into the darkened interior. I walk to the other side running a hand across the polished sheet metal and lovingly examine the swept fenders, the twenty inch chromed wheels, the telescoping, double predator-eye headlights. Everything about the car says quality, wealth, power.

But what about corruption, what about greed?

Doesn't it say that, too?

The chauffeur stands patiently holding the other door open. For me. I'm reluctant to let the five hundred and fifty horsepower, twelve-cylinder, tuxedo-clad beast out of my eyesight, even to sit inside of it. The driver smiles, prouder than the owner, if possible; probably he's prouder of this machine than of his own children. He's seen this look of mine before and lives for it. You can see it on his face. This is his baby. He'll always be there to have the fabulous car ready. Ready for Magic Simon, the Lord's own golden-tongued messenger.

Sliding in, I'm enveloped by deep black leather. The door closes softly, and solidly behind me. Double paned, bullet-proof glass and sound insulation instantly shut the outside world away. I'm alone with the Reverend in a leather-lined metal womb. Simon says nothing. He seems to be enjoying my awe—my worship—of his lovely car.

This is why he has this, just for suckers like me.

I look up to the panoramic roof and a soft blue and gold light bathes my face. The good man has had his roof glass replaced with stained glass, and coffered in dark mahogany. The picture is the gold cup of Christ on a field of blue. The Holy Grail in heaven. The Grail obtained.

"Well, how do you like Our little chariot?"

I'm too flabbergasted by the thing to answer. Besides, as he knows, it's a question that doesn't require an answer. My father's own S Class paled by comparison, a mere passenger car where this is truly a chariot of the gods. It is Apollo's own ride, pulling a celestial body across the sky.

"It's..." it's outrageous, over the top—and what on earth do they say when they see you in this thing?

I love it.

"...it's totally awesome."

He smiles the proud smile and nods to the driver to go. I look around some more in disbelief, reclining the huge seats, fiddling with the ventilation, turning on the movie-disc player and turning it back off again. One thing bothers me. Nags me. I don't know how to ask it.

"What... what do they say?" I indicate the opulence around me, "...to all this?"

He nods, knows what I've been thinking, is waiting on it perhaps.

"John, the Lord wants Us to be rich. It's His will."

There's conviction in his voice but it is the sound of an answer, long ago prepared, a tried and true one. Either that or he's said this so long, he believes it.

"The scriptures tell us that Jesus was a wealthy man, John. Did you know that?"

I blink stupidly at him. Scripture is not my strong point. Actually, I thought he was a poor Jewish carpenter. Born in a manger and all that. I doubt him, but I can't make myself express it.

And what the hell do I know?

"Wealthy?"

"Yes, John. Wealthy. Powerful. All of this," Simon warms to his subject, "Jesus' cloak was so valuable, Roman soldiers gambled for it when he was crucified."

Yeah? The soldiers I know also gamble for toothpicks and MREs. I think, too, of my sailcat crucifix, buried beneath the palm, entombed with a lost treasure.

"Well, I knew the soldiers gambled for it, but –"

"– Yes. And He drank from a cup of gold."

Simon lifts a finger to caress the golden image above.

Well, what the hell. Maybe he did.

I decide to humor him.

"Yeah, and He probably would've driven a Maybach too, if he only could've!"

The good man laughs at my weak joke and claps me on the knee.

"John, We think you'll do just fine here. Just fine."

"I pray so," I say, hopefully believably, hopefully under control. "I do hope so."

I see the morning sky eyes again, her hair, her face. Only this time, she is frowning.

⅄

# TELAMON

I **got to admit** it, Reverend Simon did me right. Lying on the bed after a session in the Jacuzzi, hands behind my head, silk lined terrycloth robe wrapped tightly around me, I just take it all in for a while. Calling that thing a Jacuzzi is an injustice. Having once been shown the raised Carrera marble—what to call it—roman bath thing, complete with marble columns, broad stone stairs, decorative glass tiles and blooming gold floral fixtures, I had to try it as soon as Simon's lackey had left. I'm aware of a crazy grin on my face, but I can't help it, this is too much. And it's not like I haven't seen opulence or wealth or decadence before. I've seen plenty, or at least I thought I had, until now.

Going from a metal shed and stolen pool pads to the personal rooms of Caesar in one day is hard to process. But, just like that, after the brief interview (more like a show and tell, really) Simon christened me his "Production Assistant" and set me up in his pad behind the main sanctuary.

In a normal church, these rooms would have been the sacristy. But this is a normal church like Vegas is a wholesome town or like Rap stars are blue collar workers. This is the pimp-daddy apartment of all time. Here's where, between sermons, events, and telecasts, Simon changes into his many suits and robes. What's interesting is that there are only two ways into the apartment, and they're both hidden. When they showed me this place, I immediately became partial to the entry off of a nondescript service corridor. It looks so much like a utility closet you'd never even guess what lies behind it.

This bed is just insane.

I run a hand down the silk duvet, white as the driven snow and so stuffed with goose down my head sinks in past my ears. I laugh and make a snow angel, or rather a bed angel. It's like being on a throne, lying on this larger-than-King-sized thing rising up from a marble edifice in the very center of the room, like a keep within the potentate's fortress. I sit up and try to wrap a hand around one of the enormous bedposts but can't come close. They're not even bedposts really, they're the columns of a temple, the temple within the temple as it were. They too are of solid marble and capped by ornate capitals way, way up there towards the ceiling.

Thing's gotta be twelve, fourteen feet tall, at least.

And the whole shebang is capped by a billowy canopy. I take my hand away and lie down again, looking up at it now, far above me. And what a canopy it is: blue as the sky, hemmed in gold rope, dripping gold tassels, gathered up in the heavens in delicate folds.

Finally, I make myself get up, meaning to find my duffel bag where the guy said he stashed it in the closet. But there is no closet, at least not like any I've ever seen. It's a whole wall of high gloss burled wood panels and not a single knob, pull, or fixture to be found in the whole expanse between the stone base of the floor and the cornice twelve feet above. Cautiously, I touch a panel, and a door glides open silently, hydraulically.

Awesome. I want some of these.

If I ever have a house, that is.

Inside is a bank of Simon's suits. Must be a hundred in there. I'm reminded that these are, after all, really the changing rooms he uses in between sermons and telecasts. I shut the door again and try to decide again which door hides my meager belongings. Each panel of wood matches with a precision I've never seen, and suddenly I realize that's not all there is to it. There's a scene composed of the very wood grain itself: of clouds, of mountains rising from rolling dales, subtle and amazing and unexpected in this otherwise overwrought grandeur.

I think of Bal and what he'd have to say about all this.

Nothing, that's what. He'd just look at it, and he'd have nothing to say.

But it is beautiful.

Finally, I touch the right panel and find my bag sitting all alone in an empty closet. I throw my robe on the floor, and there's a guilty thrill standing naked here. I don't know why, but there's a distinctly uncomfortable feel too—as if I'm being watched.

I am being watched.

Looking up, I study the enormous figures worked into the ceiling frescos. How could you not feel watched by those guys? And then, I see him. The incredible audacity of this man. Upon entering the room the first time, I'd seen the paintings more than twenty feet above me, of course. I'd thought them excellent copies of the Michelangelo in the Sistine Chapel but that's not what these paintings are, not exactly. I'd seen the real ones once, and like those indescribable works of art, the God in this scene reaches his divine finger out to bestow the gift of life unto man.

But this is not Adam.

I still can't believe it.

The figure in the painting is Simon.

What for Simon? Who are you trying to impress? God?

Is this really how you see yourself? Or am I just jealous?

I look around me at the opulent trappings, breathless, suddenly wanting to flee, also wanting to stay forever; I want this too, I know I do. And yet I don't.

Could this ever be me?

Who's to say that in the darkness of the decisions and decisions and decisions one faces over a lifetime of chance and uncertainty that I wouldn't reach out and grab for the same thing—this kind of power, this kind of wealth; this kind of worship? Yes, that is its name, that is the beast lurking here unseen in the corners, hiding from the light—it is worship—the deification of a simple man. And who am I to even know myself, much less to be a judge to other men?

"Sir?" a girl's voice.

Crap, crap, crap.

I scramble for the robe to cover myself, fall over my bag, legs, arms, everything flying everywhere. Grabbing the robe, and standing up, I try to recover some dignity, but it's no good.

"Yes?" My voice cracks. Hasn't done that in years.

Standing there is a young Mexican woman holding a tape, cloth, and pins; she's averting her eyes gracefully, incredibly managing not to laugh at me, a faint smile sitting on her lips maybe (and who could blame her?). Looks like a tailor or something.

Where the hell did she come from?

I never heard her enter, and the thought of the people here just being able to come into my room is shockingly disturbing. Very.

"I'm here to measure for your clothes, sir."

She looks at me now, already sizing me up, suppressed mirth and embarrassment still there, but kindly.

"My clothes?"

"Yes, your suits, sir. Mr. Simon's orders, sir."

"Oh." I frown. Suits, I don't want suits. I hate suits. Simon's words in our meeting come back to me now.

"John, if you want to be at the Wealth of God," he told me, looking over my ratty clothes, "you always gotta' look sharp. Let's do something about that shall We?"

I'd not understood what he meant then. Unfortunately, now I do; I sigh.

"Okay, well, I guess."

She comes to me now, unfurling her tape.

"By the way, my name is John," I tell her. "And, please, you don't have to call me Sir."

"Yes...John, please..."

She gestures for me to hold out my arms. I do and my robe comes open, leaving me hanging in the breeze again.

"Sorry!" I quickly wrap it shut again, and notice that she's giggled a little this time and averted her eyes, but not too quickly.

Was that a bit of a glance?

She's actually kinda pretty. I try to calm myself.

"Wait, a sec, let me get something else on." She turns away and fixes her eyes on the floor while I hastily put my tightest underwear on, some jeans, and my nicest t-shirt, which isn't saying much. "Okay, let's try this again."

The girl lingers over her work, lightly touching me where she measures. I watch the black hair, the slender brown limbs, the diminutive girlish body under the simple dress. It's driving me crazy and I have to resist the urge to lift her with a hand, to touch her.

"John?"

Oh great, now I've got Mike barging in on me, too. And just how many people can get in this place, anyway? "Over here, Mike," I say, as the girl finishes up.

"Simon sent me down here," he calls as he comes around the bed and looks me and the girl over. His brown shoes sparkle and radiate like diamonds. "What are you doing?"

My tailor hustles away without a word, without looking at either one of us.

"Getting measured for suits, apparently."

Mike gives me a confused look, looks to where the girl departed, then looks back at me.

"I guess Reverend Simon thinks I need some," I add, trying to clarify that it wasn't my stupid idea.

"Oh," he pauses, looks down and kicks at a carpet fringe a little. "Well, what are you going to be doing then?"

"He said I'm gonna' be the Production Assistant."

At this Mike looks up at me quickly, incredulously.

"He made you what?"

"Ah, Production Assistant..." I say meekly. I'm getting nervous vibes from Mike's look, and thinking that maybe I don't know what I'm getting into here. "...is that good?"

"Do you have any experience with Productions or Theater or anything like that?"

I shake my head that I do not, getting more scared by the second. Suddenly, Mike snaps to attention, touching his finger to his ear, and I realize that he's got a tiny earpiece there. He seems to be listening to it.

"Yes," Mike is saying, "yes," a nod, "yessir, I'll do it," and then: "Thank you sir, God bless." He takes his finger away from his ear slowly, a distant look on his face, then he addresses me. "Right. Production Assistant, yes, as we were saying, that is good...very good." I grin, relieved. "It's just... well, you'll be helping me a lot, John...and Reverend Simon too, of course."

Mike starts to walk, beckoning me to follow him with his hand. It is a precise mimic of Reverend Simon's gesture. I move to follow him towards the wall of wooden closet panels.

"Uh, where are we going?"

"Control room," Mike says preoccupied, not even looking at me. He touches a panel, and the door glides open. He steps in.

"In the closet?"

"Not a closet, John." The voice comes out to me, as if in a tunnel. I hesitate, step in the dark closet, see that this one is actually a dimly lit hallway.

Very cool, a secret passage.

I hustle to catch Mike up. When I do, he looks at me briefly, reflectively, and continues talking, almost as if to himself.

"It's a hard job. The PA will be responsible for ensuring that the entire sermon goes off without a hitch. The props, the cameras and audio, the floods, the angels, the pyrotechnics; there are controls for all of these things."

Interesting. I nod my head. "Sounds like fun."

Mike looks at me dubiously.

"Well, it's very complicated," he says. "It all has to be done exactly on cue..."

"Oh."

"...Or the sermon will fail." Mike stops before a door, puts his hand on a security pad, and looks straight at me as the door swings open of its own accord. "And Reverend Simon really, really doesn't like it when the sermon fails." He steps in, leaving me there in the hall with the thought of Magic Simon's wrath.

"Oh."

I feel the palms of my hands start to sweat, like they do before a big match; I rub them together, looking at them, as if I've never seen them before. Sweating, like they were before the big match with Clarke. Just like that.

And look how well that worked out.

The control room is dimly lit and large, filled with blinking lights, wall mounted monitors, the quiet machine sounds of a nerve center not in use at the moment. On the far wall is a huge window that overlooks the main sanctuary, now dark. Two full banks of work stations step down the room toward the window. Empty swivel chairs in each position. Looking around me, I'm stunned, now nervous, now scared.

This place; it's like mission control.

Mike's just standing there with his hands on his hips, looking out through the windows into the darkened sanctuary. The huge space stretches before him like some vast cave in the night. Tiny, orange Exit signs float in the nothingness of the black gulf. He doesn't turn to look at me, but he's heard me enter. In quiet tones, he speaks: "The Reverend's talked about creating the position for some time now. 'Take the burden off,' he told me, 'it's too much...'"

There's the sound of genuine pain in his voice, and I feel ashamed.

"...Take the burden off," Mike goes on. " I never thought he'd actually do it." Now, I know.

This was your job, wasn't it Mike?

"I'll have to help, of course," he says, recovering himself a little. "Yes, I'll train you. You have to understand how he operates, his subtle cues, the timing.. This is actually good." He's saying the words more to himself. "This is good, yes, yes. I'm the youth minister after all. That's my main job."

I nod, but Mike doesn't see me.

"But it'll take time," he smiles at me now. "There's a lot to learn."

"I'm sure there is," I assure him, and Mike keeps smiling, having talked himself back into relevance. But his is the smile of resignation, as if he senses the inevitable: that he'll lose some of his closeness to the great Simon, like losing a part of himself.

And he'll lose it to me.

Mike picks up a tiny earbud from a drawer at one of the stations, toggles a switch or two on one of the panels, and hands it to me.

I put the device in my ear, a white noise, then quiet, then the rich, deep voice comes: "Ah John, there you are, there you are." It is Simon. I look at Mike and give a thumbs up. "Welcome to the inner sanctum of the Wealth of God," the voice says, "Welcome to Us."

"Hello, Reverend Simon," I say into thin air, "Thank you..."

But the voice like a phantom is gone now, as if it were never there at all, and I close my mouth slowly, my words still hanging on my lips, forgotten. I'm left wanting, somehow. I had it only for a brief moment, but I'm left selfishly wanting for more: more of that closeness, that nearness. Somehow, I feel that I would do anything for the Great Man with the voice like a god.

He only has to say the word.

Mike spends hours showing me the system, and at the end of it, I'm totally exhausted, but it was interesting and even exciting to see what spectacular things you can do with this set-up, the show you can put on. I hadn't seen anything when I'd witnessed my first sermon. There's more you can do—a lot more. And I think Mike's feeling better, too. He's seen that I can learn this, and as we walk back through the secret passage, I get a new sense of camaraderie from him.

"See Mike," I say to him, "that was fun. I'm going to like the job."

"Yeah, well wait until there's twenty people in the control room all yelling at you, and five thousand people in the audience, and a hundred thousand tuned in, and Simon working his magic out there, and then see how much fun it is!"

But he says it with a laugh and a smile, and he is glad after all, and pleased I think, to have found a willing pupil.

"Yeah, well, I'll get ready, you'll see. I'll do you proud."

Mike smiles and claps me on the back. "I'm sure you will, John."

"And who'd a thunk he'd make a wayward hitchhiker the Production Assistant to the Wealth of God? If ya'll hadn't picked me up, I'd probably be sleeping in a ditch."

Mike smiles back appreciatively and opens the door to my room.

"Yes, who would've thought? But the Lord does work in mysterious ways, John."

I nod. So does the Reverend Simon, apparently.

"Yeah, that, and I work real cheap."

But it's a bad joke and Mike looks at me quizzically. Quickly, I add: "But, seriously, I am very grateful to you and Reverend Simon and Elizabeth. Thanks. Thanks a lot. I don't know how to repay you."

"No repayment needed," says Mike; "it's the Lord's work, not mine. The Lord's work."

I watch him leave the room, and then I look overhead to the looming figure of Simon painted up there on the ceiling, receiving the gift of life from God.

The Lord's work? Well, maybe Mike, but I wonder...

And just then I catch a glint in Simon's painted eye and a disturbing thought occurs to me. I'd seen the video monitoring system in the control room. There are cameras all over this building, all over campus, and they are always filming.

Is it the Lord watching over me? Or is it Simon?

It takes a couple of weeks of solid learning before I can even think of managing the basics of an entire sermon by myself, but it's more fun than I've ever had working before. I spend hours and hours in my control room, playing with the equipment and getting to know the other people who work here. There seem to be a thousand dials and switches controlling every technological trick imaginable. I have to learn how to operate all the stations myself, and, as the only full time production employee, I'm supposed to be the leader of the effects show. When I'm ready, I'll be telling the other production people when to run their miracles, and I'll do some of the effects myself. It's something new every day. I'm particularly fond of flying the angels out over the sanctuary. It's like playing with a super-sophisticated remote control toy, and I have to make myself remember that these are real women and that their lives are at stake. I learn these controls the best, for it's a strange and powerful sensation, seeing the girls float out over the void by your hand. I can't get enough of it. I know now why the Wizard built Oz.

The big day arrives. My first sermon at the helm is about to begin, and I'm wracked by nerves. I tug on my new tie for no reason and look down at one of my new suits. They'd come yesterday, a dozen of them at least. I'd been proud then, looking in the mirror at myself and wondering if I'm becoming my father, grudgingly admitting that indeed I do look good in them. I'd even gone to show Elizabeth, feeling like some GQ model, or something.

Remember how her eyes had shone?

But now it just feels silly.

I brush my jacket down for no reason. The other controllers are here, the room is abuzz, and the telecast has already begun. Watching people file into the sanctuary, my palms sweat again.

"John! You ready with the cues?"

I jump. It is the sniveling director, yelling in my ear bud. He's talking to me from down on the stage where Simon is almost ready to begin. In this game of 'Simon Says,' I'm to listen for the cue phrases from the sermon itself and trigger the miracles accordingly.

"Yes," I reply to him, "ready."

Mike watches over me, the veteran passing the torch to the rookie on the day of the final exam. I've now seen several sermons and worked the machines to perform the small miracles, but I've never run one of the productions before.

Today's the day. Try not to screw up, John. Not today.

"Lights!" The director barks the command for the show to begin.

This is an easy one. I point a finger at the light man; he's already expecting it. He nods, flips a switch and turns a dial. The sanctuary lights go out; there's complete darkness within.

A dazzling spotlight snaps on, illuminating Simon. He stands alone in the darkness, looking up, directly into the heavenly light. He raises his arms, dramatically clasps his hands.

This is the cue. The show is on. I'm on my own. But it's hard to concentrate. He ascends a stair, like some dapper leopard. The crowd is already enthralled, and I am too.

"Waters of the Lord!" he implores the heavens.

His arms are held wide now, his face is upturned to God.

Nothing's happening.

Crap, I wasn't paying attention; that was a cue phrase. This is one of my controls.

I race to the station, spin the blue dial and press the blue button. Lights flood the stage and cataracts of water burst forth in a thundering river. In my earbud, the sound is so terrifying, I jump back.

Goddamnit, now I've over-flooded it.

I reach for the dial to turn it down, but a hand restrains me; there's a whisper in my free ear. It is Mike. "That was just fine," he says, "just fine. You're okay. Try to stay calm."

I try to slow my breathing, to quiet my laboring heart.

"Voices of Heaven!" Simon's cue words ring loudly again.

Another of my controls. Quickly now.

Snatch the stage lever, spin the fog dial, pump the pedals.

"Easy, easy, easy now," whispers Mike in one ear while Simon belts out his sermon in the other. I give the hand signal to the choir guy. "Not too fast."

In the video link-up, I see the choir materialize from behind a cloud bank just as their voices burst simultaneously into song.

"Beautiful. Well done".

It's a strange sensation having two voices in my ear. It's as if both God and Gabriel are competing in a game of miracle one-upmanship.

"Heralds of God!" proclaims Simon, and his voice thunders over the crowds in a stormy wave. I don't know what he's been talking about, so concentrated am I now, but those were the cue words—'Heralds of God'—the ones I've been waiting for.

It's time for the angels.

I check the video screen one last time. The girls are all ready to fly. I place both my hands on the twin joysticks, feeling Mike tense behind me as I do. This is the hard part. This is the best part.

"Come forth!" commands Simon, the demi-god. "Heralds of God! Come to me!"

I nudge both sticks bottom left. Angels swoop low over the gasping crowd. Diaphanous gowns flutter out behind the flying girls in their speed. My hands move the sticks again. The angels slow to a hover, hanging low in the cavernous space, just above the delighted audience.

"Hear the suffering of the people and bring their lament to the Light!"

At these words, I punch the yellow button and move both joysticks in a smooth counterclockwise motion. The girls spiral up in an ever tightening cone to the spectacularly bright spot on the distant ceiling, becoming silhouettes as they do. I punch the black button, and total darkness descends into the sanctuary.

The choir stops. There is total silence.

Simon and I let the congregation sit there a moment in utter darkness to reflect on what they have just seen and heard. In the crowd: only the sound of awe. The effect was perfect.

The show's over. I move the angels quietly back into their hidden docking stations.

"The lights," Mike whispers, "get the lights."

"Oh, yeah."

I bring the spot back onto Simon and slide the dimmer for the house lights up enough for the congregation to see the offering plates. In my ear, the good reverend is now imploring the flock for money. Today there will be more soldiers for Simon's Army, more maniacs for the Simoniacs, and even a few inductees into the Reverend's Inner Sanctum, but that's it for me.

"Oh, that was good," congratulates Mike. "That was just fantastic, John! You did it! Couldn't have done it better myself."

"Thanks," I reply humbly, and it was, wasn't it? It was pretty good.

Mike's ecstatically proud of me. Simon seems relaxed and happy out there. And I am proud, I realize. I've never felt like this on a tennis court or in any job before.

I can do this. I can actually do this.

Still. Something nags me about it all. A little buzz in my mind that says something's not right; an unhappiness I just can't quite put my finger on. It asks: will I ever be happy anywhere, will I ever feel good about something?

I wonder, sometimes, I really do.

As the weeks pass, I get really familiar with the equipment, more relaxed, and I start to make improvements of my own. Mike doesn't even come to the sermons to supervise anymore. He leaves them to me and spends most of his time working with the youth groups. Some days I don't even see him. But I become more and more indispensable to Simon, and he integrates me deeply into the support functions of his world.

We've gotten some new equipment, too, including a cool remote control that allows me greater freedom and requires no other controllers. They were all unreliable volunteers anyway.

I finger the device, so much like a TV remote, but with two tiny joysticks and a roller ball. It's been a big learning curve, and no one besides me has been able to master the new gear, including the Director. I smile with a new thought.

Pretty soon we won't need him either.

But that's evil. Shame comes over me for thinking this, and I wipe the smile from my face. His is a paid position. He's got a family. This is his life. My Pop might have been the kind of guy to want him fired, but not me, no matter how much he antagonizes me.

That's not me. Still...

In the corner of my eye, I catch a glimpse of her and turn to watch the monitors for the security camera feeds. Even in the tiny picture frame, Elizabeth looks radiant.

"Welcome to Oz," I say, breaking in on the PA system for that sector.

She looks up at the camera, laughing, and waves. I wave back and blow her a kiss.

Good thing she can't see me.

Strange how Simon is.

That'd been his idea too, having her help me. He saw one day how good I am with the new equipment, especially how I was adding small flourishes and enhancements to the miracles, just screwing around really. And just like that, on the spot, in front of everyone, he'd said: John, work out a new angel routine for my new sermon. The Director's jaw dropped at that. Everybody's did, but especially his. It's the Director's job to come up with the routines, not mine, and everybody knew it. But nobody said anything; nobody confronts Simon.

The Director's mouth worked itself like a fish out of water, but no words came out, and I'd turned away to hide my laughter—hide my fear too. Simon took it all in, I know he did. The man's sharp like that. He smirked at us almost, then he added another twist to his evil social experiment. Elizabeth, he'd said, help him. And then he'd turned and just walked out, leaving everyone standing around in uncomfortable silence.

The door opens, startling me a little and the remote drops from my hand with a clatter.

"Hi, John, what's up?" Elizabeth says, looking down at me while I fumble around trying to pick up the device. There's a smile in her eyes.

"Oh, hey, uh, not much."

She's wearing a warm-up suit and a gym bag, and I'm wondering what she's got in there, and what cool thing to say to her, but I can't come up with anything. So I just stand there, looking at her, as usual. Finally, she breaks the awkward silence.

"So, you need for me to be a test angel again today?"

"Oh, yeah, let's do that," I respond, relieved to have something to talk about. "I think we almost have it."

We spend the next half-hour whiteboarding small changes to the new routine we've been working on. And though I like being close to her here, working with her, I love to see her out there even more, floating across the chasm, performing the routines we've created all by ourselves. I wrap up the planning.

"That just about does it I think, you ready to fly?"

"Ready," she says.

And I can see she's excited, too. Picking up her bag, she practically dances over to the exit to the angel bays. She opens the door, turns back, and holds my eyes for a moment.

"Oh, John, do..."

"Yes?" I ask, heart in my throat. I'm thinking furiously about what she might ask, hoping she'll say, what? Do you love me? Do you want me?

"...well, I just, oh, do you think this will be beautiful, this routine? I'm so worried about it."

"Oh." I'm disappointed. I could swear something else was on the tip of her tongue, but she couldn't bring herself to say it. "Well, it'll be no problem. It will be beautiful, you're..."

Now it's my turn to choke. What I want to say: you're beautiful, you're the most beautiful angel I could ever imagine; I want you; I think I love you. I do. But I can't.

"...really good at this choreography stuff. Thanks, thanks for helping."

She smiles, turns and steps into the hall, and lets the door go again. Was that disappointment in her eyes? Did she want me to say something more? Did she? The door clicks closed behind her, and I am left alone in the dim room.

I can see her now on the video monitor as she gets ready in bay one, and I try not to look, try not to watch her taking off her warm-up suit.

You're a voyeur John, that's what you are.

A filthy perv.

But I can't help it. I can't. It's thrilling seeing her in this way, silently in black and white, her beautiful body revealed in a black leotard and a simple t-shirt. She dons the angel wings and pulls on the harnesses. A longing in me so intense, I can almost feel her, touch her as she adjusts the straps around her thighs, under her arms, her breasts; she must know I can see her, but she doesn't turn away. She looks up now, right at the camera, and smiles at me.

So beautiful.

She gives a thumbs up. She's ready to fly. I move her slowly, slowly out of the bay and over the sanctuary where I can see her through the window. Now I pick up the audio. An unmitigated pleasure, controlling her every move this way. It's a dance, a dance of high wires, of computers, of circuitry. She trusts me implicitly and completely in these private sessions; I make her swoop low over the empty seats, and she flies in a Supergirl pose, fist out, cleaving the air, laughing in simple delight at the thrill. I bring her up now in a soft arc, floating her like a dandelion on a breeze; it's a new move, but she anticipates me, and flutters there in space; it's as if we are together in the heat of a slow tango, but without the inhibitions of actual contact, we are freed for an even greater intimacy.

Now the ascent to heaven. She adds the twist of a slow pirouette, reaching out to her sides with perfect white arms, palms turned up, eyes to heaven, like some marbled goddess of the air. Sadness seeps into me.

Why can't we be like this when we're actually together?

In her physical presence, I have a hard time even speaking to her. We—she?—can't allow our intimacy to extend into the personal realm; something holds us back. But I am sure the thought is there in each of us, the vivid memory of our dancing lingering within.

I know it does. It must.

She finishes up the routine with mock drama, and we laugh, and I bring her back in, switching back to the video monitor. As she lands, she looks at the camera, right into me, and I see it. I know it.

Something is there.

It is in her eyes, in the way she softly purses her lips, not a kiss, but almost, almost.

Back in the room together, she wraps her arms across her chest, as if she's embarrassed to be seen now. She quickly packs her things to go, and we break into a different dance of furtive shy smiles and careful innuendo; nothing more and with nothing said. As the times before, when we've been alone like this, experienced togetherness like this, I can't bring myself to ask her out and can't express my feelings for her.

I can't do it.

My father claws his way in my mind. Loser, he smirks in a chant. Loser, loser, loser...

Can't disagree with that.

The door shuts behind her with the sound of finality, and my heart sinks once again. I turn out the lights and slump in the chair, gazing at the twinkling of electronics, like stars, false ones though they be. I'm not even sure I'd know where to take her, anyway. All my time is spent at the church now. Thanksgiving and Christmas have come and gone. New Year's, too. I worked right through them—three sermons each day, all telecast live. No one, not even Elizabeth, asked me over for dinner, and I picked a present from the Church collections.

Like a thief.

Murderers and beggars, Dad lectures again, cannot be choosers.

Just shut up, Dad. Shut up. Now.

The microphone in my ear crackles to life. I know what's coming.

"John," says the voice of the god-man, Simon. "John, come to Our office. Now."

Not a thief. Not a beggar. I'm a slave, and I don't even have a car.

$$\lambda$$

# A MOUTH OF DOUBT

In the moment of my dribble, the rich brown leather feels just right in my hands, and I pull up from way behind the three point line.

"Game winner," I call.

I cock my arm and shoot, and the ball leaves my fingertips with a lingering touch. The wrist snaps outward just so, the shot's off, the game clock expires, and the ball's in a perfect backspin, up in a gorgeous high arc. I hear the satisfying rip of the net as the ball plunges through the hole.

"Nothing but net."

I raise three fingers in triumph, although no one's in the gym to see my heroics.

Should' a played basketball instead.

Dad liked basketball.

The ball bounces back my way; I sprint up to collect it, and go for a sweet layup.

Call it.

"Reverse left-handed putback."

In the middle of my move, there is white noise from my earbud.

"John." Simon's voice, in my ear.

I miss the shot, landing awkwardly, and kick the ball to the bleachers.

Damnit, Simon, can't you ever let me be?

"Yes, Reverend?"

"Come to Our office."

The link closes as abruptly as it had opened. I collect my jacket, straighten my tie, and start the walk to his office. The walk of the damned.

Why has it been getting to me so much lately? Why—because the Reverend Simon is nearly always with me now, and because I'm not sure about him anymore, not that I ever was—that's why.

And where is all this headed?

I wake to his voice. I go to sleep with his voice. The voice, ever-present in my ear bud, is alternately and randomly demanding, peevish, kind, or instructive, often in the same set of commands. It is always delivered from on high, and I never forget that I'm required to serve. His voice has become like my own consciousness, or merely a louder consciousness than mine, buzzing more abruptly, more aggressively than my own. In my thought lately, Simon's voice has even begun to supplant that of my father's. And I'm not sure Simon's isn't worse. In just a few months, I've moved on from being a mere Production Assistant. I am also the Personal Assistant, the Man's right-hand. I seem to be perfect for all of his uses. Everybody's noticed the special treatment, too. I'm beginning to feel hated here.

But it's not my fault.

At Magic Simon's office, the great man's great wooden door is closed. I knock.

Nothing. There's no response.

I raise my hand to knock again, but before I can make contact, the door cracks open, and a lady slips out so fast I almost knuckle her on the forehead.

"Oh, ouch, sorry," I say quickly, embarrassed.

I've never seen her before. She's a bleached sort of pretty and looks married. Strangely, for someone who almost got rapped on the head, she doesn't make eye contact with me. She just mumbles an apology of her own and runs off, like an escapee. The door bangs shut behind her, and I'm left wondering what to do now. I wonder if Simon's ever been married.

"Deliver the script to the Director, get them started in half an hour." Simon's voice in my ear again. The link closes. The door remains shut.

"Reverend? You there?" I tap my ear, nothing.

Oh well.

I turn to rummage through Simon's outbox, and the document is there.

"Here's your script for today's telecast," I tell the Director, handing him the sermon written just like a screenplay. "The Reverend wants to begin in thirty minutes."

It seems a simple enough statement, but the Director, short, badly balding, bespectacled whiner that he is, takes the document without so much as a word of thanks. He just looks at me through magnified eyes so that I can see the scorn that much more clearly. It's as if he's saying: I'm the Director here, boy; I don't take orders from you, and tell Simon he can kiss my ass. Of course, he says nothing of that. In fact, he says nothing at all to me; he just rudely turns his back to address his crew. I don't really blame him. He's got to be sore about my handing him his assignments this way, as if Simon can't be bothered to even speak to the man any more.

Actually, I've been wanting to apologize to the Director, to say that I have nothing to do with Simon's orders to him, that I never even asked for this job. I've been looking for the right words to say, the right time. Maybe this isn't it.

"Commandments from the Mouth of God, guys," the Director says loudly to his crew. "Better snap to it." His voice is mocking, derisive. He didn't even try to say it quietly.

He wanted me to hear that.

Astonished and hurt, I try to hide the look my face must have revealed, try to turn and walk away slowly, as if I haven't heard. Laughter behind me. Anger swimming up within me.

Damnit, it's not my fault. This isn't my doing. Simon, you hypocritical ass.

I find myself walking back up to the office.

You've got to see me; you've got to talk to me.

But it's hard to think of what I'll say to him. All I can think about is this: The Mouth of God. So that's what they call me? The Mouth of God?

It's true, then, they all hate me.

It's a tough realization and a lonely one, too. Here I am, sequestered away at the Church twenty-four by seven, like a wraith, and I'm most of these people's only link to the increasingly private Reverend Simon.

Why wouldn't they hate me? Why shouldn't they?

What is he doing to me?

Elizabeth is the only one who seems to understand. He treats her pretty much the same as me, always calling on her to do little details of other people's jobs—no matter what she might be working on at the moment. But with her, it's just so he can see her, just so he can be close to her. I'm sure of it. That's really starting to bother me, too.

The way he looks at her.

Lascivious animal, he's always finding clever ways to touch her: a quick hug, a light brush of the hand, a quick arm around the shoulder. I have to admit he's good at it, and maybe I am just jealous, but it seems to be even more pronounced when I'm there too, like he's flaunting it or something. And when she turns to leave, he'll wink over at me, like he's saying: look at that piece of ass, will ya'? It makes me sick, and I know she doesn't like it.

But then I wonder: do you know that, or do you hope it, John?

Could she actually like him too? Surely not.

At Simon's office, the door is cracked, and I stick my head in without even knocking. Simon's standing right up next to his floor to ceiling windows, facing them, lording over all the church grounds. He turns to see who it is and smiles broadly at me. A gold ringed index finger orders me to come over and I make the walk across the expanse of carpet playing a game with myself of what I'm going to say to him. I imagine taking charge of this conversation and getting him to agree on calling an employee meeting where he'll clarify each of our positions, the group's goals, something. And in this imaginary meeting, we'll establish better communications with the whole team, and not just have me and Elizabeth as go-betweens. And speaking of...

"John, just the man We wanted to see."

"I am?"

"Yes, yes."

Simon is smiling wickedly.

"Come over here and see this."

He turns again to look out the window and waves me to his side.

"Look down there," Simon says.

When I get there he drapes an arm around me in a fatherly way, and points down to a huge black and red powerboat. The thing is sleek and sexy and menacing and very, very cool.

"Wow. More of the Lord's good will?"

"Yes, she is a beauty, isn't she? My earthly reward for doing His Will, just as the Wealth of God is, and these good people that I have all around me are." He claps me on the shoulder and beams at me as the boat is being pulled away.

I'm stunned at what he's just implied, and without the least trace of irony. I'm the same as a powerboat. Same as a fancy car. Like everyone else here at the Wealth of God, I am simply a possession of the Church. His possessions.

We are Simon's earthly rewards.

It's a sobering thought, and it's starting to make me mad. But, at the same time I can see his point, and that makes me even angrier, for what is life anyway, but the pursuit of material possessions and the quest for a paradise on earth?

Damnit, look at me.

Here I was coming up to set things straight, and now I'm feeling like something he bought at the mall. And I'm buying into it. I feel sick. I don't know what to say, don't even know where to begin with him, but before I can articulate what I'm thinking, Simon's hand stretches out to me. My attention snaps back to him. He's got something, something very familiar.

"Speaking of which, John," he says, "We bestow some rewards of Our own. Here, a surprise, just for you."

"You do?"

Simon says nothing. He just wraps my hand around the hard metallic object. Tentatively, I open my fingers. But this can't be. On a string with a card, it is: my Porsche key. My scalp tingles, a peculiar feeling travels down the back of my neck, then my spine, like hackles rising. My first reaction: run, flee, hide. But I control it and enclose the key back into my fist, not looking at him. The note says:

"Your Earthly Reward, Parking Garage, 3G—enjoy!"

My Porsche. I can't believe it; he has my Porsche. I can't say anything at all. I can't process this. No one knew. No one here knew I ever had a car at all.

But he found it. He knows my secrets.

He smiles his panther smile, steel eyes glittering with purpose, then he turns his back and goes over to look out his window again with hands clasped behind his back, saying nothing more. Magic Simon indeed.

The key burns in my hand. I turn and just barely restrain myself from running, and Simon's smile is burned in my mind, like the storybook cat's, grinning there before me as I hurry through the halls.

There in the parking garage I find her, right next to the Maybach. She's gleaming and beautiful, and she is my very own car. I know it like you'd know your own mother. Maybe more. I open the door and slip slowly into the car, running my hand over the newly cleaned upholstery. Definitely mine.

You left me, she whispers. Don't do it again.

I stop. Another sudden shock.

I see a long, coarse, black hair; it's almost woven into the fabric of the floorboard carpet. With a pinch of my fingers, I pull it out and examine it closely.

Incredible. Even after all the cleanings. And I think of him, out there, somewhere, absent these days from my dreams and my sight. I toss it away like it was dirty.

The car fairly purrs as I let it idle on the spot. Buffed to glossy perfection, working beautifully, interior shining—the car is even better than before. Remade, reborn, renewed.

I back the car out quickly and smoothly, throwing into first while still on the move. I pick my ear bud out and toss it away as I accelerate past the Maybach. In my rearview mirror, I see the damned thing skitter to a rest in my now empty parking spot.

I drive. Recordings of Simon's sermons compete in my head, alternately and simultaneously babbling and laughing hysterically and crooning and whisperedly soothing.

It's an hour before I even really think about anything at all and another hour before it occurs to me to think about where I should go or what I should do. It's just me and the wind in my ears and my very own voice has a say in my very own head.

What does this mean? What is he playing at?

But my own voice has no definitive answers.

From within, another voice comes, a new voice, a big and brassy voice. A vision, a vision, it cries. You need a plan or you are done, you are had, ix-nay, finite, no delays.

No, no, silence. But the voice goes on and on and on.

I ignore it as best I can and drive.

As night draws near, I find myself all the way over in Victoria, sitting in some rusty corrugated steel-sided barbeque joint, eating good greasy sausage and ribs from a plastic plate. No cops have followed, no threat seems imminent. Obviously, I haven't been reported. What is up here? My mind wanders over all that I've done since I ran that very first day. Not exactly a good show, no, not at all, and verses are in my head:

*Run and leave, run and hide, no house, no home, no girl to call my very own.*

I shake them away. But what choices did I have? I tell myself the lies: about getting caught, about exposing myself to risk, blaming the accident for everything. Lies, all of it. Almost like I've deserved all this, for I have done it unto myself.

Should I leave the church? Is that what he's saying?

But he'd written, "Your earthly reward." Is he actually saying: I know your secret, I have spoken for you, and I forgive you?

Damnit, why the riddles?

Because it's a choice. He's giving me a choice.

Stay or go. Return from the wilderness, or flee back into it.

Or is it a threat?

I know your secret. Leave and you will be reported.

But if I felt trapped by him before, now I will be totally and utterly in his thrall. My staying is all his vision of success, not mine, not mine at all. If he says drink the Kool-Aid, I will have to drink the Kool-Aid.

"Want some more, Honey?"

I look up at the waitress for a long moment, confused by her intrusion on my thoughts. I've heard that somewhere before, somewhere long ago. The pretty night-gowned lady. Back there in the woods. It seems like years since I met her. I don't even know her name. I think of Gloria, too, and Adela, of Elizabeth.

Do I want some more? Do I? I don't know.

It's not a rhetorical question, idiot.

"Honey..." she says, and the déjà vu moment grows stronger, "...you all right?"

Looking up at the waitress, I shake my head clear. She's overdone and overweight, but okay with it all, and seems kind beneath the crusty exterior. I'll bet she's seen more down-on-their-luck kind of guys in this place than you can shake a stick at, and yet she still seems to care.

"Yeah, sorry, just had my mind on something else."

She smiles and nods, cocking a hand on her ample hip.

"Well, that's fine, now don't you let whatever it is worry you too much. So, you want some more ribs, or not?"

"Oh... okay. I mean, no thanks, I'm all right. I'm full. I think I'm done here, if you could just bring me the check."

But I'm not, I guess. I'm not done with all this.

Where else can I go?

I've got a good job now. A real job. It's the best money I've ever made and the most responsibility I've ever had. I'm the magic behind magic Simon. Religious mumbo-jumbo or not, he needs me, and that's something.

Isn't it?

Of course, I'm sure he'd known everything all along, or figured it out before I even went into his office that first time. That explains why he was so intrigued with me, why he wanted a meeting, why he set me up so nicely. I'm his reform project; I'm his little social experiment, and now he is definitely testing me. Probably, knowing exactly what he was doing, he had also sensed just when to give me those keys. I wonder how long he's had the Porsche ready, waiting for the right moment. God, how I imagine him laughing now, everything playing out just like he thought. How the man does presume himself to be one of the glorified. One rung below Jesus. Or just maybe: one rung above. I know I've been manipulated, but somehow knowing it makes me feel a little better because I know he needs me now. Whatever the circumstances of my arrival were, I have the one thing in my favor: he does need me.

Back in the car, meandering slowly east, I'm heading back. Back to the Wealth of God. My eyes wander up into the sky, purpling now with the darkness and streaked with long, deep, pink and orange clouds; a scene so dramatic as to be garishly unreal, like some bad painting done in bright acrylics by a two-bit craft show artist. Or by Simon. I have to smile at the thought. I sober up at another.

Does *she* need me?

⅄

# JOHN THE BAPTIST

Sitting in my control room, listening to the hubbub of the staff preparing for the sermon, the whining of the Director grates above them all. I finger the earpiece. I'm ready, but Simon is curiously silent. I think back to my return to the church. Reverend Simon was right about that. He knew I'd return, and I did. I parked my car exactly where I'd found it, and the earbud was there on the garage floor, too, exactly where I'd thrown it, scratched but still working. Thankfully, it had been silent when I put it back in, and it had stayed that way for a whole day. Probably he saw the whole thing and knew when I switched it back on. I'll bet he was smiling with bared fangs. But I'm right about his needing me, too. Why else would he have done what he did for me? Like a spoiled only child who has every toy but no one to play with, he's realized what he doesn't have: real friends.

Am I that friend?

Can someone like Simon ever really be friends with someone?

Probably not.

But it's maybe as close as he can get when he thinks of everyone as his possessions. He must like the thought of owning me, like a slave or something. Strangely though, the realization still gives me some confidence. After all, Simon does want only the best of possessions. He must think I'm at least good.

"Well, what's the Mouth of God have to say? Where's Simon? What's up?"

It's the Director, and he is glaring at me from behind his cokebottle glasses, as if it's my fault Simon hasn't shown up yet.

"Beats me. He'll turn up."

I brush him away with a sweep of my hand, finding it easier to defuse him these days. His snide remarks bother me no longer. After all, I realize with some pride, I am (in a way) the Mouth of God, even if maybe a doubting one. They're just jealous of my friendship with the friendless tyrant. A thought: do I have any friends? Maybe on the basketball court; Elizabeth seems to truly like me, maybe Mike too. Not many others though, I have to admit. At least I have my car now, so I can go out when I want. Maybe I'll meet some new people over in town. Maybe I'll work up the courage to ask Elizabeth out to dinner. Maybe she'll even go, if I can find the right words. All I need is the right thing to say and the confidence to do so.

Simon's absence isn't really a concern to me yet. In truth, it's hard to even concentrate on prepping today's miracles with the crew. I've done this sermon before, anyway.

What's the Director so upset about?

I adjust the audio at his command and sneak a glance at a couple of the angels getting ready in the bays. Where does he find them all? They're all beautiful. None of them is Elizabeth though.

Turning away again, I look at the video feeds from outside; it's a beautiful Sunday morning. Can't believe I'm in this dungeon; I'd rather be out playing basketball or something. For a moment, the vision of the tennis court comes to me again, but only for a moment. It's disturbing. Sighing, I think about my match with Clarke; the pain's going away. Although I hate to admit it, even to myself, I miss the game.

Well, I still have the one racket. Maybe I should just get all new ones, and make a new start with the game, not taking it so seriously any more.

"John?"

I snap back to the task at hand. It's the Director again. He's out on the sanctuary stage.

"Yeah? I'm here."

"John, wake up. Cue the angels. Let's do a test fly-through."

"Okay."

I check the angel bays again on the video monitor. Only the angels named Rebecca and Heather are there, in bays one and three, ready for their test flights. Bay two is empty.

Funny, I thought I'd seen her already today.

She's the new one. I remember her because she's a buxom, blonde, with a voluptuousness that in youth is beguiling, but later sags and droops. And she has an unforgettable name.

"Looks like Boopsie is AWOL today. We'll have to fly with just Rebecca and Heather."

The Director sighs.

"Whatever. Why can't these girls show up when they're supposed to?"

He's whining again. I wonder if he does this at home, and I feel sorry for his wife.

We make the test runs and decide not to fly at all since the routine looks weird with just two angels. I think briefly of trying to get Elizabeth up to sub-in, but change my mind.

Too bad. She only flies for me.

Selfish, yes, but the thought of her out there in front of everyone is not something I can stand. I do wish Simon would show up earlier for these things though.

After all, it's really hard to change on the fly.

I smile at my own little pun and relax again. He'll figure it out, he always does. Again I'm reminded of how pantherish Simon is out there, like a great prowling, preaching predatory beast; he'll always land on his feet. People are filing into the sanctuary now, and I dim the house lights a bit, ready to darken them entirely just before Simon's grand spot-lit entrance, like God's rock star. The organist begins hammering away, sounding the bass pipes of the biggest organ this side of the Mississippi in a way that'd make the Phantom himself jealous. The excitement of the show catches up to me now. Simon's absence looms larger. A shocking realization: only three minutes to go.

"John?"

Finally. It's Simon's voice in my ear, but something's clearly wrong with him. He sounds strange, breathless, distracted.

"John?"

"Yes, I'm here. Are you okay? We're about to go live."

"John, you have to do the sermon," Simon says, ignoring my question.

Alarm rises; what did he say?

"John, are you there?"

He's still out of breath. I'm worried he's having a heart attack or something.

"Yes."

"John, listen to me. You must do the sermon."

This can't be happening. What the hell? Is he dying?

"What? What are you telling me?" I'm trying not to scream. "I can't do the sermon! What are you talking about? Are you sure you're okay? I can't do the sermon!"

"John. Do the sermon."

The command is issued with absolute finality, and he switches off. My earbud is dead. Two minutes until Showtime. I slowly remove the device from my ear, trying not to hyperventilate. The Mouth of God could use a vomit bag just now. I can't believe this is happening to me.

I cannot believe this.

But he'd said it.

Do the sermon. Do the sermon. Must do the sermon.

Walk now. Down the little hall to the stage. Slowly, slowly. It is long and long again; the door to the stage: a miniature thing, a playhouse door; it's the rabbit hole. The Director screams something in my ear; he's heard what Simon said. Now he's screaming and screaming. None of what he says is relevant, nothing is relevant any more. Switch off. Toss the earbud. There is only The One Command. The command to face the crowd.

Jesus Christ, Jesus Christ, if you're out there, I could use you now. Help me.

No reply.

I open the door and step out to profound silence.

A trembling walk to the dais. The shining thing, floating in an ocean of darkness, it thrusts up into a column of light, and it is: so very empty.

Waiting for me.

Wearily, I mount the stairs and raise my eyes into the face of the congregation. Standing there, gripping the pulpit, blinking into the roasting spotlights, nothing comes to mind. Sweat beading on my forehead. Palms shining with wetness.

Not one single little iota of anything. Nothing.

My head, so often filled with words and strong images, is quiet, completely stilled. The crowd is clearly surprised to see me, a young dandy they've never seen before. They're mutinously expectant; they sense something is wrong. In my illuminated state, I can only see these people as faint ghosts; they're hazy and indistinct, disturbingly like wraiths floating in the dark. I can feel their angry questions beginning, too.

Where is Reverend Simon? We came to see Reverend Simon, not this clown. Where is he? Where is he? Where is he?

Simon's not here. The bastard.

And still I stand here. I can hear everything so clearly, it's as if every one of the thousands of people in attendance each has a personal microphone: the cough of a guy in the back, the whimpering of someone's baby, some teenagers whispering in the balcony, the fidgety uncomfortable noises of people who came to see someone else.

Someone other than me.

I stare out and into the yawning black space full of people. My brain is incapable of firing a single verbal synapse. I hope my mouth is not agape. A thousand annoyances clawing at my person. I worry with my choking tie. I scratch the suddenly itching tag of my underwear, tug at the uncomfortably constricting jacket arms, stomp down on the brand new Italian leather shoes that are now biting my toes unmercifully.

Try to remember. Any of Simon's confection sermons will do.

Can't remember a one. Not a word. Still nothing.

Unbidden, I think then of him. The Monster. Wondering if he's really out there. I tell myself it's impossible, impossible; it always was. Still, I strain to see him. I want to see him somehow, and then, strangely, I begin to feel as if I am looking for myself out there. Then the eyes of the masses begin to penetrate the gloom of the sanctuary as if each and every one of them are looking right through me with glowing x-ray beams. Me, up here, exposed and unproven in front of everyone. Me, on God's stage. I can't bear it and I look down at the pulpit. The high gloss oak grain surface is completely devoid of anything resembling a scripted sermon. I rap it loudly with my knuckle, focusing the scrutiny of all the eyes on me even more intensely. I wonder if the pulpit is made of real wood or particle board, and decide for sure that it is particle board.

Cheap bastard. Buys himself a Maybach and this crap for the sanctuary?

At least this gets me thinking again, gets me back to being me. My own voice sounds in my head, quietly, but confident of the advice.

Stick with what you know.

I see a tennis ball flying at me, spinning, dipping madly, yellow fuzz buzzing like an angry bee. I volley. I rally.

"Dear People!"

I begin with such joyous relief that I'm almost in tears already. My eyes kindle fire, and my smile broadens with the peaceful feel of my complete and utter thanks.

"In the game of life, there are winners and losers!"

The words fill my head now.

"The winners keep their eye on the ball, Dear People. God's ball!"

I catch the imaginary ball, grasp it in mid-air, and show it to the crowd.

"God's yellow, shining ball of light and love, People. His Light! His Love! Winners keep their eye on it, and let me tell you, it burns what it hits!"

I stagger back, struck by an unseen overwhelming force, recover to the pulpit, and raise my arm in victory.

"But they rally, Lord, and they stand tall, and it impacts them, and fills them, and they see nothing else but His light and His love, these winners. Nothing else at all!"

Now I'm blinded by an imaginary light so bright, I close my eyes, raise my face to the brilliance of the spot light.

"Not weakness, not enemies, not your faults, nor the faults of anyone around you, not anything else, Friends—winners just see this bright ball of Light and Love! And when you have this, and you hold it close to you," I bring my arms around myself in a close embrace, "and you let it fill you, then you are all winners! Every single one of you."

I open up, arms wide, point to the crowd, encompass them all with a single grand sweep of my index finger.

"Winners!"

I'm down on the stage now, pointing insanely to people in the audience, picking one out as I pick them all out. The spotlights follow.

"You! And You! And You! Are you filled with the Light of His love? Are You winners in the judgment of the Court of God?!"

And indeed there must be something like a fiery light burning in my eyes to judge from the audience's pleasantly surprised reaction: a grudging approval of my dramatically sincere delivery. A few heads are nodding, but most shake their heads. No, they say, we are not Winners. We are not.

I slowly lower my arm and pause in deep reflection. I remember that one glorious time on the court where I had seen nothing but the ball, large as a beach ball, floating there in front of me, light as air. The game had been so easy, so perfect on that day, and my father had been there to see me win it. It was something like pride that I saw in his smile.

"What are we without His light and His love, friends? What are we?!"

I open my arms again in a wide entreaty of the entire congregation.

"Who are we?"

My hands splay out on my own chest in a gesture of self-examination. Prowling and circling around the stage.

"Where are we?"

I leap up the stairs and cast my gaze down to the glossy pulpit, bowing. My voice lowers, is caught by the microphone and whispered into the ear as a private revelation for each and every one of the spectators. It all starts to happen involuntarily. I am completely caught in the spirit of the moment, listening to the words of my own stream of consciousness.

"We are nothing."

"Amen," a voice comes from the crowd in tentative acknowledgement.

"We are nowhere."

"Amen," two, maybe three voices joining in now.

"We are lost."

"Amen!" The tide of the sentiment is swelling now. The audience is reacting to me.

"We are losers."

"Amen!" It is unanimous now, loud, with passion.

"We are all losers," I shout. "All of us!"

"Amen!" The audience belts out their agreement.

My voice pauses, but in my mind: a skyscraper forms above me. Around me. The structure of my own heaped failures takes shape and towers. Losses and longings crowd together and pile, clamoring for vertical space in hypertime: Elizabeth so near but her touch never felt; my empty, empty existence here, forever groveling, always in fear of discovery; the fiasco of my One Big Chance and the disappointment I saw on Bal's face that day when I disavowed the game that was my only dream for the future; the running and running, and the losing of my very sense of self; my failure to ever live up to the trust of those who cared for me and helped me; of feeling like there is nothing, nothing in this world that I can do to live up to any of the expectations that have ever been set for me.

Not now. Not ever.

My voice returns strong and wise, but beneath it: the shivering feel of trouble to come.

"I am here before you today, People, unproven and unknown to you and with nothing but the strength of my words as testament to what I say, and I say to you that I am not a Winner. I have been drowned in the crucible of loss!"

I jump down again to the stage. Spotlights trail me like police choppers.

"Look at me!" I command, jabbing a finger at my heart. "I look like you, talk like you, love like you! I *could be* you! How does it come to pass that I am among the losers who have fled from His Judgment? How?!"

Heads shake, faces in the gloom breathing in my every word. No one knows.

"Let me tell You, it is a hard life, a lonely life, Friends. For without His Light and His Love, we have no soul, we Losers. Ours is a life of dread, a life on the lam, running from ourselves as we run from the responsibility of loving Him."

More and more now, I feel the alarming oncoming rush of heavier things, more painful things, of threatening things. A mother who never cared, who couldn't stay. A mother who left me. Granpa, the one person who truly loved me and understood me, dying alone and estranged in the filth of a forgotten VA Hospital. And Gloria. Years of confusion and hope, resulting in nothing. Thrown away. Again. Images and feelings twisting around themselves and growing. The structures of my soul, too quickly forming. Walls built of despair. An edifice of defeat. Cracking and crumbling now, swaying precariously. The confessions of my entire life. Building. Right here on the stage in front of complete strangers.

"It happens so easily, Friends. So easy, you don't even realize it is happening. Because it's the small things. The everyday things. Small losses that happen each and every day. In every way. Losses that build up and pile up and accumulate because you did nothing. Because you failed every day to act upon His command to be a Winner. Because you resisted Him. And as the failures grow, the burning Light of His Commands become so painful and so demanding that you reject Him all together."

I weep openly, then, right there on the stage. All the pain, all the frustration, all the overwhelming guilt of failure; all of it that has been hidden away behind the quietude of my persona, or taken out in the meaningless expression of my sports. All of it just pours out, runs down my face, streams onto the pulpit, and pools there, glistening in the powerful light for everyone to see. Again, I mount the dais; slowly this time, the preposterous weight of myself bearing down upon my shoulders. I cannot look at them, these people before me; As an audience, they barely exist at all. Not as beings of flesh and blood. They are my past, they are my executioners, they are the judges of my soul.

And I am moved further and without conscious thought, to more.

"And when you reject Him, your life is nothing!" My voice rises to a yell. Heads nod vigorously. "Your life is empty of meaning and direction and Heavenly Love. You are a Loser and He will become wroth to see His creation wallowing in the idleness of sloth, shirking the responsibility of His Love." I am wailing, but I don't care.

"And if you still resist His just and divine punishment. If you forsake Him. If you raise your hand against Him and beat Him back and beat Him back and beat Him back..."

I hammer the pulpit with the meat of my fist, over and over again, beating Him back and trying to stave it off, but I can't. I am helpless.

It is coming.

" ... then you are a Killer!"

A sobbing shriek. The smallest of pauses. My fist still poised to strike again. A last look at these people before me and I am aware of a new silence among the witnessing crowd, aware of their nervous discomfort, of their sadness, too, but this awareness is far, far on the periphery of the internal locus of my thought because in it, the thing comes swiftly crouching, and the thudding echoes of my beating hand only recall it all the more. Hulking up out of the recollective gloom, like a roiling world-encompassing thunderhead, as if the wasted years of my life preceding it were no precedent at all and there was no moment before *The Moment*, it comes to engulf: the instance of The Fall. And with this final burden, the structure of my being yaws and leans, is overwhelmed, and comes groaning down and grieving from its heights. And in the falling, it takes a final form: the shape of my own dead father.

I scream it.

"I am the killer! I killed my father!"

My hand strikes the pulpit again, cracking it.

"I am the killer of the Light and Love of the Father!"

I lower my head to my arms, right there on the podium and I cannot but think of this one truth: I am a killer. Always will be. I do not exist and there is no one in my life who loves me and there never will be because I am nothing, a non-entity, a living breathing husk.

I kill the ones who love me.

Whether we knew it or not.

The tears gush and gush, out and onto the arms of my suit jacket. I said I'd never shed another for him. Not for him, not for anything, but I cannot stop them. I do not try. There is a time and a place, and this is it. And so I let them come, until there is no sound, save for the sound of my crying, and until my mind is emptied of everything, save for the vast and formless aftermath of my loss. The silence of the sanctuary is so complete now, I feel as alone as if I'm the only person on the planet, like Adam before the creation of Eve.

An entire congregation is moved.

First one lady starts, then another. Now a man or two, and then the whole front section breaks down. Now they are all weeping together, weeping with me and for me, pouring out their own failures and trials and tribulations on sleeves, on handkerchiefs, on hands, or simply letting it run down their face to drip onto the pew or into the opulent carpet. It is a single body of self-reflecting pity and sadness and failure, those thousands of crying people.

A single body, weeping as one.

I look up and around me, astounded, my eyes seeing the wonder through a bright crystal of my own tears. The whole sorry existence of my life has hit home and poured out of me, but, seeing the crying masses now, I discover a new thing.

It is the existence of us all.

New hope comes now. New words.

Quietly, I find them.

"We are all killers of the Father, People. By our lack of action. By our bad thoughts and by the lack of our good deeds. By the lack of our honesty with ourselves and with the Father who is in Heaven. In this way, People, we all kill the Father. Until even the memory of His touch and His love ceases to exist and we are left with the nothingness that is the empty reaches of hell."

Still crying, I smile a broad smile, a real smile.

My voice surges with new power.

"But be not afraid to cast off your transgressions!"

My right arm makes a powerful throwing motion.

"Cast them off into the endless sea of His waters, and, there, let them be swallowed unto the very substance of His Being. Throw them off then and bask in His everlasting Light, bigger than the Texas sky, for He is all around you and in all of you, if you can but feel and touch Him again."

The roof of the building ceases to exist for me. I spread my arms to embrace the entire sky, rinsed clean from the storm and cobalt blue and shining beautifully.

"Pursue not your vain and materialistic passions People, but rather cast them off and venture forth into the wilderness alone with nothing but your Faith, Friends, to confront the demon within."

I grip the pulpit hard now, look into the eyes of each man, woman and child I can see, all riveted as one to my every word.

"Faith and Love! Faith in the forgiveness of the Father! Your Father! For He is but testing you! Testing you in the quest to fulfill His will! For His is the Light and the Will and the Love that will give you the strength to confront the beasts of your despair! He will lead you from the Wilderness!"

I pound the pulpit with my fist and the sound thunders through the speakers.

"You will triumph over your demons, People!"

"Amen!" They're right there with me, victoriously emerging from a long, dark forest.

"You will emerge from the wilderness!"

"Amen!"

"You will emerge from the wilderness as Winners!"

I thunder down on the fragile pulpit with both fists, breaking it clean in two. In my elevated, victory-drunk state, I kick the thing aside, raise my fists and face again to the sky, and sink to my knees among the splintered remains of the shattered pulpit in total triumph. In that exact moment of verbal and physical ecstasy, the falling of the pulpit throws my remote control to the floor, and, by incredible chance, the miracles occur.

The unprepared angels are thrown from their bays, screaming bloody screams of real terror. The river boils forth in a flood's torrent. The main and most powerful stage spotlight illuminates too quickly to its maximum, bursts, ignites, and burns real fire down from the heavens with a white hot flash radiating directly into my upturned eyes. I can see nothing but white burning light; I hear nothing but screaming angels and gushing water. I shoot to my feet.

Then I roar.

I roar in pain. I roar in delight. A huge smile of agonizing inspiration lights my face.

"Who among you will come forth!?"

I'm shouting at them.

"Who among you will come forth and cast yourselves into the waters!?"

I'm yelling at them, a complete lunatic.

"Who among you will be reborn as Winners!"

I'm commanding them with a voice that I've never known I had, never even known that it existed. I've never felt this way before.

I still can't see, but I know where they are. I feel for them through the blinding whiteness in my eyes. In sightless, but powerful sweeping motions, I beckon the entire congregation to come up and be saved. I command them to come forth and bathe in the miraculous waters.

And they do.

They come in droves. An entire flock herds forward at my command. They'd jump in and drown themselves, if I told them to. But I don't. I can't.

This is not me.

This is not who I am.

This is not me.

The voice in my head is my own again, quiet and calming. My sight returns to see thousands crowding towards the stage, massing to be re-born. Somehow I find Mike in the throng. I point to him to come forward, command him to baptize these people with the last vestiges of the power that was so recently and miraculously mine.

And he does.

It's possible he'll save thousands of people this day, but I won't stay to see it. I run from the stage, heading for my room, driven to be away from this. I'm frantic to be in my own inner sanctum behind the control room. I want to throw myself on my bed. I'm confused by all the wild emotions that have just swept through me, used me, and left me again as a wreck. Most of all I want her. I want to lay there with her holding me tight. I want to look into those eyes. I want to cool my own burning orbs in the morning sky of her cool blue eyes.

I want her.

✦

# ANGEL WINGS

I run through the control room, throwing the doors shut behind me as I go. Finally, I get to my own room, shut my door behind me, and lean up against it with closed eyes still burning, letting it support my weight. It is a profound sense of relief to be away from the mindlessly blind mob that I myself have created.

Let Mike deal with them. Let Mike save them.

Sweat pours down my stiff collared shirt and stains my tie. Blindly, I tear them both off, toss them onto the floor, lean back against the door again, breathing more easily, longing for quiet and a soft embrace.

But, instead of quiet, there is noise. I perceive the rhythmic squeak of bed springs and hear the moans of pleasure. I open my eyes. I am not alone.

Tattooed angel winds spread wide and blue from the pulsing dimple formed just below the small of her naked back. The wings flap, lift her, bounce her along. Beguiling, how her wings soar above him. She lifts them both, lands back onto him, soars above him again, and lifts them both, over and over again.

This is where you've been?

This is what kept you?

I did that for you, and this is how you repay me?

In my room? On my bed?

Simon. Simon and our missing angel. Here in my bedroom. In carnal flight. I want to scream at him, punch him, throttle him. I want to yank her off him and slap her to the floor. But I can't. I can hardly move. I'm mesmerized by the flapping of the wings, drawn to them almost more than I can force myself to be repelled by them. He notices me then, looks around her, and up at me as I lean there stranded against the door, riveted by the softness of her eagerly pulsing body. He grins an evil grin.

"Join us." He grunts it out, not pausing in his exertions.

"What?" I can't believe this. I can't be thinking this. He can't be thinking this.

"Join us."

This time he smiles his beatific smile, and it is even more evil than before. Even in this state, even prostrated as he is beneath this girl, even so, he can smile his damned smile, implore me into his folly, and make me think that perhaps this is acceptable, that somehow, for us, this is okay.

"Join us, John. Our angel here, she..." he looks up at her, pleasuring herself up there, building herself to crescendo in an erotic trance, ignoring us altogether. "Our angel does generously give of her many gifts."

He smiles again. A smile that would allow him to get away with anything. And does. Slowly, despite myself, I walk towards them. As if traveling through an endless clear water, I'm made languorous by the conflict in my emotions. I see my own hand leading me forward, reaching out to touch, to feel the angel wings.

I'm there now, standing beside them, enraptured by their flight. Without conscious thought, I extend a single finger out to the throbbing wings and hesitate there, no more than a millimeter above soft white skin and feathery inked down, so close I can feel the heat.

The door bursts open.

I turn towards the intrusion. And I see her. She stands there in the doorway, bright and smiling, a joyous look in those lovely blue eyes, seeing only me somehow, only me. It is a look, I think, of love.

"Oh John! John, that was so inspirational, so moving! I'm so pro... so..."

She sees us now. All of us. Her mouth opens in slow motion, and her mind belatedly comprehends what her eyes have told her. Now she sees me, frozen there with no shirt on, my hand poised still; she sees Simon sprawled out on the bed naked, almost in a perfect likeness to the painting of him above; she sees, too, the fallen angel. She sees it all. And in the presence of a truly beautiful person, the wings, still flapping there above Simon become vulgar and wretched, as if they're the black wings of a vulture, beating at carrion.

There are no words that I can say to her. There is no explanation that I can give to her. I can't even explain this to myself. All hope that I ever had, or ever will have, of being with her leaves me in that moment, evaporates into the sweat and sex charged air.

"Oh."

It's all she says. She looks as if she'll faint, her hands drop, and her bright face dims. And at that very instant, Simon comes. He comes like a lion, roaring psychotically up to the heavens. And when he roars, the angel comes too, a gruesome creeping sound like the bleating of a slaughtered goat.

The effect is electric, a lightening shock of immense proportion. Elizabeth goes rigid, stiffening straight as a board. On her face is incomprehension, then pure horror, and then burning hate, all roiling there on that unblemished surface in undisguised waves of emotion.

And seeing this, Simon laughs. A shock far more disturbing than the sound of his climax. He laughs and laughs and laughs, an insane, shameless, jarring laugh, so loud it echoes in my empty brain; it alternately reviles me and mocks me, again and again. And whether he laughs in demented pleasure or from the depths of his black and debauched soul or even from sheer lunacy—maybe all of those things—I don't ever want to know.

Elizabeth clenches her fists, and her look changes from black despair to an unfathomable revulsion, then to something far worse. And in the moment that she turns to run, I realize with horrible certainty what it is. It is the look of a person who has completely and totally lost her faith. And I know with that same certainty, too, that I will never see her again.

Not ever.

Dazed and grieving beyond reason, beyond hope or light, I have just enough sense to pick up my shirt, to stumble out the door, and to close it behind me. I'm left with the final sound of Simon's laugh, the final image of clawing, groping, bestial ecstasy. I close my eyes, lean on the door behind me; it is an image that I'm sure will never leave me, no matter what I try, no matter where I go. And go I must, though I've got nothing to go to and know of nothing I can do.

I've staggered back somehow to sit in my control room. Only one thought repeats itself over and over: trapped, trapped, trapped. I am trapped here, alone with a madman, a deceiver, an antichrist. Dumbly I turn to watch the video screens. There in the sanctuary, Mike is still at the task of saving people. I watch his hands as he helps each person up from the endless stream. They are loving and strong hands, cradling each head and each back as he lifts them out: adults, the aged, babies; one and all they are dripping wet and helpless as children. And the look on every one of the faces emerging from those waters—every single one—is the otherworldly look of the reborn.

ᐱ

# BLACK MAGIC

The baptisms take a long, long time, and I watch them all, not caring. No, come to your senses, I do care. Why else would I stay here, watching this?

I did this by my hand, by my words, by my actions.

Or was it—was it something else, Someone else?

The last person, a little girl of perhaps twelve, emerges from the water into Mike's hands. A glow of light shines from within her, a smile so large as to soften even my anger, to tinge gray my soul's black ambivalence. Mike smiles too, happy tears streaming down his face, and he seems to be a true rock rising up from among all the fabricated stone, the sets, and the machine trickery, as if the entire church were built around him and upon the foundation of his person. In him, I see a man transformed, and I know he has truly found himself and his calling. Unlike me, he will never wish to be anyone or anywhere else. This is who he is now, and I cannot bear to see it anymore—and whether it is from jealously or my own baseness or something else, something darker—I don't know, but whatever the consequences, I must leave.

An automaton, I walk the secret passages meeting no one, passing secret doors and touching the knobs of each of them with a finger, as if I might pass through them and into a new life in some other time, or into some other place entire.

If only, if only.

This one. The door to angel bay one. Elizabeth was the last one to fly from here. I climb the narrow stairs to see what she saw, feel what she felt before the plunge, the leap of faith entrusted to my hands alone. I know not why. And there, up above the sanctuary, in the very rafters of the ceiling, I reach out, hold the steel cable, lean out, far out over the now dark space below me. All is vacant; the last of the reborn have left for new lives, new dedications, new temptations, and which of them will achieve all that they hope for?

Who are the lucky ones? Why?

My weariness knows no bounds, and I descend again into the secret halls, this labyrinth of the Wealth of God.

"John! John! Have you heard..."

The excited voice distorts, echoes in the narrow space and sears my ears, wrenching me from the solitude of my vacant wandering. It is Mike. I look up and see him.

A changed man he is, he is.

But I cannot speak and try to turn away; try to just walk away.

"...I see," he says.

Now an arm is around me, supporting me, guiding me with the new strength he has found. It's the strength of the new man.

Look away. This flash emotion.

I am crying again, sobbing even.

I don't want you seeing this, knowing this.

"John, it'll be okay. I know, too. Elizabeth came to the elders already. She told us about Simon."

Incomprehension. I look at him. He's refracted by my tears into multiple persons, many beings.

"Come on, John, come with me."

He soothes, murmuring nothings.

Elizabeth told us, he'd said.

Elizabeth told.

In the staff break room, back under control. I drift away to sit on a stacking chair against the wall, not knowing what do with my hands: now in my lap, now clutching my temples, the bridge of my nose. I'm not looking, and I'm trying not to listen, but can't help it. I can't. A barrage of angry voices assaults me: the church elders and disgruntled employees, dripping vindictives one and all;

they're in an uproar still. I hear the Director's voice loudest of all, he sneers at me; even through the gesticulating crowd, he's gloating. The fallen angel, she's only seventeen, a minor.

"A child, a child!"

They scream with evil deliciousness, men and women alike, and only the thin veneer of virtue remains. Nausea engulfs me now, waves of it. The noise becomes incoherent babble, a thousand grotesquely slobbering heads, posturing and snarling apes one and all.

Almost, John, you almost...what would have been?

Had she not come in, what would you have done?

Could you have?

But in all their talk, there's nothing about me, nothing at all. One more thing cuts through the noise: I'm not implicated; I'm not even mentioned. Mike is serenity in the middle of the lynch mob, trying to calm them.

She is nowhere to be seen.

I'm sure she's left the building, the grounds, the church altogether.

Where to, Elizabeth? Where to now?

I get up to leave, and no one notices, not even the Director.

She gave me that.

The tears may have stopped but the pain will not. I slip out again into solitude, and the door latch clicks behind me like the locking of a vault.

At least she gave me that. She didn't tell them everything.

Secrets, no more secrets.

Stay out of the hidden passageways, John.

I walk through the spacious main halls. People are literally running through them, by me, with sidelong knowing glances. I see the poison spread with bitter virulence, from the heart outward into veins, into capillaries, it seeps out through the skin itself, this shell of a church; it burns in shocked furtive whispers, in crying sobs, and in wickedly vindictive smirks, too. Not everyone loves Simon. Hate, it seems, prevails. Surreptitious looks are shot my way in passing, involuntarily I flinch. I know what I would have done, could have done, wanted to do. She knows too, and yet she saved me.

She saved me. And then she left me.

I want to hide. I go to a gym in the very back reaches of the campus; it is blessedly empty. I turn the lights out, bar the door, and lay down on a foam exercise mat under the light of an EXIT sign. But I see the word inscribed on that sign still, through closed lids. That one word, my luckless destiny, burning redly as I try to descend into thoughtlessness.

Without these walls, the great green lion is toppled from its boulder in a splintered crash. An angry mob roars, and the beast is trampled. Broken fiberglass pierces many, mingling bright red blood with intensified fury. Focused now, the jilted minions throng at the huge razor cross schisiming the perfect sky, and they grasp at it with purpled hands. The great symbol sways drunkenly, but its metal roots go deep in buried concrete, and they hold, they hold. Checked in their fury now, the horde considers and the group conceives.

Now chains and roaring trucks appear to grapple with the soaring bright thing. Insanely shouted screams and belching engines and earth burned by scorching wheels, and down, down it finally comes to impale the Earth with a wrenching metallic groan.

Victorious, the crowd roars with malevolent confidence and swarms up the grotesquely twisted mass of still shining steel, yelling and dancing. Emboldened now and restless with rage atop the fallen cross, the mob sees the church, and with one voice takes up the cry to destroy it. Like a horde of black ants they flow down, split up in crawling lines around the lakes, enjoin again into a single mass, and descend onto the church itself.

I lay there, disembodied, and watch it all, watch it all come to ruin: the buildings, the gyms and steeples and meeting halls, the main sanctuary itself with rafters falling sickeningly; and it all crumbles down around me in a cataclysmic sundering of the very ground.

My eyes snap open. My clothes are soaked in sweat, the taste of dust is in my mouth, and the feel of perdition is all around me. But nothing. Nothing has happened. The church still stands. The persistent electric hum of the EXIT sign drills into my brain. I'm bathed in the unnatural red light of the sign. I light my watch: 3:21 AM. I know what I need to do, have to do. I just don't want to do it—again.

Furtively, I walk the empty halls back to my room, staying close to the walls. I try not to look up at the cameras, wondering if he is somewhere up there, watching me. I take the service corridor and edge open the un-marked door. The bed is still ruffled from the girl's flight. I try not to look at it again, but I can't help it. The impressions of their bodies are still there.

Just look away, look away.

Quickly, I open the closet and gather some of my things. Randomly almost, I throw some clothes into a duffel bag I've picked up from some Church vendor somewhere to hide my gun. It is in there, a metal tumor of sharp edges and the dense weight of it a burden now. I want it no longer, but can't throw it away. Can't leave it here. I take a pair of jeans and wrap them around the weapon and I look to see what else to bring. Nothing but my perfectly tailored suits hanging there. The gifts of Simon. I run a hand down the pinstriped one, remembering how sharp I had looked in it on that first day of its delivery. On my body, it was truly transformative. I was then a Something, a Somebody-Else. Someone good. I lift the suit off the rack and start to put it in the bag but then stop, holding it up. In the end: just a suit of cloth.

This isn't me. I toss the suit to the floor.

This is Simon.

Hurry away now. No one to see.

In the garage, the Maybach's not there. In all the yelling yesterday, I can't remember hearing anything about Simon's whereabouts. Unbidden, I get the image of him there in the backseat banging Boopsie's head up against the stained glass Grail.

Or he's dropping her off a bridge somewhere.

Slipping my car out unnoticed, I still can't shake the feeling that all of this isn't really happening, that this is the dream I'm driving through, all alone.

Slowly, I cruise the drive, the electric fountains spray muddy water into the tepid air, the lakes look black and oily in the ground lights. The emasculated lion eternally advises people to BE BOLD, and a single star is to be seen in the sky above the steel cross, shining dimly.

This place will still be here when I'm gone.

Probably, it'll be here long after I'm dead.

Doesn't He care?

I turn onto the road. No answer comes to me, and He does not speak to me. There is no guidance but my own. At the highway, I make a decision. Go to Houston. It's not hard to see how; I just point the car towards the polluted brown and orange bloom of artificial light. The beginning of the burbs, miles and miles of burbs, is easily visible on the Northeast horizon like levels of purgatory or burning embers in the night.

Houston, all the way in. I drive the weathered and diesel-grimed concrete canyons, nearly empty at this time in the morning. A dually-driving maniac closes in on me at what has to be ninety miles an hour; he swerves around me at the last second, nearly losing control. He lays on his horn as if somehow I'm to blame—like I'm a dog crossing the road, and next time maybe he'll just crush me. I grip the wheel tightly and resist shooting the bird, but only just.

The acrid smell of exhaust as the pickup roars away. Running lights fade into the electric glow. He's running, too. Running from something, probably drunk. Wasted and trying to get back before his wife wakes up, or her husband, or who knows what. This Houston air feels dirty, like I could rub my arm and roll off greasy curds or clumps of filth. Like swimming in Lake Texarkana.

Remember, Mom, you took me there once, back when I was a kid, and you let me swim in there. I emerged happy and covered with a muddy shade of brown. You'd shrieked as I came out, as if someone had turned your little boy into a manikin made of clay. That'd been the end of that and I was never allowed to go in again.

Probably, you just didn't want to get the car dirty.

Dirty is how I feel, and all I want now: just a shower. There's not enough money for a long stay, but it'll last until I figure things out. A budget motel coming up looks okay.

Checked in, I shut the hollow door behind me. The shabby room is empty and sterile. I shut the vinyl window blinds tight, but they don't block out the constant drone of the cars on the interstate or the yellow electric street-lights from cutting in between the slats. No matter. A window unit gives some white-noise, some cool solitude. I shower and cast myself naked onto the paper thin sheets face down, lost in a misery I can't shake.

Awaking to the glare of a cold white sun, I forget a moment where I am. Thick lines of black and white light spray across the featureless room, across my cold and shrunken body. I see the bag with the gun and hear the sound of traffic and I remember. Wrapping myself in the thin blanket, I rise to make the cheap coffee.

TVs in every room, said the sign, and so it is. I turn it on to listen as the coffee drips.

It's all over the news already. The story of the powerful and rich evangelist committing abominable acts in the Church with a seventeen-year-old girl is electric. Cameras are everywhere. The reporters, paparazzi, and other lovers of The Fall crawl over the Church grounds: in the bushes, at the doors, interviewing the congregation, cruising the parking lots. I see them on the TV and think of vultures, of the wings of vultures. But I can't stop watching, can't get dressed even. It's perverse.

Evening comes, and I'm still on the bed, lying down, head propped up on a pillow and body spread-eagled. This stupid head of mine. It's pounding and pounding from the wash of blaring TV imagery, from gnawing hunger, too. Finally, I muster up enough energy to turn off the tube and dress. Opening the door, I'm faced with a line of traffic, smog and noise.

I don't want to drive.

Walking along the access road down to some fast food burrito joint, struggling through the weeds by the curb, I feel like someone's going to swerve and hit me. Of course there's no sidewalk; who but a vagrant would walk here anyway?

But there's a TV in the restaurant, too. It sucks me in, holds my attention in mute reverie, and I see it all again and again. Apparently Mike has been elevated and he leads the sermons now. The show goes on.

And who is running my control room?

A bitter laugh. To think what an idiot I am. Was.

Any fool with two thumbs can do that job.

Over the week, a pattern emerges: fast-food, TV, disturbed sleep. In the stupor of my new ritual, I see it all spewed forth by the miracle of mass media. Simon crawls back like a beaten animal. He eyes Mike on the stage with a feral look, and I see the panther again.

Wonder why those fools there can't see it, too.

Here's a beast who will bite you again and again. But now he's groveling, begging for forgiveness, and they're all caught up in the vanity of their own goodness and the belief in a God who cares, who forgives, who changes people.

Yeah, right. God?

Who's really out there?

Incredibly, Mike seems to believe him. The elders believe him, and the congregation is swaying that way. I can see it even on the small screen. Like a reformed politician, Simon is winning them over, one at a time. First, they give him back the morning telecasts. Hearing his voice again is repugnant to my ears, as if he is still speaking to me directly through the earbud. But, of course, he is not. The effect is disturbing, and it makes my skin crawl. But I continue to watch. Next, they give Simon the afternoon shows, too. Finally, he gets all the broadcasts back. I watch them all, and he is even more a presence in my head than ever before. He's doing all the original sermons now, and he's telecasting an inhuman number of additional hours to recover his lost congregation. He speaks directly to the camera in a personal appeal. Disturbingly, the look in his eye seems to glint especially for me.

It says: you were there; you wanted to; you're as guilty as I, but you are unforgiven.

He plays the fallen part well.

"...I have suffered," Simon reasons with us sorrowfully. "He humbles even the mightiest among us..."

And he has all of his original charisma.

With each telecast, the audience is wowed with a new and better miracle, better ones than I ever conjured up, and I wonder again whether it is Mike in my control room, restored to his former station and faithful to the end, or is it that Director?

"Forgiveness!"

Sometimes Simon shouts it.

"Forgiveness..."

Other times it is a plaintive sobbing whisper.

He works the word into every sermon, every message, over and over again. I stare in disbelief at the disingenuous delivery, but, as the camera pans across the congregation, I see tear-wet eyes, shining with the light of his words.

Am I the only one who sees it?

Am I wrong to be skeptical?

Is it like he said? Is it me?

Incredibly, the disillusioned congregation, many of whom were so recently reborn by my hand, is returning in masses. Simon forgives them all of their sins, even as he forgives himself.

"We have experienced a hell on earth. Learn from Us. Come let us all be saved again. Let us be saved together. He will forgive us of our sins!"

I even see him sink to his knees, head hung low, tears on his face: a beggar in a three piece silk suit.

He's never done that before.

"We will overcome!" He shouts and raises his fists.

"You will overcome!" It's an order.

Simon even has a guest celebrity preacher come in and re-baptize him along with all the willing faithful. He, and thousands of the congregation, are born again in a made-for-TV special, telecast live to the U.S. and Great Britain. It's a stroboscopic flurry of white lights and spinning angels, and it is accompanied by the choir with five hundred simultaneous voices lifted in one mighty song. He emerges last, dripping wet from the baptismal waters, fists raised defiantly to the sky. He's triumphantly born again, and the audience loves it.

Magic Simon is back.

⋏

# Revelations

Listless and awake again tonight in my bed, I can't forget her. From the balcony to-day, I thought I'd seen her walking into the lobby. I'd felt the tingle of my flushing face, gripped the rail with sweating palms, and leaned dizzily over to see.

To see, to see those eyes.

I'd run down the stairs to her then, barefoot and wild-eyed.

"Elizab –"

I was almost shouting, but the startled girl had turned at that moment and shrunk away like I was some lunatic, and her dull eyes were terrified. I stared at this girl; she was nothing like her, not even close. Quickly, I'd mumbled an apology and slunk back to my room, feeling like an escaped pervert, like a fool.

You're lucky the poor girl didn't call the cops.

And what if it had been Elizabeth? What if, by some miracle, she'd come here looking for me? Why would she? And what would I say to her anyway?

"Hi Elizabeth, thanks for coming. You know, just because I was standing there half-naked and touching a minor's ass doesn't mean I was going to engage in anything. Really, I was just about to report Simon myself. And, by the way, would you like to marry me?"

A bitter laugh. I bury my head in the pillow.

He's there again. On the goddamn TV. He doesn't even bother to look sorry now. The old swagger is there. The past put behind him. Elizabeth, at least, had tried to do something about this charlatan. In an instant she'd seen him in a true light, and then she'd acted.

She almost brought him down.

A strange thought: perhaps it was meant to be like this. Maybe this is really all part of the grand plan, His plan. Watching Simon now, groveling on TV, I don't know. The sight still makes me slightly sick; but perhaps this really is some sort of miracle. It looks like an act, and I can't believe his behavior is sincere, but maybe, just maybe, it is.

And what of forgiveness?

Shouldn't I be asking for it too?

Am I supposed to forgive Simon?

Am I the hypocrite here?

Who will forgive me?

A chill runs down my spine, and I remember the blinding light and the power of someone else's voice in my own, someone wise and strong and understanding of the secrets of the universe. Someone powerful. It was there, right there on the stage for thousands to see. It was me confessing. But what was that really? Was it the free association of a desperate mind? Or was it more? God never spoke to me, those words just came out, they were just there when I needed them to be.

I look at Simon on TV, remembering some of his sermons. He can do it every day, three times a day. Is it really God speaking? Would something like Simon really be an open mike for the Almighty? Would I?

But perhaps he is going through this same thing, and I'm just too blinded by my own cynicism and sorrow to see it. Perhaps he has really changed—but by the Lord's hand, or by his own? Or, not at all?

With Simon's voice low in the background, I jump up to go to the bathroom and brush my teeth. At the mirror I stop and put both hands on the sink rim.

The same John Sharpe.

I lean in and take a longer look, the square chin, the week's growth of beard, and now the eyes. I hold my own gaze, looking for something different, something better. But they are my own beautiful green eyes, as she had called them, way back there in the woods, and they are neither my father's eyes nor my mother's eyes. They are mine. Did my experience up there on the stage really change me? Was it some sort of epiphany? I rub my chin; I feel the same, look the same, but there is something new in me, I think. The look there is not the one I know, not the one Dad knows. I'm capable of more, capable of command, of on the spot thinking, of doing what I have to do. Somewhere, deep down, I know there's some powerful reserve of will and strength. It's not God speaking to me or religious ecstasy.

I smile at myself, a good smile.

It is me.

Simon shouts in the background, but I don't look back. I pick up my toothbrush and clean my teeth. It feels good, such a simple act of renewal.

Simon, you sycophant, I have to see.

The watch alarm sounds; it's 8:00 AM. The familiar vertical strips of light between the window shades. Stretching out, I feel good. Slept better than I have all week. I'm leaving here today. One way or the other, I'm leaving, and I won't be coming back.

The 914 coughs to life, and I thread my way into the trafficy snarl of rush-hour. Even going against traffic, we're still moving slowly in my lane. The other side of the highway is stopped completely. I see grim faces and angry people; some speak on cell phones, some just sit there dejected and tired, dreading another day in cubeland. A vaporous sward of fume and exhaust rises and hangs over the entire freeway, making its way in, choking me almost.

Times like this, I wish I had one of those SUVs, like Mom used to have. Blast the A/C and ride along in your big metal tank, oblivious to the poison all around. But that's not real life, that's all fake. Like the lion: BOLD but fake.

I wonder if he'll even see me. Maybe not. Maybe he thinks I ratted him out; maybe I'm just not useful to him anymore. I don't know. What I do know: I have to try.

Driving past the lion, I'm uneasy. For some reason, I feel like security might come out and pounce on me at any second. I park in visitor parking instead of the garage. Just sitting here struggling to get out of the car and make myself go in. The church buildings loom, more solid than ever, and somehow forbidding now. In the space of a week, the whole place has become foreign to me, feels closed to me.

Get up.

I walk in, straight into the offices. No one at the reception questions me; it's as if I never left. Maybe they never noticed me in the first place. In the halls, a few people actually wave, and I return the greetings. The Director pretends not to see me.

Simon's door is cracked, meaning he's there and available. I walk right in, trying to open the door with authority; I mount a determined look. He looks up with a curious glance and smiles widely.

A false smile? But, no, not when the man himself is false entire.

I open my mouth to speak, but before I can form the words, the phone rings. Of course, he picks it up. I snap my mouth shut again and try to frown my disapproval.

God, I hate it when he does this. Could be a goddamn cold-calling salesman, and, if I'm in the room, he'd take it. And in this moment, my resolve begins to vanish. Whoever Simon's talking to is someone he actually wanted to speak with; he becomes so engrossed in his conversation that he doesn't notice any of the dark and unhappy looks I give him. He doesn't seem to notice that I'm there at all. I'm just a worm in this august presence. I turn to go, to salvage something of my pride by just getting the hell out of here.

There's no point in speaking to him now, anyway. I've seen what I expected to see.

Simon sees me. He glances in my direction and holds up a finger. It's just one finger seen out of the corner of my eye, but it commands me. Wait, it says. Wait. And, damnit, I do.

Standing there shifting my weight from foot to foot, I try to think of what to say instead of listening in on his quietly spoken phone conversation. But I can't help catching some of it. I hear something about how the church has "already recovered," and that "Our little incident" may have actually helped the TV ratings. The congregation is actually growing again. I catch something of the name of the person he's talking to. Someone named "Tip," perhaps.

His voice grows lower. He's quietly going over income and speaking about some fancy financial instruments now. Sounds like Simon will be increasing the capital in his funds. I catch the order to "spread it around," then he drones on forever about small cap and large cap funds, indexes, and bonds. It's all very boring, like listening to Dad was when he talked business. I don't understand it, not sure I ever will.

Good, seems like he's wrapping it up now. Chuckling, he closes the conversation.

"Stay sharp."

He emphasizes the sharp and hangs up the phone. It's a good-bye between old business cronies. The realization hits me hard; suddenly it grips me. I flinch involuntarily.

Oh my God, I know it now.

It's Chip, not Tip.

"You said 'stay Sharpe,' didn't you?"

On Simon's face: the briefest of flinches. It is enough.

Chip Sharpe. My father. This can't be. But it is "Simon, you were speaking to my father. You were speaking to my Dad, weren't you? That was him."

"Yes," Simon says tersely.

It was my father. And he is alive.

Delirious happiness comes over me. I could hug Simon, I could jump steeples, the arches of the soaring roof; I could spread arms and float, no remotes, no cables. An angel freed from its snares of twisted steel. The heaviness of death, lifted.

Simon watches me curiously. Gray predator-eyes glint with detached amusement. The feelings give way though to something else. The thought like a sniper's shot: betrayal.

They knew. All of them.

They knew it all along, and nobody told me. No one. All this time. All these places. It wasn't ever me. Not ever. It was my father. And he knew. You stupid, stupid, stupid idiot. You are such a worthless, gullible fool.

A scream grows inside of me, a sudden violence. I want to smash something and crush it into dust. Burn it to ashes. The tears want to start, but it makes me angrier, and I stem them within a swelling rage.

Just as Simon is about to speak to me, I turn and kick open the office door. A satisfying smash of sheetrock sounds as the steel handle impales the wall. I don't give a goddamn anymore about Simon and whatever lie he'll tell me, whatever lie he's telling himself, telling everyone. All I can think about is my father. That manipulative, lying bastard. My father. I run for my car, almost blindly.

The engine screams to life; I'm redlining it, my tires burn. In my rearview mirror, I see Simon himself, running out the door behind me and waving me back.

"Simon, go to hell where you belong."

It's a six hour drive to Texarkana, but the tank's full. I slam the car through the gears, accelerating out the driveway in a reckless, red anger. The lion flashes past; I want to ram it.

Next time.

I don't want to stop. I just want to drive it straight through. That's what I'm going to do.

Chip Sharpe, Chip Sharpe. I should have known.

⋏

# WHAT MATTERS

**My father is** sitting there in his leather chair. A glass of twelve-year in his veined hand, two sparkling cubes in crystal, as always. He looks up at me as I enter the room, my bag on my shoulder. Fists clinched, I draw up and stare him down; he's been waiting for me. No apparition this. A father of flesh and blood. I should go to him; I should tell him how glad I am. You're alive, I'm so glad you're alive. But I cannot. This too: I wish he were dead. I scrutinize him with a wind burned wild-eyed glare. He's just like I remembered him. He's in his best business mode: composed, calm, in control—seems even larger than he is. The look on his face: I'm sure he's got some speech prepared. His mouth opens to speak, to control the situation. He starts off with it.

"John –"

"– Don't start in with your bullshit on me! I thought you were dead. I thought I killed you when I pushed you down the stairwell. And you knew that, and here you were the whole time alive and well and playing with me, like I'm some sort of pawn in your demented game. Your own son? Were you ever going to tell me? You let me believe I was a murderer. What? Did you like the sound of that? John Sharpe, your son, a murderer? You knew, right?"

He nods, yes, and starts to say something.

I interrupt him again, shouting. I drop the bag on the floor. A metallic clunk as it hits the floor hard. And it spills out of me then and there with my father looking on, working to stay calm. How he's manipulated me. I didn't even know it. I was too stupid to see it. The Sheriff. The highway department. Someone at the racket club. The Challenger. Simon, especially Simon. All of them. All his doing.

"All your cronies right?"

I sweep the world with my arm, all-encompassing, shouting the questions at him. He just nods his replies, says nothing provocative, stays calm.

"Just like my whole worthless life!"

An agreement of silence, not even a nod.

I sink into the chair set there especially for me. I'm babbling to him, almost incoherent now. "Can't you see how this makes me feel? How worthless this makes me feel? How worthless you've always made me feel. I've done nothing, nothing at all my whole life. Nothing I wanted to do. Why can't you, just once, support me instead of tearing me down?"

"John," he says calmly, "don't forget, you did leave me for dead."

There's nothing to say to this. As if I could forget. As if I hadn't seen him a thousand times, lying there at the foot of the stair, in vulgar repose, eyes staring.

"When you wake up on the ground and discover your only child has just pushed you off a balcony and run off without even calling the ambulance, well, your first reaction isn't too charitable, you know?"

His words strike a chord. Shame, loathing, the old enemies infuse themselves within me again. Feelings so familiar as to be my malcontent friends. And I suppose it's true. I could've done that for him. I could've at least called. But he looked so dead already, so gone. I don't know what to say. I can do nothing but look at him.

"I mean what the hell, John? What kind of person..." But he doesn't finish his thought. He's stopping himself from getting worked up with visible effort. He takes a long pull at his drink and forces himself to look away from me.

It must be the look on my face. It must be. It's the look of the dolt, the one he hates so. I am staring at him. But I refuse to accept this. He's not going to make me feel bad about myself again. Not anymore.

"I'm sorry," I say. He looks up again. "I am sorry. I mean, I panicked, it's true. I ran. That was stupid, but I didn't know what to do. I didn't mean to. You looked so... so dead. All I could think about was going to jail.

"And Dad, I know what you think about me. I know you've always thought I'm an idiot. But I am not. And believe me, I've felt horrible about what happened. You can't imagine. But you saw to it that I was going to feel even worse. Man, did you ever see to that."

"Yeah," he says, "yeah, I suppose so."

He gets up, walks over to his mini-bar to refill his drink, and I notice for the first time: he seems old. He's still formidable, still got his swagger, but it's something else, something more measured or thoughtful perhaps. He has changed.

"John," he begins quietly, swirling his drink in a slow spiral, "did you ever imagine that it wasn't difficult for me, too? Can't you see that? But there are some things you just don't run from. There are some things you have to own up to. Killing your father is one of them, accident or no. I know what I did was harsh, I know it, but believe me, I have only ever wanted you to do the right thing. Call it tough love, if you want, but..."

"Tough love?" I begin yelling at him, mad all over again. "What a bunch of crap. That's not what this is about, and when have you ever loved anyone? Never, that's when, because you're not capable of love. You don't even know what the word means. My whole life, I've done nothing but try and please you, but there is no pleasing you. And if someone doesn't meet your expectations, well, that's it, man, you've got nothing else to do with them. It's over with them. But I'm your son, Dad! Your son! You don't just throw me away because I didn't turn out quite like you expected!"

He actually seems a bit taken aback by my outburst.

Was that painful, Pop? I hope so.

I want to hurt him; his calm infuriates me.

"And I'll tell you something else. I'm not the son you think I should be because I don't want to be like you. I never have. Is that a Big Surprise? Yeah, hard to imagine, huh? Who wouldn't want to be like The Great Chip Sharpe? Well, not me. You can have your miserable life and just go on ignoring me, just like always. What do you care? You don't care because you don't love me and neither did Mom. And why? Because neither one of you ever could bring yourselves to believe that I could be it. That I was the only kid you were ever going to have, and what a failure that was, huh?"

And for the moment, he seems to grow larger, red flashes in his eye, the fighter I know he used to be asserts itself. He starts to raise his hand against me. I know he could beat the living hell out of me.

Let him.

But he controls it. Surprising, but it is there: he truly has been hurt by my words. I shut up as he looks at me reflectively, his stony demeanor hinting at a pain beneath it. And now I start to feel ashamed; I wish I could take back the words, but I can't. I stay silent, sullenly refusing to meet his searching eye.

He sighs, drains his drink, sucks one of the ice cubes, and suddenly neither of us can look at one another. I unclench my grip on the chair. He pours himself another.

Standing there by the bar, looking at his glass, he has a look on his face that I've never seen before: regret.

"Can I have a drink?"

My father looks up, surprised. "Sure, sure," he says, as close to meek as he ever gets. He makes me a scotch just like his: two cubes and a splash of water. I haven't ever liked scotch; maybe I used to reject it because of him. I don't know. It doesn't matter. I take a long sip. The rich smell of the peat. Like a residual memory of soft gray rains on green fields. Of ancient stone sheep folds. As if dredged up from my own childhood or a past life. Of the Sharpes who stayed. False memories all, I know, but better ones than these.

And then something in me shifts. My anger's exhausted. I am an empty husk and I can no longer feel bitterness or sadness or guilt. It is gone and deep down in my guts or in my brain or in my heart, somewhere, something else wrenches into place. A machinelike progression. And after that: curiosity.

"How'd you do it," I ask quietly. "You know... how'd you manage it all exactly?"

He knows what I mean, and he relaxes a little. He's clearly relieved to be back in his element, to think about something other than one of the greatest— and only—failures of his whole life.

He looks at me quickly and strangely then, thinking.

"John, I know you don't believe me, but I really didn't. Here's how it worked..."

The women in the woods? He'd actually heard of them. "Those are no 'wilt-ing daisies,' he says, "that was a dangerous situation, and that one woman, their leader, she's the worst..." He says he thought I went out there on purpose, thought I knew of them all along. He's hiding something. I know him well enough to know. 'Close to the truth, but not the whole truth,' as he always says.

But I let it drop. And the Sheriff? He financed the Sheriff's campaign. The man owed him a few favors. "But he's a good man, John, a good guy. Probably he would've helped anyway." What about Herbert? What about the Highway Department job? Well, that was actually the Sheriff's idea, he tells me, "... and remember, John, you found the marijuana fields. You helped him, so he returned the favor. I did nothing there. And you won those guys over in the end, didn't you?" He actually smiles at me.

Is that pride in his voice?

"I heard Herbert said good things about you before you left. Good things. And Dodgen's a man who tells the truth."

Quickly, fleetingly, I see it there in his eyes. It *is* pride. This surprises me, and I look down again. "Well, I'm pretty sure they hated me," I say, remember-ing Bobby's horribly twisted face in a flash and wanting to forget it again just as quickly. "But okay, well, how'd you manage the teaching pro job? All the way down in Galveston?"

"Well, when you just left the highway job like that, I thought you were gone for good. I thought I might never see you again." He hesitates on this point.

Does that thought actually scare him?

"Robert called me," he continues. "Said he saved your life in Jefferson. Said you looked like hell, too. I started to regret my decisions at that point, and I called the Sheriff. He remembered you'd told him something about going down to Galveston, and I started thinking you might show up at the Country Club down there."

He smiles smugly, like, yeah, he knows me.

"Then the Bakers called again, and –"

"– which one, Robert or Gloria?"

He makes a show of remembering. There is something there, a flash. It was Gloria, I know it, and he is hiding something there. Could it be? Him too?

"– Gloria called actually, why?"

Yes, definitely. Hiding something.

"Just wondering."

He considers my words and we stare at one another, trying for one another's thoughts.

"Well, I guessed you were heading down there because of the Bakers–"

"—I wasn't."

He holds up a hand.

"Okay, okay, well, I thought you remembered that they had a place down there. Gloria... always liked you, too. But it doesn't matter. We figured it out.

"Robert called too, by the way, and he re-signed me to manage his affairs. I have to thank you there. If you hadn't run into them, they'd have never come back to me. That's a big account you helped bring in."

"Glad to be so good for your business, but I was starving to death at the time."

"Yes, well," he flashes his CEO smile but it fades quickly when I don't return it.

No remorse. No, I will not forgive you of this.

"Sorry about that," he goes on quickly. "But anyway, I figured you'd show up there for sure by that point, and Gloria made the calls to Zingleman."

"How do you know Zingleman?"

"Gloria Baker's on the club board down there." He answers quickly. "And anyway, I already knew Zingleman."

Yeah? I start to ask how.

"And he really did need a teaching pro, and, John, well, you really are well qualified for that." He smiles at me. "It wasn't a hard sell."

Hold on, there was something else, I remember.

"You got that guy fired."

A faint look of remorse crosses his face, briefly.

"Don't look so offended. That guy was going to get fired anyway. Zingleman just needed an excuse and you provided it."

Maybe. But still.

He reads my face and senses my loathing.

"Don't look at me like that; no one's innocent here. And don't forget about the Challenger."

I remember the Sharpe sign at the table, the empty, empty table. His appearance to me there. Or the appearance of his ghost, walking in grotesque reality. But then he wasn't dead. Was never dead. And do the living have ghosts?

"Zingleman didn't hesitate to use me there. Called me right up, and bold as brass asked me for a big sponsorship. He knew, same as I would've, that you wanted to play in that tournament. Oh no, Zingleman's no innocent here. He's no idiot, despite the show he puts on. He sensed you could be useful to him, and all he had to do was fire one already malcontent tennis pro.

"And, besides," he says, like I should be happy about it, "you got your shot, didn't you?"

I nod. Yes, I'd gotten my shot, I did. But.

He searches my eyes.

"Isn't that what you wanted?"

Yes, Goddamnit, that's what I wanted.

I feel sick. I still say nothing. How can I explain to him that, in fact, it makes me feel worse to know he bought me a wildcard into a pro tournament—if it's even possible to feel worse about that debacle? I can't begin to answer him.

Pop pauses a moment. He seems to struggle with himself when I don't respond.

"I wanted to be there. I wanted to –"

"– You did come. That was you."

"Yes. That was me."

"So you just decided to show yourself five minutes before the biggest thing in my whole life! My dead father, come to life? What the hell!" I'm out of my chair, slamming my drink down, screaming out. I'm advancing on him, fists clenched. No stopping, no stopping. "You want me to fail, you asshole! That's what it is. You always want me to fail! Goddamn you!"

"John, John, John," he says, holding up his hands and he does not rise and does not look at me, and the guilt is writ there painful and large and genuine and, as I stand over him once again, I see him helpless and dead at my feet.

I check myself. Just in time.

"Please sit down," he says quietly. "Believe me, that's not what I wanted." Still he does not look me in the eyes and does not challenge me, and slowly I back away to sit again, burning still, but unsettled by something I had never seen in him before: defeat.

Finally, he looks me in the eyes again, and something of the Chip Sharpe I know comes back over him: he of the relentless drive, he of the uncompromising, indomitable will.

"I am sorry. It was a... I know... a distraction."

"A distraction? That's all you have to say? That was the colossus of all distractions."

He nods, and then I'm surprised that he is giving me this much, for it is far more than he has ever been willing to give before. A long pause. We study each other, saying nothing. He pulls heavily at his drink.

"You played well... despite the circumstances."

I stare at him sullenly.

"I meant to meet you well before, but... anyway, I'm sorry. When you ran off like that, we thought the worst. We thought you were suicidal."

"I'd have thought that's what you wanted."

He holds up a hand for me to stop.

"Okay, okay, John. Enough. You have every right to be angry, but that's too much. Me and Gloria were worried sick. You can't believe it, I know. But we were. Everyone was. Zingleman, Robert, everyone. Nobody knew where you went. We called the cops out to look for you. Everything. Zingleman said your roommate and his girlfriend stayed out all night looking for you and came back to find you'd disappeared."

I think of Bal, of seeing him on the beach and how he'd stood there knowing I was very near and how he'd moved on, deciding to let me go my own way.

But now Pop's getting angry. "And John, Goddamnit, wakeup! I may be guilty of it, it's true, but all you think about is yourself. Do you think people don't care about you, that they don't worry about you? They do, they do. You think throwing you out was easy for me? That any of this was easy? What else would you have had me do?"

I shake my head, thinking of all the things he said to me that day, has always said to me. How he treated me. And I start to say something about it, but can't now. That was another person. Not me. That was a life other than mine.

Only, it wasn't.

And then I think of Bal and Adela and Zingleman out looking for me all night, of the frantic phone calls, of everything, and I feel myself close to choking with the conflicting images in my head, the wild emotion.

Awkwardly, my father moves as if he is about to come over and put an arm around me or something, but he doesn't, he sits down and swirls the ice around in his glass pensively. He waits me out a little.

"When Zingleman called," he continues softly, "no one had any idea where you'd gone. I know you probably won't believe this, but it was pure luck that you were picked up by Simon's employees that day."

"But how did Simon know."

"By a stroke of good luck, you did call Zingleman, and he simply called the number back later. He spoke with whatshisname –"

"– Mike."

"Mike, yes, he spoke with Mike and told him you might be in trouble and asked where you were going. Then Zingleman called me, and I called Simon. He was most accommodating."

"Why the hell didn't you break it to me then?"

"John, I know how this all seems, I do, but I thought you had it figured out in Galveston already. I thought this was your way of reaching out to me to tell me. By this time, I didn't think you wanted to speak to me."

No, that's not true, I shake my head. No. I did.

"You've got an independent streak in you John, you do. What I've never understood is why you didn't get out on your own earlier, why I felt like I had to finally force it on you."

"I don't know..."

"That Simon's a piece of work, isn't he? I wasn't sure whether I was sending you to God or the devil, but –"

"– The devil."

"Yes, well, he is one of my best clients, John. Actually, I'm a bit surprised you didn't know that. But then you never had much interest in my business, did you?"

I look at him and shake my head.

"Anyway, my fund made him filthy rich, as if he needs it with the income he's got."

"You got the filthy part right," I blurt out. I'm disgusted with Simon all over again, remembering the unrepentant look on his smug face. "Man of God, yeah, right, Simon is the antichrist who thinks he's God."

"Well, maybe," Pop says. "He's a strange guy, but I thought his offer to take care of you was genuine. He seemed grateful to have you there."

He pauses, looking at me closely, and in him, I see the same look flash, the one I always saw in Simon. The look of unapologetic deceit.

"Anyway, it sounds like you learned some real skills and did well there, and I know he doesn't tolerate incompetence. From what I heard you were happy there for a while?"

Again the look. I nod. Yes, I was happy there for a while, I was. But I can't take this. He's going too far. Simon is a monster who deserves no understanding, no sympathy, no gratitude.

"Grateful to have me there? Simon doesn't do anything out of gratitude! Did you pay him? Did you give him something? That's what Simon understands. Taking, that's all he understands. Taking and taking and taking. Don't you get it? He thinks just because he wants something, that it's his—by divine right! And here I was, the whole time, taking and taking and taking, too. Not even realizing it. It's not right, how I got those jobs. Don't you see? I took some guy's job. Again. You took it. Here I was thinking I earned something, that I finally got somewhere on my own, but, oh no, all I'm doing is grafting, like some parasite, just like Simon, that corrupt pervert."

Pop's taken aback at my outburst. This is not his way of thinking, not part of his worldview. I'm pacing around, and I don't even know when I got up. I'm angry at him, at Simon, at myself, especially at myself. I remember her eyes, her look at that moment. My failure. My failure most of all.

"Yes, too bad about Simon's little... indiscretion."

I stop and stare at him. He really doesn't understand.

"Indiscretion! You call that indiscretion? He was screwing a seventeen year old volunteer in my bedroom! In my bed, Goddamnit! I caught them at it! He asked me to join them!"

I'm yelling again, the wound reopened. I see myself on the stage, under powerful lights, then the vultures wings flapping grotesquely. I see her leave forever. I see it all in a flash of intense pain, and I crash back into my chair, gripping the arms tightly.

"You call this, this *Thing* your client? You think I should be grateful, that this was somehow good for me? And you told him to take me in!"

I point my finger at him angrily.

"You."

The last one gets him, it hits him hard. Good. For once, it seems I've caught my father completely by surprise, made him reconsider his actions. For once, he has no reply. Not a sound in the room. Finally, he takes another drink and drains the glass in a long pull. The ice cubes rattle against the shining crystal. He pours himself a third.

"I didn't know about that." He looks at me. "Yeah, I knew about the girl," he quickly adds, "but I didn't know about you... that he..."

"You shouldn't have anything to do with that guy, you know. Not if you have any ethics at all."

Pop is surprised to hear me speak this way to him; even I'm surprised to hear myself.

He takes another pull at his glass. Quietly, almost painfully, it comes out of him.

"Look, John, you're right. I don't want that kind of... John, the Reverend Simon will be my client no longer."

He pauses, as if he's trying to think of something else to say but can't. I rise to my feet, and, for the first time all evening, I am able to look him in the eyes with conviction in my voice.

"Good."

I didn't mean for it to, but somehow that came out vindictively. But he seems pleased with me somehow. Maybe it was the firmness in my voice. He makes a decision.

"Look," he says, looking up at me, "stay here. Come back and live at home."

I stare down at him. Then he tells me something else, makes me an offer to stay and work for him in his very own firm. I don't know what to say or what to think. Part of me is repelled. It feels dirty, and I want to run out of here and never come back again. Ever. But part of me does want to stay. I hate the very thought of it. But it is there. I can see the life that he offers, have lived it all my life. Maybe I have changed and maybe he has, too. Maybe this can work. And there's no black and white here, he's right about that. Did Herbert and Zingleman and Simon hire me for my qualifications? Hell no, they didn't.

"Let me think about it."

He nods. He understands.

I pick up my bag and start to walk up to my room.

"John, wait... there is something else..."

I look back at him and see him struggling with himself and that look I've seen on him tonight: it is there again. Maybe not defeat. He is working to tear out the words, as if they're his own flesh and guts.

"Gloria," he says. "Gloria is your real mother."

⅄

Somehow I think this room should be different, but it's not. Everything's just as I left it. A shrine to stupidity. There are a couple of old rackets leaning in the corner. I lie on the same faded blue bedspread. On my last day here, I'd already started taking down my posters, and only one of them is still on the wall. Otherwise it's all just the same. If anything the room feels larger than I remembered.

As if nothing just happened. Has ever happened.

With the corner of the bedspread, I dry my eyes for the last time and stare up through the skylight, remembering the last time I'd looked up there. Animal forms in the clouds. Tonight, none at all. I can just make out the first stars of this clear evening. I am tired, so tired now. But should I go to sleep at this moment, I feel as if I could wake up tomorrow, in this place, and nothing would be different. My Dad will have already left for work, and the house will be empty. I'll get my gear and go to the club. I could fall right back into that life. But I can't go back to my old life now; I mustn't.

I stand up. Something important. I have to know.

My fingers dial the number slowly. I wonder if he'll be there. He picks up on the second ring, and grunts a greeting, as if somehow he knows it is me.

"Bal?"

"Yeah, hey John. You doing okay?"

"Bal, are you for real?"

He only pauses a second.

"You at home?"

"Yeah. Bal, I mean..."

I can't find the words. From Bal: silence.

"...did my father, did he, well –"

"– Does it matter?" Bal says abruptly.

Does it?

At first, I don't know how to answer.

"Yeah. Yeah, I guess it matters."

"I don't even know your Dad. Don't want to."

"Yeah, I know."

"Don't do it," he says.

We pause there a second. I hear the faintest of white noises on the phone. He's so quiet; I can't even hear him breathe. With the receiver still to my head, I hang up the phone. Even when I hear the dead noise of the broken line, it seems he's still there, waiting and listening. I pick up my car key and examine the worn plastic stub, tracing the Porsche emblem with a fingernail.

I sit on the bed and place the bag in front of me. Slowly, I unzip the bag and my hand easily finds it. I remove the clothes and grasp the grip and examine the timeless blackness of the thing, and I wipe it down with a shirt. I get a magazine out. It is full, and I push it into the grip until it clicks solidly into place. I pull the slide back and let it go, listening to the metallic ripping of the springs. Then I drop the magazine and eject the chambered shell and put the bullet back in the magazine and do it all again. I get up and I stick the .40 cal into my waistband, and I can feel the cool metal against the bare skin of my back. It is pleasant, almost as if it belongs there.

Shutting the door to my room, the click of the latch has the feeling of finality, and I hold the door knob a second longer, not wanting to let it go.

Walking slowly back down the stairs, I see the Sharpe family crest, hanging there proudly.

Dum spiro spero, it says.

While I have breath I hope.

As if they even know we exist back in Scotland.

But here, too, are the pictures of us as a family. I stop. Haven't looked at these in a long, long time. Almost forgot they were there. He has changed nothing here since she left. All of us are happy and young and smiling. We are always smiling. Were they real smiles?

All a fake.

"Goodbye," I whisper.

I look down the stairs then, down into the living room; he's sitting there in his chair, gazing into the oily luster of his drink. His two ice cubes have melted down and glommed together now. A delicate double ovoid shape. The symbol of infinity. It spirals slowly in the glass, round and round and round. I wonder if he sees the same thing I do, or something else entirely.

I go down and pause at the bottom of the stairs, facing him. He doesn't look up.

"Goodbye," I say. I pause to reach behind me, and I feel it there. He glances up at me briefly, but says nothing. "I am sorry. You know?"

He just nods. Then he looks up again and a strange look comes over his face. A night for strangeness, this.

"What have you got there?"

"Nothing," I say. "Nothing at all." Right hand extended to shake and left reaching behind my back, I go to him.

"Goodbye, John." He sighs, says nothing more.

⅄

The car feels good beneath me. The wind through the Targa top is cold in this clear night air. Warm heater drafts swirl up around me. Highway 59 South scrolls quickly in and out of view, flickering to life in the dim yellow beams. Occasionally, I catch the gleam of eyes in the night.

Coon or deer. Maybe a coyote.

When there is no one coming, I pull off and stop the car and pull the gun out. I hold it in my lap, just looking at it.

Quickly now. Before someone comes.

I drop the magazine between my legs and throw the gun deep into the black of the pine forest. It disappears utterly and completely into the void and I cannot even hear its landing. I am compelled to go and look for it again, but I overcome it. Now I take the bullets out of the clip and count them all and they are all there.

All accounted for.

I throw them in the woods and I throw out the now empty magazine, too. Nothing makes a sound, and I wonder if anything was ever there at all. But it was. I sit there a while longer and I slow my breathing. I feel better.

Hands back on the wheel, car's still running. Heel to toe the brake. The accelerator now. Clutch out, gear in. I speed up on the shoulder and smoothly pull back onto the road, going the speed limit. Roadway again, reeling into existence.

A bright orange jumpsuit bursts into view.

All the breath catches in my throat. I hit the brakes and stare, almost driving off the road, slowing to a crawl. He's on the right shoulder. His back is to me, but I know it.

It is him.

I still can't believe how huge he is. His hairy head is a blackness, absorbing the night. I roll up to him slowly. He knows I'm there, but he doesn't turn or run; he just keeps walking. Then he lifts a long lanky arm and hikes his monstrous hairy thumb.

I stop and pick him up.

# Acknowledgements

It took a long time for me to do something about writing and publishing this book, and I could not have done it without the help of many, many people. My special thanks go out to my father (whom I have never shoved through a second story railing!), my mother, Alice McGowan and her book club, Nancy Lemann, Daryl Scroggins, The Writer's Garret of Dallas, The Writers' League of Texas, the good folks at The Summer Literary Seminars, Louis Sachar, Meghan Tinning, Matt Twomey, Catherine Zoueki, Kristy Hall, and The DMIL. And, of course, to you D'Jelma, thank you so much.

# ABOUT THE AUTHOR

Born in Hawaii but raised in East Texas, Brannon Perkison lives in Dallas, Texas, with his wife and two children. When not writing telecom marketing copy at work, he meddles in his wife's architecture business, draws cartoons, coaches the chess team at his son's elementary school, and plays more tennis than he really ought to.

Perkison based *The Do-Nothing* on German bildungsromanen, novels of self-discovery and formation. In 2011, his manuscript was a finalist in the Unified Literary Contest, a quarter-finalist for the Amazon Breakthrough Novel Award, and a finalist in the Writers League of Texas manuscript contest, the largest such contest in the state. In the same year, a fellowship from Summer Literary Seminars gave Perkison the opportunity to workshop *The Do-Nothing* manuscript with Louis Sachar.

13869493R00193

Made in the USA
San Bernardino, CA
09 August 2014